TURN BACK
By
Margaret Afseth

Amazon/kindle Edition

ISBN: 978-0-9921638-1-5
Publisher's note: This novel is a work of fiction.
Names, characters, places and incidents are either
products of the author's imagination or used
fictitiously. All characters are fictional, and any
similarity to people living or dead purely
coincidental.

This book is dedicated to Wes, my encourager, and
the love of my life. I miss you.

TABLE OF CONTENTS

Prologue:

Like naughty children, they were playing just beyond the edge of the protective planetary barrier out in outer space. As a guardian, he should have known better, but she was so delightful, and he so enamoured watching her play like a sunbeam against the obsidian backdrop, he had allowed her to move farther and farther away from safety, not realizing the distance.

And then, it was too late.

He did not even sense the diminutive four-passenger space vehicle. That region of space had been unoccupied by others for so long, he had become too confident, lax.

She saw it first, attempting a rapid shape-correction, but the transport beam caught her mid-change. She vanished so abruptly it took him a moment to realize what had just happened. In that instance of hesitation, he also was caught in a similar ray, and transported to the small craft. Unlike her, he had no time for a form change, though for him that mattered little. He was but a warrior, and a male.

The energy drain of the transport beam was not enough to kill him, but was sufficient in strength to render him powerless and senseless. When he awoke, they had separated them.

****

The guardian male struggled valiantly against the chains. The others planned to keep him alive for sport, but Yt found their pleasure at taunting and torment revolting. The 'Better One' was much younger than past captives, and this one was half human, or the drain ray would have killed him right off. Redro and Wollof liked nothing better than to toy with humankind.

The laser-like weapon of Redro's glove spat a red-hot beam at the victim, cutting a second deeper, hideous slash where an old one was still raw and festering.

Yt hissed in sympathy, and turned away.

"Leaving so soon?" laughed Wollof. "He'll need your tending when we're done."

"You can call me when he is no longer conscious. I am bored, and have better things to do."

"What's better than torturing a half-one?"

"The animals need to be let out to pasture..."

"Go then, enjoy your menial labour." Redro sent another hot missive toward the helpless prisoner.

****

Something furry crawled beneath her to hide.

She was lying on bare boards covered in dirty straw in what smelled like a cattle shed. The ammonia odour of urine, and the pungent stench of manure caused her eyes to water even while still closed. The lids seemed frozen, or at the very least glued shut by dried sleep goober. Though she made a tremendous effort, she could not open them.

Someone is standing nearby.

She heard the wooden bar gate slid across the front of the stall; laboured rasping breathing, as if through a facemask or someone blowing through a metal pipe.

What is that?

She remained motionless, feigning unconsciousness.

A claw-like hand passed beneath her body, moving the sack dress slightly. Something small, quick, and warm squeaked when caught. And she knew the rodent was gone.

"What are you doing in the prisoner's cell, Wollof?"

"My lunch got away from me," the creature near her responded in annoyance. "I'm hungry! Couldn't let it get away, could I? So I chased it in here. Never meant to go near the female…just after my lunch!"

Redro laughed derisively. "Well, it's not like you could have her in that condition anyway. Silly thing is caught half dormant; neither human nor Light being."

"What do you mean?" Wollof asked, approaching the door.

"Don't you see how she looks human? We know she's Light; we caught her. She was trying to disguise when we hit her with the transfer beam. Look at her eyes."

"They're half closed. I can't see them."

"Exactly. Her eyes are blue with no slit. I checked when we brought her back. What I don't get is why this one and the warrior were so far out in space when their base is somewhere here beside our installation."

"They are both very young; suppose they were playing out there? I didn't know they had them that immature."

"The male is an adolescent, but yes, the female is definitely below puberty. Puzzling. That's probably why she made such a mess of going dormant." Redro laughed mockingly. "Can't be as old as Yt, and you know what he's like. Stupid; slow."

"So, what's wrong with her eyes?"

"Must have figured if she changed her eyes we wouldn't know what she was. Made herself blind in the process."

Wollof hissed with excitement. "Let me be the first to have a go at her. If she can't see me coming…"

"Better not. She may be dormant, but I hear, when awake if they sense you, they have this painful reflex that shocks the hell out of you."

"Did she shock you when you looked at her eyes?"

"She was out cold, and drained of her energy…"

The voices drifted away as they moved off. But they had forgotten to close the barrier slider, and her prison was left open.

Yet, she could still feel another nearby.

Why is it hiding?

****

Yt stepped from concealment when he was certain the other two had gone. They had left the gate to the cell unlocked, open wide. If he took her away at this moment, they would think she had escaped on her own. But they believed her too injured to get far, and he knew that was indeed the case.

Where can I take her?

Maybe humans might help?

He bent, lifted her, throwing her across one shoulder, then pressed the teleport button on his belt. An instant later he materialized in the shadow of a hospital. A man was just exiting the doors at the lighted front of the building.

I cannot stay to make sure she is cared for.

Yt dropped the female, pressed his belt again, and vanished.

****

Redro was growling angrily when Yt appeared back at the stall.

"Where'd you hide it?" he hissed venomously. "Tell me! Or I'll make you pay!"

"I put her where the humans will take care of her…"

"You stupid imbecile!" snarled Redro. "We can't go into their units. We can't get her back now! Your infantile behaviour needs correction! Don't you understand yet, we inflict, not mend? You act like one of the arrogant 'Better Ones'. Are you Healer like they, that you bleed for their offspring?" He dug his claw mercilessly into Yt's shoulder, and hissed. "You'll come with me now to the torture platform where I will teach you the meaning of cruelty; what is expected of you."

Dragging the young male by his arm, Redro stormed from the stables, not stopping until he reached the captive boy warrior.

"Now!" thundered the superior. "You will torture this one until he shrieks for mercy; till you hear his squeals in your head!"

"Master, please, I'll do anything else..."

"You will not! Idiot newborn!" Redro was so livid spittle flew as he yelled. He picked up the glove weapon on a nearby table, and viciously tossed it to Yt. "Coward! Weakling! Slacker! Put that on! I will stand here to watch you. Make him scream!"

****

An hour later the 'Better One' boy hung from the wall, sagging in the shackles. He was covered in angry open gashes, raw and bleeding; his eyes were swollen shut, blood seeping from beneath the edges of the lashes that swept his cheeks. He appeared not as a living male, but as a hammered meat carcass.

Yet, he had uttered not a sound through it all, never cried out in mind or verbally.

Yt abhorred what he had done; loathed Redro for forcing his hand. He felt like an animal; wanted somewhere to scream and lash out at his world. For that matter, he'd like to take on anyone who might challenge him, or get in his way.

Redro laughed, elated. "Now you get it! Doesn't it bring the pleasure? Makes the ire come to the surface; gets the blood boiling so you make a good predator. You'll learn yet!"

Yt hissed, and spat at him. Redro raised his fist and struck the younger male across the face. Yt staggered back.

"Let the anger come," Redro encouraged. "Then you will finally be one of us!"

Wollof came from behind and cuffed him across the back of the head, adding his form of challenge, as well. A sense of a presence watching made Yt turn toward the prisoner.

The boy had regained consciousness. His eyes half open, he watched Yt's humiliation. Yet, what was mirrored there was not condemnation nor agreement, but sympathy. It was as if, though one was chained and the other not, they were comrades, prisoners each, in a different form.

Yt heard the words inside his head: Don't let them win. You are better than that.

As if the effort to project the thought had drained him of what little energy he had left, the guardian boy went limp.

Yt shivered visibly, grappling for control over the negative emotions, as if the encouragement of his victim meant more than life itself. The effort made him gag. Then as he righted in his own mind, the stench of blood and the appalling sight of what he had done made him retch, spewing all over Wollof.

Shame shot to the surface within Yt. Wollof cursed. Redro laughed.

"Sissy!" he hissed. "Worthless Healer!"

Yt turned and fled.

Wollof made to pursue, but Redro held him fast.

"Let him go," he decided. "He's nothing but a half-wit; useless to us. Out there, he'll go dormant; I've seen it happen with others. They can't rationalize how they were born, so they revert back to the in-between. He won't last long among humans. They will teach him the same as we, to be violent just like us."

****

Yt took flight, running with all his might, fleeing from the barn, down the long driveway between arching trees on either side. He reached the railed double gate at the end of the roadway, pushed it open, and plunged headlong into a field of corn; running, running until he reached the pasture, then through it; never stopping, always fleeing, as if somehow he could escape reality. When he felt he was far enough away, was certain they had not followed, he hit the teleport button on his belt, thinking wildly of the big city where he'd left the unfortunate female.

But nothing happened. They had already rendered the instrument inoperable.

He wrenched it angrily from his waist, tossed it fiercely to one side, and took off running again, toward the distant mountains, and the city that lay beyond them.

Yt would rather be anywhere else than where he had been born.

When he was too exhausted to proceed, he stopped to catch his breath.

Somewhere around here is the Healer base. But...probably they will not even let me inside. And...they are likely not even here.

He felt utterly hopeless. Despaired.

My only other recourse is the humans.

But, if they saw him, his life would be nothing. They would end it.

There is nowhere to go. I am not going back! I'm not!

I wish I could be dormant; in the in-between state they would think me human. But...I don't know how...I don't know how...to become human-like.

Having rested enough to have his second wind, he turned toward the nearby highway, took off at a walk, going parallel to it.

His longing to be different was so strong in his spirit he could near taste it.

When a beat up pickup truck came over a rise, he quickly hid in the ditch. The old farmer pulled to a stop almost even with Yt, and his heart pounded in his throat, but the old man merely needed to relieve himself. When he got out to take care of nature, Yt climbed into the back and hid among the straw bales.

In the night, the boy awoke feeling cold. He tried to burrow deeper into the straw, but found his claws were now hands, the scales had become smooth skin, and the reason he was freezing was that he was naked. Yt shivered, realizing he had become an in-between.

****

The emergency room was crowded, the staff rushed. When the young girl was rolled in, the attending physician merely made a cursory evaluation. He quickly noted the child was blind.

Her breathing seemed normal; pulse rate a bit fast, but there was no obvious reason for her to be unconscious.

Probably faking it. She's most likely a street imp wanting a bed.

As he listened to the heartbeat, it abruptly arrested.

"Heart's stopped!" he yelled. "Crash cart!"

The white sack dress was brutally ripped away, exposing a budding adolescent beneath. A cart rolled to position; the paddles trust into his hands.

"Charge!" he ordered frantically.

The machine whined, quickly rising to peak.

"Clear!"

One second the young girl lay still as death; next her body jerked violently with the impact from the electrical charge.

He looked away to the monitor for only a moment, then back again, ready to order the renewal of the charge.

But the child had vanished from the gurney.

****

She had purposely tricked him, deafened him to the heart sounds, just long enough to fool him into reacting. The energy was sufficient to enable her to teleport.

But…it was not enough to get her home.

Result: destination unknown.

And with the artificial energy jolt…memories of the life she once had, vanished as completely as she did.

CHAPTER 1

Amadeus drove through the obsidian night, with streets so slick and rain saturated it was dangerous, through sheets of needle cold water that blinded his view, yet concentrated little on what he was doing, or where he travelled. Thoughts morbid, he dwelt on Claudia's impending demise.

As a young couple, the two had come to America some thirty years before. His dreams had been extensive then: set up a private clinic; have a grand home; start a large family. But they had refused to let him practice medicine in his new country, even though he'd been licensed in Austria.

The grand home had not materialized either. He had not only been forced to wait on that, it had taken years just to save enough for their small cottage.

And Claudia was still barren.

Now there would never be progeny, no childish laughter; no pleasurable excursions; no interaction with anyone. Even Claudia would soon be gone.

His wife was dieing; he'd faced that fact, but had considered it in the more distance future; until now.

Today Claudia had refused any farther chemotherapy. And, she had requested to depart this life from her own bedroom.

How am I to care for her? Her meds are beyond my reach. My paycheck is too small to hire a nurse. I cannot afford to take off from work to sit with her. What am I to do?

He did not see the young woman until the last moment, when she dashed in front of his vehicle; he nearly hit her. Amadeus braked abruptly, tramped down hard, the rear end of the car sliding to the right on the greasy pavement.

The smell of burnt rubber hung in the air as he rolled down his window, prepared to shout at her for being so careless. Then he recalled he had not been paying close attention himself.

She moved around to the driver's side, a shadow of a woman, in her early twenties. No wonder he hadn't seen her, with her taupe complexion, dark loose curly hair, and eyes as brown as the shadows that hid her. Her nationality was certainly of India, and she'd been slinking like an illegal.

When she spoke her voice was so soft, her English so broken, he could barely understand the words.

"I hungry...please, sir...you have spare change?"

His heart went out to her. Suddenly, he remembered he hadn't eaten himself since morning.

What can it hurt? Might as well feed us both; it'll get my mind off Claudia.

"Get in I'll take you for a burger."

The car felt so warm after the freezing street she felt drowsy. She had been so uncomfortable it didn't matter if the man raped her. If he gave the promised meal, it would fill her belly; if not, at least she could get warm.

She had escaped over the side of the boat just as the port authorities boarded the craft from the other side. This was America; she had thought…Florida, a place of sunshine and warmth. Here was the land of the free, land of opportunity.

But it definitely hadn't been that for her.

On the long trip over here, mother and father had both died of cholera, leaving her to fend for herself, and now in this country, they considered her an illegal. She was not permitted to work, which meant no food, no shelter…unless you wanted to call the streets adequate cover. Three weeks of such conditions had soured her view of this new world. In her opinion, the lot she'd been dealt was less desirable than what her family had escaped.

Jamara shivered. She had not expected the monsoons of winter.

"There is a blanket behind the seat. Pull it out and wrap yourself in it; you'll get warm quicker."

The English language was hard for her to speak, but she understood it well enough. Jamara did as she was told.

"Do you have a name?"

Of course I have a name. Doesn't everyone?

"Jamara."

He pulled into a drive-thru, and moved up to the intercom. After ordering for both of them, they sat in silence waiting, moving forward slowly as each car pulled up to the window, received their order, and moved off.

At this very place, she had found edible food in the dumpster, and been rudely chased away, when someone caught her fishing for what others threw away.

After the man paid for the food, he moved the vehicle to a quiet place in the parking lot, then passed her one of the burgers, a pack of French fries, and a large beverage.

He did not seem hungry, merely sat staring off into space, watching the sleeting rain drumming on the car hood. Jamara, on the other hand, quickly woofed down her share.

As she was finishing, he turned to watch her.

"Here," he offered quietly. "You can have mine, too. Don't have much of an appetite today."

He looked so sad, as if his world had collapsed in his lap, and he couldn't quite think what to do to make it right again. As she polished off the second meal, he returned to his fixation with the weather outside the windshield.

When the food was all gone, she sat beside him almost dozing. He finally came alert, turned toward her.

"You live around here?"

She wasn't quite sure how to safely answer. "No room."

Realizing it was time to go back outside, she began to fidget, uncertain what to do. "I thank," she said carefully, inching toward the door.

"No need to hurry. It's pretty nasty out there."

He sat thinking, seemed to desire nothing more from her, so she stayed where it was comfortable.

Finally, he frowned, and turned to her again. "You aren't a hooker, are you?"

Unfamiliar with the word, she simply waited.

"Do you…ah, give favours…to men?"

Jamara frowned. That she had understood. "No sell!" she declared curtly.

It is time to leave! she decided.

But she couldn't find the door handle in the dark.

"Oh, sorry. I'm not looking for that believe me. Just relax. I was just wondering…what you're doing out here on a night like this."

Jamara fumbled for the latch; there didn't seem to be one.

How do I get out of this thing?

"Do you have a job?"

"No…job."

"You live out here? On the streets?" He gestured beyond the glass.

Jamara nodded.

"Well…that won't do…"

Once again, he sat thinking. She decided to wait it out; she wasn't anxious to go back out into the elements.

"Do you…do you think you could care for someone who is sick?"

Stunned, she peered at him intently. Had she understood correctly?

Aboard the ship, I cared for my parents until they succumbed to weakness and dehydration.

Would that qualify?

"I do," she agreed hopefully.

"All I can give is room and board…I don't know how much money I can pay otherwise. See…my wife's dieing…"

"I come. I help," Jamara declared excitedly.

A tentative smile played at his lips. "Okay!" he laughed self-consciously. "Then…let's go home!"

CHAPTER 2

Claudia was gone. She had passed away just three weeks to the day he had brought Jamara home to care for her.

Today, when they had closed the casket, it had seemed so final, like his life was no longer of any use without her. Amadeus felt as if he had died as well, left behind to maintain a mere shell, until his demise should be discovered. The ache in his heart throbbed raw and agonizing.

Jamara too was very upset, though it appeared she was more conditioned to death. The young woman had become attached in the short time the two women had spent together. It was understandable, as they had been so intimate, the elder bathed, fed and comforted by the younger.

Claudia had at first rallied, taking upon herself the task to give the younger woman a better grasp on the English tongue; teaching Jamara how to survive in a culture of which she was unfamiliar, and generally expanding on the preparation for life itself. And the younger woman had learned well: to cherish and love her mentor, and both her benefactors.

Jamara became the daughter Claudia had never had; Claudia replaced the mother Jamara had lost, thus enriching those last days for both.

Then one night, in her sleep, Claudia left them both. And now, Amadeus was again faced with a dilemma.

What am I to do with her now? Jamara is half my age...it isn't proper for her to stay alone with me. But I just can't send her back out to the streets. She's still an illegal. There was never any time to see she got her papers...I thought it best to hide her, but maybe that was wrong? Now, it might be too late.

His worry had him pacing.

"I'm going for a walk on the beach, Jamara," he called out.

From the kitchen, the clatter of dishes stopped. "You do not want lunch, master Damas?"

He chuckled softly. She always called him that because she found Amadeus too hard to pronounce, and that had also been Claudia's pet name for him, but the memory cut deep.

"No, thank you. Not hungry. I need some time alone to think.

"Don't think too hard, master. It make you sad."

****

Laying on hot sand feels so good!

Sighing, she rolled over, staring with unseeing eyes at the place where the sun above should have been roasting the land. But the warmth was blocked by shadow; someone knelt beside her.

"Just lie still," a voice laden with concern cautioned. "So stupid of me! I've left my cell phone back at the house in the pocket of my suit jacket. That means I'll have to find a payphone to call 911. I'll have to leave you..."

He speaks aloud. Why is he using verbal?

Confused, she attempted to answer in audible as well, but her voice was scratchy from disuse, and came out a whisper. "Where...is this?"

"Sh! Don't try to talk. You've been in the sun too long, obviously dehydrated. Here, I'll just close your eyelids so your eyes don't become damaged. The sun's still too bright to be staring into it like that."

As his hand passed over her lids, she reached up and caught it, following the arm up, to place her palm to his face. Now, she had an image of his features by mind sight.

"Why, you're blind," he said with concern. "Who would do this to a blind child?"

Do what? she wondered silently, but he seemed not to understand.

Her mind now also showed her what he saw: the dirty shift she wore ripped open in front to the waist. In embarrassment, she tried feebly to pull the tattered pieces together across her naked budding breasts, but her hand shook uncontrollably.

"It's okay, dear. I've seen a young woman naked many times when I was in practice. Don't let it concern you. Here I'll put my hoodie over you, and no one will see."

He wrapped her in comforting flannel, a hooded jacket of some sort. She shivered, for it blocked away the needed sun.

"I need to go get help...call the police. This should be reported, so they can find who did this to you...and emergency services..."

He thinks I've been violated?

"No," she croaked out, her voice too hoarse to come out above a whisper. "Please...they will find me, come after me."

"You're afraid your attackers will come back? The police will protect you."

"No! Only you. No others!" In her agitation, she tried to rise, to flee.

"Easy...easy there. If you're afraid, and you don't want anyone else, I can take you to my place up the beach. Just be calm. No one's going to hurt you. You're safe with me."

Never safe, she thought. *I'm among humans.*

His hands moved gently, carefully down her sides. She knew he was determining the extent of her other injuries. "I'll carry you," he decided. "You seem too weak to walk. The sun's drained your energy."

No. No, she disagreed in thought. *The sun gives me energy.* But once more, he failed to read her.

He lifted her easily, and though she tried to fight, her body was uncooperative. Her head lolled like that of a feeble infant, falling to rest against his muscular chest. As he walked, he questioned her to distract her.

"What's your name?"

"Ka..." No longer able to speak aloud, she went to thought. *...ra.* Then got the first syllable out verbal again. "Le..." But as the sense of things began to fade, she finished in her head. *...ave me in the sun.*

"Kali? Okay, Kali, no need to talk anymore. We're nearly there."

Sound was growing faint; feeling had already fled.

"That's it. Just sleep."

With those words, his presence eased from her mind.

****

"Jamara!" Amadeus yelled, kicking open the screen door, catching it with his hip.

Her dark head poked around the doorjamb of the kitchen.

"Master Damas!"

"I found her on the beach," he explained, answering the shock registered on her face. "Open the door to Claudia's room. We'll use that bed."

Jamara quickly ran ahead, opened the door to a side room, hurried across the threshold to the bed, and stripped back the covers. When she stepped back, Amadeus lowered his burden carefully to the mattress."

Jamara cried out with indignation, as the bunny-hug he'd placed around the child fell away exposing what lay beneath. "She only baby woman! "

"Yes, not more than twelve or thirteen."

"Why someone do such a thing?" she demanded angrily.

He had no time to explain the immoral behaviour of other men; this situation was already uncomfortable enough.

"She must have gotten away from her attackers," Amadeus reasoned. "Go get some hot water and towels. She needs cleaning up...and I need to examine her to see how much internal damage was done."

Jamara frowned at him.

At her puzzled look, he elaborated. "A large man can do a lot of damage to a young girl…" Still, the woman looked at him uncomprehending. "Inside…" he clarified.

Her face ran a gauntlet of emotions, not the least of which was livid anger.

"I catch this beast, I cut his man thing off!"

He could not help himself; he grinned at her indisputable ability to express her basic thought, considering her limited grasp of English.

"Go get the water, Jamara…hot please."

Jamara stormed away to do his bidding.

As he was undressing the young girl, she began to come around.

"Kali…can you hear me?" he asked softly, so as not to startle her should she fail to remember him. "Don't be frightened. You're safe in my home. I need to examine you to see if you're hurt inside."

He expected some sort of resistance, but what happened had him backing away in uncertainty. A visible electrical static appeared around the pre-teen, zapping and hissing across her body.

This is no ordinary girl, he surmised.

As he retreated, the phenomenon faded. Once again he stepped toward her. A faint shimmer returned.

"I don't intend to hurt you, Kali," he reassured. "I just need to determine if you are hurt inside." The static came back full force, so he decided to back off for the moment. "But...it can wait..." The deadly electrical energy abated once again.

It must have something to do with fear, Amadeus told himself.

Jamara entered the room carrying a basin of steaming water, and towels thrown over one shoulder.

"Set them on the night stand."

When she had complied and stepped back, Jamara noticed the child upon the bed had been stripped naked, and gave him a dark look of disapproval.

"I clean her up!" she stated bluntly, in that no nonsense tone he had grown used to over the past few weeks.

Amadeus nodded agreement. "Be careful. I'll just stay in the room to make sure everything is alright."

Jamara frowned at him, but said nothing more. He watched as she began bathing the girl. To his amazement, nothing happened; no static energy; no resistance from the pre-teen; nothing.

It puzzled him.

Is it the fact I'm a male? No, can't be. I undressed her...but that was when she was unconscious.

When Jamara made to cover Kali with the sheet, Amadeus stepped forward. "Just leave it. I have to assess her injuries."

This time he was careful; he attempted to sidetrack her.

"Kali," he said as he bent over the bed. "I'm going to have a look at your eyes. Is that okay?"

She nodded.

Cautiously, he touched her cheek. When nothing happened, he moved up to the eye. He lifted the lid. Beneath, the iris was a cloudy blue; the white of the eye blood shot. He checked the other eye. It was the same.

"Did something happen to your eyes, Kali? Or were you always blind?"

The child was silent so long, he wondered if she was deaf as well. Then she finally reached up, and lightly skimmed her fingers across his features.

Is she seeking to familiarize herself with what I look like? If so, that's good. Maybe she didn't realize I'm the man from the beach.

"Remember me now?" he asked. "I'm Amadeus. I won't hurt you...at least, if I do, I don't mean to."

She dropped her hand, but said nothing.

Amadeus straightened. "Close the drapes, Jamara. We need to get this exam over with."

As Jamara obeyed, Kali began to whimper.

"Light..." she pleaded, the word coming out forced, as though her throat were sore, or at the very least, extremely parched.

"It's okay, Kali. We will open them again when we're finished. We don't want people from the street to be looking in while we do this."

Amadeus pulled a penlight flashlight from his shirt pocket. He had gotten in the habit of carrying one ever since Claudia had first taken ill.

He bent near Kali again. "Can you open your mouth for me?"

The girl complied without objection. But as Amadeus leaned in, the light on the instrument abruptly died. "Ah. Stupid thing," he hissed annoyed. But in the second before the beam had died, he had seen enough to know there was no problem.

He slipped the flashlight back in his pocket, dropping it there out of force of habit, thinking absently he would replace the battery later.

"Well, your throat seems fine," he remarked. "Why is it so hard for you to speak?"

"Aloud...is harder."

What on earth does she mean by that?

Amadeus stood thinking, wondering how to get the girl to relax. The overhead light began to flicker, almost went out, then brightened again. He hadn't realized Jamara had flipped the switch coming in.

"Kali, would you like something to eat...or drink?"

"Water..."

Good idea! There's the problem. What's the matter with me? She's dehydrated.

The light flickered again.

Great timing for a power outage, he thought sarcastically.

"Jamara, will you fetch her a glass of water, please?"

"I have made soup, master Damas," Jamara offered. "I bring some also?"

"Sounds good," he agreed. *And that will keep her out of the room awhile, so I can get this done.*

It was evident, what he planned to do with Kali was as abhorrent to Jamara, as it was distasteful to him. Each time he had mentioned it, she had appeared uneasy, so he decided it would be easiest to do the exam without her.

The light dimmed a third time. It suddenly dawned on Amadeus. *Is the girl maybe doing that?*

Moving to the foot of the bed, he cautioned quietly, "Kali, I have to examine you down below…to make certain you are not hurt inside."

Kali began to whimper apprehensively, then abruptly went silent, as if steeling herself for the inevitable.

The light dimmed one more time; came back again.

Amadeus touched the girl's feet with both hands.

He was totally unprepared for what happened next. A sudden burst of static energy shot from the heels of the young preteen, travelling up his arms, hitting him full in the chest with such force it threw him back against the opposite wall, slamming him hard, with a violence that seemed more wrathful than energy based.

He lay there stunned, his body tingling, as if he had just put his finger in a live socket, and been zapped with a high electrical charge.

Jamara rushed into the room. "Master Damas!" she gasped. "What happened?"

Amadeus sighed heavily, the numbness in his limbs subsiding slowly. Shakily he stood to his feet.

A bit confused, he passed his hand across his face. His speech came out slurred and incoherent, as he tried to process what had just taken place. "I think…"

That wasn't just fear. Is it me? She let me touch her eyes…

The child had some sort of defence mechanism.

But…she never does it with Jamara.

That puzzled Amadeus.

"Jamara, will you touch her feet?" When the woman hesitated, he appealed more forcefully. "Please? I think you'll be okay."

Jamara reached out and carefully surrounded the small foot with one hand.

Nothing happened.

Maybe she doesn't have energy for another jolt?

Then from the bed Kali spoke, a controlled anger evident in her tone. "No male touch me…ever…in that way."

Amadeus relaxed. *So that's it. She doesn't want the exam!*

"Cover her, Jamara," Amadeus said surrendering. "And put a gown on her. Use one of Claudia's old knighties. I'll be outside."

He turned, and as he left the room, he surmised: *Guess there is no way a man could have raped her with that kind of reflex.*

****

Seated on the porch swing in the back yard, Amadeus waited. Darkness closed down with the night, and still he sat thinking.

He heard Jamara return to the kitchen for the soup, but it took only minutes, and she was back again. Apparently, Kali had refused the offering, for the bowl was returned to the refrigerator.

The screen door squeaked, as Jamara came out onto the porch.

"She will not eat. She cries…"

Amadeus sighed heavily. "I'll go talk to her."

"I come too!" It was as close to a demand as Jamara would dare. Apparently, she didn't trust the two of them together.

What am I going to do with these two girls?

"Yes," he agreed.

The room was as dark as a cloudless night when they entered. Kali cried out plaintively as soon as she realized Amadeus was in the room.

"Please…light," she begged tearfully.

Is she afraid of the dark?

"Aw…child." Amadeus flipped the switch by the door. "Leave the light on from now on, Jamara."

He came and stood by the bed. "May I sit down beside you, Kali? Or will you zap me again?"

Enormous tears stood in the child's eyes. "I…can not…help…what happened."

His heart ached for her. *No matter what she is, none of this can be her fault.*

"May I sit beside you?"

Kali nodded.

He eased carefully to the mattress beside her. No evidence of the former light show appeared.

"Are you able to see the light, Kali?"

"I feel it…makes it better."

"O…kay. And, why won't you eat?"

The young girl made no answer.

"I am going to touch your face, okay? To see if you are running a fever."

Tentatively, fully expecting to be shocked again, Amadeus reached out. Her skin felt like ice, freezing. It was so cold it almost burned his fingertips.

He frowned. Before, she had felt hot to the touch.

Are her reactions opposite to normal human beings?

"How do I help you, Kali?" he pleaded. "I don't know what to do for you."

"Need energy…" Kali sighed softly. "Light…"

"You mean…like sunlight?"

She nodded weakly.

"It's night outside."

She slid lower on the pillow; seemed almost to give up at that disclosure.

"Will something else work?"

A tear trickled from beneath her half-closed lids. Kali turned toward the bedside table. She reached out toward it, her hand trembling.

Amadeus turned to look at the stand. Placed upon it, over in the corner, was a small wicker basket that held chocolate bars and paper wrap candies. They had forgotten to remove it after Claudia's death. He had always kept it well stocked with treats during her convalescence.

Suddenly, one of the bars jumped to the hand of the girl. Shocked, he stared at it, as if he were seeing things that weren't there. Then he raised his eyes to the face of the child.

She has telekinetic ability! And why should that surprise me?

Kali whimper softly, trying to undo the wrapper, yet seeming too weak to do so.

"Candy? The candy will help?" he quizzed. "Here I'll unwrap it for you."

He fed it to her carefully, one piece at a time. In awe, he watched her relax once it was all eaten. Her breathing slowed, evened out, and she slipped away into easy slumber.

Astounded, awed, Amadeus rose cautiously, motioned to Jamara to go before him as they vacated the room. They left the light burning.

Such a simple solution, he marvelled. *If only I'd asked in the first place, it would have saved me the pain.*

He left the door slightly ajar as they moved out into the hall; so he would hear her should she wake in the night.

Later after Jamara had gone to bed, he pondered his situation while sitting on the sofa. He knew this child would have to be kept hidden. To hand her over to authorities would be like giving a cat to vicious dogs. They would probe, and test; experiment. He couldn't sentence her to that.

Once again he was responsible for a stray, but this one...

Well, no way can I send either of these girls away now, he decided.

Jamara would be needed; he could not do this alone. And Kali? As different as she was, she would still need female nurture...and sheltering.

Well Amadeus, you found her; brought her home, he told himself. *You'll have to take responsibility. I guess I can always pretend they are my daughters.*

CHAPTER 3

Amadeus worked as a stockman and janitor at an east end medical clinic. It was the closest he could get to medicine without having a licence. While Claudia had been sick there had been no time for testing. Now, he did not dare apply, not with Jamara an illegal, and Kali in his trust.

His hours were convenient, from one PM to just after eight, but the pay was only minimum wage; it would make it difficult to support two young ladies.

Jamara could not take an outside job until she got a green card, and to apply for that she would have to prove when and how she had entered the country, which in itself, presented a problem. As Amadeus understood it, she had jumped ship in fear of authorities. It was unknown to him if her parents had bought passage legally or had paid to be smuggled in on a cargo ship. He wasn't sure how to get around the lack of documentation.

Amadeus was also looking into underground employment, where you were paid in cash and worked on a day-to-day basis; these employers were not likely to check your place of residence or identity. There were ways to skirt the system, a world beneath the law thriving covertly. You could also trade and swap. He just had to find the connections, obtain extra jobs for them both. Their survival would depend upon it.

It might not be the honest way to go, but he was already far past breaking rules.

And as for Kali, there was no way she was employable. It was now two weeks since he had found her. She was doing better, but still talked little. The young girl easily found her way around house and yard, even though sightless, but she preferred to hide away behind the high backyard fence, sitting in the sun.

She would sit out there for hours.

Though still favouring chocolate bars, she had progressed to normal foods.

Amadeus worried. If he found work for Jamara, Kali would be left alone. The pre-teen would also have to take on some of Jamara's household duties. It created a quandary. On one hand he wanted to keep her safe, yet she needed, in his opinion, to be kept busy. He did not like to force work upon her, but they would all suffer if each did not do their part. And everything would fall apart if authorities discovered their situation.

Tonight Amadeus was later than usual; it was after ten o'clock, because he had stopped to pick up groceries before heading home. He parked the car in the alley behind the market, left the vehicle running and unlocked, as the area usually had little or no vagrant traffic, while he loaded the bags of produce in the trunk. When he slid behind the wheel, darkness had already descended.

He raised his eyes to the rear view mirror to make certain all was clear, swung his arm across the seat to watch as he backed out, only to realize he was not alone in the car. On the rear seat, covered with the blanket usually kept there, his back toward the front seat, a filthy young boy was curled in the fetal position, asleep.

Amadeus pulled in an annoyed breath. *Oh, man! Not another stray. What is this anyway? You'd think I was a magnet for the misplaced. I should take up sheltering them as a profession.*

It was cold outside, had been raining again. And the youth appeared utterly exhausted. Amadeus did not have the heart to force him from the car, back out into the freezing night.

He can't be any older than Kali. Ah, heck! What's one more?

The man backed carefully out into traffic. As the boy did not start awake, Amadeus drove away with his passenger.

Once at home, after unloading the groceries and putting them away, he returned to the car. The young boy child slept soundly, so Amadeus lifted him and carried him inside, making him comfortable on the sofa. The fellow slumbered on, dead to the world around him.

The girls had gone to bed; Amadeus had eaten, just sat down in his favourite chair to veg out before the television with it turned down low, when half way through the programme he was watching, the boy abruptly sat up, looking disoriented.

Amadeus couldn't help but grin. The child looked so comical, his eyes huge, a frown upon his brow, as he attempted to process where he was.

"Well, young man. Did you have a nice nap?"

The adolescent hissed like a snake.

What kind of reaction is this?

"Well, no need to be so nasty," Amadeus chided pleasantly. "Are you hungry?"

The young fellow simply sat there, glaring angrily.

Appears I have another non-talker on my hands, he mused. *Better get used to it, Amadeus.*

If the young boy stayed, there would be another man in the house. And…if Amadeus could trust him, he could safely leave Kali alone.

The man stood to his feet, started toward the kitchen. The child rose from the sofa, and trailed after him, and whether from modesty or chill, he had the presence of mind to take the blanket with him.

Amadeus pulled out a frying pan, placed it on the burner, and turned on the gas. "Do you like eggs?" he quizzed, going to the refrigerator.

Making no comment, the young fellow took a seat at the table, pulling the blanket up over his shoulders.

Must still be cold.

"Do you have a name?" Amadeus enquired, fully expecting to be ignored again, as the boy seemed as uncommunicative as Kali had been that first night.

He cracked a dozen eggs into the hot pan. Amadeus reasoned they could have what remained for breakfast in the morning.

Scrambling the eggs quickly, he decided to add toast to the menu, and popped four slices of whole wheat bread in the toaster.

The boy's eyes followed his every move.

When the toast popped up, Amadeus buttered the pieces, scraped the eggs into a bowl, and brought it all to the table.

He went to the cupboard to fetch a dinner plate and utensils. When he turned back the youth was eating from the bowl with his dirty hands. He had already wolfed down half the contents.

Amadeus chose not to be annoyed, merely chuckled. "I guess you were hungry, after all. Want some milk to wash that down?"

The boy licked at his fingers. The bowl stood empty.

As Amadeus turned from the refrigerator with a full glass of milk, he was surprised to hear the young man speak. His tone was amazingly amicable, the voice more matured than expected.

"In your tongue…my name is Ty."

Amadeus raised an eyebrow quizzically, and set the glass on the table.

"You can talk, after all."

Ty ignored the sarcastic remark, lifted the glass, draining the contents with one gulp. At that point Amadeus noticed the toast had disappeared from the plate as well.

This child is a ravenous wolf!

The man took a seat at the table opposite the boy, and for long seconds they sat staring at each other. The anger had lessened in the eyes of the young one.

Here was an enigma, Amadeus realized. The young man sounded adult in his thinking when he spoke, but in body was undernourished and small for his age.

"How old are you?"

"In human? Nearly fourteen."

What an odd way to put it.

Amadeus considered his options: He could ask the boy's help, or tell him what to do. It was a choice between treating him like an adult, or like the child he appeared to be.

The man decided it would depend upon the actions of the teen himself.

"You need a bath," Amadeus observed bluntly.

Ty hissed at him.

Amadeus was taken aback.

"Well…if that's how you feel about it…"

They stared eye to eye, but the man found no rebellion in the eyes of the other. That puzzled Amadeus.

Was that just reaction?

"On the other hand…" Amadeus decided to take the firm approach, giving him an option. "If you are to stay the night, I'd prefer you take a bath."

The answer that came back was quick, curt, and unexpected. "Don't know how."

"What was that?"

"Never had one. Don't know how."

Amadeus was astounded. *Is there a language barrier here?*

"You're pulling my leg? Is there another word for it in your dialect? Do you know what a bath is?"

"It involves liquid." The boy again hissed unhappily, and the man realized his reaction had to do with an aversion to water.

When the young man hissed a second time, Amadeus became annoyed. "Will you stop that! It's impolite."

They glared at each other across the table for several seconds, but Ty did not hiss again.

"Okay." Amadeus decided to go with treating him as the boy he appeared. "Bath it is! Follow me."

But when the man arose and headed for the hall door, Ty remained in his seat.

Amadeus turned at the doorway. "Second rule," he stated firmly. "If you stay here, you obey me. Now come!"

He turned his back abruptly, proceeding into the hall, testing to see if the young fellow would challenge him. In the bathroom, he turned on the taps to let the water run. When he turned around, and Ty was standing right next to him, he almost ran into him. Ty had also left the blanket behind.

Going to have to watch myself with this one. He moves with the stealth and agility of a jaguar.

When the tub was full, the water no longer running, Ty stood looking at the water in uncertainty.

"Get in," Amadeus ordered.

"It hot," objected the boy.

"Warm," the man corrected. "Get in."

Ty looked at him one more time, his eyes begging mercy, almost terrified.

Does he think this a punishment?

Tentatively, Ty lifted a leg, stepped over the rim, then stood waiting in the liquid.

"Sit down."

He splashed down with a thump, water sloshing over the sides at the impact. Amadeus ignored the resulting mess; he could always clean up afterward. He'd teach the boy to tidy after himself at a later time.

Amadeus handed Ty the sponge. "Use soap."

The youth stared at the tool in his hand, as if he had no idea what the man meant.

Amadeus sighed. Obviously, he really didn't know how to take a bath. So he took the sponge away again, soaped it thoroughly, and began to cover the boy's back.

It was then he noticed the deep ugly scars.

Like criss-crossing tracks, some still raw, they covered every inch of the child's back. Amadeus, to prevent embarrassing the boy, chose to ignore what he saw, and scrubbed more gently.

"How do you like it?" Amadeus asked softly, as he came around to the boy's chest.

The boy had had his eyes closed, a look of rapture on his face. He opened his eyes, surprised. "It is…good."

Amadeus grinned. He was making progress.

When Ty was clean, he looked decidedly different, almost a handsome boy. He had startling blue eyes, and blond hair under all that grime.

If I didn't know better, I'd think he was Kali's twin.

Amadeus went to fetch his own robe from his bedroom for the boy. When he returned, Ty still sat in the warm suds. The man pulled the plug.

Ty looked at Amadeus as if he had been struck.

"Well, you can't stay in the water forever," Amadeus reasoned. "Come. Step out, so I can towel you off."

Compliant, Ty did as instructed.

Dry and covered, the man led the boy again to the sofa. Without being instructed, Ty lay down, and by the time Amadeus brought the blanket from the kitchen, the boy was sound asleep.

Amadeus shook his head. He had never realized a child could be this abused.

What kind of animal would treat a young boy in this manner? Beat him, not even tend his wounds, or...even teach him to bathe.

As the man fell into his own bed, he wondered if Ty would still be in his living room in the morning.

He was.

CHAPTER 4

The next day was a day off for Amadeus, and as these were a rarity, he slept late. When he entered the kitchen all three foundlings were at his table. Ty was actually eating with a fork, which seemed to somewhat impede his progress.

Much better for the digestion, thought Amadeus. *Jamara has a persuasive touch. That should help. Or I wonder should I give the credit to Kali?*

Ty and the young girl sat side by side at the long side of the kitchen table. As if to reassure him, moments before, Kali had reached across, and touched the boy's hand.

"Master Damas!" Jamara scolded as she caught sight of him. "Such a mess you leave in kitchen and bathroom. Not good example for young ones!"

Amadeus sighed. He had been too tired, in fact he'd forgotten, to clean up last night.

He grinned sheepishly at Jamara. She sounded just like Claudia.

As he took his seat at the short back end of the table, the woman placed a plate of bacon, eggs and toast before him.

His gaze went to the window, while he dug into his food.

"I see it's stopped raining. How about we have a barbecue tonight? I'll cook," he added to appease Jamara.

"Not in the dark," Kali objected. "Please."

Ty looked up, a fork full of eggs halfway to his mouth, in obvious wonderment that Kali dared to bargain with the master.

"Why not?" Amadeus quizzed.

But it was Ty who answered for the girl. In that low tone bordering on menace, he stated matter-of fact, "'Opposite' see us."

Amadeus frowned. *What the devil does he mean by that? Does he know something about her attackers? Was he one of them? And his terminology...then again maybe, it's that language barrier thing again.*

"We could have it for lunch time," Jamara suggested. "Or afternoon early...before dark..."

It took Amadeus a second to bring his mind back to what she was referring. Oh, the barbecue!

"Yes, we could do that," he agreed amicably. "Will that be okay with you, Kali?"

She nodded. It was unusual for her to be talkative, and the last thing Amadeus wanted was to discourage her interaction.

The boy might be good for her, he reasoned. *Might even draw her out. She seems to want to mother him.*

"You find another in the night?" Kali stated pointedly. It was as if she was asking where, how or why. He wasn't quite certain which, so he went with the norm.

"Yes, I did. This is Ty."

"He...a male?" She said it almost like the fact troubled her.

Amadeus chuckled. "Well, the way I see it, now I'm not at the mercy of two girls. He evens out the household."

"Master Damas," Jamara scolded. "We not gang up on you."

Amadeus laughed good-naturedly.

"I see him?" Kali interrupted plaintively.

So that's why she keeps touching him.

He met the eyes of the reluctant boy. "Ty, because she is blind, she needs to touch your face to get an idea of what you look like. Will you let her?"

"I am not to touch the females," Ty returned with some force, dropping his eyes, and returning to his meal.

Well! Talk about peculiar, Amadeus thought in amazement. *At least I won't have to worry about that.*

****

He belly full, Ty returned to the living room couch to think.

The younger female smelled familiar; like the flowers of a fruit tree he had once seen; the one with berries the size of a robin's egg, only red and juicy. He thought, in this tongue, they called them cherries, but he wasn't sure.

It seemed like he knew this Kali, but he could not place from where.

"I'm going out for a while, Jamara," Amadeus called. "Will you be okay with things?"

"Okay, master Damas. I watch twins."

The man laughed. "You mean Kali and Ty?"

"Yes. They look like twins."

"You noticed that too, did you?" Amadeus chuckled to himself. "I should be back in about an hour," he added.

The screen door slammed. A moment later Ty heard an engine start up; after an interval, the car pulled away.

Ty sat thinking. With pleasure, he remembered the bath of the night before.

This man had been good to him, not like some he had encountered on the streets, those who had kicked him, and chased him away. Amadeus had fed him, soothed his aching cuts.

Ty no longer remembered how he had gotten those; he remembered it as punishment, but not the how or why.

He never wanted to go back to that hazy memory time. This was a far, far better place, warm, and they had plenty of food. He could obey the man, if that's what it took to stay. He had always obeyed, and this master wasn't cruel like...he would not, utterly refused to, remember the other one's name! The past would be forgotten, dead!

He would remain here!

Ty got up from the sofa, and walked back into the kitchen, determined to do what it took to remain part of this family. The room still held cooking smells, and even though he'd eaten his fill, they stirred within him a new need for more.

Kali had gone outside, but Jamara remained, puddling in water.

She likes to be clean.

Maybe he liked it also. He was still making up his mind on that.

He decided, he would go outside, let the younger female touch his face.

She will not like what she feels, he reasoned. *I am ugly now.*

The outside door was open, only the screen needed to be conquered, or so he thought. He made for the barrier. Jamara moved deftly into his path.

"You not dressed," she stated tersely. "Must wear clothes to go outside."

He looked down at his nakedness. In his old world clothing was no problem, and besides, he had the robe.

Why does this female insist on ordering me around? he thought with annoyance. He felt like hissing, but the master had said not to do that.

"The mister give me this!" he argued, pulling the garment tighter around him, closing the front so skin no longer showed.

"Not for outside!" Jamara corrected. "I get you something else; an old pair of jeans and shirt too small for master Damas. Come with me!"

Ty frowned. He did not understand why this was important. To him it seemed rather silly, but then he had not known to bathe was a good thing. So going on the premise she was right, Ty followed after Jamara, much as an obedient pup would follow a mistress.

After searching through a box at the bottom of the closet, Jamara came up with something like the man wore.

"Put this on," Jamara ordered, pushing the garments into his hands. "Go to the bathroom to do it."

Ty grunted.

Okay, he would look more like master. *The bathroom must be the place the man gave me a bath.*

"Go on!" Jamara insisted impatiently.

Bossy female!

****

Ty seemed to take a long time to dress, but finally he came from the bathroom wearing the jeans and shirt. Immediately, Jamara realized he was far too small for them to fit well.

"Hold still," she ordered.

Bending down she rolled the legs of the jeans into a cuff.

He has no shoes either, she noted. *Did the mister find him naked? Master Damas needs to buy him clothes; maybe that is where he go?*

As she stood up, Jamara noticed Ty had not bothered to button the shirt, and his zipper was undone.

Quickly, she pulled up the offending zip, hiding her embarrassment, by moving on to the buttons of the shirt in one swift motion, and securing them one at a time, from the bottom up. Ty watched her every move, as if he'd never seen it done before.

She rolled the sleeves of his shirt to the elbows, then stepped back, surveying him.

"There! Now you are fit to go outside."

Without a word of thanks, the boy went out the door into the backyard.

****

Ty moved silently, slipping up beside Kali seated on a stool in the middle of the yard. He assumed she would not know he was there, and he hoped to have the advantage. But a second later, she reached out a hand to the side, and like a sleeper who could not help but cooperate with the fantasy world he dreamed, Ty encased the small member in his own.

As their hands joined, warmth flooded over him; peace and safety felt here, now, with this blind one, who seemed to see inside him, to know without explanation. She was inside his head, making all things better; all the past agony and pain fade from his thoughts, memory stopped, only the now remained.

Ty sighed. He had found his place; it felt good.

She gently tugged at his hand, guided until he stood facing her. Her hand travelled up his arm to his face. He flinched.

You will not like me. I am ugly.

Kali smiled as if she'd heard the thought. Touching first his eyes, one at a time, then his nose, and finally his mouth, she softly reassured. "I like you."

His heart gave a funny stuttery jump.

"Go get another stool; sit with me."

The stools stood against the back wall of the house. Ty obediently ran to retrieve one, setting it down beside her, but her attention had abruptly shifted, and Ty thought she was unaware he had returned.

He moved cautiously behind her; still she paid him no mind. He reached out his hand to the cap of blond curls. His touch was gentle, the feel so soft, like feathers on a newborn chick.

Ty sighed, and then...Kali moved; smiled as if amused.

She had let him touch her.

****

Jamara had finished with the dishes. She moved to the screen door to check on her two charges before she began preparing the salads for the barbecue. Two stools sat side by side in the middle of the yard; as usual, Kali sat on one of them. What surprised the housekeeper was Ty stood behind Kali.

What is he doing?

Ty reached out a tentative hand toward Kali's blond head.

Oh, watch out boy! She will sting you!

The adolescent touched the curly crop of fair hair. Jamara cringed, fully expecting what had happened to Amadeus to happen to Ty. But...there was no reaction.

He withdrew his hand, came around to stand beside the girl. This time he quickly reached out, and suddenly, touched her arm. The mere unexpected movement should have startled Kali into stinging him, but it did not.

Ty ran his palm down her arm. Kali turned and smiled at him.

Amadeus entered the kitchen, his arms loaded with parcels, which he let fall with a thud to the tabletop. Jamara had been so intent on the episode developing outside she had not heard him drive up.

"Where's Ty?" he asked, anxiously gazing about. "He didn't leave, did he?"

Jamara put her finger to her lips, signalling he should be silent, and motioned to look in the back yard. Amadeus joined her at the screen door.

Ty and Kali now sat side by side, holding hands.

"She did not sting him, master Damas," Jamara proclaimed in awe.

"Well...I'll be," Amadeus marvelled. "Most peculiar."

CHAPTER 5

In the weeks that followed, as they adjusted and assimilated to a new life, the 'twins', already psychologically traumatized, soon completely forgot their hazy origins. Accepted for what they were, excused for what they could not be, sheltered by loving caregivers, the two had little reason to dwell on why they were different.

They became family. Brought together by adversity, they now pulled together, learned to treasure and care for each other, excluding all others, save for Amadeus and Jamara.

It was six weeks later when another noted Kali's unusual nature, and circumstances once again rocked their sheltered comfort zone.

On the day in question, Amadeus entered the side gate just as a fight broke out. Ty was mixing it up with a burly older teen twice his size. Why the dark haired neighbour boy was in the yard at all was a mystery.

Ty held him clamped around the waist in a two armed vise-like grip, and was trying unsuccessfully to throw the other off balance, but the larger boy kept his feet firmly planted two feet apart, balancing, so the manoeuvre wouldn't work. Laughing hilariously at the feeble attempt of his irate weaker opponent, the bully remained immovable.

Kali stood back, near hidden under the shade of a nearby tree, her arms wrapped around her, as if to comfort herself; her face was a livid mask of tortured fear.

"What is going on here?" Amadeus thundered, setting his grocery bag on the patio table.

Ty made no response, seeming not to hear, so Amadeus had to forcefully separate him from the taller young man, who continued to laugh even after the boy had let go.

"Ty, explain yourself; what is this about?"

The boy made a motion with his tongue and teeth, as if to hiss at Amadeus, but when he realized who had manhandled him, he seemed to think better of the action. Even so, his words came up venomous, and resembled a spitting mad panther.

"He makes insult to Kali!"

Almost instantly, the other boy came back with a defence. "All I said was she's weird." His voice was the deep timber of a seventeen year old that had already gone through puberty, making him sound more man then boy. His manner and tone dripped with distain and sarcasm; his lips curled in an out right sneer of disrespect.

"And were you invited into this yard?" challenged Amadeus with annoyance.

"I came in on my own, mister," the teen retorted belligerently. "Thought the little lady needed some real company. I see her out here alone ever time I pass...I've watched her...I know what she can do...moving things without touching them. Just wanted to ask her to show me how she does it."

"He teases her!" Ty cut in. "He means to do her harm; I feel it. Kali feels, also."

Amadeus looked toward Kali. It was apparent she was considerably upset. She was trembling; shaking almost as bad as the night he'd found her. And that, more than anything else, caused his protective anger.

"You leave this yard immediately!" he ordered hotly. "And don't you ever come back!"

The intruder snorted derisively, turned his back, and leisurely made his way to the alley gate. When he reached it, he turned back, and sneered.

"You better watch your back, mister. You have no idea who you're talking to. I could come back here, and have her any time I want, or…I could go to the cops. They'd sure be interested in what's going on at this house, especially with all the freaks you've gathered. All it takes is one call…"

He let that sink in for a minute, just stood there for impact, then he turned abruptly, walked into the alley, and casually sauntered away.

"Inside! Both of you!" Amadeus hissed angrily.

Both young people ran, as if he'd lit a fire behind them.

Once all were safely inside, Amadeus slammed the door, and turned on the two.

"Kali! Don't you realize, you have to be careful? Don't use your power outside where others might see you. Act normal!"

Kali began to cry at the insinuation, and the man realized just what he'd said. But Ty, as he often did, jumped in to protect, before Amadeus could soften his stance.

"You, stop! You, hurt her!" Ty admonished bravely. "Or…I fight you too."

Amadeus almost laughed. Considering Ty had lost the last battle, and he was even sturdier then that opponent, the boast was an empty threat.

"Now, Ty…"

In her quiet weeping, Kali turned into Ty. His arms went around her so naturally, it was as if he had been comforting her all his life. Amadeus marvelled at the bond they had established in such a short time.

"Ty, I never meant to hurt Kali…" He was trying to reason away his guilt, but the pair would have none of it. "You two don't realize how serious this is. If others know what Kali can do, they'll bring in police, doctors…they'll probe, and test her…"

It was as if Kali saw the visual of his words. "No doctors!" Kali pulled away from Ty, panicked. "No police! He is right Ty! I am sorry…Amadeus. I will be more careful."

Amadeus sighed. "It's probably already too late," he decided, speaking his thoughts aloud as they ran through his mind. "If he reports me to the authorities, I could go to jail."

"Why you go to jail?" demanded Jamara, just then entering the kitchen, her arms loaded with parcels she dropped haphazard on the kitchen table. "What happen?"

"A neighbour boy was harassing Kali, and Ty and he got into it."

"Why you go to jail, master Damas?" Jamara asked a second time. "You do something too?"

Amadeus sighed. *Even she has no concept.* "I'm responsible for you...none of you have any realization...I'm breaking the law...just by keeping any one of you."

"Why they punish you for being good man?"

How do I even explain?

"None of you are my children...there are all sorts of things they can charge me with..."

"But you help us," Jamara defended.

Ty cut in. "Explain," he demanded quietly, suddenly appearing more adult then Amadeus felt at the moment.

"I can be charged with child abuse...just because I didn't turn you over to the proper authorities when I found you. You are just children; I am considered the adult..."

"I am not a child!" Jamara stated with dignity. "I keep house! You pay with room and board, clothing."

"It doesn't matter! You are an illegal!" Amadeus thundered in frustration. "By law, I am harbouring a fugitive. Kali was attacked; I didn't report it! By the time they finish with me, I'll be in jail for the rest of my life. And you...you'll be in the system...or out on the streets."

"Ah, stupid laws!" Jamara stamped a small foot angrily. "Why make you pay for caring? This world topsy turvy!"

"You want us to go?" Ty quietly asked.

"No! No! No!" Amadeus declared vehemently. "That's the last thing I want! And it wouldn't help anyway. They'd only think I did away with you. Listen you guys; I'd do it all over again given the same opportunity. But…if that kid does go to the police…they'll put you two younger ones into foster care; Jamara will be sent back to India…"

Ty seemed to be the level headed decisive thinker of the group. "How we help? What can be done?"

Amadeus looked at him in surprise. He had anticipated rejection, disagreement, panic, but not that he had a strategist at his side.

He pulled a chair from the table, and sat down to think.

How do I handle this? Even if nothing happens this time, there will come another.

Amadeus looked up at the three. Their eyes held the expected fear, but more so trust was mirrored in them. They expected him, had faith, he'd find a solution.

"Do all of you want to stay with me?" he asked pointedly. "We'll live in constant jeopardy."

"We are safe with you," Kali stated resolutely.

Ty nodded agreement. Jamara smiled triumphantly.

Amadeus ran his hand across his whiskers to hide the pleasure he felt.

Oh boy! he thought. *It's their lives or mine. And they'd never survive on their own.*

"Well, this much I do know," he reasoned. "It's unsafe to stay here any longer."

"We hide, master Damas?" Jamara quizzed.

Amadeus nodded solemnly. "Girls, begin packing. Ty, you come with me."

"Where?" The sudden panic in his voice, told the man, Ty thought he was being put out of the family.

"You are going to help me get boxes from the recycle bin," Amadeus reassured. "But first I need to find a car lot, where I can switch the car for a truck. Can't do it legally; it'll have to be a concealed acquisition."

Ty actually grinned.

"We'll cross state lines…I'll say you are my children. I need to withdraw what money I have… We'll all have to get jobs. Kali can't, I know, but she can keep our home base clean. And if they find out about her, we'll take off again."

And so, Amadeus became a fugitive himself. Hiding secretly, yet in plain sight, he took his adoptive family beneath normal society, shielding his menagerie of dysfunctional children with assiduousness, moving on when authorities came too close, always one step ahead. He no longer considered his welfare important. Apart from the children, he was nothing; they were his life, caring for them, his sustenance. Kali's safety was always the finally equation.

CHAPTER 6

The species was subdued and in mourning.

Since the children had gone missing three years ago, they had kept at bay the agonizing sorrow that might overwhelm them if they took time to dwell. Fanning out across the universe in hope, they had searched bare planets, asteroids, even suns to no avail, until it was determined there was only one place left they could be: the planet where they had been born.

She had first felt the boy, but his pain had been too severe to latch on to the location of the young guardian. His essence was now too weak to follow.

In another part of this country, she had also sensed the girl. The last time she had picked up her signature, it had been near water. They had followed it to an empty dwelling, confirmed she'd been there through the lascivious mind of a nearby young male. The trail had gone cold from there, the trace too faint; it too had come to nothing. Their treasure had simply vanished.

That had been two years ago.

Even as each city, town and village came up empty, she still believe they were here... somewhere. Most others had already returned to home base in defeat, grieving.

This was the final small hamlet, the very last street. If they failed to find a trace today, she too would have to give up...admit the cherished loved ones were lost...forever.

This morning she had been almost certain she had felt the girl again. Yet, there had been no sign of their youngest offspring, though they had searched all day. Perhaps it had been only wishful thinking.

The female sighed. *It is time to end this, to leave the planet's surface before darkness closes down in the area...to go home. I will never return!*

Why Almighty Creator, do you not show me visions like you have at other times? Have you deserted us? Why could you not have warned me, so I could have prevented this? We are incomplete without them, without her. Why? What purpose did this serve?

The shout startled her from her reverie.

"Ty! It is time to come in! Ty!"

The female froze.

That voice! I would know it anywhere!

She scanned the area for the source of the call. A husky fair-haired boy of about seventeen was shooting hoops on the driveway of a residence. The basket was attached above the garage door in front of him.

He let the ball fly one last time, the shot perfect. As he caught the return expertly, the voice called a second time.

"Ty!" She sounded so annoyed, like a sister scolding her sibling. "Supper is ready! You need to wash up before they come. Will you get in here? Please!"

It is her! There is no mistaking it.

The old lady came visible on the street next to the driveway, and just behind the young teen. As the boy turned to go inside, she hobbled after him, hurrying to keep up. He did not notice her.

When the screen door closed too slowly behind him, she caught it with her cane before it slammed shut, holding it open, and passing through deftly after him.

Aware of her suddenly, seeing her only in peripheral vision, he spun ferociously, then realizing she was just an elderly person, he relaxed again.

"You can't come in here, grandma," he objected. "This isn't where you live."

In thought, she chuckled, impressed both by the respect in his terminology, and his first aggressive response. *Good! He is protective. He's become her defender. That is how she has survived.*

She decided, however, it was best to carry out the charade, for now.

"I am tired." Which was true; she was exceedingly weary. "Just let me rest a bit," she pleaded in a tone of quiet exhaustion.

He did not soften, at least not yet.

"Not in here! This is not your home!"

"But…I have family here…" Again, the statement was quite factual.

"You are mistaken," he declared in annoyance. "Go back outside."

She remained, silently waiting, pretending not to comprehend, sending him a memory, a residue from the past. He stiffened in shock.

****

A picture of a forgotten time ran through Ty's mind. He remembered a young defenceless woman seated on a chair in an empty room. In appearance, she resembled Kali, much as she looked today. He stood threateningly towering over her, badgering her belligerently.

'Remember me, Ty, when we meet again,' the female of the dream-memory requested. The words had made no sense at the time.

At first she had seemed helpless...but her power had been greater than his, his weapons useless. She could have ended his life right there, but she had spared him. She had been the first to give him kindness.

He drew in a sharp breath at the vivid recall, wondering: *what does that incident have to do with now?*

Was that memory...or just hallucination?

Then he remembered something else. This old lady smelled of vanilla...and cinnamon, just as the girl of the memory picture.

The scent! That's what made me think of her.

But Ty preferred to forget. Long ago he had decided to keep the dark knowledge locked away, hidden. He had denied that time, that place. He would not go back there!

Who is this old lady? She cannot be the same person! She's just a confused old woman.

"Ty...whatever are you doing out there?" Kali called impatiently from the kitchen. "Will you get in here, and set the table. Amadeus and Jamara will be home from work any second. They'll be tired; doing yard work is hard labour. They'll need to eat, so they can relax."

He knew she was right. She was the more compassionate one, always putting others first. He wished it wasn't such an effort for him to do the same.

Ty decided it wasn't worth the effort to deal with this puzzle at the moment, turned his back on the senior, and walked the few steps to the kitchen. The old woman followed like a puppy behind him, but he ignored her.

"Gosh, but you're pokey today. What's the matter with you, anyway?" Kali complained petulantly. She stood, her back to him, by the stove, stirring a pot of stew. "Wash your hands first," she ordered.

He tossed his ball to a chair in the corner, and headed to the sink. When he moved past Kali, she immediately sensed the second presence in the room, tensed visibly.

"Who is with you?" Kali turned to the door, sightless eyes tracking, searching out blindly what she could not see.

"Ah, it's okay." Ty touched her shoulder in a gesture of comfort. "This old lady followed me in from the street. She says she's tired and would like to rest. She's a little confused, harmless. Thinks she lives here. Let Amadeus deal with it."

"You can't be here," Kali declared bluntly. "We don't know you...our father will be home soon."

The senior simply laughed delightedly. "Amazing," she said softly. "Easy to find someone; just follow the voice."

Her own voice had a most unusual effect on Kali. The girl frowned, as if puzzling over where she had heard it before, then shook her head, as though dismissing her own conclusion.

"You're right. She does seem a little mixed up. Ah, I don't think it'll hurt to let her rest a bit. Amadeus always tells us not to be unkind. Maybe, you should set an extra plate. She can have supper while she relaxes. I've made plenty."

Ty pulled out a table chair for the old lady.

****

"What is this?" Amadeus asked warily, as he entered the kitchen after taking his shower. "We have a guest?"

"She's a bit confused," Ty explained. "Wandered in here off the street. She thinks this is her home. Followed me in when I came inside."

"You didn't notice her sooner? You're letting your guard down, son," Amadeus scolded gently. "That's dangerous. You know better."

The boy dropped his eyes, uncomfortable. "Sorry…"

"You know what happens when we trust strangers…" Amadeus turned to Kali. "You've been…careful?"

"She feels safe, Amadeus," Kali reassured. "We've set a place for her. There's plenty."

Ty lifted eyes searching for a reprieve.

"You feel the same?"

The boy nodded.

"Well…okay then."

Amadeus had learned to trust their instincts. The judgement of his twins never erred; their measurement of character was flawless.

"I guess, she stays for supper, but as soon as it is over, she goes back to her real home." He turned to the senior seated at his table. "Do you remember your name?"

"Of course, dear. I'm not senile. I'm Sonia."

He laughed. *Feisty little darling,* he thought. And deciding she was indeed harmless, took his place at the table. Because he was tired, and hungry, he forgot to practice his own cautionary warning.

Amadeus let his guard down.

Sonia grinned, narrowed her eyes, like a tiger about to pounce. A second later the expression vanished. Dishing out his food, Amadeus missed the suggestion of threat.

****

Each time Jamara passed a dish, Sonia declined. "I do not need to eat just now," she finally stated quietly. "I will simply sit and visit."

The way she sat there reminded Amadeus of Kali, how the girl often sat and listened, filing away data from those around her while they were unaware.

After a time, he began to suspect there was more to the old woman then was obvious. She seemed neither confused nor aged, but alert, watchful and clear minded. From the first initial introduction, she sat quietly observing them as they ate and interacted with each other, as if she were judging their relationship to one another. And even though the four were careful to speak only of general circumstances, it was as if Sonia picked up the hidden thoughts. She missed nothing.

Finally, growing suspicious, Amadeus decided to wait it out. Something was not quite right here, but he would let it play out...as long as no harm came to his family.

Kali, also observant, soon became agitated that the lady would take no sustenance.

"Please...you must eat," she pleaded when she could hold her peace no longer. "I know you like stew..."

Amadeus came suddenly alert.

"Great-gran, you taught me. You made this very kind for Sky the first time you ate together..."

A look of shocked horror fled across the girl's features as she realized what had so unexpectedly come from her mouth. Kali tensed, anticipating a reprimand from those around her.

Ty looked up stunned, fear jumping into his eyes. Jamara's chin came up in sudden disbelief.

Sonia simply grinned, as if this were what she had been waiting for all along.

She chuckled. "Took you long enough to place the voice," she said quietly. "But then dormancy does tend to dull the senses."

Amadeus stupidly let his jaw drop.

Alarm and panic fought for rule on Kali's face.

"Who are you?" she cried in a terrified squeak.

"Why, just who you said, dear," Sonia admitted amicably.

Ty's eyes went wide.

Kali digested the information for a second.

"Then…what am I?" she softly whispered.

"You don't remember?"

Kali shook her head.

"What do you recall?" Sonia probed carefully.

"Only this life, now…with Amadeus, Ty and Jamara."

Sonia seemed to consider that statement with much deliberation, yet when she again spoke she took the conversation a different direction.

"If you were asked to leave the others, would you feel…unbalanced?"

Kali came back with a quick answer, as if the enquiry was not as unusual as it sounded. "It would hurt terrible," she cried out in anguish. "They are my family…now…I…I don't remember…"

"Us," Sonia finished for her, nodding sadly. "Perhaps, the memories will return," she reasoned, as if arguing with herself. "If you were given a choice, would you remain with these…friends? Bare in mind, you will never be safe here," she cautioned. "And with the same consideration, remember, you continue to jeopardize their lives as long as you are with them."

Kali went silent.

Sonia's words sent a shiver of foreboding through Amadeus. He was remembering that first night.

"I found Kali on a beach in Florida," he volunteered. "She had been attacked..."

Sonia's eyes sought the man.

"After you brought her to the safety of your home," she demanded pointedly. "What made you flee from it?"

Amadeus was surprised. *How does she know that?*

"It got dangerous...for all of us," he excused. "At the time I had the welfare of all three of my charges to consider. Someone saw her using telekinesis; he threatened to expose her."

Sonia nodded. "Ah yes, I know of whom you speak. His mind was a disgrace to humanity, especially for one so young. He would have indeed done her harm. However, because you fled, it has taken us much longer to find her."

Amadeus felt like a small boy being reprimanded. Until this moment, he thought he had not erred in judgement.

"I can not blame you, Amadeus;" Sonia reassured. "I honour you for your choices. You have kept our treasure safe, which is an exceedingly great accomplishment. You did your best under the circumstances, and I realize you have made sacrifices to do it. But...you have no idea the dangers that lurked near you."

She seemed to dismiss him then, turning to Kali. "You still have kinetic ability?"

"I can bring objects to me."

"Humm…" Sonia mused. "You are caught between dormant and whole. That explains why you are blind." She looked again to Amadeus. "Does she shock you?"

Amadeus laughed in spite of himself. More and more he was beginning to appreciate this lady. "A couple of times, she sent me flying. Funny thing though, she never does it to Ty. So it can't be a male thing, or is it just me?"

"Males."

"Ty is male," Kali broke in.

"A compatible equal will not get shocked."

Equal? thought Amadeus. *Ty?*

Before he could ask, Sonia posed another question.

"Why do you call my great granddaughter, Kali?"

Amadeus was surprised. "When I found her, that's the name she gave me."

"Did she now? Are you certain?"

He frowned, uncertain now that doubt had been planted in his mind.

"Show me the memory."

"What?" Amadeus looked at her with sudden trepidation.

"Think of that time."

Are they telepathic, as well?

"Yes," she answered, seeming to know what he had thought. It sent shivers up his spine.

"Please do as I ask?"

Amadeus revisited the event in his mind; the memory brought other things also, things he'd kept at bay these long years: the grief he had been struggling with at the time; the quandary over Jamara; how finding the girl had solved his problems and taken his focus from bereavement to nurturing. He remembered his attempt to examine Kali…

"I've seen enough!" Sonia declared curtly, her tone coloured by annoyance. "I don't blame her for shocking you. You are fortunate she was energy depleted on that night or you would be dead."

His face grew warm with the reprimand. *Was I inappropriate? I never meant to be.*

Sonia visibly softened.

"Past behaviour will be forgotten…forgiven." Addressing Kali, Sonia revealed: "Your real name is Kara, dear."

"Kara?" Amadeus said in surprise. "How did I get it so wrong?"

"Let's see if we can reconstruct," Sonia suggested. "Kara was unaccustomed to vocal speech. She was also severely destabilized. It requires more energy to vocalize than to transfer thought."

They talk to each other telepathically? No wonder she was so quiet at first.

"No doubt Kara said…"

"I remember now!" Kali cut in. "My name is Kara. I said Ka…out loud."

"And completed it silently," Sonia finished.

"I wanted him to leave me in the sunlight, but couldn't get the words out."

"And what most likely came out verbal, was the beginning of the sentence," the old lady reasoned. "Le…from leave."

"Of course," chuckled Amadeus. "Kal…le! Well, Kali or Kara; I think both suit her."

Sonia went suddenly serious again. "Kara? Do you remember that you were not alone when you were taken?"

The girl's face changed to virtual terror; it became obvious she was recalling something extremely unpleasant. Reading her expression, Ty ever the protector, jumped to defend.

"Leave her alone! It hurts to remember. Nothing good comes of remembering the past."

Sonia narrowed her eyes, searching the young boy's face. For long moments, she said nothing.

Is she probing his memory? Amadeus wondered. *Can she see what I've never been able to get out of him?*

Something traumatic had happened Ty; he had always known that, but the boy had never shared details.

Kali was still reliving her own horrors. Suddenly she shot to her feet screaming, beside herself with panic, anguished and concerned.

"Ram! Ram! They have him! He's still a prisoner! They torture him!"

Amadeus' blood froze in his veins.

Sonia moved with amazing agility for one so aged. She was up, had circled the table, and stood next to the girl in three quick movements.

"Easy child. Give me your hands; I will share your pain. I can relieve the memory."

"I told you not to hurt her!" exploded Ty, who had come just as swiftly to the girl's side.

Sonia turned abruptly to the boy, her eyes narrowed in threat. "You do not want to do this, boy! I can be your deadliest enemy, or an irreplaceable friend. Which will it be? The choice is yours." Ty seemed to be reviewing, as if remembering another encounter. "Good!" Sonia stated, as if she knew what he'd decided. "Be still now, and go sit down!"

To the man's amazement, Ty obeyed, like a whipped cur at a master's scolding.

Kali had calmed herself some, but was still sobbing hysterically. "It's my fault!" she moaned. "So stupid! Stupid! Stupid me! I had to play unprotected in space...and he let me! He always allowed me whatever I asked."

"I know, dear," Sonia agreed quietly. "His one weakness. Give me your pain, little one. Allow me to help."

Kara offered trembling hands, and the minute the two linked, the girl steadied visibly.

"Ah, great-gran." The teen folded against the senior in abject misery. "I am so so sorry."

"Sh! Sh," Sonia comforted. "You were only six." Sonia eased the girl back to her chair. "Okay now?"

Kara nodded. "I need to go sit down. Stay calm. We will deal with one thing at a time."

"What about Ram?"

"Now, we should be able to find him."

Sonia feebly moved back to her own chair. It stuck Amadeus as strange, but now the woman did appear confused, and…hurting.

The whole matter was puzzling.

"How long did you say Kara was a captive?"

Sonia looked at him as if she had forgotten he was there; her mind seemed far away, on other matters. She sighed, compliantly yielding to his intrusion.

"Only mere days," she admitted. "But for Ram, it has been three years."

"But…you said she was six?"

"Kara is only eight."

"What? That doesn't add up," Amadeus declared argumentatively. "And she looks…"

"She's in a dormant state. In human she is sixteen; by our aging cycle, only eight."

"Half the age of a normal human being? What are you? Am I to under stand you are non-human?"

"Does it matter?" Sonia reproved. "Is that what's most important at this moment?"

He pulled in his breath. She hadn't denied it. "I guess not," he admitted, chastened.

"We need to take her where she will be safe. She has become attached to each of you; are you prepared to come with us? It will help her to adjust."

"Of course." For so long Amadeus had put his needs last in regards to the children, this required no consideration. "Whatever I can do to make the transition more comfortable. Do you mean, you want Jamara and Ty to come also?"

She nodded regally, as if she were the queen granting entry to her court. "For Kara's welfare, it is most important for at least Ty to join us."

Amadeus turned to look at the boy, and for the first time saw the sheer panic mirrored in his eyes. The man knew this was not a time to force.

"I think Ty needs to make that decision for himself."

Without hesitation, the boy spoke up. "I come."

And both Amadeus and the old woman understood the effort, the courage, it took to say yes.

"I will come, also," Jamara agreed.

CHAPTER 7

Life had changed drastically for Amadeus when he had taken on his family. Once again, he knew his world had tipped off kilter. The first time he had expected to be constantly running until the young ones no longer needed his care, but this time he had no idea what to expect.

He had learned to anticipate the unusual from Kali, or Kara, as he must now call her. Ty too was distinctive in behaviour. With Jamara there had been the cultural variance. But all four had learned to balance with each other to survive.

This journey upon which they were about to embark, would be nothing like the past existence they had put together. It was obvious; they were expected to leave everything behind. If these beings were indeed non-human, their way of relating to life would be foreign, as well. What was the usual to the three might be totally dissimilar to their hosts.

What will life be like with them? Where will we be going? Off planet? How will we get there? In a ship? Maybe they live in another dimension?

These questions spun through the mind of Amadeus in the seconds he waited.

As one, all four were expecting the answers to come from Sonia; waiting for the old lady to guide them. However much he anticipated the bizarre, Amadeus was unprepared for the actual alien reality.

Sonia rested only minutes, seeming to be pondering her next move, her options.

"Guardian. Come visible," she ordered of the empty air.

Amadeus immediately reasoned, as they were telepathic, she spoke to someone other than those present in the room.

When the gigantic man appeared beside the old lady, Ty shot to his feet, knocking over his chair, and hissing in sudden fright.

"Ty!" reprimanded Amadeus, though he too found this being formidable. "Calm down, boy. Don't be rude."

He knew he was asking a lot of the teen, for he himself felt quite disconcerted. He had not expected the males to be so much larger than tiny Sonia and Kara.

The being was near eight feet in height, with a dark molasses skin tone, and Arabic-like features, complete with the beak-like nose. However, the eyes were his most arresting attribute. They were brown, the pupils like those of a cat, they were brown, the black slit centre near indiscernible at first glance.

Amadeus couldn't blame Ty for his alarm, considering how well muscled and broad shouldered the man was. And the human man had the odd sense; this male had been in the room the entire time.

"He is only my protector, Ty," Sonia reassured softly. "You need fear him only if you mean harm to Kara or myself."

The guardian's eyes silently met the anxious gaze of the boy; they narrowed like a vigilant panther, but he said nothing, simply crossed his arms over his chest, and stood waiting.

"I wouldn't hurt Kali...Kara," the teen defended carefully. Ty picked up his chair, and returned to his seat with a show of bravery, but Amadeus noted, he was trembling.

Through the subsequent conversation between Sonia and her men, the boy watched uneasily. As the giant continued to ignore him, very gradually, Ty began to relax.

"It grows dark," Sonia observed. "Blanket the area, warrior."

With a slight evidence of fear, Kara raised her head. "They can see us in the dark," she recalled. "That's why they noticed me in space."

Neither the guardian, nor her great-gran chose to comment on her words. Amadeus, however, took note of the disclosure.

That's why she never liked the night.

"It is done," the giant told Sonia. "Do you wish me to summon Joel, my Lady?"

Sonia shook her head. "Too risky. Too many 'Pure' together...they'll pinpoint. Tell him to stay on home planet; send me Eric instead. We will set up temporarily at Sanctuary. Technical centre should still be functional. Let me know when he has our safety guaranteed."

The male closed his eyes. Amadeus assumed it was to concentrate.

Is he sending a mental message to a space ship, or across the far regions of outer space?

Sonia waited.

Jamara had never liked being idle. Now she rose from the table, clearing away the dirty dishes and leftovers. Just as she returned after finishing, the guardian opened his eyes.

"Eric says, he can see to it the enemy base is sightless; give him just a short period more."

Sonia agreed.

Jamara gasped as a second giant appeared out of nowhere. This one was not as large as the first. He was six to eight inches shorter, still well over seven feet, with a leaner build but still robust. He seemed of Navajo breeding, with tanned darker skin and the proud bearing of such a nationality; his braided hair and buckskin clothing leaving no doubt of his heritage. His eyes were turquoise with the vertical slit in rust brown. And he seemed no less intimidating.

Kara sensed him the moment he appeared. "Great-grandpa!" she squealed in delight, rising from her chair with arms open wide.

"Easy, Sky," Sonia cautioned. "Her memory is intermittent, and there's no telling what powers might come to the fore."

"So, she might sting me." Chuckling, the native dropped to one knee. "Ah, little one," he said fondly. "Look at you. Will you permit my touch?"

Kara was shivering with anticipation. "Yes! Oh, yes! Oh, yes." Unchecked tears slipped down her cheeks.

Sky folded her gently against his chest, closing his eyes. It was obvious he too was struggling to hold back his emotions.

So this is Kali's family, Amadeus mused. *How did they ever come to lose her? And this is the old lady's partner? He looks too young.*

It was then Amadeus realized Sonia must be in disguise.

Kara is dormant. What does a female look like, if these are their males? And does Sonia hide for her safety?

Sky stepped away. "She is rather well balanced considering," he reassured. "She feels safe to touch. Negative emotion is neutralized. You do that, love?"

His analyse makes him sound like some sort of physician.

Sonia nodded. "I did. Emotions are still mostly dormant; connection limited."

"Aw…" he chided softly. "Not a good thing to risk here." A look of mild rebuke passed between them. "You put yourself in jeopardy."

"Wasn't any alternative at the time."

Sky shook his head, turning once more to the girl, and passing a hand across the half closed lids. "Your great-gran will have to see to those eyes as soon as we are safe," he decided.

He looked again to Sonia. "Any word of Ram?"

"I think we will find him at the old farm house," she declared evasively. "Outside of Sanctuary…"

Sky pulled in a sharp breath. "Aw, no! If so, his condition will be grave. It'll take much more intense balance…long term even."

Sonia closed her eyes, as if the thought grieved her immensely.

"My Lady?" the larger guardian interrupted. "It is safe now to proceed."

Sonia opened her eyes, looked to Sky. "Are you prepared also?"

The Navajo nodded, stepping to Kara.

"Okay," Sonia ordered. "Stand please. Amadeus, Ty and Jamara, join hands. We are about to jump to Sanctuary. Brace yourselves."

Before Amadeus could ask questions, whether jump meant to teleport, the room vanished. And immediately, they were in a cavernous room of granite.

****

I remember this place! Kara thought excitedly.

It was as if just being here gave her internal sight in place of the physical she lacked. Turning, she saw with her mind's eye her great-gran had changed form. Now she was much younger, taller, exceedingly more beautiful, with short blond curls and purple slit eyes. The way Kara remembered her.

Sonia immediately took control, the ruling monarch of their species. "Go fetch Ram!" she ordered curtly.

And the guardian warrior Djura obeyed, instantly vanishing again.

Without preamble, Sonia turned to her great-granddaughter. "Now, young lady," she declared. "I will not leave you another minute in this state."

As she stepped to Kara's side, Sky objected. "Maybe, you should wait for privacy," he warned.

"Not another minute!" Sonia disagreed.

Wrapping Kara in an embrace, she had already begun the process.

Inside the girl's mind, the world tipped violently. Past visions slid by rapidly: people, friends, family, events; and Kara had recall once more. As the room righted again, she was eight, and...she could see. She was also once again in align and in union with the species, one with her relatives.

Yet Kara felt a lack. Something from before was missing. She did not have the ability to assess what it was.

Rather than dwell on her deficiency, she turned her attention to the new faces around her. For the first time she had a visual of Amadeus, Jamara and Ty. Amazement was evident on each face, mirroring her own surprise.

They appeared so much smaller than she had imagined.

But Ty was not a disappointment. He was a handsome teen, strong and as tall as she, but...

Oh, how terrible was the hurt inside his mind.

Kara shivered in foreboding.

****

Amadeus had no time to appraise his surroundings. What he witnessed immediately upon his arrival, and afterwards, totally kept him tilted.

Firstly, the vision of Sonia in her true form rendered him speechless, but the second, the abrupt and sudden healing of Kara, left him doubting his senses.

When Sonia embraced the young girl, they seemed to meld into one another, becoming a glowing single image brighter than he could safely endure. The air around them crackled, and immediately Sky appeared affected as well. That man dropped to one knee as if the wind had been knocked from him, gasping with the force of something Amadeus could neither locate nor understand.

It was as if these three worked in conjunction; the females took energy, draining from the lone male of their kind present. The whole incredible experience made your teeth ach and your hair stand on end. Amadeus shuddered at the power of these creatures.

Moments later, the light phenomena dimmed again, Sky rose to his feet, seeming unaffected now, as if merely suffering for that second, and all returned to normal...their normal.

But when he looked at Kara, he had trouble believing this was the same girl he'd nurtured these past three years. She was now a stunning beauty, a much younger replica of her great-gran; the incredible treasure they had sought. And Amadeus could understand now why Sonia had called her that.

A budding ravishing beauty, un-matured yes, but the distinct reproduction of Sonia, she had shimmering hair of gold-blond and the amethyst eyes. Without a doubt, her vision had returned...for with eyes wide open, she scanned those present in the room. It was also obvious, like her matriarch, she saw more than the mere surface physical.

****

The moment they arrived, Ty too remembered Sanctuary.

I have been here before! This place is bad for me! Feels closed in...we are underground. These live hidden...because of us!

Sheer panic took his breath away.

He had no time to think...before the healing began. It seemed in an instant, Kara was whole, unbelievably gorgeous...perfect.

And now...absolutely beyond reach...unattainable to him ...forever.

Ty felt he could weep. His body would not stop trembling.

From the day he'd been born, he'd been taught the 'Healers' were a deadly force to be annihilated, wrong because they were different, opposite from his kind.

But he had never seen them heal before...at least not like this.

His mind felt confused. This terrified him!

He had been ingrained with the belief they would torture him; kill him.

He'd been with Kara for years!

Ty's terror spread, so he could barely stand.

Then he felt Kara in his thoughts, soothing the fear away, telling him to forget how he'd been raised, not to panic. Sonia slipped in with her.

Together, they were comfort. Ty began to visibly relax. Then they broke the connection, and the boy...found he missed the union.

Kara was still lost to him. He knew it!

CHAPTER 8

Jamara was fascinated by this new world: walls of shinning granite, beings of light. Creatures that went in damaged, came together, then exploded; coming out whole and beautiful on the other side, like a rebirth. It was intriguing, appealing; she felt as if she had entered Nirvana.

When she had left her native land of India expecting America to be her paradise, she had been disappointed. She had never even dreamed she would end up in a place like this. Jamara stood spellbound, wondering what would happen next.

Kara, the one I called sister, is one of these?

Then Jamara's state of bliss unexpectedly dissolved.

Two giant guardians materialized, with a smaller figure between them. The younger male was badly injured, weakly struggling, fighting valiantly against those who held him.

Sonia cried out in anguish at sight of him.

Kara began to scream in sheer terror. Ty cowered, as if he were guilty of inflicting the damage done to the wounded one.

Tears of empathy fled unchecked down Jamara's own cheeks.

"Kara!" Sonia pleaded. "Your fright increases his blind terror. Control yourself! Be quiet; calm."

As Kara went silent, Jamara sought also for control, thinking somehow it might help. But the sight was heart wrenching.

The one who resisted was a mere boy, his clothing in tatters, each rent revealing raw, angry flesh beneath, deeply slashed, festering or bleeding. His eyes had swollen shut, but even though he could not see, he still fought, writhed and thrashed, thinking those who had rescued were his captors.

"Help us, mother!" implored the larger of the guardian pair. "He doesn't know us. He won't stop struggling."

The second also added an appeal. "He will kill himself!"

Sonia and Sky stepped together; touched hands.

And the boy between the two seemed to drain of energy, going limp in a dead faint.

Dread crawled up her spine. *Are they able then to take the soul as well as to heal the body?* Jamara wondered.

"Ah," the second guardian sighed in relief. "I thought there, we were certain to lose him."

Sonia and Sky stepped apart.

It was then Jamara noted the boy seemed to be her nationality.

How can this be? she marvelled.

"Take him to the healing chamber, Lance," Sonia suggested. "Keep him confined for a time, so he doesn't hurt himself. His mental state is fragile, may not balance when you heal him. It is likely to take several deeper sessions to right him. He has endured captivity too long."

Jamara shivered. *This must be Ram then. Who would be so cruel?*

Together, the two guardians vanished with their burden. And just after they were gone, the warrior that had been at the house, slowly, gradually came visible.

He also was slashed viciously, but his wounds were fresh.

Sky winced at sight of him. "Aw, Djura."

Weakened, unsteady, the valiant male almost fell, dropping with a heavy thud to his knees. Sky in an agile turn, caught him as Djura sagged against him.

"Was it long enough?" gasped the loyal defender. "I kept them occupied as long as I could."

"Mission successful," Sky reassured.

Horror leaped into Amadeus' face. "What kind of weapon does this to you?" he demanded urgently. "When you seem to have such power."

The injured warrior made answer. "Negative-energy laser."

"Don't you have a defence?"

Ty's reply shocked Jamara as much as it did Amadeus. "They will not fight back."

And, just how does he know this? wondered Jamara.

Sonia ignored the comment, addressing her partner instead. "Sky, will you take Djura to his quarters. You need to wait a bit to heal his wounds. There is insufficient balance left to heal both at once, and…"

"Ram comes first," Djura pointedly declared. His voice was hesitant, weak with the strain from the sever pain he must be feeling.

Together the two males disappeared obediently.

Amadeus waited until they were gone. "Why won't you fight back?" he demanded, not even considering the information might be incorrect.

He simply assumed Ty knows what he's talking about, Jamara marvelled. *Why?*

But the conversation continued, and Jamara found Ty had been correct.

"We are a peaceful, non-aggressive race," Sonia admitted, her tone brooking no argument.

Astounded, Amadeus still tried. "But…with such an enemy, surely…is that wise?"

"If I were to will it, I can send an adversary to the ends of the universe," Sonia stated bluntly. And it was obvious she did not mean it as a boast. "By mere thought," she emphasized. "Would you have us be predatory?"

Amadeus appeared suddenly apprehensive. "No…of course not! I follow your reasoning, but…" He shook his head uncertain. "I'm afraid I could not be so amicable."

Sonia smiled softly. "At least you are honest."

Four ravishing females, all different from Sonia and Kara, suddenly surrounded them.

****

Amadeus felt suddenly overwhelmed, not just because he was the only male adult in the room, nor because these women were all over six feet tall, the red head maybe even seven, but because he was wondering if perhaps he had made a wrong choice in agreeing to come here at all.

He had been so used to making decisions regards the welfare of his charges; it was hard to relinquish control. It was now all out of his hands. And to add to the quandary, the things he had learned since coming here, made him realize he had placed the young people in the midst of some sort of inter-species war.

There was nothing more he could do for Kara, but the other two he felt still needed his protection.

Is it possible for me to remove them from further endangerment?

The female with the scarlet hair seemed on constant alert, just as the warrior guardian Djura had been. He wondered if she might be his mate; their attitudes were so similar.

Ty seemed so terrified of these creatures, yet he seemed familiar with them. That puzzled Amadeus, but it also touched off a warning.

Ty had always been a good judge of character.

Will Sonia allow me to take the other two away? wondered Amadeus. *Now that Kara is safe with them, and obviously normal again, why would she object? Maybe the kids could visit somehow?*

Amadeus was so deep in thought, he startled when Sonia spoke.

"Karine?" The largest female with the auburn hair turned in answer. "Will you and Angel please see Kara to her chambers? She grows weary."

"Yes, my Lady."

A blond, blue-eyed female stepped to join her, and the two linked hands with Kara, vanishing abruptly.

Addressing the remaining pair, Sonia continued. "Morgan, you and Chantel take Jamara as well. See she is made comfortable in Jade's old quarters. I think she will like it there."

Suddenly all the women were gone, effectively removing Jamara from his care, and leaving only he and Ty alone with Sonia.

Immediately, one of the former blond males reappeared at the matriarch's side. It seemed the men were extremely protective of her, never leaving her without a means of defence.

"Amadeus, this is my youngest son, Zane," Sonia introduced. "Zane is half human. Sky is not his father."

He raised a questioning eyebrow at that. *They can interbreed with humans?*

Sonia chuckled. Obviously, she had read his thought. It caused a hot flush of embarrassment, as Amadeus had forgotten they were telepaths.

"It is a long story, Amadeus. Bear with us, and sometime we will reveal more." Then she added, "We are not your enemy. Tomorrow, you may ask Sky anything you wish, on any subject that plagues you." Amadeus frowned, puzzled. "He looks forward to sharing your companionship, as you both have medical background."

I was right then.

Sonia turned to her son. "How is Ram then?"

"Healing well, but...the mental health, as you anticipated, will take much longer."

"And Djura?"

"He is healing back at this moment…with Lance's help."

"Lance is my oldest," Sonia explain. "He was the other who help bring Ram home. Zane?"

"Yes, mother?"

"I think we should fit the humans with transporter belts, and the bands for climate control that we've used previously. They will then have more freedom."

"Okay. I'll get Eric on that."

"It can wait for after sleep break," Sonia decided. "We all need some rest."

Zane nodded. "Where would you like these two housed?"

"Ty seems a bit disoriented, unsettled," Amadeus dared to intervene. "We don't mind a room together."

Amadeus' reasoning was, if he were alone with the boy, he could question him and discover how Ty knew about certain things. But Sonia was not about to fall for that ploy.

"Ty will be alright," Sonia stated quietly. "Would you like a room of your own, Ty?"

"Could I be outside?" the teen asked timidly.

Sonia smiled. "You may go outside as soon as you have the transport belt. You are not our prisoner, Ty, and may roam free as you please, but…I would prefer this time you sleep inside. Okay?"

Ty nodded agreement.

How did he even know there was an outside place? wondered Amadeus. *They never mentioned it.*

"There is a whole valley between two mountains," Sonia revealed, the fact a surprise to the man. "You also may explore, Amadeus." Then once more, she added gently to the boy. "You are safe here, Ty."

The teen's eyes filled with tears.

What is going on here? thought Amadeus. *What is it Sonia sees that I've never gotten out of him?*

"Zane, I think Ty would like Joel's room. His favourite colour is green."

"They could each have a chamber in the single male quarters," suggested Zane.

The boy's head came up in sudden fear.

"Aww..." Zane said sympathetically, as if he'd read something in the young teen's mind that had been until now guarded. "We all have been there at some point," he reassured. "Come." He took the boy by the hand. "Life's too short to worry so. It will all work out. I'll take you to your chamber."

Sonia chuckled. "It will be okay, Ty," she whispered. "You just need to think some things through."

Suddenly the other two just seemed to walk into nothingness. Amadeus stood alone with Sonia.

She quietly looked at him. "You are a good man, Amadeus," she decided. "A little unsure at the moment, but you will work it out. Trust me, the children are safer with us than they were with you. Even Jamara will find new life here."

He felt like he was being reprimanded; yet still she sought to comfort at the same time.

"Even you could find solace here, if you give us a chance. Do not flee, just yet. Give it time."

Amadeus dropped his eyes. There seemed no secrets from this woman. *Can I live with such openness? My last three years have been spent as a fugitive.*

"The fleeing is over...the hiding is not. Out there you will still be a renegade. You have left your society; can you fit back in? There will be questions to answer..."

Amadeus sighed. She made perfect sense. "But what of Ty? If it was just me, I wouldn't care."

"Ty is not of your kind..."

Somehow, that did not surprise him. "Is he of your species then?"

"To a degree."

He frowned. *What did that mean?* But he knew it was better not ask for clarification. In time maybe he would learn more if she decided it was beneficial.

"And what of Jamara?"

"Is it for you to govern her life?"

So she is removing them each from my care. He shook his head, surrendering.

A silence dropped between them. What am I supposed to do with my life now?

"It would please me greatly if you would remain..." She had read his thought, and was answering. "Get to know us better. Stay a few months, then make a decision."

"I thought you'd be leaving when Ram recovers…"

"Something else…will prevent that," she countered evasively.

When she did not elaborate, he realized she meant for him to wait and see. She was certainly not one to share a confidence unless it assisted her purpose.

Probably, I wouldn't find the revelation to my liking any way, he decided.

"Sometimes Amadeus I see a future that may be troubling," she admitted. "I do not tell because it might harm to know ahead of time."

He hadn't expected that disclosure.

"Okay. I'd like to stay…and study you," he agreed quietly. "May I ask one question?"

"Most certainly."

"They all guard you, both the men and women; they obey you without question. What is your station in your society?"

She chuckled. "Right to the point," she praised, delighted. "I am what is called the "Leader Female'. It is more than simply a designation; far more involved than mere leadership. Our species is one combined unit. I hold them together…physically, emotionally and mentally. I am their life source. If you seek to remove the entire race, the best way would be to eliminate me."

Amadeus blinked, shocked beyond words.

"To kill you, would…destroy the entire species?"

"All thirty of us."

At first he wasn't certain she was serious. His jaw had dropped stupidly at the new revelation. Then he realized the trust she had placed in him, the risk she had taken, and he was humbled.

When he could speak again, he attempted clarification. "There are so few of you?"

"You see now why any child is greatly treasured?"

It took his very breath away.

Then Zane returned, to take him to a sleep chamber.

****

At the new quarters, Zane turned back just before he meant to go. He studied Amadeus for a long moment, then decided to speak.

"Never before, has my mother shared our secret weakness with a human. To be so trusted with this knowledge…she must see something special in you," he reasoned. "Apparently, she also sees that you have a part to play in our future, or she would not have embraced the risk." Zane shook his head, marvelling. "As a people we have learned to rely on her second sight." He met the human man's eyes, his own suddenly hostile. "Mark me, we will be guarding her! Do not take lightly what she has confided to you…and share it with no one else. Or we will deal with you."

"You think I would do her harm? How could I even…I'm merely a human. And, I was once a physician. My Hippocratic oath is the core of me."

"It is not the first time hurt has come to us from the bosom of mankind."

"I am sorry for that, Zane," Amadeus declared regretfully. "But do not lump me with all of the human race. Some can be trusted."

Zane nodded acquiescence. "Fair enough," he agreed. "I hope her faith in you is well placed."

On that note, he jumped to his own quarters to be with his pair, Chantel.

Zane remembered the cruelty of another human, how she had tormented his partner before she and he had come together.

That had been one human, Darla, but others had stood watching...doing nothing. And the brutal one had received her due, not of the species preference either, but by her own choice.

Will this human be like my Chantel...or another Darla? Zane wondered. *This one is male. With the exception of Wade, we have never found a trustworthy male human before...*

Whatever will we do with him? Zane puzzled. *Perhaps my mother sees something unexpected?*

CHAPTER 9

Like an infant listening to her parent's chatter in the night, as she lay awake, Kara could hear her great-gran conversing with her partner. Perhaps, because they were unused to her presence, the pair had not blocked her from reading them. It was obvious they were unaware she listened in.

She should have tuned them out, but Kara was curious. Now she wished she had not been. They were discussing her, and what she heard caused insecurity to flood over her like a smothering waterfall.

"Ah, Sky," Sonia moaned grievingly. "They have done such damage to her mind. She is no longer the innocent Kara I nurtured and trained."

"I know," he agreed. "I feel the difference too. Were she fully human, they would call it brain injured…mentally challenged."

"There in lies the problem. She is part human. Because of that, I am at a loss how to fix this. The amplified abilities needed to be 'Leader Female' have suffered impairment to the extent I doubt she will ever be fit to support even a part of the species, let alone its whole…especially should we increase in numbers. She may someday lead, but we as a unit will not survive it."

"Dear one, remember all the times we have been on the brink of extinction," Sky reminded. "In each episode you found an answer."

"Not I, Sky. You know better," Sonia disagreed. "It was the Almighty Creator provided the solution in each case."

"And so it will be again. Nothing happens without a purpose; that is what you always tell me...even though we challenge or do not understand the reasoning."

Sonia softly chuckled. "Tonight we reverse our rolls. You are ever my encouragement."

Kara felt him kiss her, and she shivered at the unusual sensation in her great-gran. She knew it was time to block away her empathy. And so she did, going to mere thought-listen.

"Is it possible to re-train her?" Sky asked suddenly.

"Not unless her powers resurface. They have wiped clean the duplicate records I gave her. If something happens to me, even if I could again transfer that burden to her, some of the histories will be lost. She alone held those. I transferred memory past, the infinite detail to her. I now hold only the limited version. The other is still somewhere there in my mind, but I cannot re-transmit again. I never realized their weapon had been fine tuned this well."

"Why did this not happen to you when they used the ray on all of us?"

"I believe it had something to do with the fact she was caught in between change, half dormant; half whole. All they need do to make it work is to create such a state in me, and the weapon would have the same result...and you can imagine how that would end."

"Is this a new model, or the old modified?"

"They were testing the prototype on her, modifying it while she was unconscious. She has that memory, but cannot recall it herself...and they are unaware of their success...its effect. They were simply toying with their victim."

"I thought this weapon was exploded. And we destroyed the prototype ourselves...also the plans."

"There was a copy on another ship. Those here did not at first know its purpose, or use. They rebuilt it for something to do; Kara was the test subject...all experimental. They are still unaware it can kill us all."

"The weapon and the plans must be destroyed again!"

Sonia sighed. "I'm one step ahead of you. Already done. But it still leaves me with this problem; how to undo my great-granddaughter's handicap."

But Sky was still mulling the defence issue. "They only have small weaponry left?"

"Until one of them re-invents."

"Aw," Sky groaned exasperated. "Why must they always be so malevolent?"

"You know why. I am more worried my girl will not heal back."

The whole revelation made Kara feel like crying. Mostly she heard, they found her inferior. The way it appeared, at this moment, she was the same among them, as when she was among the humans...abnormal!

She had lost something irreplaceable...she was broken...and great-gran couldn't fix her...no one could!

Silently Kara began to weep. She shut away their thoughts, wished for oblivion, then cried herself to sleep.

****

When Kara awoke many hours later, Sky had already gone about his duties, but Sonia was in her sitting room reading, awaiting her great-granddaughter's rising.

"Great-gran?" The matriarch looked up, and smiled, as the girl entered the room. "Great-gran, I know I should be like you, but I'm wrong...in my head. Why can't you fix me?"

"Oh, honey." Sonia put down her book, and stretched out welcoming arms toward the child. "Come here."

Kara felt like a petulant infant who had cried so much her head hurt. She crawled up on Sonia's lap to be cuddled. It seemed perfectly natural, after all she was no teen; she was only eight in their years.

"What makes you think your head is not right?" Sonia wanted to know.

"I...was listening to you last night," she admitted hesitantly.

"Aw...my mistake. Foolish of me to forget you were there," Sonia chided herself. "What was said...I want you to know, we love you no matter how you are. It is like when someone gets sick...or injured. You do not reject them for it. It should make no difference. Love continues; in fact it grows more because of the weakness in the other. Isn't that so?"

"But, I don't want to be broken!"

Sonia gently kissed her forehead. "Tell me, little one, what causes the most hurt in you right now?"

"I feel your love, but...I also am aware of your displeasure..."

"I do not reject you, child. My frustration is with myself...my own inability to heal you."

"Am I not...whole? I can hear the thoughts of others; speak to them back without verbal, and I am aware of the feelings around me. I can do everything they can...I am one with them..."

"Yes, what more do you want? What plagues you so?"

"I want to heal the hurting ones...Ty and...Ram, but I can't seem to remember how ...or be included when the others do it."

"That is because we are keeping you separate from the process. You are not well enough yet. If you take part in healing with us you would be injured more, so we prevent your inclusion."

"It isn't me? My healing ability doesn't need fixing?"

"No dear. That works just fine. Besides, you are still very young. Capacity to heal grows stronger with age; as you mature your talent will increase."

"I'm not so broken?" Sonia smiled reassuringly, and nodded. "I'm used to thinking myself a teen. Now, I'm feeling like a child again..."

"And so it should be." Sonia caressed Kara's hair, smoothing it back from her face. "Doesn't it feel good to leave responsibilities to your elders? Enjoy life, little one. Play as you used to..."

"Ah, great-gran. I miss my momma. Where is she? Why hasn't she come? Doesn't she love me anymore?"

"Ah, honey..."

Sonia pulled her in tighter. The comfort felt good. It had been so long since she had experienced the intimate touch of another. Yes, it is better to be a child. Right now she couldn't handle being adult.

Sonia's fragrance of vanilla/cinnamon was reassuring, so soothing. It brought back memories of other times in her arms. But then, Kara also recalled another scent, the essence of caramel...her mother's personal bouquet.

Kara raised her head, and demanded a second time. "Where is my mother?"

Sonia sighed, pulled the girl's head down against her breast. Silently, they sat there, and Kara began to cry sensing something ominous.

"Sh, dear! Sh."

"Is she dead?" Kara could think of no other reason for her parent not being there.

"You have a new baby sister," Sonia revealed softly.

Kara's head shot up with renewed excitement. "I have! When can I see her?"

"She was born the day we found you."

"Yesterday?"

"Yes, dear. I did not know myself until just now, when your mother mind showed me. She was keeping it secret for when we would return, but because you are upset with her, she was forced to tell me now. You have spoiled her little surprise." Sonia chuckled good-naturedly.

But Kara's thoughts went in another direction, as the negative reality struck her. "Will my sister replace me?"

"Oh, most certainly not!" Sonia returned vehemently. "Her anticipated arrival caused the search for you to be intensified. You will never, under any circumstance be replaced!"

"But…is she another…'Leader Female'?"

"No dear. She is just a normal."

"I'm not normal?"

"Aw, dear…how did you become so insecure? Living among humans has twisted your thinking. You are special…your abilities are profound!"

Unbidden, tears sprang to Kara's eyes. "But, mine aren't working! I'm supposed to be like you!"

"Not exactly like me. Each of us is different, each important, irreplaceable. You will have your own place in our society as you grow older."

"But now, I will never be the 'Leader Female'."

"Never say never, dear. I have many times seen the unexplainable happen. And I choose to believe this problem will right itself in time. Do not give up."

Kara sat silent for a time, considering this advice. Her great-gran's love flooded into her senses, and for the moment she basked in it.

"When will my parents come?" she finally asked.

"They will not be coming, dear," Sonia regretfully disclosed. "It is unsafe to bring the infant to this area of space. The enemy is too close...she is the first child born to our species since...we began our new lives."

"Can't they leave her with gran...and the others?"

"She is half human, very fragile," Sonia attempted to explain. "The separation from her parents would break her bond to them. That would mean she would go dormant; it might even kill her at this stage...and after what happened to you, I'm not certain your parents would survive such heart break."

Kara suddenly was filled with unreasoning jealous anger. *The baby is more important to all of them than I am! They love her more!*

"Oh no, dear! That is not so! Each life is of equal value; all are important! This baby is vulnerable, unable to function without her parents. Until she is stronger, they must be continually joined and with her... They have always loved you dearly. Don't you remember how they spoiled you when you were dormant? They have been searching these long years at my side. Only this birth prevented them being here."

Sonia stroked Kara's hair with each word; the soothing caress made the separation more bearable. The girl began to realize her great-gran was attempting to do for her what her parents would have, had they been here, what they must do for her small sister instead.

"As soon as possible, we will go to them," her great-gran assured. "Would you like to see your little sister now?"

Even though her face was smothered against the matriarch's breast, Kara nodded. She wasn't going to give up that pleasurable sensation for anything.

Immediately their two minds were one with her mother Jessica. They could feel the soft downy head beneath her hand; feel the velvet skin as she caressed the new infant. The three were cuddling the sleeping child together. Kara sighed with the pleasure of it, suddenly overwhelmed with love for her sister. Tears of longing filled her eyes, and spilled over. Moments later Sonia broke the connection, and it felt like she had lost something dear.

"Oh, when can we go home so I can play with her?"

Sonia chuckled. "It will be weeks before she does anything more than eat and sleep, dear. When we get home, she will see and enjoy you more."

"When?" Kara pressed.

But Sonia would not specify. "As soon as we are able...Ram must be balanced before we can travel..."

"Why won't you let me help with that? It would speed it up."

Sonia remained the ever-calm adult. "First you are too young to take part in emotional healing, and…your own mental state is too fragile. It would unbalance you beyond any repair."

Frustrated, still a little angry, Kara attempted to cool her emotions.

"What about Ty?" she finally asked.

"Aw, yes," her great-gran observed, as if there was more behind the question than was obvious. "You have known since you first met him, this one is a damaged one, haven't you?"

"Yes." Kara sighed. "I could always see cloudy images of torture in his memories, but he tries so hard to forget, to fight remembrance. And now, he seems separate, I can't read him, can't connect with him."

"I am preventing deeper communication," Sonia admitted.

"But, why, great-gran?" Kara pleaded, feeling defeated. "What did I do wrong? Have I done him harm?"

"No. I feel that right now to watch his struggles will hurt you. I will spare you that at all costs. His emotional/mental state needs healing. Trust us to do it, before you attempt closeness. After that, he will come back to you whole."

"How long will it take, great-gran?" Kara asked mournfully. "I need him. I feel like everyone I care about is lost to me."

"Be patient, dear child. You yourself are not well. Your mood swings fluctuate too much," Sonia reasoned. "They will soon right themselves. Until then you could do more harm than good. All will return to normal eventually."

"So much healing needed, and I am so useless…I might as well still be dormant!"

Sonia went quiet for many seconds, then slowly, very softly she confided. ""If for any reason, at any time in the future, you do not want to remain with us, I can put you dormant again, but…you will be minus all abilities. You would live a normal human life span, die very much younger, and…never remember us."

Kara burst into tears. It sounded to her like rejection, hate. "What kind of choice is that, great-gran? I would lose all…"

Sonia sighed. "At some time you may wish it… I would only do it for your safety. I do not wish it."

Finally, Kara said it aloud, the real reason she felt disjointed, the most important loss to her mind. "Ty…isn't like us. But, he is the one I need."

A half smile played at the corner of Sonia's lips, as if she still held an undisclosed secret.

"Very true…but two lives are in this balance, not yours alone. He must make his own choice. Will you permit him that privilege?"

"Oh, great-gran…this hurts too much!"

Sonia's arms tightened around her again, and once more Kara felt her affection, sunk into it.

"Give it a month…even two," Sonia suggested wisely. "Much can change in that time."

Kara gave a disparaging sigh. "Well…at least, I'm not the baby of the species any longer," she decided.

Sonia chuckled in delight, bent and kissed the top of her head.

CHAPTER 10

Amadeus woke with a start. It took a minute to orient himself, and to realize Sky stood beside the bed.

They had spent considerable time together the few days Amadeus had been here, and he had come to appreciate the male, as well as the guardian way of life, as he understood it.

He knew he had much more to learn; they had only just touched into the knowledge these people held.

"Would you like to sit in on a healing session?" Sky inquired at a whisper.

Amadeus quickly sat up. "Indeed. I would count it an honour."

He had witnessed Sonia heal Kara, but since then had learned there were other ways and forms of doing it. He very much wanted to watch; however it was done.

"Your 'Keeper' was programmed to respond to both vocal and silent commands. I recommend you use thought rather than speaking aloud, so you do not disturb the others. It is quite early," Sky cautioned. "When you are ready, come. The unit will guide you to where we are. No need to hurry; we will wait on you."

With that the physician vanished abruptly.

It took some getting used to, the sudden way they could teleport from place to place, and when it was done with him in tow, it disoriented him considerably. Amadeus supposed eventually, he would adjust.

****

Half an hour later, Amadeus entered the healing chamber, a small fifteen-foot square room. He had chosen to walk rather than use the teleport belt. He did not particularly like jumping on his own, what with the sensation and a fear of materializing inside a granite wall. The distance wasn't that far, anyway.

On a cot against the far wall, Ram lay asleep, his rest obviously fitful.

To one side stood Sky, Sonia and Djura with a second female.

All Amadeus could see of this one was her beautiful wavy gold-red hair flowing loose down her back. Djura had his arm about her, which by what the human had judged of the warrior, seemed totally out of character.

Amadeus had seen the female only once before, when he had arrived in Sanctuary, and he gathered that this was the giant's partner. Djura seemed so aggressive each time they met; he had never considered the male might have the capacity for affection. Clearly that was a grievous misjudgement.

Sky stepped away from the others when Amadeus entered. As the physician approached, a chair formed directly behind the human.

The healer meant it litterly, when he said I'd sit in, Amadeus observed with amusement.

"A few guidelines for our safety," cautioned Sky, going right into the process without preamble. "First we must never be touched while healing. You are here to merely observe. Never has a human witnessed a session such as this; it is a most private affair, but...it was Sonia's request to have you present..."

"You would rather not have me here?" Amadeus quickly questioned bluntly.

"Not that," Sky hesitantly admitted. "This will not be a pleasant experience." His gaze went to Sonia, as if he were seeking a change of heart, then finding none, returned his attention awkwardly to his human counterpart. "You will observe my female in disparaging circumstances. In her words, she will...'lose it' in the presence of a human. I am not at all comfortable with that."

Amadeus grinned, suddenly understanding where he was coming from. The male was embarrassed for a human to see the imperfect side of his mate.

"I promise not to hold it against her," he reassured. "We have all lost it at some point or other in our lives."

"You misunderstand," Sky defended annoyed. "Sonia will not be rude to the patient or you. She heals Ram of an unbalanced state, and...could well exhibit a like state herself. This is the first of many sessions where she will enter his mind, joining with him in memory to relive events. As she does it she softens the hurt impairing him."

Does he mean she sees what the boy sees? wondered Amadeus. *And...*

"Feels what he feels," Sky clarified, finishing the thought.

Amadeus shivered at the prospect.

And here once again was another of their disconcerting habits: the way they answered what you thought was a private reflection. Amadeus was not sure he'd ever get used to their knowing his every thought.

"Then this is not like a physiatrist drawing a patient out?"

"It is, but yet, much more."

"Why would Sonia do it then, and not you?"

"She is the stronger healer, our female 'Healer Ultimate'. Actually, we will be working in conjunction; I am her support person. My powers tend toward physical strength; hers are of the mind. I am also male 'Healer Ultimate'."

"Let me understand, you do this with your minds?"

Sky nodded. "Physical strength will also be drained in the process. That is why Djura joins us; he is the ultimate male strength. I know you have noted his superior capabilities, and in your mind have given him the label of 'Warrior Guardian'. For your information, the moniker pleases him."

Amadeus felt the sudden warmth of embarrassment, but he was almost glad they had read his mind this time.

"Karine, Djura's pair is here as his emotional female support balance. When we drain strength from him, he sometimes may go unstable."

"Is he dangerous…ah, to others then?"

Sky chuckled softly. "Karine will keep him tame."

Again embarrassed by his own timidity and self-absorption, Amadeus steered the conversation back to the process. "So, just how does it work?"

"Sonia goes in as primary healer. When she becomes too weak she drains energy from me..."

And suddenly the human understood what had taken place at Kara's healing. Now, he knew what to expect.

"When I am no longer sufficient, I become one with her, and she then drains from the second male. Should all of us go down, do not panic. You cannot help us. It would be most unusual, if we failed to heal back within a short period."

Sky once again repeated his warning. "At no point are you to touch anyone of us. This is imperative. A touch from you would not only kill that person, but also the entire species...we are all connected, a unified entity. What happens with one effects us all."

Amadeus remembered what Sonia had told him, and the resultant warning from Zane. Suddenly he wondered: *Is this a test of trust, of my reliability?*

But Sky showed no evidence he had intercepted the thought of the human. He simply finished his explanation.

"As we have learned about these healing abilities, over time we have perfected our methods..." Then he disclosed one last important fact. And the revelations that followed shocked Amadeus to the core. "Our headbands are not the same as yours. They diminish our image so that you are able to view us. Should we choose not to wear them, you would not see us at all. If by chance we are indiscernible to you, that will be when you need to worry…"

"Why would that be? What would it mean?"

"At any other time, it might mean the band has been knocked off line, but today…it will mean, we cannot heal back. Should that happen, simply order your 'Keeper' to take you out of Sanctuary."

Stunned, Amadeus quickly demanded. "Why? Are you dangerous to me?"

Sky's smile was guarded. "Sometimes…not now."

"And…am I to understand, your lives hang in the balance on this?"

"They do at every healing. But I doubt it will go critical this time. Sonia is strong, and two 'Healer Ultimate' are seldom inadequate. We do know our limit; how far is safe to go in this session. It is Sonia's hope that what you see here today, will be of value to you in the future."

With that Sky turned, rejoining the others, seeming to dismiss his audience. Amadeus sat back to observe.

****

The four took their positions. Sonia moved forward to within four feet of the sleeping couch, and eased to her knees, then sat back against her heels. Sky did the same directly behind and to her right.

Djura took up a position approximately three feet from them to Sonia's left. He stood in his usual guardian stance, feet slightly apart, arms folded across his chest. To his left, Karine quietly stood watch.

It was very apparent when Sonia made contact.

Her eyes closed; she tensed, and moaned in anguish, as if even entering the boy's mind was wounding. Then she relaxed, seeming to fall into deep sleep where she sat.

For many seconds nothing happened. Amadeus clearly received an image of searching through dark, fog-shrouded corridors. Then abruptly, he felt a disconnect.

Sonia cried out. The sound turned to a scream that echoed stridently across the room.

So startled was Amadeus, his body tensed painfully; foreboding crawled up his spine.

What has been done to this young man that even Sonia cringes? wondered Amadeus. *What manner of enemy tortures them in this way?*

For all his questions, that one was still left unanswered.

Acutely intent, all four involved in the healing were deeply immersed in what they were doing; not a one seemed aware the human remained in the room. I came to Amadeus then, why Zane had been so on the defensive.

Why I could so easily touch them, he realized. *I could kill the whole lot of them if I chose.*

And they were trusting he would not do it.

That alone sent the shivers of dread through him.

Sonia choked away the scream. Plaintively, she whimpered, like a small hopeless child. Sky took her into his arms, enfolding her in embracing comfort.

Unexpectedly, the young man on the bed grew calm; his breathing slowed; peaceful slumber ensued. No longer, it seemed, was he subject to unpleasant nightmares.

But Sonia appeared to have switched places, his memories having transferred to her mind. She jerked and thrashed wildly, and Sky caught her flailing hands in his own, held them tightly to quiet her. As soon Sky made contact with her clenched fists, his features took on the same agony.

They really are living it, Amadeus realized. *The healing is not easy on them.*

Djura voice came in thought to the human. *Many days will be needed for them to heal back from this. And this is only the first session of many.*

Amadeus shuddered. "Is it always this bad?"

Please, do not speak aloud, cautioned Djura. *It will distract them. And yes, healing is always painful, but more so this time. Rarely do we need to mend one of our own of emotions and memories such as these. Forgive me. I am needed. I must concentrate now. Save your questions for later.*

Sonia began to shudder spasmodically. Amadeus realized she was suffering excruciating pain. Now he did feel guilty at seeing this powerful being at her worst, but never would he judge her for her frailty. It was different when you realized how all had come about, and he admired her for the courage and sacrifice she was willing to expend for this boy, who by human standards would be the least of their species.

In the eyes of this woman all were equal, none expendable.

She was the matriarch, the ruler of this race, and that alone was hard for the man to wrap his mind around, but the fact that this lady was the old crone who had entered his kitchen only days before and changed the lives of all present upon their meeting, gave his mind such an unmeasured incredulity he wondered at times if he had escaped into madness.

As a human, Amadeus also marvelled at Sky, who though of lesser function was paired to this compelling creature, giving love and support beyond expected rationale, never faltering in furnishing what was required.

A brilliant luminosity appeared around the healer pair. They seemed to blend and meld into each other.

This is the joining, Amadeus realized. *Didn't Sky say this happens when they come to the end of their strength?*

Djura dropped to one knee, panting.

Alarm filled his soul; Amadeus shivered.

The voice of the second female entered his mind. *Fear not, human. That emotion can unbalance us. Stay calm; we are still fine. But the session must end soon. We can do no more at this time.*

Amadeus took a deep, relaxing breath.

The auburn beauty reached out and caressed Djura's cheek. The warrior guardian sighed audibly, as if she'd given him a refreshing draught of water. And then the courageous, normally stoic male burst into tears, sobbing brokenly, totally emotionally unbalanced.

Amadeus had thought such a thing was mere speculation; to observe the reality of it was shocking. It was as if this powerful defender had been unseated like a helpless child. He lived, had borrowed, the emotions and pain of the younger guardian, and the length and intensity had been too much for him.

Karine wrapped Djura in a gentle, affectionate embrace, like a devoted mother cuddling a young one. They too began to glow, then blended into one.

Not realizing he held his breath, Amadeus waited. Will they come out of this? Have they gone beyond the limit?

Abruptly the glow over the lead healer pair vanished. They became separate, two from one. And almost at the same time, the other couple duplicated their action.

It was over!

Sky rose to his feet, supporting Sonia. She turned wearily to Amadeus, smiling.

"Thank you for causing us no harm," she praised softly. "We need to seek rest now..."

Why would I ever wish you harm, dear lady? Amadeus thought with incredulity. *You do not realize the treasures you are.*

Then suddenly, Amadeus was back in his sleep cubicle, sitting on his bed. And just for a second, he wondered if he had dreamt it all; it seemed so very unreal.

CHAPTER 11

It was the next day that Amadeus discovered the beauties of the sunken garden. Tucked away in the midst of all the granite caverns with no visible sunlight, he wondered that it grew at all. It was a breathtaking view; even the larger trees were in bloom, and the rose bushes and lilacs were flowering at the same time as the tulips and daffodils; spring, summer and fall all together in one place. He marvelled at such an accomplishment, and knew it was not duplicated anywhere else on earth.

The area was lit by subdued light from inside the stone walls and the ceiling. A softly bubbling brook meandered under small bridges across each pathway. It was quiet and peaceful here, so Amadeus began to walk the trails, silently sorting through the events of the past week.

It was not until he came upon the caste iron bench by a low wall that he realized he was not alone.

Sonia looked up startled; as if she had let her guard down, had not been expecting to be disturbed, and was unaware another was near. Her cheeks were moist; she brushed at them self-consciously.

She's been crying? Amadeus marvelled in shock.

"Is everything alright?" he asked with concern.

But the normally composed female turned his disquiet into an opportunity for a private intimacy.

"Sit with me." Sonia patted the seat beside her, and though a little reluctant to invade, Amadeus lowered himself to the bench.

"Even those who seem to have it all together, can at times feel down," she admitted softly. "After a healing session, I have difficulty with emotional balance."

After what he had witnessed, he felt for her distress.

"Where is Sky? Shouldn't he be with you at a time like this?"

"That male needs to rest!" she declared as if annoyed. "Sometimes he will not, and I have drained on him most grievously. So...I left him sleeping."

Amadeus almost laughed at the attitude, but he schooled his mind and features to meet the need. "Is there anything I can do? Perhaps call one of the other men...or is there one here with you?"

He scanned the area about them searchingly. Amadeus knew a male could be standing right there, invisible to him, guarding Sonia to protect her.

"I am alone," Sonia quietly disclosed. "Sometimes, I am permitted a quiet time alone." She laughed softly, at her own words, adding frankly: "There is no one in Sanctuary who means me harm..."

He was glad now he had decided not to stand his ground, or to flee with Jamara and Ty. The matriarch apparently had judged him to be safe.

Out of the calm that fell upon them, he finally asked. "You were crying. May I ask why? Perhaps, if you share, I can ease the burden."

At his offer, Sonia smiled tentatively, but expertly side stepped with an indirect reply.

"To be honest, from what I've seen of our futures…you someday will be my saviour."

"Me?" Amadeus gave an uncomfortable laugh, both surprised and a bit disconcerted. "How could that be?"

"At present, I do not see it well."

"And, what you see…made you cry?"

Sonia laughed delighted. "Such visions have been known to do worse to me," she admitted candidly. "But this time…I have only pieces…usually it is not so limited. Perhaps my age catches up to me."

Amadeus grinned at the opening presented. "How old are you really?" he probed tenderly.

"In human…eighty."

"As I gather, it's half that by your reckoning…forty? That's still young. I think it most likely you are simply mending…not yet completely…healed back."

Sonia nodded, pleased by his correct use of their terminology. "Today I am feeling old." She sighed. "Do you realized, what is this place where we sit?"

Amadeus panned the scenery around them. He remembered, back behind them at the convergence of the three paths, a statue of a young boy, but he had not bothered to read the inscription beneath. Now he also saw a like plaque on the wall in front of them.

Before he could read it, Sonia continued.

"This is our memorial garden. The commemorative inscription ahead honours one of the first casualties we suffered during a previous sojourn on Earth. That was my brother Myron."

"Aw, so sorry. Now I understand," Amadeus sympathized. "You must miss him."

Sonia's eyes budded tears, one spilling slowly down her cheek. "He represents my first error in judgement," she confided. "I did not succeed in showing him the love he needed. I considered another's anger first; let my own irritation rule my heart...because of it, in the end, he hated us both. I banished him for lack of conformity, and...he took his own life...nearly eliminated the whole species. We were very inexperienced then."

Shocked, Amadeus was uncertain how to respond. He had never expected to see into the core of her this way.

"Is this why there are so few of you?"

"No. The reason for that is another battle, much before my time. I will leave that for another to tell." Sonia rose to her feet. "Stay a while," she suggested. "Enjoy the garden."

With that she vanished, and the human felt guilty for displacing her from her quiet spot.

He turned to read the plaque on the wall:

'In memory of the warrior Myron
Brother to Sonia and Joel
A loss great to their souls'

He realized her tears were those of mourning; not for the future had she feared, but it was regret of a past she could not change. Rapidly, Amadeus was becoming aware, this female was nothing like she had appeared at first meeting.

How did she get caught between her two brothers? he wondered.

CHAPTER 12

Jamara found it hard to assimilate to Sanctuary. This new world was so alien; here she felt no longer needed. She had gone from servant to royalty, so it seemed, and she was not sure she liked it.

Kara was most often secluded away from her care; Amadeus seemed busy with Sky, Sonia's pair, and she seldom saw Ty at all. Even he had separated, either off by himself or with one of the males. She realized both Kara and Ty were better off, but what was she to do now?

Jamara was lost here…again an immigrant floundering. She had no idea where she belonged, how to integrate, or what to do with herself.

These beings were like nothing she had ever seen before, in character so unlike humans, not merely larger, utterly foreign and uninhibited by cultural differences. They lived the mini united-nations, and actually got along. It puzzled Jamara.

As the east Indian woman pondered her circumstances while alone in her sleep quarters, three of the alien females appeared out of nowhere, their sudden arrival overwhelming, almost threatening to the smaller human, what with the closeness of their presence in the confined space.

Jamara knew each by name: Angel in her thirties was eldest; Morgan looked about the same age but was far the more restrained, and Chantel seemed younger, of the quieter type, about three years junior to the other two.

"It is not healthy to spend so much time alone in your chambers," scolded Angel. "Come with us, Jamara," she urged. "We want to show you more of Sanctuary. We'll start with the banquet room and our history record. We haven't visited it for a while."

Before the human had time to question, or refuse, to even take a breath, Angel and Morgan had each taken an arm, and jumped.

As the sensation of displacement wore off, Jamara had time to gaze around. She found they had transported to a gigantic room with tables and benches that would accommodate at least fifty. But it was the over all area that had you catching your breath.

The appearance of the room caused you to feel as if you had stepped into the outdoors at night. It was decorated to appear like a sunset of early spring, with flowers painted along the bottoms of the walls, so vivid and convincing you needed to touch to make certain they were not real. On the opposite wall from the door, the sunset graduated up in colours from light to dark, eliciting a feeling of both warmth and coldness at once. The ceiling was as star-lit as a genuine sky, depth and distance as authentic as any view of outer space.

"We wanted you to see our memory wall," Chantel exclaimed excitedly, almost before she was fully visible. "I remember the first time I viewed it...I was absolutely overwhelmed."

It was then Jamara noticed the oval picture renderings painted on the two opposing walls, and on either side of the doorway.

"The murals depict the history of this generation," Angel volunteered. "From the battle scene that destroyed the former race, to the left of the door, around to the battle in which we females became 'Aopato'."

Jamara frowned puzzled. *Became...what? What is she saying?*

Morgan chuckled. "You are confusing her. Start at the beginning. And I think; only one should do the telling. She has a hard time following when we complete each other's thoughts. Let her ask questions. You forget what it was like before we were telepathic."

Jamara's jaw dropped, and she wanted to ask, when, how, why?

But Angel was apologizing. "Oh. Yes. Sorry. I have been insensitive. After three earth years we have gotten used to talking in sequence, completing the words before they're spoken. Instantaneous processing is normal to us now. All we need do is think and the others know...we've forgotten how to be human."

Jamara was speechless. What with the females hardly letting her get a word in, and the revelations Angel seemed to be alleging, the human felt slow of mind.

"What do you mean?" she finally asked. "You were never human..."

Angel grinned; Morgan winked knowingly.

Chantel chuckled. "Oh, yes we were; every one of us! We were much like you. I was a paraplegic in a wheelchair when I came here. We were all born right on this planet."

Jamara ignored the insinuation of deficiency, seemed not to even hear it. "Not human though?"

"Very human," Angel clarified, backing Chantel's admission. "We were not always like we are now. Not any of us! Even Sonia was once human-like...a dormant, as she calls it."

"Like she be..." Her amazement was causing Jamara to fall back to broken English; the correct words escaping her thoughts in the confusion. "In form...when I see first? That dormant?"

"Similar. That was what she looked like then," Chantel agreed.

"But, at that time she did not know what she was," Angel cut in.

"And no, she wasn't dormant when you first saw her, just in disguise," added Chantel.

"I not understand diff..."

"She just uses the dormant form to put humans at ease," Angel supplied.

Chantel tried to lead them back to the original conversation. "The first of this generation looked human-like."

Jamara was totally confused now. Rather then ask another question, she simply went silent, waiting for them to make things clear.

"Oh there! See, you've done it again," Morgan reproached in annoyance. "You don't explain; you don't let her speak. Calm down, both of you."

Finally! thought Jamara. *Maybe Morgan can say it so I can get it straight.*

"You tell!" she ordered forcefully. "Others be quiet. Make more sense from you."

Morgan laughed, and drew in a quick breath. "Okay. First let's just sit down on the benches," she suggested.

When they had taken seats, Morgan began at the beginning.

"Notice the image to the left of the door?" She pointed to a five-foot oval in red against the blue-black granite. Inside this frame was a battle scene with a spacecraft hovering over a planet's surface. It was shooting red and blue beams, toward fleeing figures holding babes in arms, and small toddlers by the hands. The terror etched on the faces of those helpless humanoids sent shivers through Jamara.

"That is where it all began. The first race divided into two separate factions. One annihilated the other, but just before their 'Leader Female' perished she sent some of her male guardians to hide children in dormant form on planet Earth."

"Here?" Jamara demanded in shock. "Right here?"

Morgan nodded. "But once all the adults were killed, the enemy took to hunting for the hidden children, and in time killed them all, as well."

"But…some survived?"

"Not of the original group. It took the enemy many years to find them all, and some lived long enough to reproduce with humans. Some of our partners, the guardians, are offspring of that coupling."

"The guardians are half-human?"

"Yes, all except for Joel, Sonia's brother. She and he are 'Pure'."

"How can that be, if all of the first kind took human partners?"

"Well, this is how their story goes. Sonia's parents were both original children. Somehow, they found each other, and even though they were dormant, they successfully paired. They had three offspring: Sonia, Myron and Joel. Sonia was the only one to take a partner, and he was human."

"Sky?"

"Oh, no," Morgan disagreed. "Sky is an original guardian offspring."

Once again Jamara was confused.

"Sonia's human former partner died of cancer when their children were just babies. They had four offspring of there own: My partner, Lance; Jade; Rhea and Zane, Chantel's pair. After all of them broke dormancy, Sonia took Sky as her consort. He too had a previous spouse who is dead."

Jamara blinked, uncertain. It was hard to keep everything straight. Before Morgan could continue again, she cut in.

"Who Angel's partner?"

"Eric," Angel supplied. "He's one of the original guardians."

"And Djura?"

"Oh, he belongs to Karine…the older one of us. Remember, the red head with green eyes," offered Chantel.

"The very big one?"

"That she is; over seven feet tall." Morgan grinned. "Do you want to hear more?"

"Yes. Think I have straight."

"Okay, then," Morgan went on. "Both Sonia's girls took human partners...this all took place before they broke dormant."

"Only females can mate to humans," Jamara speculated aloud.

"Now, I never realized that," Morgan mused. "It does seem to be supported, because Rhea's daughter Jessica also paired human, and reproduced; that's Kara. Jade's daughter is still too young..."

"No!" interrupted Angel. "Sonia says that is incorrect. Sky, when paired to his human, produced a girl child."

"Oh...okay," Morgan accepted. "I stand corrected.

Once again, Jamara was perplexed. "When Sonia say this? How? She not here."

Morgan grinned knowingly. "Better explain Angel.

"We can tap into Sonia's memory bank even when she's sleeping or at a distance. She is the record keeper, just as Kara...ah, was suppose to be."

It was getting all way to complicated.

"Let's returned to our history lesson, shall we," suggested Chantel.

Morgan again took up the account. "Anyway, Jade has a daughter, Nadia; Rhea has three children: Jessica; Tyler and Shawn."

Jamara wished clarification. "Sister's have human partners?"

"You mean Jade and Rhea? No, not now," Morgan admitted. "You see, both lost their human first mate to car accidents, and later paired again with an original guardian."

Jamara blew out a breath. *So complicated.*

"Both husbands die?"

"Oh, gee, we are getting way off track. If we tell you every detail..." Angel complained frustrated. "We'll just tell you the basic for now, okay?"

"Be my guest," Morgan offered.

So, Angel took up the narrative. "When Sonia broke dormancy, she released her two brothers, and they found ten other surviving offspring from the hidden children. These were all male: ten guardians, added to the two 'Pure' brothers. Out of Sonia's family of twelve, there were only six females. This comprised the entire species."

"Is not now the same?"

Angel laughed, understanding instantly her misconception. Jamara had not come in contact with all living Aopato. "Oh no, dear. There are thirty of us now, fifteen of each, male and female."

"Correction," Morgan interrupted. "We now have an extra female. Kara has a new baby sister."

"Oh, right!" Angel agreed.

"But...how you find other females?"

"They are us!" Chantel cut in. "Nine humans...became paired to the extra guardians."

"But...how you get to be..."

"Aopato?" finished Angel.

The other women chuckled. They had finally come full circle, back at the start.

"The guardians advertised on Earth for women...the thing is, we didn't know we were meant to be wives," Morgan revealed.

"Another time we will tell you the full story of the guardian pairings," Chantel agreed.

"In the end," Angel continued. "Sonia blood-healed us all, and made us only half human...except for Ziva, of course. Somehow, she turned out 'Pure', as was fitting, considering she was to be Joel's partner."

"The credit for that belongs entirely to the Almighty Creator," Morgan affirmed. "Sometimes, when we least expect it, we are given a miracle."

They believe in a supreme being, Jamara realized. *Like Amadeus does.*

"Anyway," Angel went on. "That last picture, to the right of the door frame, depicts the final scene of the guardian pair healings."

Jamara followed her gesture to the indicated picture. Again it stood out, painted against the dark wall in a red oval five-foot frame. Inside, on a background of smoky fog-like pure-white light stood a strikingly gorgeous female, surely taller than Karine. Her raven black hair flowed across her shoulders and down her back in a cape of waving curls; the bronze tan of her skin was flawless, and dark long lashes near hid the unusual eyes. The slit was silver against a chocolate brown colour; her gaze held you mesmerized.

The man, who stood beside this beauty, though shorter than Djura, stood as powerful and commanding as that protector. His eyes were unlike any Jamara had seen to this point, the colour of polished silver with a slit of rust, and they held an unmistakeable pride for his new companion.

The two seemed to transport you to another plane, one of love, tenderness and self-sacrifice. A sigh of longing escaped the lips of the human.

Angel brought Jamara back to reality. "Ziva is our only 'Warrior Female'…extremely, unbelievably, powerful physically; stronger than Djura."

"And she was once human?" Jamara clarified with awe.

"Yes. She gave her life for Joel."

"She is dead!" cried Jamara in disappointment.

"Oh no. She is very much alive," Morgan declared, as if such a fact was not as unreasonable as it sounded. "Sonia preserved her essence in the headband she was wearing; one like you wear. She then brought her back after healing the body, and of course presented her to Joel. It was the most romantic moment ever."

"You saw this happen?" Jamara quizzed doubtful.

The three answered in unison. "Oh, yes! We were a part of it all."

"But, come now," Angel suggested. "See the other memory pictures on the walls."

As the female placed her arm around the human, leading her about from frame to frame, Jamara no longer felt threatened by these beings. Now they seemed more like sisters, a pleasure to commune with, to share and to laugh together, something she had never had before.

"This one," Angel pointed out. "Is Sonia as a baby."

The picture was of a small child of perhaps two, climbing a ladder to the roof where her father stood.

"But…she looks human!"

"Of course. She was dormant," laughed Angel. "We have told you. We were all born here. Even Sonia."

The wonder of it all finally sunk in.

Then Jamara saw another picture nearby. This was one of a woman in a wheelchair.

"This is Chantel?"

"Not that one," Chantel disagreed. "That is Jade. She spent more than ten earth years that way; she was injured in the car accident that killed her first husband. Sonia healed her as she broke her dormancy. And when I came, Jade healed me."

"Oh, oh!" Jamara moaned with yearning. "How wonderful it would to be able to heal another."

"It hurts even more when they will not let you," Kara's voice came from behind them; her tone so forlorn Jamara wanted to hug away the ache.

She turned surprised, for she had not heard the young girl arrive.

"I thought we left you sleeping," Morgan said, slipping her arm around Kara's shoulders.

"I couldn't help but hear your chatter in my head," the younger female declared petulantly. "It woke me."

"We are sorry," apologized Chantel.

"You are lonely, dear," observed Morgan.

"Everyone is so much older than I am," Kara complained.

"Nadia is to come soon," Morgan placated. "Your cousin comes to be with you."

"She is closer to your age," agreed Chantel, then to Jamara added: "You should also like her. Nadia is our 'Music Ultimate'; her father was Eritrean."

"From Africa? Here on Earth?"

"'Course from Earth," Kara retorted rudely. "How many times do you have to be told; we were all born here!"

Jamara stepped back confused. It was hard to recognise this girl as the same one she had nurtured the past three years; Kara as Kali had always been so pleasant and even-tempered. It seemed at the attaining of outward beauty, an inner ugliness had surfaced to come between them. Her scent was that of cherry blossoms, but the mood was like the tree was dead.

Morgan apparently took notice as well. "What troubles you, little one?" she asked quietly.

"What were you doing in here?" Kara asked, avoiding the subject, turning to gaze about the room.

"We were telling Jamara our history," Chantel defended.

Kara scanned the pictures almost angrily. "I remember the pairings…I didn't forget everything!"

"Aw, honey," Morgan sympathized, pulling the child against her in a comforting embrace. "The far past history isn't as important as what we personally remember, anyway."

Tears filled Kara's eyes. "But…I lost something important…I'm good for nothing now."

"That's not true. And it was by no fault of your own."

What are they talking about? Jamara wondered.

"We love you however you are; don't you feel it?" pleaded Morgan. "When you have healed back completely, emotionally, it won't be this hard to balance on your own. It will get better. Maybe the memories, the record, is still there beneath the surface, but the fear of hurtful experience holds you back…blocks it."

"Oh, Morgan." Kara finally gave in, disclosing the real scourge beneath. "Great-gran heals Ram without me…as if I'd ever do him harm."

"Aw, sweet…" Morgan folded the sobbing child to her bosom. "Your emotions are too unstable; you are not well enough…"

"I feel…excluded."

"Come." Morgan beckoned the other two, and together they made a circle about Kara, joining hands. Jamara stepped away, realizing she wasn't meant to be a part of what was to come.

Suddenly the four seemed to meld as one. For seconds, they remained so, then Angel and Chantel stepped away, and the other two were separate once again.

"Better now?" Morgan asked.

Kara nodded sheepishly. She laughed self-consciously. "I guess I was off balance again. Great-gran's healing back, resting…and I'm missing her…" she finished lamely.

"We are always here for you," Angel offered. "All you need do is ask. Sonia doesn't need to be your only balance."

"Oh, let's go to lunch," Kara suggested cheerily. "I'm starving. Come on, Jamara. We'll all show you the valley afterward."

Jamara shook her head perplexed. The girl was like a yo-yo, swinging back and forth emotionally in mere seconds. She was a totally different person now.

What just happened here? she wondered. *And what do they mean by balance?*

"It is when our emotions go out of whack," Kara explained reading her question. "The others simply put me right."

Jamara's eyes went large with shock. *They can do that?*

Kara laughed. "And yes, I also just read your mind. We can do that too. Up until now, the other females have tried not to upset you, but we can all read each other, and you. I could read you even when I was dormant, but I never said anything, so I wouldn't scare you away."

"I think...and you hear?"

"We all do," Angel admitted softly, apologetically. "We've tried not to embarrass...we keep quiet."

"You see everything I think?" Jamara asked in horror.

"Don't sweat it," Kara soothed. "It can be fun. You can talk inside your head. We can know without speaking; I can keep others from hearing you, and we can have secrets...it saves you asking, or telling out loud...so, now, let's go eat."

And on that, Kara took her one arm and Angel the other; the next thing they were in the huge lunchroom kitchen, with Morgan and Chantel following right behind.

CHAPTER 13

Eric sat at the screens of Technical centre, Sky just behind him, leaning in across his shoulder for a better look. They were intently watching the activity at the enemy outpost.

Sonia had remained a step or two back allowing the men room, watching from a different angle. Neither man realized she was having difficulty standing. For some months, she had hidden her actual physical appearance from everyone, and it was easy now, to dull their awareness of her feelings as well.

They would only worry unnecessarily, she reasoned.

She doubled forward, stifling a gasp, as a wave of discomfort cramped her abdomen. When she straightened once again, she knew she must seek privacy, or Sky, with his heightened sensitivity to her, would notice.

"Sky," Sonia declared, in a voice as controlled as she was able to muster, deliberately giving the appearance of boredom. "I'm going to the lookout ledge."

"Okay." Her pair waved a hand in dismissal, preoccupied by what they were viewing. "I'll join you shortly."

But as she jumped, Sonia was aware she would have to keep him distant for a time. That was always difficult, would make this all the harder, even though she knew what was happening was a mere practice run for the future event.

****

Half an hour later Sky materialized beside Sonia, on the log bench overlooking the waterfall. He reached out to slip his arm about her shoulders, but Sonia pulled away and would not let him touch her.

Did I wait too long? he wondered. *Is she annoyed because I had my attention elsewhere? That's not like her.*

He sensed pain hanging it the air. *She needs balance; I thought she was healed back.*

He reached across to take her hand.

"No! Leave me on my own," Sonia ordered curtly.

This is not just healing back; she's blocking me. Sky withdrew his hand, sitting quietly in surrender to her wishes. He knew better than to question. She would explain when ready.

"You seem slower at recovery this time," he probed carefully.

"This was the last deep session," she reasoned. "The rest are simple talk sessions. And should be easier."

"At least allow me to give you comfort," he pleaded. "I will hold back on energy, if that's how you wish it."

A reluctant smile fled across her lips. It was clear there was suffering there she was hiding. "You forget…it is not you who do the giving of that, but I who automatically draw from you. The thought is appreciated. Not this time, okay?"

He sighed, but could not resist one last try. "You are litterly shaking with the effort to control the pain…you cannot hide from me, you know."

"It will balance!" Sonia declared firmly, a touch of temper behind the words. She stood abruptly. "I am going to rest!"

She then vanished, leaving a stunned Sky on the bench alone.

Sky frowned and spoke aloud. "Something is very wrong. Never has she gone separate like this before."

Djura came into view beside him. "And not for many years has she blocked me from following to guard her."

Sky quirked an eyebrow. "Where has she gone? I have no sense of her; she has closed me out completely."

"She went to… your sleep chambers. But she has erected the barrier."

"She wishes to be that alone?" Sky marvelled in disbelief. "I fear this constant emotion healing is too much for her."

"Your orders, sir?"

"We leave her…as she wishes. Sanctuary is fortified; as long as she remains within its borders…"

"We have humans among us," reminded the warrior.

"I am certain they are of little threat. She has no doubt blocked to humans, if I am not allowed in our own bedchamber."

Djura chuckled, amused by his dilemma.

Sky briefly felt a twinge of annoyance, yet easily excused the humour; he was more perplexed and concerned at his pair's behaviour.

"Go enjoy some time alone with your own partner," he suggested absently.

Djura grinned good-naturedly and vanished, leaving Sky to ponder life curtailed and incomplete, something he had not endured since he had first become consort to Sonia.

****

Sonia was dreaming: She was dormant again, sitting on the outside patio of the senior housing complex, where she had lived just before finding out she was something other than human.

Lena, the woman she called the 'puzzle lady', sat with her. The wizen old woman appeared not to have changed in the least, although she was now one hundred in human.

"Well, it's about time you come back to see me," Lena scolded. "Where you been for the past five years?"

"I've been…away," Sonia evaded. "So how has life been treating you since I left?"

"Never better! Never better! I'm still kickin'."

"I don't see Laura," Sonia noted, gazing about. "You two were always inseparable. The only time I remember you not being together was when you were mad at her. Are you fighting again?"

"No. I ain't fighting!" Lena declared indignantly. "I never fought with her."

Sonia decided not to push; Lena's memory had always been selective at best.

Lena dragged at her cigarette, blew smoke rings in the air. "Laura's dead," she finally stated bluntly. "So's Ellie; the one with the bad feet."

"Ah, no. Both of them? Laura was younger than I am. What happened?"

"Well, Ellie...they cut off one foot..."

I thought I'd healed her crooked toes.

"And she was never the same after that; said there was nothing wrong with that foot. Kept insisting it got better, but the doc wouldn't listen. Anyway, finally, she just up and had a stroke, and that killed her."

She took another drag at the cigarette.

"And Laura," she went on. "She got pneumonia...you know how frail she always was; wasn't strong enough to fight it. Went quicker than a wink."

Sonia sighed, chiding herself for not keeping better tabs on these old acquaintances. If she had been here, she could have prevented their deaths.

"If I remember right, Laura always did have asthma..." she recalled.

"That one was slow," declared Lena in dismissal of the topic, her way of fending of the loss, Sonia realized. "At least now I don't have to take care of her no more."

Once more she drew heavily on the weed in her mouth; blew a smoke ring, and coughed.

"You need to stop smoking," Sonia warned. "Or you'll get cancer, and join your friends."

****

"Ha!" spat Lena. "My father lived to be a hundred. Smoked 'til the day he died. Never got cancer."

Lena felt immensely proud of that fact. She had the longevity gene.

"Aren't you already a hundred?" quizzed Sonia.

"You bet! Hundred and one next month. Just as sharp as when I was sixty. Gon'a live forever." She laughed, and broke into a fit of coughing.

"We had the same birth date," Sonia remembered.

"Ya, but twenty years apart; you were just a spring chick."

Sonia chuckled. Her image flickered. Beneath the old lady persona, Lena saw a second image superimposed from the waist up, one of a much younger, slimmer woman with violet cat-like eyes. Then as abruptly, Sonia was the complete elder senior once more.

Lena rubbed her eyes. *Maybe I do have to stop smoking. I'm starting to see things.*

"Eyes ain't what they used to be, though," she said to cover her unease.

****

"Sky?" Eric by thought messaged called from Technical centre. "Isn't Sonia supposed to be on a sleep cycle?"

"Yes. Why?"

"I think you better come here; see something."

An instant later Sky was beside Eric. "What's the matter?"

"Look where your pair is." Eric pointed at one of the monitor screens.

Sky leaned in, closely peering at the image, and gasp in shock.

"She's out in the human population?"

"Feel out for her, Sky," ordered Eric.

Sky reached out to deeply probe his pair. "Why, she's asleep! She's sleepwalking! She has never done that before."

"And she's out there without a guardian."

"Man! What a time to do that! And at that place yet." Sky shook his head worry taking the upper hand. "The stress must be really getting to her. She's got to ease up…I'll go get her," he decided.

"Are you going to wake her, Sky?" Eric asked with a grin.

The healer chuckled. "Not until I get her back safely home…maybe, I won't even then. I'll just put her back to bed."

****

Sonia was reading quietly in their chambers when Sky entered for his own sleep session. She seemed calmer now, and he sensed no pain or animosity toward him.

He took the seat beside her on the divan; she did not draw away. He knew not to probe deeply; she might still wish to remain private. She would fill in the reasons for the episode, if it were necessary for him to know.

"Do you realize what you did during your sleep break?" he asked, amusement colouring the statement.

Sonia looked up puzzled, immediately entering his memories for the source of the jest in his tone. "Oh! I didn't!" she exclaimed in horror, as she read what had transpired.

Sky grinned mischievously. "From now on, I'm going to have to watch you when you sleep, keep a closer watch so you don't go on unscheduled dangerous visitations."

Sonia made a face, wrinkling her nose in that way she did when she was embarrassed, annoyed by the very suggestion. "I'd never get to sleep! I thought that only a dream," she admitted. "I was actually there?"

Sky grinned, and nodded solemnly.

"I was sleepwalking? Me? The holder of the 'Aopato'? How embarrassing!"

Sky chuckled. "Aw, well," he consoled. "I love you, even when you aren't perfect."

Sonia smiled appeased; lifted her face acceptingly to be kissed.

CHAPTER 14

Ram lay on his cot, thinking. He'd been moved to the joint guardian quarters because they now felt him well enough.

For so long he had been in isolation, but finally Sonia had decided it was safe for him to be among the others. The ugly memories were receding; the horrible nightmares had stopped. He could tell the difference now between tortured imaginings and reality.

But he had been chained for so long, a prisoner for an eternity it seemed, his emotions did not feel restored; he did not know what to do with himself now that he was free.

He often exploded in anger. It was hard to forget what had been done to him, hard to excuse the rescue that had been delayed for so long.

At first he had waited hopefully, hung on to the expectation with every fibre of his being, longing day after day. Each time they had come to cut and slash his body, he had held on because of that anticipation.

For a long time he had believed, dreamed that Kara had made it back; rescue was on its way. It had made it bearable. But deliverance had never come.

The others will never understand what it was like...chained all alone...for years... waiting...and each day being disappointed.

The agony and torment had been beyond endurance. Each time he was near healed, his captors returned, and the horrible nightmare would continue, endlessly, until oblivion swept over him. Toward the end consciousness was seldom and the stupor more prevalent, desire and trust faded away, sputtered out, evaporated, and at the last was non-existent.

And that's why now; it is hard to forgive the abandonment.

He had learned to hate his kind in the process.

In captivity, the days had blurred together: morning, and the daylight that had come through the small window high above him, his emotional pain deeper than the physical, like a canker for which there was no balm. Then night and darkness, again torture, excruciating physical agony, oblivion, and daze-like reawakening, then at last a fitful sleep. Each new day's light brought the circle once more, over and over, until he had learned to blame not those that held him but the ones who failed him.

Yes, he had learned to hate his brothers!

I can no longer be a guardian...for a guardian must love.

His people wanted him to continue on as before. They were willing to see him through the rough patches. They assumed he could carry on as if none of it had happened.

But to him, the reality would always be there, a hell of burning injury, an agony constant and forever. He could not escape what was now an integrated part of him: distrust, dread, rage and loathing, not just focused on them but for himself most of all; because he could not be or see differently.

They do not realize…I cannot do what they ask.

He had forgotten how to be like them; to share, to let them see in.

And worst of all, he did not want to.

Ram wallowed in his hate…for them!

They refuse to comprehend how corrupt, hideous, lacking, and unwanted I feel; what I have become.

He was uncomfortable here! He was different now! He could not heal back!

The figure of a guardian slowly came visible in the doorway to the sleep chamber.

"Hi," he said quietly. "May I come in?"

Ram shrugged against the pillow. "Don't care; do whatever you want."

His memory was hazy, but he did recall this one was one of Sonia's sons. Ram thought they had called him Lance.

The male entered, moved to the edge of the bed, then sat down beside the prostrate teen.

"Do you remember me, Ram?"

"You are Lance, Sonia's oldest son," the boy returned sullenly. "Don't remember much else about you."

Lance nodded, choosing to accept the statement as cooperation. "Will you try to trust me? Will you come with me?"

"Where?" asked Ram listlessly.

"Outside," Lance suggested. "I'd like to take you fishing. Would you go for that?"

"I don't think I want to be outside."

"Sunlight feels good. It's been a long time since you felt it. But…when you are ready."

Ram sighed, vacillating between rebellion and need.

To feel the sun would be nice.

"Okay," he reluctantly agreed.

Lance rose with him as Ram slipped his feet over the edge and stood. The older guardian enclosed to boy's hand in his own, and immediately they stood together at the edge of a pond beneath a softly cascading waterfall.

They were in the shade here, yet still the sun burned hot. Ram wasn't used to such heat.

How long has it been since I've seen direct sunlight, been out in the open spaces like this? The feeling took his breath away.

Lance motioned to two flat boulders nearby. As they sat, the older one produced dual fishing rods, and handed one to Ram.

The minutes drifted by in the mindless state of doing nothing but staring at the water waiting for a bite on his line, and Ram had time to think. His companion had been right, he realized.

The sun is warm…and it cheers me. There is comfort in companionable silence.

After a time, Lance spoke.

"When I first arrived at the guardian quarters, I too had been used to being confined. There had been bars around me for so long, I had forgotten what it was like to be free."

Ram remembered now, Lance had been in a human prison for ten years, accused of a crime he did not commit.

"Sometimes…" Lance said it so softly the words were more mind than verbal. "Even though the men I was now with were never anything but loving to me, I felt I should be despised; where I'd been, what had been done to me, should make me repulsive to them."

Ram's fingers tightened on his fishing pole.

"I found it difficult to forgive…I hated all humans, even though only a few were the ones guilty of doing me harm. Even the halves reminded me of my former state, and I found it hard to trust, because of their mixed-species breeding."

"What did they do to you in that human prison?"

"You really do not want to see that Ram…"

But Ram did want to see, and in the willing, entered the man's mind. Lance did not block him; he let him feel, let him see a memory so humiliating, so degrading, it set Ram to trembling, shrinking back in horror from his mind.

He had never envisioned such perversion; never knew such indignities could be done to others.

"I guess," Ram admitted after a time. "What they did…was worse than being constantly ripped apart…left bleeding…day after day."

"No Ram," Lance disagreed. "It wasn't. To the one who feels it, every man's suffering equals in devastation. Yes, I was violated…but so were you, only the method differs. They played with my sanity, and though I was still dormant at the time…it stays fresh in my memory, is just as humiliating, just as devastating…but, with you…"

He took a shaky breath, as if fighting to ward off and control emotions he had long since buried, thoughts too painful to bear. "You have a hurt beyond mine. We who should have been there for you have helped to damage you."

Ram's chest filled with an unfamiliar tightness; so forceful it took his breath away. Anger welled up, cutting like a sharp knife.

"I waited and I hung on," he cried viciously. "Why did you never come?"

Lance was quiet so long, Ram gave up that the guardian would ever answer. The silence dragged between them, cutting a hole in the fabric of their newfound companionship.

Ram felt betrayed all over again.

At last Lance spoke; it was obvious he chose his words with care. "I cannot excuse our failure. But…I can explain it…partially." He took in a ragged breath. "We lost connection to you…to both you and Kara, almost directly after you were taken. We did not even know then that you had been taken aboard a ship. We thought at first you were hiding, playing games. We searched the immediate area; when we realized you were actually missing the trail was cold; it stopped midstream. Perhaps because of distance we could not sense; we have since learned to communicate over extended space, but it takes a certain deep concentration not every one of us can produce. We were not able to do even that at the time of your taking."

Lance studied the gently lapping water of the shoreline, as if seeking advice from its calm surface. "When we realized you had been taken all the way back here, that it was the only place left, we immediately followed, but we could never link again with your energy signature; it was as if you were deliberately hidden from us. We believe now it was your weakened state, or you were mostly unconscious, that prevented us from finding you."

"Then how did you find me?"

Lance again hesitated.

Ram's eyes narrowed in anger. "Tell me!"

"A memory in another's mind led us to you."

"Who? Kara?"

"Partly Kara…but another, as well."

"I want to know who…who knew where I was but refused to rescue?"

"Ram…vengeance is pointless, believe me," Lance cautioned. "We are so sorry we failed you…"

"Apparently, there was another who failed me worse than you! Just tell me who it was!"

"I cannot. Only Sonia knows…"

Anger boiled inside Ram; he wanted a target, someone to rail at. But the teen knew, Sonia was not his enemy. He could not fight her, nor did he want to. Sonia had rescued him.

He remembered her mercy, as she had led him to confront the worst of his harrowing experiences. She had lightened the burden; dampened the agony. It was as if she had been there with him, endured every slash, felt weakness as it overpowered him, experienced the loss of hope each new day's end had brought.

No, he could not be angry with Sonia. She was his love anchor.

"I can never fathom the rejection you feel," Lance admitted regretfully. "But I can see, that to be violated by those you love is harder to endure than any sin against your body. Trust must be rebuilt...we must earn it. We beg your forgiveness..."

Quietly, Ram began to sob. His fishing pole escaped from his grip; he covered his wet face in trembling hands, shamed by this newfound weakness. Never in all his captivity, had he wept.

Guardians should not cry...like a female, he chided himself.

Lance put his arm around the boy; Ram drew away. So the guardian sat there and allowed him his tears.

"Please, Ram," Lance finally pleaded. "We ask that you at least try to forgive us...accept the now, that you are with us...safe. We love you."

Ram gulped at air, trying desperately to control his crying jag. He didn't even understand why the tears kept coming. Lance simply waited patiently.

"We cannot promise to never fail you again...but we will always love you...no matter what you may choose to do..."

Ram shivered with the effort to hold in his rampant emotions, and listen.

"I think I can relate some," Lance said hopefully. "I know how it feels to lose hope. You reach a point where you resign to conditions…and it's even harder to realize it's ended well; the former is what you cling to, as unreasonable as that is."

Lance has been there; if anyone can understand, it will be him.

"How did you do it?" Ram asked, brushing away a final betraying tear. "I don't think I can fight the anger. I hate, sir! How do I stop that?"

"My key was to remember to leave what took place, back in the past where it happened. It has no part in the present," Lance declared fervently. "I am a guardian; love must rule in me. If I hate, it renders me powerless; our abilities come out of our love…"

A tear trailed down his cheek, betraying the boy in Ram, once again.

"Let us help you. Let us show you our love, so you may learn to love again, both to forgive yourself, and others."

"I'm not fit to be a guardian!" exploded Ram. "I failed in my duty. That's how I got there!"

"Aw, no, Ram," Lance objected. "It could have happened to anyone of us."

"I shouldn't have left her play out in space!"

"She was very headstrong and persuasive back then…"

"Don't you dare blame her!" Ram fired back defensively. "She was just a…a baby."

"And were you much more? You were only fourteen, not even full adult," Lance excused. "You are too hard on yourself. And see, there is still love inside you."

Ram shivered, tears forming again. "With all my heart, I wish I could undo what's happened to her. My mind's eye sees her damage...I wish I could make her like she was; undo all the injury I caused."

"You can!"

Ram wiped at another errant tear; stared disbelievingly at Lance.

"How?"

"By getting well yourself. Let us make you whole. In time, as she sees all has gone back to normal, her mind will come back in line."

"How...how do I do it? Tell me! I will gladly try."

"Come into union with us again. Let us mend, and show you love."

"I didn't know I was out of union! Show me how," pleaded Ram brokenly. "Show me, please."

"Let me embrace you." Lance opened his arms in invitation. "Come home, Ram."

Ram stood up; Lance moved to meet him. As their arms came around each other, the boy folded against the older guardian sobbing, then merged into the comfort of the other.

****

Lance came into his mind, and Ram floated in a sea of love. Sonia was there with them...and so were all the others.

I am not alone!

Lance does understand.

****

The shadowed sun filtered through the trees. The boy dozed against his shoulder. Lance smiled, and smoothed back a lock of hair fallen across the child's brow.

An hour slipped away, and still the man sat, soaking up the light and warmth for both of them, as would a father with a sleeping son.

Now we can work in tandem, mother, Lance thought to Sonia. *The real healing can begin.*

Ram will never feel alone again, I promise.

Finally, the older guardian slipped his arm beneath the teen's legs, lifted and stood with him, then teleported in.

At the sleep chamber, Lance place Ram upon the cot, covered him, and stepped back.

Neither of us will ever be alone again, he decided. *You and I, Ram, have a special bond, unlike any other.*

CHAPTER 15

Ty had fled as far away from the others as possible. Once out in the valley he went with the need in him to be gain height, so when he discovered the falls to the side of the stone bridge upon which he stood, he decided if he got above the waterway, there might just be an outcropping on which he could sit.

He knew the risk when he used the teleport belt to go to an unknown spot, one where he could not see his destination, but he took the chance anyway. If he lost his footing in the jump, he would plummet to his death, but he didn't care.

He was surprisingly rewarded for his daring. Not only was there ample ledge, but a log bench stood conveniently place overlooking the falls. Here it was private, inviting solitary retreat, as if planned just for him.

It never entered his thoughts the spot might already be spoken for.

He sat down with the idea he would make it his own personal private space, his hidcy-holc away from the powers that be; his lookout ledge. The drumming falls beneath his feet was muted; sound cushioned somehow, yet bird song came clearly; the sun felt warm, and the valley view below was spectacular.

Fields of grain stretched for miles; vegetable patches, fruit trees of every kind. Ty marvelled at the food available here. His view wandered to the far horizon, and he felt a new found peace.

The perfect hiding place! I'll keep it as my secret spot.

Ty sighed in contentment. *No one will find me here.*

He had been feeling so trapped, so lost…inferior to all the others. He felt like he only half belonged, yet knew somehow he was meant to be here.

Ty had long forgotten how it had all begun, back when he and Kali came together. Jamara had been the first to name them the twins. But now, since they had come here, Kali no longer joined him. As Kara, she seemed to have forgotten him, gone distant. Ty felt incomplete without her.

She had always been his comfort, but that closeness felt gone now. Even Kali seemed hurt by the fact, perplexed and confused, as if she didn't know how it had happened, or how to fix it.

Kali had the others of her species to comfort her; he had no one. That fact unbalanced him; bewildered and baffled. His emotions betrayed him; the feeling that he deserved the same treatment made no sense in his mind, yet it loomed inside him, like a spoiled child wanting attention.

Since arriving here, his nights had been filled with nightmares; dreams of things barely remembered, of doing shameful deeds, unapproved actions that made him unworthy.

Why do I feel I have hurt Kali's kind?

They called her Kara now, but that name alone filled him with dread, as if there was something behind the moniker that he should respect and venerate.

Why should I fear her? We have been emotionally one, as if, almost...joined.

But Sonia had stepped in, taking Kara's place. And the 'Leader Female' adequately supplied his emotional needs. She was gentle, loving, not at all what he had expected. Even when not in the room with him, he felt understanding from her; care...as Kali had supplied his needs from the moment they met.

Kali had made the nightmares pass. She had made them seem...less real.

But sometimes it seemed Sonia allowed his dreams...maybe, so he would remember.

The terror visions shook him. Now he had to face them...apparently on his own.

I do not want to remember what was done!

Sonia appeared to know...and he felt no judgement from her.

Why should I even be judged? What was it I did?

"How did you get up here?" Ty jerked visibly at the angry, disembodied voice, when it spoke as if from the empty air.

The young guardian boy that had been injured came visible behind the log bench.

"This is Sonia's private lookout shelf! Her special place!"

This is Ram; why is he so angry?

Ty backed to the opposite end of the seat for safety.

"I...I didn't know," he stuttered. "How was I to know?"

"Well, now you know! Get out of here!" Ram ordered venomously. "Get down! Why did you come up here anyway?"

"It felt closed in inside...crowded."

"Too bad. I told you! Get down from here! Go away!"

"Who are you...to...to tell me I can't be here?" Ty demanded defensively. "What right do you have to order me around? Why do you hate me?"

Ram moved around the edge of the rail back, sat heavily, as if still unsteady on his legs and he needed the support. He glared, unrepentant of his outburst.

"I know what you are!" he spat. "I remember what you did to me!"

Ty's eyes went wide in sudden fear. "What did I do?" he cried in panic. "I don't remember! I don't remember...any of it."

"Ya, right! You do too!" thundered the other teen.

"I don't," Ty pleaded, raising his hands defensively palms out, as if expecting a blow at any time.

"How convenient!" the other returned sarcastically. "Well let me enlighten you. You tortured me! You were 'Opposite' then!"

Ty's spirit dropped to his bowels; his body went cold in dread.

"No! No!" he wailed. "I couldn't be one of those horrid things. You're mistaken." His voice dropped to a bare whisper. "I'm human. Honest! I'm only a human…please. Mercy."

"Then how come you know to whom I refer? No one mentioned what we call you."

Ty blinked; he was right. *How did I know that?*

"Because you were one of them!" hissed Ram.

"Is there a problem here, boys?"

Neither Ty nor Ram had noticed Sonia materialize behind them.

"Ram?" she asked a second time.

"He's in your private lookout spot!"

"And why is that such a terrible thing?"

Sonia was suddenly between them on the bench. "There is plenty of room for all. Come here, dear."

The matriarch opened her arms, and Ram folded against her. She wrapped him in an embrace much like a mother with a petulant son, holding his head comfortingly against her breast.

Ty felt suddenly envious, wishing Sonia would do the same with him. He so needed to be loved at this moment.

"Ram is not himself yet," Sonia excused. "He still is troubled by negative emotion; sometimes he cannot tell dream from reality. Is that not so, Ram."

"My Lady, I remember. It was not a dream!" Ram pleaded, agitated. "I remember him hurting me."

"Is this a complete memory?" Sonia prodded. "Or only part of one?"

"He feels like the one, but…he doesn't look the same now."

"Come Ty." Sonia slipped one arm about his shoulder, including him in her embrace. He was quite willing. "Together, we will sort out this puzzle."

Ram calmed some.

"He said I was an 'Opposite'," Ty ventured fearfully. "Why does Ram hate me?"

"Do you remember hurting him?"

Ty shook his head.

"Okay," she decided. "Do you both wish to know the truth?"

"Yes," agreed Ram without hesitation, then added an apology to Ty. "I know I still go unbalanced sometimes. I am sorry, Ty, for being unkind. Sonia helps me to balance by her touch."

Ty was surprised. He too felt calmed by her presence, yet the unknown terrified him.

What if his dreams are reality?

"If...this will help Ram," he agreed hesitantly. "I am willing, also."

"Good." Sonia gave each a one-armed hug. "This is what we will do. I will link us together in mind; then we will go back to when Ram was hurt."

"You can do this?" Ty asked amazed.

Sonia nodded. "Ready?"

Before Ty could object, he was with Ram inside his memory; it seemed like his own nightmare, the one he'd been struggling with a long time.

Ty remembered the filthy barn tower, the tiny window high above, Ram chained to the wall, his arms pulled over his head, higher than the boy's normal reach; his toes were suspended, not touching the ground.

Ty not only was experiencing his own agonizing fear, but the tearing of the guardian boy's chest and arm muscles, the taste of blood in his mouth as it oozed around his teeth. Ty felt his nausea rise up, coupled with Ram's all encompassing weakness; his own revulsion; then Ram's forgiveness. He was having trouble sorting out which feelings belonged to Ram, and what belonged to him. They felt one and the same.

"Both of you show me," Sonia suggested softly. "What do you remember? We'll put it together."

It was difficult to face. Ty did not want to remember; he felt even Ram wanted to forget. Yet, Sonia seemed to be forcing them both onward.

Together they looked up, and saw a giant lizard hissing and spitting angrily, dragging a smaller reptilian by the forearm. Ty felt himself fighting that hold, trying desperately to impede the process into the room, dragging at the walls behind with his tail, digging at the dirt covered boards beneath with clawed hind feet, screaming inside his head with rebellion, yet making no sound except the audible hiss.

Ty remembered now how he had fought with every fibre of his being, and every effort had been futile. He wanted to deny even now what he was...had been, but Sonia would not let him.

He recalled how Redro had shrieked at him. "Now! You will torture this one until you hear his screams inside your head!" Ty understood the tongue even though he knew it as 'Opposite' speak, a language he never wanted to listen to again.

"Master," Ty heard himself answer in reptilian hiss. "I'll do anything else..."

"No. You won't! Idiot newborn!" The larger creature tossed a glove-weapon at Ty. "Coward! Weakling! Slacker! Put that on! I will stand here to watch you. Make him scream!"

Ty pulled from Sonia's grasp, shooting to his feet, screaming frantically. "No! No! I don't want to be 'Opposite'! I don't want to be 'Opposite'," he whimpered. "Please, don't make me."

Suddenly, Ram was on his feet as well. "It was you!"

Sonia reached out and caught the two young males, pulling them each forcefully back onto her lap. For long moments she held them close, with such and iron grip they could not escape, until both went limp in surrender.

When at last she eased her grip, both boys were weeping quietly.

"I didn't want to hurt him, Lady," Ty cried pathetically. "I remember...Redro forced me..."

He knew even as he said it, the excuse was lame; a poor reason for cruelty.

"Why?" questioned Sonia quietly. "When you had an aversion to torturing the prisoner, and you had avoided it to this point, was it different this time?"

"It was my punishment," sobbed Ty. "For setting the female free."

Ram's jaw dropped in shock.

"Aw," Sonia nodded knowingly. "Ram? Do you understand?"

Ram swiped at the moisture coursing down his cheek; tears of anger had turned to sympathy.

"He saved Kara," Ram proclaimed in awe. "I remember too now…they were always hurting him. I told him by mind thought not to let them win."

"And I didn't," Ty returned triumphantly. "I ran…right after that. I went dormant…but I forgot…I forgot about you."

"Oh, oh Ty. I forgive that," Ram whispered gently. "I understand now. You couldn't help it."

Ty broke down then, and Sonia cuddled him close.

She looked to Ram. "Do you think you could help each other heal now?" she asked quietly. "Be…brothers?"

"Yes, my Lady," Ram agreed. "We are of the same species," he whispered.

"For now," Sonia cautioned. "We will keep his secret between we three. Okay?"

Ram nodded.

"I don't want to be 'Opposite'," Ty pleaded again. "Please don't put me back with them."

Sonia touched his hand reassuringly. "You will never be 'Opposite' again, Ty. Do not fear. And, you are welcome here. Now, Ram," she added. "I will leave you two alone. I think I can trust you not to fight anymore."

Sonia chuckled when Ram blushed to the roots of his hair.

"Be friends now," she instructed wisely. "That comes first."

'Be friends; be brothers.' Her words echoed softly in Ty's mind.

Be brothers, he thought in awe.

"Be brothers!" Ram said aloud. "And, we will!"

CHAPTER 16

The little Shitsu kept pace with Sonia as she walked leisurely along the sidewalk of the tree-sheltered cul-de-sac. The tiny puppy seemed to sense their presence even though it could not see her, or Sky who shadowed his pair.

At the entrance to the crescent a speeding Camero zoomed around the corner, squealing its wheels in the rapid turn, the driver in a hurry for no apparent reason. The diminutive dog by their side took offence, darting forward defensively, challenging the neighbourhood intruder, chasing along the side of the left front tire where the lone occupant failed to notice it. The thumping of tunes, loud on the stereo inside, drowned out the high pitched frantic barking of the small protector, and when the wheel turned to take the second curve, the youth behind the steering column was not even aware a very fragile, fur-covered quadruped was in the monster's path.

There was no shriek of tires, no attempt to brake, only a whomp and a soft fluid scrunch, as tire passed over victim. The vehicle sped away out into the connecting street, the driver totally oblivious, unaware of the mortal damage he had caused.

In the centre of the thoroughfare, where it had been dragged, the Shitsu lay sprawled. One back leg at an unnatural angle, gasping in the throws of death, deep oozing gash along its side, blood dripping from the jaw, and a cut across the eye…the small defender lay dying.

Sonia gave an agonized cry; went visible, not as an aged senior as was usual, but fully Aopato; young, gorgeous, Amethyst eyes and all.

The distraught 'Leader Female' had fled across the space so rapidly, knelt and immediately began healing within seconds, that Sky had no time to even think to give a mental warning.

Ah, female! Sky thought in frustration. *Have you no sense of where you are at all?*

Sky decided it was wiser for him to remain invisible and out of the way at a distance, where she could not so easily draw from his energy, resulting in them both being exposed and defenceless out here in a human neighbourhood.

He watched as the great ugly slash appeared along her side; Sonia gasped as if finding it difficult to breathe. A welt showed itself along the forehead; another just below the knee, and her hip went disjointed.

But Sonia was on her feet directly, healing back as she moved, the mending of a small canine taking little of her healing power. Still wholly visible as an alien, cuddling the miniature dog against her face, she carried the slowly reviving animal to a rundown shack four houses down. The unhealed mark still visible on her forehead, dragging her injured limb up three steps to the door, she rang the bell.

Sky held his breath.

It seemed to take an eternity, while Sonia stood exposed in bright sunlight, before the owner unlatched the inside door. At the very last moment, before the second door was thrown open, she metamorphed into her customary old lady guise…but her injuries were still apparent.

Sky sighed with relief. *At least she has the presence of mind to do that much!* He shook his head in disbelief of what was happening, yet was powerless to stop it. *In full view of humans no less! You, girl, are so fortunate, this street is quiet today.*

The octogenarian in the doorway peered out with dimming vision. "Yes? How can I help you?" she asked in a voice as aged as she appeared.

"Is this your dog?" Sonia ask, her tone scolding.

The white haired elder leaned in close, then chuckled. "Sheba," she croaked. "How did you get out again?"

"You should watch your pet better," rebuked Sonia. "You could lose her to a speeding car."

"Aw, but she's okay," excused the senior with a dispassionate air. "Come baby. Come to momma."

She reached out to take the tiny Shitsu, but Sonia held it firmly, turning away. She was not willing to release it to one this careless.

"You should watch your dog more carefully," Sonia again repeated. "She could be killed by a vehicle."

"Oh, she's forever getting out," the human excused testily. "I can't always see her. You're a naughty Sheba, aren't you?"

Up to this point, the owner had not realized the dog made no sound. Had it been dead, she would not have noticed.

Sonia held on tightly. As her owner reached a second time, the animal stirred in Sonia's arms; a wet tongue came forth to lick the human hand.

"Come to momma, Sheba," coaxed the woman.

The Shitsu barked excitedly, as if in welcome to a cherished companion, and began to squirm exuberantly. That was Sonia's undoing. She released her hold; the animal left to the arms of its owner. Immediately the elder was laughing, as the wet tongue delivered sloppy kisses.

The human turned, and without even a thank you, the door slammed behind the two. Sonia was left standing, forgotten. Still limping from her unselfish healing, the female eased from step to step, and…vanished.

Sky blew out an exasperated breath of frustration. *Now, where did you go?* And muttering in annoyance, he followed Sonia's light trail to its source.

Where, he found his pair back in their chambers, fast asleep upon the couch.

"Oh, female! You will be the death of me yet!" Sky declared, as he stood in the hall. "This has got to stop! You are going to explain it to me…"

Lance appeared at his side. "Anything I can do? You seem rather upset."

"Stand guard at our chambers," Sky ordered. "If my pair goes anywhere follow her, but don't wake her!"

Lance chuckled. "Sleepwalking again?"

Sky growled in annoyance. *Everybody knows.*

"She just healed an animal in broad daylight! What if an 'Opposite' had shown up? And she wasn't even in disguise; she was visible, in her true form!"

Lance quirked an eyebrow. "Getting dangerous…"

"Tell me about it! I can't believe this! Whatever has gotten into my female?"

Totally discouraged, Sky vanished without another word.

He needed help on this one; he meant to get some advice!

****

Sky sat Indian-style, cross-legged, in his own private spot, not on Sonia's lookout ledge, but just above and to the left on another smaller outcropping. Before he was paired, when he had been a simple guardian, he used to hide here to watch over the 'Leader Female'. He had not felt the need to get away from everyone for a long, long time, but this day had troubled him so greatly, he required it now.

Reaching out to Joel on home planet by thought transfer, he made the connection quickly, and began the mind-to-mind conversation.

I don't know what's wrong Joel, Sky pleaded. *I hoped you could help me sort this through; being Sonia's brother, and 'Pure' as well. Maybe you have knowledge, ability, I am not privy to.*

Not certain I can be of much help, Joel answered. *I'm still only a male. Have you tried the females? They would be the ones to ask if this is a female thing.*

173

Sonia hides from us all. Her behaviour is so unlike her; so irresponsible, I fear it will get us all killed. Could it have something to do with the fact she is 'Pure'?

Joel laughed. *Brother-in-law, you are the physician! If you cannot see the problem, what would make you think, I would know something you do not?*

You can tap into records, the histories, where others cannot. Sonia is your sister; she allows you to see when she keeps it from other guardian sight.

She shows you more than the men, man! There was a time when I saw very little...when I was...apart.

But your relationship is better now...

True...we work more as a team. But females share more with other females. It is the same, as with the guardians.

Is there nothing? Sky sighed disconsolately. *I am at my wits end. I fear I may have somehow been responsible. Have I hurt her in some way I am unaware of?*

You ask that of me, with my record of mistakes?

Sky chuckled, realizing the reasoning behind Joel's comment. *Well, I figured seeing you had experience in that area, you might see what I had done.*

Have you considered it might be something simple; not your doing at all?

Sky sighed. *I have this feeling it is something I started...though for the life of me...I can't fathom what I did.*

Just what makes you think that?

Embarrassed, Sky revealed his real dilemma. *We have been paired more than four, nearly five, earth years, and...she has never before wished to sleep single when we had the opportunity...*

Joel laughed outright. *The honeymoon is over, eh?* he teased.

Not funny! hissed Sky. *No. But lately, she certainly is acting peculiar. This sleepwalking isn't even by her knowledge...Joel, no one has ever gotten behind her mental control before. It's like someone else is manipulating her, like she's a puppet. This worries me! Could the enemy have developed a new weapon?*

Does she seem in pain?

I know she is! But she won't let me ease it when I notice the need. And even then I feel she is hiding the full pain level from me.

Sky drew in his breath, hesitating, reluctant to share the rest. *There is another thing... for months...she will never let me see...her naked reality. She shows me what she thinks I want to see.*

What did you do to her? Joel exploded protectively. *Did you shame her...or try to force her?*

Never! I would rather die! Why would I ever do that? Never! Never! Sky cried, mortified. *I have never considered her ugly, even in the dormant form...not even in my private thoughts! Nor would I consider gratifying myself alone.*

Okay, man! Easy. I never meant to degrade you. I shamed myself to even consider such thoughts. I felt

I was...approaching from all angles. Forgive me, please.

Sky was silent, shaken still by the implied ideas Joel had put forth.

Give me a few moments, begged Joel. *I will search what records we have here. Perhaps, I can find a comparison.*

Sky schooled himself to a calm, more reasoning attitude, as he waited for Joel to make contact once again.

Joel came back, chuckling.

I might have a solution you had not considered, he stated cheerily. *What sense do you get just before Sonia withdraws from you?*

Sometimes, it's as if I startled her; other times, as though she is shamed by her appearance, and does not want me to see.

I've got the answer! Joel declared triumphantly. *Remember, Jessica? How she withdrew from the common collective, even from Wade, just before we discovered she carried the new little female? And all along Sonia knew what we did not. Are you absolutely certain the females are not keeping something from us?*

Sky gasped in shock as the implication hit him. *You jest!*

And why would I do that? Is it not possible?

At our age?

You are thinking like a human, Sky, Joel rebuked. *We are 'Aopato', and they are always fertile.*

Sky could barely breathe with the wonder of this revelation.

My pair is...with child! he marvelled in awe. *She hides it from me?*

Joel chuckled at the male's predicament. *I guess it is your fault after all. You did do something...*

Sky visibly faded from view, his embarrassment very physical.

Let me know how you make out on this, Joel suggested, as he broke contact.

Sky was so litterly astounded, he found it hard to believe their good fortune. Then the full impact hit him.

Sonia will not be able to travel back. She is Earth bound, until the child delivers. I cannot take her to safety!

CHAPTER 17

Sonia lay half dozing on the sleep couch, when Sky entered their chambers; even now her imaged shimmer, shifting to the usual ravishing beauty he was used to seeing.

"May I join you?" he enquired quietly.

"I am very weary, Sky," she objected sleepily. "I feel as if I have not slept at all. Please, I would rather be alone."

A mischievous half-grin fled across the male's face. *Of course she will feel so; she has been wandering the streets, and...healing.*

"I will sleep in the guardian quarters if you wish it, but...we need a talk time, my love. It is very important."

"Must it be now?" she asked petulantly.

"As soon as possible; needs immediate attention. Waited too long already..."

Sonia sighed, resigned. "Very well."

Behind her, against the stone wall, a pillow prop appeared. Sonia shifted up and back to a seated position, then moved over to make room for Sky.

The physician took his place beside his pair, lying on his side, supported by one elbow, facing her. He waited, studying her.

She appeared well, though tired, her girlish figure adequate and proportionate; the way he enjoyed it, but now it seemed a travesty, a charade, an illusion, and he saw it for what it was: a concealment, a secretive veil. He would have no more of it.

"You hide from me," he rebuked quietly. "Why?"

Immediately she was in his mind, probing, enquiring, perceiving, and as she read her annoyance grew. He never held back from her; he had no secrets. He loved her unconditionally.

"I see I'm found out," she observed, without contrition. "You and Joel have been talking."

Sky frowned his disapproval. "Keeping such a secret from me was wrong," he reproached. "I could have helped…"

He moved his head, his eyes pointedly seeking her abdomen, still unchanged.

"How far along are you?"

Sonia sighed dejectedly, and finally revealed her true form. She carried the little one without showing excessively, but by position it was clear she was in the last trimester.

"The other day, when you did not want me near you…you were in false labour?" he accused.

She nodded.

"Your emotions have been fluctuating?"

"I am handling it," Sonia declared obstinately.

Sky frowned, annoyed by her inflexibility.

"Why would you keep this from me so long? You must have been already carrying when we were searching for Kara."

"At first I did not purposely conceal." Sonia met his eyes straight on. "Men can sometimes be very unobservant."

He shook his head, a pang of guilt prodding, but he ignored it, to face the more serious infraction. "You deliberately made me dim to this. You know that's the truth of it. The blame is not entirely mine."

She averted her eyes, ashamed. "I'm sorry. You are right. You have always been my perfect mate. It is me...I am a biting she dog today."

He couldn't resist the chuckle that escaped him.

"It would have been better if you'd have left me be."

"Oh, I think not! Now, what is the true reason you hid from me?"

She hesitated a second, then decided to risk all. "If you touch me when I am unprepared, the child within will bond instantly to you."

He quirked an eyebrow questioningly. "And this is undesirable, why?"

"There are things you are unaware of..."

"I am physician, Lady. Fill me in."

"We are two 'Healer Ultimate'. It will not be the same as with Jessica and Wade."

"How so?"

Sonia looked away, would not meet his eyes. "It is rare, but...we can produce a 'Double Healer'..."

Sky frowned, searching his physician's memory. "I am unfamiliar with this term. Explain, please. Do I understand correctly? You are protecting me?"

Sonia met his searching gaze, her eyes flooding with tears. "It has been agony...to keep you distant..."

"Why?" he pleaded, puzzled. "Why is it necessary?"

Sonia sighed. "A 'Double Healer' is most aggressive from the moment of conception, but especially in the last months; it controls its environment tenaciously. It has the urge to heal beyond its ability. Should it initiate and need healing back it will kill to get the energy it needs...until we can teach it how to do it right. It cannot be taught while still inside the mother. Also...it will protect its host, me, viciously, if it feels threatened. It operates on pure instinct, not by the reasoning process."

"You carry a 'Double Healer'!"

"Yes," she whispered.

Sky drew a sharp breath. "So if I touch you, and you fail to shield me, what will happen?"

"It bonds to you. It will love you, but you will be secondary until after birth. If it feels threatened by you, or perceives you have caused me hurt...it will attack you."

Sky laughed suddenly at the irony of his position. "So, by it's reasoning, when the birthing process begins, it could decide...I am the reason for your pain...and kill me?"

Sonia began to cry softly. "I don't know, Sky. It is an unreasoning infant. Don't blame it; it doesn't know any better."

"Why didn't this bond develop when we were healing Ram?"

"It was distracted. We were healing, something it desires above all else."

"So I'm safe when you are healing?"

"Not really. We were one when we healed back. It couldn't tell us apart. And...you had already given me your energy."

"So dangerous!" Sky moaned. "If I had known..."

"What? You would have stopped me? With my compunction, and the infant's..."

"I would have tried to do Ram on my own...a different way."

"The child gave me added power..."

"Aw..." Sky's breath exploded in frustration. "On one hand benefit; the other lethal. What a fix."

"Deadly mostly to you," Sonia objected. "Anyway, the hard healing is past. However, now the child craves more..."

Her eyes filled with tears again. "Oh, Sky. I fear I have given our child a death sentence. Though it will have unbelievable healing ability it is cursed to always heal back alone, separate, because it has no equal. It will be forced to live without a pair."

"Much like it's mother was," Sky observed. "And that was worked out..."

"But this is a male!" she cried disconsolately. "When it reaches maturity, at thirty of our years, sixty in human, he will go into a madness should a compatible, strong enough female not be found to pair to him."

"Are you by chance his 'pair compatible'?" Sky asked suddenly.

"Yes. I am equal in strength at the moment," Sonia admitted. "But when he reaches full healer power at thirty..."

"We will worry about the future when it comes, Loved one," Sky decided. "For now...its protection reflex will be more aggressive toward me in defence of you. Am I correct?"

Sonia nodded, and took to weeping again. "I can no longer protect you, Sky. He's become too strong."

Sky's heart ached for her dilemma. "Oh, female. Let me hold you," he pleaded. "I am not afraid. It can be no worse than the day we paired, and I do not want to be separated like that again."

She brightened. "You think?" she queried hopefully, wiping at her lashes, deciding to be positive.

"I offered you my life that day, remember?" he countered softly, reaching for her. "And I have never regretted it."

Sonia melted against him unable to resist any longer.

"See, you needed me. Let down the shield slowly. Let him get to know me."

"I'm afraid, Sky," she admitted. "For you."

"Don't be. I still have free will, and my life is mine to give if I must…"

"I could not bare to lose you…"

"It will not come to that," Sky said with conviction. "This predicament would not exist unless there is a way through it. The Almighty Creator has always shown us the answer in the past. The help will be there when we need it."

"Sometimes, in the living it," Sonia confessed. "I tend to forget…"

"We all do. But this day, I am not surprised you cannot see as clearly. You are much weakened…all this healing in your condition…"

Sonia frowned. "But I've been asleep most of the day…"

Tongue in cheek, he asked in a teasing tone, "Have you now?"

Sonia turned a suspicious look on him, suddenly realizing what he implied. "What did I do this time?"

Sky laughed outright at the worried look on her face. "Only healed a small broken animal."

"I what?"

"And you did it in broad daylight in your true form."

Sonia gasped horrified. "Was I seen?"

He shook his head, grinning.

"Stop teasing me," Sonia scolded perturbed.

Sky chuckled, and playfully tickled her.

He sobered. "Are you going to drop that shield, so my boy can get to know me?"

Sonia wrinkled her nose in reluctance, then silently surrendered.

"Are you sure you want to risk this?"

"Most assuredly. You are taking the chance to carry my child."

Sky immediately felt when she lowered her protection.

The third mind barrelled in: young, questioning, probing, an eager exploring essence of curiosity. He was near over whelming, such a full, real powerful little creature. No one could ever say this foetus was a mere blob of tissue. It was a living breathing entity, most definitely!

Sky laughed delighted. "He is undeniably healthy," he observed. "It is such a pleasure to know him before birth; so unlike when one is purely human. We are able to connect mind to mind even before we can touch. What shall we call him?"

"He says his name is Kyle."

"Aww…picked his own name, did he?"

Sonia snuggled under Sky's arm, almost melding to get closer. Love blossomed between them, to be experienced by the young one as well. They felt his observation and approval.

"So." Sky broke the silence. "Explain to me why he has you sleepwalking."

"He is more dominant when I am asleep. For some reason he is attracted to humans. I think it could come from all the time we've spent on this planet looking for Kara. And he has such a tremendous need to heal…"

"And the puppy?"

"He's an infant…it was a tiny, cuddly creature…small like he is…"

"Aw…of course," Sky agreed. "He is doing the healing then…from the womb?"

Sonia nodded.

"My magnificent son!" Sky proclaimed proudly.

Then he shook his head at reality. "If he isn't more careful," he said for the benefit of the small listener. "He will be the death of us while we await his physical arrival."

"Oh…" Sonia moaned. "Don't tell him that…please."

Gently, Sky stroked her hair to ease her sudden tension.

After a moment, Sonia observed, "He is aware you are easing me. He likes you…"

"Good," whispered the ever-pleased father. "Now, shall we sleep?"

"Do you think it is safe?"

Sky chuckled; kissed her forehead. He folded her against his chest, and resting his head against hers, slipped away in slumber.

Just before he escaped to that dreamland, he reasoned drowsily: *At least should Kyle take her sleepwalking, I'll feel when she moves.*

CHAPTER 18

Kara sat alone on the lookout ledge bench above the waterfall. She had come here to sort through her turbulent emotions. She felt so abandoned, excluded.

Ever since the two boys had met, it seemed Ty was always off somewhere with Ram, as if they both had traded her companionship for the other male's company. Kara could not fathom what boys found so gratifying about fishing, racing through the fields, and rough wrestling with each other to prove who was stronger. It was like their minds had gone blank, the brain turned off, and they were now only brawn.

She would like to have joined them, gone walking among the flower beds below, listening to bird song, smelling scents so powerful you could taste them…to be with either one of them, but each preferred boy-company now.

Kara reached out to search the minds of, what had once been, her two closest friends, but as always, she was blocked.

Great-gran doesn't trust me! She hides their thoughts from me. This was the only conclusion Kara could come to.

Self-pity brought tears to her eyes, while her mind puzzled at the change in the boy who had been her devoted protector these past three years.

Why is he so different now? Why does he avoid me? Is something wrong with Ty, too?

They all want me to stay among the females...away from Ty. Why?

Did they find something bad about Ty? Is Ty locking me out because he no longer likes me, or is great-gran responsible? She doesn't want me to be with Ty. I know it!

Silently Kara wept. Lonely, forlorn, imagining the worst, the young girl gave way to her fears.

I am useless! They don't want me! Great-gran does not love me anymore.

The air beside Kara shimmered.

A stunningly beautiful black female materialized on the bench next to the despondent teen. This was Nadia. She had the most gorgeous jet-black hair that hung in long spiral curls halfway down her back. Her caramel skin was flawless, and her chocolate brown eyes were unique, the only ones in existence with a vertical slit of gold.

The Eritrean half-human had the mouth watering personal scent of fresh strawberries when you had just bitten into them. Kara could almost taste her cousin she was that ravishing.

She felt envious; for Nadia was the teen she wanted to be.

Rebelliously, Kara moved to the opposite end of the bench, brushing at the tears on her lashes.

"This always was grandma's most favourite spot," Nadia observed softly, almost as if she had been conversing with Kara all along.

So Chad and Nadia have finally arrived. They had been a couple from the very first, ever since their change. *Great-gran never stops them!*

"So...I'm forbidden to be here?" Kara retorted argumentatively.

"Did I say that?" Nadia countered. "You are feeling somewhat down, aren't you?"

Silence reigned, when Kara made no answer. She attempted to gain control of her riotous emotions.

At last she could speak with some civility. "Chad came with you?"

"Yes. You remember our life before?"

"I'm not a total idiot!" Kara shot back testily. "Some memories are still there...the most recent."

"Good. Yes, Chad is with me. He is not only my guardian," Nadia admitted. "We are 'pair connected', and cannot be apart. It has happened mostly because he lost his twin. He needs...someone, or he would have died."

"I know that! I do remember recent history. And I can tap great-gran's memories..."

"Good. Then you understand why we must be together..." Uncomfortable, Nadia went silent. Finally, she added, "Gran wants us to wait another year to be paired."

"Uncle Shawn is two years older then you, only half a year older than Chad, and he and Chrystal have been paired for a year..."

"Your uncles Tyler and Shawn were paired because it was necessary, to save the lives of their partners. The new females would have died if they had not been junctioned. For Chad and I, we can wait. No threat to our lives is involved."

"Great-gran always has the answer. She's always right," Kara stated sarcastically. "Always the controller!"

"Kara!" rebuked Nadia. "Yes! She is always right!" she declared vehemently. "She is 'Leader Female'! And she must be followed, or…we all die! Have you forgotten what took place when we all rebelled?"

"I never rebelled then!"

"Then stop doing so now!"

"I am not a child anymore!" Kara spat. "I don't need you scolding…"

Nadia appeared to regret her combative approach.

"I know that," she returned softly. "That is why I reason with you now as an adult," she pleaded. "You are only eight by our years. Our maturing is different than humans. The mind grows fast in our species, especially in a 'Leader Female'…and the emotions and body take time to catch up…"

This pacification only angered Kara further. "For the past three earth years I lived the life of a teen! I cooked, I cleaned house; I was responsible!"

"Indeed," Nadia acknowledged. "But when you changed again the body returned to our normal. The mind still has the experience…"

"Do you even really understand?" Kara reproach annoyed.

"I am trying, Kara," Nadia affirmed. "I was a teen before also…for that matter, I actually was a grown woman before we broke dormancy."

Kara grew silent realizing maybe Nadia did have a foreknowledge after all.

Nadia let the quiet linger, allowing her cousin time to think.

At last she volunteered, "Do you realize Gran can't return to home planet?"

"Why is that?" Kara returned with absentminded unconcern, not following the sudden shift in subject. "Because of me?"

"No. She is in her last trimester. It is now too dangerous to travel with 'Opposites' so close."

Kara rudely snorted. "She's too old to have another baby!"

Nadia smiled wistfully. "Never too old," she disagreed tenderly. "All it takes is to feel intensely loved by your partner for your body to accept the process."

But Kara's thoughts were on herself; compassion wasn't present at all.

"Great-gran is a 'Pure'. This child will replace me."

"Oh no! Never! Unless you were to die...you cannot be replaced."

Kara drew a blank.

"It doesn't go...in line?"

"No. It certainly doesn't. Besides, this baby is a male..."

But Kara barely heard her. Her own self-indulgent thoughts brought tears to her eyes.

Another infant! Now great-gran surely will not love me.

Once again her anger flared. "She has shut me out, you know?" Kara cried bitterly. "Cast me off! She has no more need of me."

"That is not true," argued Nadia. "You two are intimately connected, more so than the rest of us. She carries us, but you two work together. At the moment, it's different. Right now, her emotions are in fluctuation...and she doesn't mean to, but she drags you with her when she goes down. You have to learn to cut away when you feel that happening ...become strong enough to fight on your own..."

Why does she have to make such perfect sense? Kara wondered in annoyance.

"Okay. Then why does she separate me from Ty and Ram?"

"I am not privy to that information. I am not 'Leader'. But there must be a good reason. She has always hidden hurtful things from us when it is what's best for us. And it has always been a wise choice."

Kara saw no good reason to separate her from Ty.

"I hate her control! I hate her!"

"Oh, Kara. No you don't. That's your emotional unbalance speaking."

"Why did you come back here anyway?' Kara demanded angrily. "Why didn't you two stay at home planet where you were safe? I've put enough people in danger because of my stupidity."

"Aw, Kara. You were young. You didn't realize the danger..."

I'm too stupid! Too young! Too blind to understand! Kara berated herself.

She could fight it no longer. She surrendered to weeping.

Through shoulder shaking sobs, breath coming with effort, she demanded, "Why...did ...you...even...come?"

And Nadia answered with calm assurance. "I came because I love you. I wanted to help you; to be your emotional balance..."

Shocked, Kara pulled for breath in an attempt to gain control. She finally realized Nadia was here not to scold but to support.

"Granny Sonia can't take much more," Nadia pleaded. "We need to take up some of her burden. I am taking...offering to carry this load."

Is she offering to balance me?

"But I am a 'Leader Female'," Kara objected. "I could fry your brain! I could cause you to become as mad as a psychopath! I could end your life with a mere thought, if I become unbalanced enough. You are just...a regular female."

"I know that," Nadia rejoined acceptingly. "But I am willing to take the risk."

Kara shook her head rejecting the thought, trying not to cry, to check her unruly emotions. "I don't want to kill you, cousin. You carry the only 'Ultimate Music' gene. That is irreplaceable, too special a talent to sacrifice. Your life is worth more...than mine right now."

Nadia shrugged, but rather than argue again, she chose to present a solution.

"Then you must learn to balance on your own. I know that is possible for you. Grandma Sonia does it all the time."

"I am not great-gran!" Kara sobbed. "I…am…immature…too young, and…I have lost the knowing how…the ability."

"I choose to believe, it is not all lost. You can re-teach yourself how. You are 'Leader Female'! Your abilities are beyond mine."

"Then what good can you do me? You can not help!"

Kara knew if they touched Nadia would be the weaker link. She would be killed.

"I can balance myself," Nadia declared confidently. "As you feel me do that, you follow my lead. With your extra strength, when your ability kicks in, you will be able to do the rest."

She is actually offering to give me balance!

"If the ability is even there at all…" objected Kara.

"It is." Nadia countered. "I believe it isn't lost, only buried."

"What if I drain on you too much?"

"Stop worrying." Nadia slid across the seat, no longer taking no for an answer. She slipped her arm around Kara, pulling the younger girl against her own body. "I trust your love for me. Use me only if you must."

But there was little choice. The connection was immediate, the drawing of the other's energy a reflex. Kara gave a great sigh, as she felt the release, the relief.

"Steady yourself..." Nadia cautioned. "Think of things more pleasant..."

Kara felt the rejection, the despair, the loneliness, and the self-indulgent resentment leaching away. But she also realized Nadia was absorbing it, and this would do irreparable damage. It would change the agreeable, enchanting, melodic-talented creature she knew as her cousin into something vindictive, obnoxious, with a jarring, discordant lack of talent. The 'Leader Female' nature in Kara found that not only unacceptable but also abhorrent. With all her strength she began to protect the older teen, and in so doing fought her own demon moods.

The last words she'd heard became her mantra: 'think of things more pleasant', but she could not recall anything in her recent memories, so she slipped into the mind of her team mate, searching, and what she found there made her laugh.

"Sonia and Kyle healed a puppy?" she marvelled.

Nadia was only able to produce a weak smile in return.

"Oh, I'm draining you too much!" Kara went rigid with the effort to withdraw from the connection. "I'm hurting you! Move away from me quickly. It will break the junction."

"No," Nadia disagreed stubbornly. "Balance...yourself," she gasped.

Kara pulled in a deep breath, envisioned Sonia holding the puppy against her cheek, and came up laughing in delight. She had broken free at last...on her own!

"See…you did it," moaned Nadia weakly. "All by yourself…"

"But I have harmed you!" cried Kara fearfully, realizing the other girl was slipping into a faint.

Immediately, Kara re-established the junction, forcing away Nadia's negative emotions, reclaiming the pain she had caused. But this time the emotions seemed different, the feelings foreign, as if they had not originated with her. The sensations were simple to conquer, and becoming less and less detrimental, eventually faded altogether, to be replaced by proper balance in both females.

Nadia swallowed back the last remnant of frailty. "And see, now you try to balance me, cousin," she congratulated. "I knew you could make it right."

Kara sat back, remaining with only hands touching.

"Are you safe now?" Kara met the brown eyes of the 'Music Ultimate' searchingly. "Are you able to balance on your own?"

Nadia sighed, and grinned. "Never better."

Kara let go of the black girl's hand. "I am so sorry I hurt you."

"Wasn't I a willing purveyor?" she chided. "And, you did it, cousin!" she declared jubilantly. "You did it!"

Kara giggled. "I'm not all broken!"

Nadia smiled and hugged her.

Kara sobered, and went to scolding mode. "Don't you ever try to sacrifice your life for me like that again."

"Can't and won't promise that cousin," Nadia declared laughing. "We never know what the future might require. Hey, how about we go for lunch? Something real sweet. After that emotional roller coaster, I crave chocolate!"

The bench on the ledge above the waterfall suddenly stood forlornly empty.

CHAPTER 19

Ty was still a loner, feeling more comfortable away from the rest of the males. He and Ram had spent much time together, but sometimes Ram needed his own counselling session alone with Sonia, as was the case today. And at times like that, Ty sought the lunchroom where he knew he could always find food.

The treats were always waiting for him when he arrived and Ty never questioned how it came to be so. He assumed it was some sort of sensor that caused the supplies to appear when those wanting a snack arrived and as no one prevented him from filling his desires, he always dug in.

The long counter would be covered with platters of cut meats, cheeses of every variety, many choices of sliced bread, and abundant varieties of fruit, multiple scrumptious desserts and beverages of all kinds. From these he could pick and choose whatever he wished.

Ty was forever hungry, perhaps because he had spent most of his childhood starving. It was like his body was storing up just in case the food supply suddenly dwindled, or as if his insides were of much deep capacity than was evident. Sometimes Ty felt, he must be as large as that formidable warrior-defender Djura, and he needed to constantly feed the ravenous beast within to keep it at bay.

The boy made himself a ham on rye sandwich, took a huge piece of apple pie, smothered it with ice-cream, grabbed a large glass of milk, and made his way to the farthermost corner away from the doorway, where he sat down, his back to the marble wall.

Ty had just finished the mouth-watering dessert, was taking the last swallow of the beverage, when Ram appeared beside the table.

"Ty!" Ram exploded breathlessly. "We need you to teach us something."

Before Ty could say anything, Nadia and Kara materialized at the doorway. Chad, the black female's protector appeared seconds later, as always when sensing the presence of other males near her, interpreting them as potential threats.

"May we watch?" Kara asked with obvious excitement.

"Watch what?" Ty wondered, puzzled.

Ram chuckled at his perplexity. "The common mind, Ty," he explained. "They know instantly, before I even get to ask you."

"Ask me what?"

"Well, Kara remembers you playing basketball…"

Ty frowned. "You been in her mind?" he objected protectively, his old habit of defending Kara resurfacing.

"No silly," Ram rebuked. "I didn't invade. We all have access to her memories. With our mind connection we each know what the other remembers."

Ty sighed. Would he ever get used to this commonality?

Wish I knew what they were all thinking the way the rest of them do.

"Sorry Ty," Ram apologized. "Sometimes we forget you can't read us. I came to get you. Zane and Lance say they are losing physical conditioning for lack of exercise, and want to try a game. There are not enough of us for a baseball game, so…"

"I can't play with you guys," complained Ty. "You'd use that kinetic power of yours to beat me. Not fair! Besides, I never played baseball before."

"Don't want to play baseball, Ty. But tell you what," Ram suggested. "We'll teach you baseball, if you show us basketball."

"I don't know how," Ty admitted reluctantly. "I only use to shoot hoops."

"Oh. Okay…" Ram accepted, non-pulsed. "You want to come shoot hoops with us? We can compete that way, can't we? Two against two."

"I don't have a chance. You've all got powers. I don't!"

"Ah, Ty," Ram complained, frustrated by Ty's inflexible attitude. "We never use powers when playing a sport. Have I ever used my abilities when we race? Why, Sonia would be forced to punish us for cheating."

"What?" Ty exploded in surprise. "She punishes you for cheating?"

"It's our rule; we agreed on it from the very first. We never manipulate while playing a game. We want the physical exercise! It defeats the purpose to use mental power. So we all agreed, if we slip up it's punishable. We choose the penalty; Sonia is the enforcer."

"She…will be there to watch?"

"No. She doesn't have to be there. We have an honour system."

Ty shook his head, baffled by the complexity. He was still dubious.

"Come on," Ram pleaded. "We've set up a court against the ball field fence."

"We are coming to watch!" Nadia and Kara proclaimed in unison.

"And we'll go get Jamara…maybe even Amadeus would like to come?" Kara added.

"Let's leave it a thing among the younger generation," suggested Ram. "Okay, Ty? I'll even jump you to the site."

Reluctantly Ty agreed; stood up. He was not much for the playing with others. He'd had too many bullying sessions with his 'Opposite' brothers. But for Ram, he would try.

****

However, neither Ty nor Ram had expected their simple play to become a species spectacle. Ram's request had been ignored completely. Supposedly, it was more beneficial for the boys to have a cheering sector.

When they came upon the scene, not only Sonia was there, but also all the rest: Sky, Djura with Karine his pair, Zane and Lance's partners Chantel and Morgan, Eric and his pair Angel. Chad had brought Nadia and Kara, and true to their word the girls had persuaded Jamara to come along. Lastly, just a bit late, came Amadeus.

How did they all get here so fast? wondered Ty. *They must have planned this before hand. They are forcing me to interact!*

He almost turned around to transport back on his own using the belt he wore, but Ram grabbed him by the arm moving him into the circle of the basket backdrop. Then the sunshine felt so good, he wanted to stay out, and soon, as they played, Ty actually forgot the spectators.

Before they started, Ram whispered, "I honestly didn't know the others were coming. It was originally just going to be the guys, but in our world, it's hard to keep a secret...I'm sorry. I know it seems like we ganged up on you, but...I didn't."

"I know," Ty sighed, resigning. "It's that common mind again. Hard to hide when everybody can see you."

Ram chuckled, giving Ty a one-arm boy-hug of reassurance. "Now you're getting it. You'll be one of us in no time."

****

The other guardians had done the preparation while Ram had gone to persuade. Along one side of the baseball diamond fence they had created a strip of cement, a basket with a backdrop behind at both ends; the distance between the two points about thirty feet, adequate room to present a challenge to all involved. This set up pleased Ram.

He was excited. It had been so long since he had played a game with his 'Aopato' brothers.

Sonia and Sky had taken their places on a bench parallel to the court. Karine sat as companion to the 'Leader Female' while Djura stood as guardian just behind his monarch. With a male on either end of the seat as well, Ram agreed their ruler was sufficiently protected, even though she was out in the open.

So also were the other females, all of which were seated a step behind the head warrior on a second bench. Nadia sat at one end with Chad at her back; Kara came next, the human woman between her and Angel, and Chantel and Morgan at the far end, Eric to the rear on that side.

The human female drew Ram's attention. She was obviously of his ethnic origin, a fact that sent a shiver of anticipation through him.

Surely I am not attracted to a human?

From the minds of the women, he read that her name was Jamara.

Tamara was a Hindi male name meaning spice. Someone had obviously fashioned a variant name for the girl.

Pretty name; like the person, he thought. *And she's very near my age.*

But no, it is foolhardy to consider her as a prospect. I have a game to play!

Ram turned away, put his mind to the task at hand.

****

Amadeus teleported into the playing field site using his own transfer belt; he had realized at the last minute the distance was too great to walk. Thus he arrived fashionably late.

As always he failed to appreciate the 'jump' method he'd used for it often left him disoriented and somewhat dizzy.

As he came upon the watching spectators, he noticed Chad immediately, recognized him as well. From the nappy tight frizz of hair on his head, to the midnight colour of his smooth silken skin, the six plus nearly seven-foot teenager resembled the black marble statue from the sunken garden, an exact likeness of his fallen twin.

In the darkness of night Chad would have been near invisible for even his eyes were brown, the black slit barely noticeable, but out here in the sunlight he stood out, formidably so.

Though not much more than eighteen, it was obvious the boy took his duty seriously. His manner suggested he was not present to join in with the other males. He had guardian duty!

Standing to the rear of Nadia and Kara, it was also apparent he was not there merely to protect his chosen female, but all six were his responsibility. Even though Jamara was placed between the larger other women, Amadeus knew, should the enemy put in an appearance the male would defend the human just as fiercely as any of the 'Aopato' females.

Chad's posture was relaxed, but he stood stoic and alert, a near mirror image of the giant Djura, who had placed himself squarely behind the 'Leader Female' and his own pair Karine.

Amadeus went to join those standing on the court. He arrived just on time to take part in the discussion.

"So how do you play this game?" Lance inquired. "Does anyone know the rules?"

Sonia chuckled at their pretended ignorance. "Seems more than one would have knowledge of the sport," she observed. "Perhaps, if you ask Amadeus."

"Come show us how to play Amadeus," Lance called as the physician approached.

Amadeus was quick to shake his head. He hadn't played the game in years.

"If I joined, I believe that would make your teams uneven. What if I just tell you how?"

"Unacceptable!" thundered Zane. "We can make it an even number. How about you Eric?"

"Sure," the tech-centre manager agreed. "I'm willing to join in."

As Eric moved down to the cement strip, Chad shifted over to take a post behind Angel putting him dead centre behind the women if defence were needed.

"That okay, Ram?" Lance queried. "Ty?"

"Don't make any difference; two or three." Ram shrugged. So Ty assented as well.

When Amadeus had joined them, the males circled around. "Well," the human suggested. "How about we make it simple? The idea is to get the ball away from the other team, and toss it in your hoop. You can steal it away while your opponent is bouncing it, or intercept when they toss to each other, or even when it misses the hoop. The first team that gets fifty shots in the basket wins. So we first need to choose the players per side."

"I think you have a problem," Sonia broke in. "Our males have an unfair advantage over the humans."

"Yes," Amadeus agreed. "They are so much taller...they'll be able to score much easier. But I don't know what we can do about that."

"I do," Zane offered, grinning. "Remember what we did in that ballgame we had just before our pairings?"

Sonia chuckled. "That should suffice."

Puzzled, unable to see into the 'Aopato' common mind, Amadeus countered. "Aw...not all of us read minds here. Would you mind explaining?"

Ram was laughing gleefully. "We go human!" he declared. "Like this!" And he metamorphed into an older man of thirty.

Amadeus went slack jawed in shock. Behind him, he heard the females giggle.

On the other side of Ram, Zane, Lance and Eric became human-like men twice their ages. Eric the eldest was now in his sixties, while Lance appeared only about a year or so younger than that, and Zane was at least four years his junior.

Amadeus grinned. "So that's how Sonia does it! Is this then your correct age...in human, I mean?"

Lance soberly nodded, grinned.

"We are still going to beat you human," he challenged. "We are equal now by both size and ability...except where Ty is concerned, of course. He's still younger, and should have the youthful strength beyond ours."

"I," Ram put in. "Am also only half your age. You have me to contend with, old one."

"Easy fellows," Sky warned. "Take it to the court."

"Not quite yet," objected Zane. "We need to pick sides."

"I will decide," Sonia offered. "That way there will be no favourites played. Eric, Zane and Ty will be on one team. Amadeus, Ram and Lance on the other. The last gets the first shot. Play well, gentlemen!"

****

Lance got the ball first. Zane was immediately in his face, up close and threatening. Lance feigned left, then right. He bounced the ball, his legs spread apart waiting for the right moment to charge away. Eric joined Zane, each blocking Lance's every move. The ball bounced again, a third time. Lance expanded the position of his legs preparing to make a toss. He bounced the ball a final time.

Ty saw his opportunity. Crouching quickly behind Lance, he slid beneath the eagle-spread limbs, stole the ball as it hit the pavement, and darted away toward the opposite end, bouncing the ball.

I may not have played the game, Ty reasoned triumphantly. *But I've seen it performed many times on TV.*

"I swear," Lance exploded in astonishment. "That boy has powers of his own!"

But as far as Ty knew he was only using speed and agility. *I have no powers,* he rejected in thought.

Ram was keeping pace with him. Neck and neck, they sped on. Ty wouldn't give an inch.

Have to concentrate! he reprimanded himself.

Ty tossed off the shot from a short distance out, easily making the hoop.

From the centre court Eric turned, and even before the goal went in, he headed toward their basket. He caught the ball as it descended, and bouncing the ball once, twice as he ran back, tossed it to Ty who was still over at the side. Ty was off and running again, repeating his previous performance before the opposing team was on him.

When they finally got the ball back, Amadeus was wiser. He and Ram played team toss until a shot was counted for their side.

Lance finally got the ball again, but by then he had forgotten that Ty was like a slippery eel; the boy once again slid beneath the inverted v-shape, and was away with the ball.

Ty had found his nitch; his combative nature had opened up; his aggression was in full swing.

He ran toward the other end, bouncing the ball in rapid succession. Ty made the throw. The orb hit the rim of the basket, rolled along it, and as those watching held their breath, finally...fell in.

Ram let out a whoop of exuberant appreciation, even though the point counted for the other side. "Well done, bro!" he enthused.

****

Jamara felt she had the second best seat on the benches, and though she had never seen such a game before, found it thrilling to watch the men in action.

When first she had watched the 'Aopato' males transform, her initial reaction was one of fear. These were not boys at all, as she had supposed.

Why Ram is older than I am! Even in human-like form he is most handsome.

What Sonia had told them that first night had not fully registered until this moment. In human, they really were twice the age they appeared.

As the game progressed, Jamara swelled with pride at Ty's apparent prowess, like a sister for a brother. But it was more Ram she was aware of, following his every move, enthralled.

He made the chills crawl her spine, her belly fill with need for a man; the rippling muscles, the evident conditioning, the alert intense participation. Jamara gasped in dread when he was pushed down, held her breath until he rose again. Ty sometimes seemed less essential; in her experience he could take care of himself. But, Ram was still recovering, and his welfare hung on the brink.

Down on the court battle raged; Jamara hung on every moment.

"Watch out for that little rascal," Lance warned Amadeus, as he stepped back. "He's better than I bargained." He turned to his other player. "And Ram! Stop cheering for the other side. You underestimate Ty. You want to lose?"

Ram only laughed.

He seems so good-natured, Jamara thought to herself. *So easily forgiving.*

But now he grew serious. He tore across the court after Ty with the obvious intent of blocking at any cost.

And that's when all restraint flew to the wind. No one had explained what was not permitted in the rules. From that point the game took on a brutality to make anyone cringe. Jamara closed her eyes many times to shut away the images, but the sounds still carried.

"Whomp!" And Ram hit the ground hard.

"Ump!" as Lance took a blow to the midriff.

They are going to kill each other over a round rawhide ball!

Men! Jamara thought. *Always the same; got to prove they are the strongest, the best, endure pain the longest. Why? I'd rather watch a gentle man.*

****

"Time!" yelled Djura.

Ram came to the bench panting. Ty beside him was limping, and Lance and Zane looked as if they could drop at any moment.

"Why did you call it?" demanded Eric hotly. "Weren't we winning?"

Djura's face remained a study of apathy, but his eyes betray thoughts of amusement. "You have reached the fifty point deadline," he stated placidly.

"No way!" Ram declared in astonishment. "You were counting?"

"Am I not the usual scorekeeper?" the warrior guardian asked with a raise of his eyebrow.

"It's over?" Ty asked in a deflated tone of regret.

"We could play another," Lance suggested.

"I think…not today," Sonia countered. "Soon darkness comes…"

The males looked at the surrounding hills in surprise, suddenly realizing it was dusk.

"Ah yes, time to go in," Eric agreed. "Another day, we will challenge you again." He morphed back to his usual shape. "This was fun!"

Amadeus shook his head as if in disagreement. "I'll be stiff and sore for days, man, but…yeah, it was worth it!"

Ram grinned, put an arm around Ty's shoulder. "Next time, we will play on our own, right bro?"

But Ty chose to differ. With a shy smile, he decided, "I like playing on a team better."

CHAPTER 20

Jamara was with the other females in what was called the human common room. Kara and Nadia; Angel and Morgan were each present. Only Karine was absent; she was companion to Sonia this day, and as the "Leader Female' preferred the library where the waterfall cascaded in soothing cadence, and she needed the respite, the other females had chosen to keep company with Jamara here.

A small 'Keeper' became visible above the women.

Morgan as the oldest addressed it. "Yes, what is it?"

"I am for Jamara."

"Okay. Jamara will receive the message," Morgan agreed, acting as spokesperson for the human.

"Your presence is requested outside, please."

Jamara knew there was a strict code of ethics regarding the single's sleep quarters, which extend even to here, the recreational area. No male was allowed in the private female common room, and it was quite customary for a male to send in a 'Keeper' when he wished a certain woman to join him, but Jamara had never had it happen to her before.

Surprised by this development, she quickly enquired, "By whom?"

"Ram awaits you outside in the corridor."

"He does? He wants me?"

Pleasure she could not swiftly hide filled the pit of her loins.

"He wishes to ask the lady Jamara a favour," intoned the "Keeper' expressionlessly.

Kara and Nadia giggled knowingly. Morgan smiled, winked at Angel. Flushing, Jamara found the blood rushing to her cheeks.

"You better not keep him waiting," Morgan suggested. "We will connect again with you later."

Jamara felt as if she had been dismissed, like a servant sent on an errand.

He was leaning casual against the granite wall of the passageway, when she stepped out. Ram straightened at the sight of her.

"You want me?" she asked, disbelieving still.

"Ah...yes." He seemed like a young distressed schoolboy, ashamed that he'd been dared by friends to ask to seek a girl's company. "I...I was wondering...ah, would you consider accompanying me on a picnic?"

Jamara drew in a sharp breath. Never in her wildest dreams had she hoped for this.

It was extremely hard for her at this moment to take his offer as serious, to view him in the guise of a suitor as she thought he meant it, considering he once again looked like a young boy half her age, but she remembered the mature athlete giving it his all on the basketball court, and that made it much easier.

"I'd understand if you would rather not be with me. I know, to you, I appear much too young...for you."

"Oh, no!" Jamara quickly objected, without thinking how that might be misconstrued.

And he did take her words at face value, as if he'd refused to mind read thoughts underneath, and was only listening to the surface words. He turned away in dejection.

This put the usually timid Jamara in the rare position of having to deviate from her normal attitude. Used to deferring to the males of her culture out of respect, and allowing them to make the choice, she must take the initiative or lose the opportunity of a lifetime.

"I did not mean no in that sense," she quickly clarified. "I mean, I know you are my age or older..." At this point, as bashfulness took the upper hand, Jamara became tongue-tied.

He turned back, a cocky grin replacing the abandoned bearing, waiting for her next words. His eyes danced with amusement.

Jamara swallowed back trepidation. "I would love...like to join you," she agreed in a soft tone, lowering her eyes, uncomfortable.

"Love?" His manner now was teasing, toying with her. "That is good."

The passage was suddenly way too warm for Jamara's comfort.

He let the moment hang, then chuckled good-naturedly. She could feel the cat-like eyes probing, but could not bring herself to look up into them.

"Shall we go...now?" he finally asked quietly. "Or would you like time...to prepare?"

Jamara at last met his gaze, to be swallowed in pools of brown, mesmerized, invaded deeply to the depth of her soul.

"If you wish," she whispered breathlessly. "We may go…anytime."

"Good! May I touch your hand?"

Jamara shivered. Never had she seen a man this courteous, nor had she ever been so attracted.

"Yes," she agreed softly.

When their hands made contact, she shivered a second time. He smiled, pretending not to notice the effect he had upon her.

And then they were beside the small pond at the foot of the giant outside waterfall.

****

Ram let go of Jamara's hand reluctantly. He made a valiant attempt not to let her heightened expectation inflame him, but it was difficult. Sonia and Lance had both suggested he seek out the females. This was to be a test of his self-control. The final judgement, to see if he would be safe out among the women…to decide if he could be trusted as a guardian again, a defender, not distracted by his own feelings and thoughts.

But Jamara made it extremely hard. He realized now, it had been a mistake to choose the human. Even the 'Aopato' females had assumed an attraction between them.

I should have picked Kara. She would have been less risky, more reliable. But I am still ashamed of my part in what happened. I was afraid she would unbalance me.

However, he could not deny a fascination with Jamara. She was as strikingly beautiful as any of their females, plus she reminded him of a time and the place of his birth, the cultured women of India. He had not expected to feel such magnetic attraction.

What am I to do now? She is litterly trembling.

He recalled Sonia's instructions. "Your duty is to protect her. You are to put her at ease in your presence, or the guardian becomes a detriment rather than a person she is comfortable with. You may choose from any of the females at Sanctuary. We will not be monitoring you, but we will not leave you on your own for any length of time either."

Put her at ease, he reprimanded himself. *What would Sky do with Sonia? I asked her on a picnic. Right!*

If she would only stop shaking, Ram wished he could put his arms around her and comfort, but she might be offended by such quick familiarity. *Did she expect to be raped?*

The continent of India was not a safe place for a woman unattended; it might well be she feared him.

If I only dared enter her thoughts to, but a guardian must give his charge privacy.

"I mean you no harm," he reassured. "I am your guardian. Intimate contact is permitted only to the paired."

Jamara gasped at the implication, and Ram realized he should have left off the reference to familiarity.

Oh, am I ever blowing this!

Ram swallowed a deep breath, and began again, deciding to busy his mind with other safer things.

****

A red and blue braided rug of strikingly intricate design appeared out of nowhere on the grass to the side.

"Come sit upon the mat," Ram suggested gently. "I am new at this," he excused. "Sonia has given me a test...to see if I am ready to be a guardian again...to make certain I can handle my emotions around a female. I am sorry if I've frightened you in any way. I did not mean to misdirect."

Oh, so it isn't what I thought, Jamara realized with disappointment. *I misinterpreted his intentions. I'm such a fool. Why would anyone want me, anyway?*

"Oh, forgive, sir. I am so sorry," she quickly pleaded. "I misunderstand...I thought... something...else."

He smiled reassuringly. "I know you did, and it is entirely my fault. I misdirected. Don't get me wrong. I do find you...very appealing..."

His image shimmered, and he very nearly went invisible. Jamara wondered if it was because he was embarrassed at having to admit the attraction.

He seemed at a loss as to what to do next. Finally, he repeated his request. "Come. Sit...please."

Jamara carefully lowered to the brilliant rug. Without further preamble, he joined her.

"Nanmaste," he greeted her in the tongue of their common race. "Welcome to my jungle."

"Nanmaste," she returned. The word in Hindi meaning 'I bow to you'.

"Well!" he exclaimed. "I promised you a picnic, didn't I?"

Jamara smiled, at once less skittish; his manner had dispelled her fears.

She watched in fascination as various savoury dishes appeared on the mat between them: Lemon coloured rice; Roghan Josh or lamb stew; Samosas and two kinds of Bhajia, one a mixture of potato and cauliflower, the other India's famous onion ring Bhajia. A cooler, called Raita, made from tomato and cucumbers, was also produced to balance the hot spicy dishes.

"You do all this?"

Ram chuckled. "Not I. The 'Keepers' will produce most anything, but I chose my favourites. I hope they are yours also. But…I am not finished. I could not make up my mind so I asked for both desserts…"

Carrot Halwa appeared along with a second dish.

"Gulab Jamuns! Oh, I haven't had those since my parents and I left India!" She had never seemed to be able to get enough of the sweet deep fried balls soaked in syrup.

"When we have the Halwa, the whipped cream will just appear on it," he told her. "And …I have real India Tea."

"May I serve you?" pleaded Jamara, warming to the idea.

Ram grinned, and nodded. "Would you like music?"

"Our music," she wanted to know, as she filled a plate with a large portion from each dish.

"Of course.

"And no waiting while I indulge, female," Ram decided. "You will eat with me."

Jamara was not going to argue with that. Handing him the loaded plate, she filled another with portions of her own favourites.

To the sound of sitars strumming in the background, they each partook, indulging in small talk about their birth country as much as the delicacies set before them.

****

Through mind connection, Ram had tapped into a Delhi radio station for the background music. He was relieved to see that Jamara had relaxed sufficiently to laugh in amusement at his somewhat dull jokes.

She was exceedingly beautiful for a human, at least to his eyes. Her long black hair fell to her waist, stray strands curling slightly at the edges of an oval face. Chocolate brown eyes framed by dark long lashes looked out from a background of silken taupe skin, her complexion flawless. When her full lips turned up in a smile they revealed perfect teeth peeking out like small white china sheep playing hide and seek from behind crimson curtains.

The meal over, Ram made the leftovers vanish, and the two sat sipping the strong tea. Birds sang in the trees as the music ended, the waterfall thundered at a distance. If he allowed memory to escape, he could almost feel the jungle cats lurking in the bushes. Like Tarzan in that old classic, Ram wished he could spend his future in such a wilderness with his Jane.

The thought fled across his mind, *is this my Jane?*

His heart pounded in his ears, excitement raced through his veins; a longing filled his chest like never before. The breath he pulled in felt ragged and painful.

I have to get control. She's a human. It can never be!

But it was already too late. Ram was smitten, falling hard.

CHAPTER 21

From the outside, Jamara's view was different. She had the added handicap of an inability to read the mind of another, and although those around her might have constant communication with each other, and the women mostly included her in such mind knowledge when ever possible, she saw only the surface expression of the man she was with now.

The meal had been most pleasant, the conversation a refreshing interlude, but as Ram suddenly seemed to brood in his silence, her first thought was to feel a disappointment, then rejection, and the only conclusion she could come to was that she had caused it.

How could I have been so stupid as to assume he would seriously consider me? It is plain he was raised caste. I have no station. Why did I think it could be different then with the other men of India? He views this as an exercise, an experiment...I'm just a practice subject!

Such thoughts ran through her head, yet all the while she smiled politely; to laugh at his amusing words seemed all he required from her. Jamara was used to doing just that. It had always been what her race had expected of a lower caste woman, and she had done it well, but this time the charade was much harder to maintain.

Inside, the burning hot cauldron was about to spill over and burn him.

His manner is so controlled it is almost callous. I am so foolish!

It was like men played at a game of self-control. Who could be best behaved, the most excellent at hiding? Those of her homeland had always been good at role-playing.

Why should this one be any different?

Jamara was weary of false pretence, of appearing unaffected. She longed for honesty, wanted to know and feel...to be cared about, touched, held.

Ram had shut himself away, and was obviously not reading her. She knew what it felt like when the women gathered her every thought. Maybe because he was a male he was refusing such interaction, but Jamara missed that perfect communion.

I am tired of this lonely game...of being left out!

Jamara stewed while Ram silently brooded.

Superficial conversation, small talk! I hate it! I'm tired of being expected to be perfect ...presumed not to have feelings. I thought I'd left all that behind in India. I am a living, breathing creature with needs of my own! If you want to pretend, use a machine!

Clearly he was oblivious to her seething tirade, and she could not explain why she felt such lack of control. It was quite unexpected.

The music had started again, changed: a monotone chant accompanied by the drone of a tamboura; a praise song to the mother goddess. It only made matters worse.

She hated it! It was jarring, nerve grating...harsh. It frightened her, brought back memories of times she wanted to forget. It felt like someone had just slapped her, was violently assaulting her.

****

Jamara had tensed visibly, and for just a second Ram wondered if he had done something. She set her cup down with a clumsy motion that rattled cup against saucer.

"Could you turn off the music, please," she begged, her eyelids closing as if to fight off tears.

Ram frowned, and broke contact with the radio station immediately.

"What bothers you so suddenly?" he probed. "I thought you were enjoying our picnic."

It felt like suddenly they had traded places, and it was she now who was unstable. He could sense the anger seething in her, and a desperate misery.

Have I somehow transferred to her? That can only happen if she is a sensitive.

Can a human sensitive...be compatible to us? I must be mistaken. There has to be another explanation for this!

"The picnic was...delightful." She was making a valiant effort to appear enthused, but the words were empty and seemed false; he could see the pleasure had gone out of her.

"The singer...frightened me. It reminded me of a time of oppression, and...the day when I was forced to flee."

His heart slammed hard against his chest. I have hurt her, he realized. I did not mean to do that.

"How can I make amends?" Ram implored. "Will you tell me of this time?" His voice dropped to soft sympathy. "I will listen…no judgement."

She raised those soulful eyes, and they brimmed with tears. Mirrored there were past and present hurts, confusion, and disbelief. It rent the empathy of his heart. Without thinking, he reached for her hand, touching without asking, to soothe.

"Please…let me take this burden from you," Ram pleaded. "Let me share it, make it less."

He knew well how another's care could change the horror of experience.

But, Jamara shook her head. "I've never told anyone," she whispered.

"All the more reason to remove such a canker."

"You have enough…of your own trials. I cannot understand what came over me. I am so, so sorry for being…inconsiderate. I spoiled…such a lovely picnic."

"No…not spoiled. I will cherish this memory…forever. Besides, I am healed…nearly. Surely, I can share the burden of another now."

She was at a breaking point; Ram could recognise it in her because he had just been there, only recently escaped his own infernal region.

"Tell me…please," he insisted. "Do not continue to carry it alone."

Quietly, the tears came, slipping slowly down the tan cheeks. And Jamara finally gave way, commenced to tell a story those who knew her would never have suspected. For years she had held it in; now it broke forth like water flooding out from a shattered dam. She could not have stopped it had she tried.

Ram saw the festering as he probed for the memory, went in as she found it so humiliating to say the words. What he saw first was burning loneliness, a condition he was much familiar with, as he had been in a similar space many a long night previously.

He did not think of shaming her for the weakness of her weeping, saw no need to squelch or quiet the female reaction. He loved her, as only 'Aopato' can, hurt with her, held her, and listened when the words finally came.

Ram tenderly caressed her hands to calm her; gently trying to put her at ease, and as a result, the story when it came out was without regard to consequence.

"My father detested the caste system, and passed that abhorrence on to me. He considered the roll of the female in our society to be both degrading and wrong. In our home, behind closed doors, my mother and I were equals. But it was only later, that hc could fully give us freedom.

"At first my parents lived with the extended family, where the household was ruled in the old manner. My great-grandfather was a tyrant, brutal and demanding. When my mother came to them as a girl bride, her main purpose in his eyes was to bring forth the next male heir. As each birth was female, the women of the family were ordered to kill it.

"However, when my mother went into labour with me, she was alone with my father on a hillside.

After the birth, they hid me, staying away in an old shack by themselves."

Jamara swiped at moisture on her cheeks. She appeared calmer as she prepared to go on, encouraged by the fact Ram was neither disagreeing nor reprimanding.

"When my parents were finally discovered, father was given a choice: kill me or be disinherited. Mother was forcibly sterilized. Father knew if he were to stay, they would cast her off, and compel him to take another wife so an heir could be born. He chose to keep me, to have my mother alone as his only wife. They were...we were cast out of the family; considered now as...lower caste."

Jamara's sadness at the memory made Ram's anger rise to the surface, but he quickly steeled it away, lest she misinterpret his reaction again.

"From then on, my father worked as a common labourer; he had been a professor at the university. Mother worked in textiles, sewing goods for export. We never had any further contact or connection to our birth heritage. It hurt father immensely."

She took a breath, shuddered. She was coming to the part most hurtful.

"My parents lived a stringent lifestyle, saving as much as possible with the idea always in mind to leave India and immigrate to the Americas. As I grew to womanhood, they hid me from the eyes of men, and...my father secretly educated me. He taught me to read and write, about our history and culture, to speak several languages, most things a male of our society would be taught, but never a woman."

Ram realized the wound beneath was about to open; it would ooze forth like gangrene from a festering sore. He cringed when she shuddered again.

"One day when I was out unveiled in our enclosed courtyard, an older man caught sight of me. He immediately came to my father, wanting me as lesser bride. That night, we packed up and fled."

Ram had held himself back from deeper mind probe, waiting to hear the words as she had experienced it. *That cannot be the only reason they left India,* he surmised.

With great difficulty, Jamara went on. "But my would be suitor was not content to leave matters be. He sent hired thugs to search for us, younger, strong, violent, immoral men. They waited until we thought all was forgotten, until both my parents were working. I was caught alone in the field where I was picking fruit..." Her voice dropped near inaudible with shame. "I was violated...repeatedly...by each one...left for dead..."

Ram shivered in revulsion, growled deep in his throat like an angry tiger. But Jamara was no longer aware of him, living it all a second time.

"Father found me; I had tried to crawl home. As he made his way through the alley leading behind our quarters, he found me covered in the blood of virgin and sodomy. I would have died in his arms but for the help of an aide worker, a physician."

Her tears were no more; she was spent with the telling, yet she continued the last of it.

"Our savings were just enough to buy passage to America for one...I was given transport as a prospective sex-trade worker. When I was well enough, my father...made the choice for me. He also persuaded the captain to include mother and himself as kitchen help aboard the freighter.

"When we took passage I wasn't yet out of my teens. It took two years to reach the shores of Florida...and by then, both my parents had died of scurvy."

"Give me no farther details," Ram broke in, his tone dripping with rage. "Only tell me, how did you break away from them?"

"When the ship reached the Florida coast the American coastguard came out from the everglades surprising us. They escorted the freighter to harbour. At the time, I was being used as a substitute scullery maid, and wasn't confined in the hold like the others. As they were being boarded, I slipped over the side unnoticed."

Ram blew out a sigh of relief. *At least she was spared the brothel!*

"Amadeus found me a few nights later, living from the scraps in garbage bins...living on the streets. He took me in..."

"To nurse his dying wife," Ram finished for her. "I know the rest as Amadeus has shared it with Sky. We do not intrude on memories unless necessary. If we had known all this, the females would have healed such nightmare recollections. Amadeus never asked about your past?"

Jamara shook her head. "I was taught to hide personal trauma."

She pulled away to sit up, suddenly embarrassed to realize she'd been in his arms all along. As she took a seat again beside him, Jamara went on to reminisce.

"Amadeus helped me...to view life differently. I was used to a man teaching me. My mother was kept away a lot by her work, and father was both teacher and confidant. He made the decisions. Amadeus simply took his place. He is...was my employer, but also taught me not to fear old customs; they have no hold unless I give it to them. Amadeus introduced me to a benevolent God, one who gives life, doesn't punish for every mistake. He told me I did not need to endure continual reincarnations in which I would pay for sins I committed in past lives...the way our people were taught."

Ram nodded. "I have come to know this Creator God also," he agreed. "It is helper to me when the immoral and malicious have their way. Our species has intimate communion with the Almighty One; we reach out and are touched by It...no, I long ago left the beliefs of my birth place..."

Her eyes filled with amazement; he wanted to cover those awed open lips with his mouth. Ram knew it was time to bring the situation back into focus, or he would do something he would regret.

"It was not for my benefit I chose the ethnic setting, and not my preference either to step back to the past. I am extremely sorry it caused you such pain." He suddenly chuckled. "Mind you, I will always like the spicy food of my ethnic origins..."

Jamara smiled, her pleasure real once again. "I too…but no longer…is it my culture. I fear, I have become…Americanized."

Ram grinned mischievously. "I think I have become a mongrel, such a mixture of all races that I can hardly decide what I am."

Jamara dropped her eyes, as Ram had reached out to take her hand as he spoke. He realized he had forgotten to ask permission, and eased back again carefully, to give her space. She folded her hands placidly in her lap, and was comfortable once more.

"I want to reassure you," he declared softly. "When I do pair, my female will be treated as my equal. I know according to the customs of India men are permitted to seek satisfaction outside of marriage, but the female must be faithful always to him. I do not intend to take relief elsewhere; she will be my one and only. I have seen that is best in a relationship. You would not be my property…you may scold me, even correct me. You are allowed to defend yourself, put me in my place if it is needed…"

Jamara's eyes went very large. "Please…are you toying with me again?"

Ram sighed. "Aw, yes. At first this was an exercise…but now, I am most serious. What you believed at the beginning, has become fact…"

Tears shimmered in her eyes. "You are not joking?"

"Never. Never again," he whispered softly. "I will teach you our way…"

Her breathing quickened; her chest rose and fell with the fever of anticipation. "Will you teach me in the quick way, like the women do...by mind transfer? I have learned thought communication already..."

Surprised and pleased, he responded with an objection. "You do realize that makes us more...intimate?"

"I know now, you will never hurt me," she reassured confidently.

He wanted to jump up and shout to the heavens. She was stealing his breath away; he could not believe her innocent trust.

Ram knew the risk. He knew he should not do it, but she had just stolen away all reason, and he was more than willing now. Without further hesitation, he took the chance, knowing well the consequences.

****

She felt the connection immediately; a love so overwhelming it stopped the senses. Suddenly Ram was inside her mind showing her a universe of knowledge, a new way of living. Even with the females it had never been like this. He had exposed his mind to her without reservation, to show her his feelings, experiences, memories.

Not only were they thinking in their mother tongue of Hindi, words were unneeded, as images flew by in rapid-fire visions, knowledge and emotions, impressions and comments, explained in seconds, feeling as one unit. Cultural placement was irrelevant; past differences forgotten; old wounds no longer hidden but gently balmed. He was comforting her, and she him, all pleasurable beyond description. They each had found a kindred spirit.

It would have been easy to remain thus, lost in each other, had it not been for the intruder.

****

The guardian cleared his throat to gain attention.

"Ram!" Still the two remained oblivious to the stern entreaty, locked in a world of common mind. He had been there once, didn't blame them. "Ram!"

Surprise registered on the boy's face as he jolted up from union. He suddenly realized who stood before them.

Lance grinned. "Getting a bit close there, aren't we? What happened to practicing control?"

Ram went invisible for a second; Jamara blushed and dropped her eyes self-consciously.

Lance chuckled. "It doesn't bother me, you guys," he assured. "I know what it feels like to find someone you've longed for...but...Ram, it is time for your last session with Sonia."

Ram nodded, stood up obediently, turned to Jamara. "I will see you again," He promised.

****

She knew when the two males went private. The females did that all the time, especially when they thought it best she not hear their thought discussion. Lance and Ram went silent for seconds, while Jamara simply waited.

****

"One thing, Ram," Lance chided softly, as the boy prepared to jump away. "Do you realize how defenceless you two were just now? Have you so quickly forgotten what results if captured?

Ram stiffened, dropped his eyes, the rebuke stinging smartly.

"I have failed in my test," he observed remorsefully, in self-chastisement.

Lance placed a hand on the younger guardian's shoulder to reassure. "You did well, but...got a bit distracted at the end."

Ram winced as if he'd been slapped.

"Believe me," Lance added. "I do understand...better than you realize. Such a thing strikes like lightning when it comes. You have been hurting so badly, and this is the other side...to find love when you least expect it, is overwhelming. I've been there...I know it is incredibly irresistible."

Ram looked up with tears in his eyes. "I am very...vulnerable still. It was indeed ...unwise."

"I suggest, next time...ask another to keep a distant watch. It will still be private, but not so deadly."

The boy nodded. "Sometimes, I still forget that help is available. In my weakness ...need, I pushed on too quickly."

Lance quirked an eyebrow. "Little late for regret, don't you think? Do not feel shamed. It has happened to each of us at some point, always unexpectedly," he added, sobering at the reminder of his own rise to pair connection. "She is beautiful...if she shares your feelings...that would be beyond wonderful!"

Ram grinned, and knowing he was now dismissed, vanished without another word.

****

233

Lance turned to Jamara, his manner changing from amicable to frosty.

Eyes narrowed in warning, he scolded disapprovingly. "Do not toy with him female. He is still much fragile."

Tears sprang to her eyes at the rebuke. "I...would never toy. He is the nicest man I know."

Lance's features brightened, and he grinned. "Good. And by the way, when you are 'blood healed' you will be about the same age..."

Mystified, Jamara drew a blank, wondering to what he referred.

"The silly human counting thing," Lance attempted to explain. "He's fifteen according to our aging method, but thirty in human. You'd be about fourteen by our tally."

Why would I need this 'blood healing'? Jamara wondered.

She recalled now, the women mentioning it in the history of the species, but they had neither explained what it was nor how it was done.

Lance had read her question from her mind, answered it. "To become...like us."

"Why?" she puzzled.

"You just became 'Pair connected' to Ram. It happened the moment Ram transported with you today...the instant you first touched. We all felt the new junction. It sent you into emotional overload."

Jamara frowned, still totally uncomprehending.

What is this 'Pair connected'? Does he mean I did harm to Ram?

Lance chuckled, amused by her confusion and ignorance. "Don't bother your head about it," he reassured. "It will all work out. Come. I will jump you back."

As Jamara linked arms, her heart inexplicable took up a rapid-fire beat of excitement.

When Lance left her at the door to the female quarters, Jamara's first thought was to seek out the women.

She needed some answers!

CHAPTER 22

Ram fully expected Sonia to reprimand him.

She had always been like a mother to him, and he knew she would never be vindictive. Sure, she was sovereign, the energy source that held this new species together. Since the first day he had seen her, Ram considered Sonia to be the ultimate manifestation of love, mercy, intelligence, and perception. But today he felt he had failed her; he had followed his own will…without seeking her advice first. She had every right to be angry with him.

Yet, when he arrived, Sonia sat quietly, smiling softly; waiting…patient as always.

He knew she was aware of what had happened. There were no secrets from her. He also realized, his personal sessions with her had come to an end.

"Am I healed?" he asked tentatively.

"What do you think?"

"I made a decision on my own…that was wrong…I think."

"Ram," Sonia chided quietly. "You have forgotten we are all individuals even though we are unified. And…sometimes our needs get the better of us."

"Then…it's okay to go separate," he observed.

"Most certainly. And to make your own choices," the monarch agreed. "But remember, in so doing, we may…sometimes, cause unnecessary consequences for others."

Ram dropped his eyes guiltily. "My choices have put the species at risk," he stated uncomfortably.

"Do you not see the danger to yourself?"

"I do," he admitted. "But, I am of little consequence."

Sonia went silent, neither disputing nor agreeing. He now could see clearly with the eyes of the whole.

How can I remedy this?

She deliberately made him speak it. "You have a question, Ram?"

He drew a deep breath to give himself courage. "My Lady...I know, because of Ty, I am no longer meant for Kara... Does that mean...I am free to choose another?"

"You have as much freedom as you desire, but remember, your actions affect the whole."

"I may choose another female...as my pair?"

Sonia nodded solemnly, then grinned approvingly.

Ram released a sigh of relief. Hurriedly, he rushed on with his next words, as if he feared she might stop him before he could express himself completely.

"I love Jamara..." But further words fled his mind; he could think of nothing else to say.

Sonia's eyes twinkled. "I see that. You also have 'Pair connected'."

"I have?" He said it almost doubtingly, as if he'd just become aware of it. "I mean she has? With me?"

"Yes. So…what do you propose to do about it?"

Ram was still somewhat stunned. Without considering another solution, he gave the most abhorrent resolution. "I could go human."

Sonia held him with her eyes, reading him deep.

"Is that what you wish to be?"

"No, my Lady…but I would do it if it would save others, and…not hurt my Jamara."

"And you think she would not be hurt if you both returned to the human world? Would you live in the Americas, or perhaps…India?"

Ram dropped his eyes, uncertain. "In India our union would not be so unusual. Females are promised at puberty…but we would never be safe. As for America…we would have more freedom…" He knew he was grasping at straws; neither would be tolerable, so he went silent.

"And what of the species you leave behind?" Sonia probed.

Ram sighed. "I am in a quandary. Jamara has learned to appreciate our way; her memory would have to be erased; so would mine…and there is always the enemy ones. I could not protect us from 'Opposites' were I a dormant. Would the others of the species still be at risk if I went human?"

"Aw, Ram," Sonia reproved, tears of compassion brightening her amethyst eyes. "Your attitude is commendable, but you are not the first to put us in this predicament. There will be no need to go dormant. I knew the minute I laid eyes on Jamara she would be perfect for you. Allow me to work this out…"

His heart jumped to hope. *If others have been in my place, and Sonia fixed it...*

"I was not the one who fixed it, Ram," Sonia corrected. "Remember, in the guardian pairings the Almighty Creator worked it out quite well."

"That is the answer?"

"Let me first understand something," Sonia implored, shifting the conversation. "Suppose you were in your teens, as you would be were you both of our species, and say instead you were in your former culture as teens, what would take place?"

"Jamara would be given to me as a child bride."

Sonia nodded acceptingly. "From here on it all depends upon Jamara. Whether her love for you is strong enough; I will not give you a child bride without her willingness."

And that rocked Ram's surety; he was not positive Jamara would choose life with him.

Is it possible for a human to love to that extent in such a short time?

"Wait in your quarters, Ram. I will call you."

The young guardian backed away trembling, bowed slightly, and vanished.

****

Sonia turned to her pair. "What do you think? Could we use another female?"

Sky grinned knowingly. "I will go fetch her."

****

Jamara was in tears, when Sky returned with her.

"I'm so sorry, lady," she cried, as soon as they came visible. "I would never have gone with him if I had known I could do so much harm. I would never have let him even touch me…"

Sky stepped away, ginning at her apparent distress. Sonia remained the picture of calm serenity.

"You seem upset, dear," she noted placidly. "What has got you so rattled?"

"Angel…explained. By becoming 'Pair connected' to Ram I've put you all at risk. If I don't pair well with him, he will…die!" Her voice rose on the last note, a sound of pure panic. "And when he dies, you all will die! I have sentenced you all to death!"

Sonia could not help herself; she chuckled at the misconception the human was under, her assumption she could not meet the requirement. "Well, if that isn't as blunt as you can put it. So, our fate rides on your shoulders alone, does it now?"

Jamara blinked, taken aback. She wiped at the wetness on her cheeks, and an attempt at composure chased the alarm. "It isn't…doesn't?"

"Aw, well," Sonia admitted. "How many times have I thought it rested with me? Isn't that so, Sky?"

Sky lowered to a seat nearby, his amusement at womanly hysteria evident in his eyes. "Females take things so seriously. It never ceases to amaze me how emotional they can get. We are forever on a roller coaster since Kara returned, with her, Sonia, and now you."

Jamara frowned, not comprehending.

"Young one," Sonia went on to explain. "Our species is constantly in flux. We are an amalgamation; with all the different personalities we are forever in trouble one way or another. It's normal for us. You have done nothing that cannot be remedied."

"Oh, tell me how…how can I fix this?" Jamara pleaded hopefully.

"It all depends on how much you care for Ram?"

"Oh, Lady." Tears brimmed, threatening to bring weeping again. "Angel also told me about 'blood healing'. I do understand…what is expected, but I only just met Ram," she reasoned logically. "I have never found someone so wonderful before. He completes me, fills a void I wasn't aware existed, but…I don't know if I can love him as he needs…if I fail to be his all… Oh, Lady, I would do anything so he is not hurt again." She drew in a quick breath, went on rapidly. "I have never had anywhere to go; I am nothing… Now, I have someone who loves me as I am, and…if I loose my life through this process…it would be no great waste…"

Sonia shook her head, disagreeing. "Everyone has value; none are any less."

A tear escaped, slipped down Jamara's cheek. "I would give my life for him. Would that be enough? Could I make him happy? Isn't he too young to pair? He might grow tired of me, and want another…"

Sonia sighed, tears of sympathy standing in her own eyes, realizing the turmoil the human faced.

"Shall we see?" she offered softly.

****

Ram paced his chamber frantically. He might easily have worn a path had not the floor been made of granite.

At last the call came to his mind. "Come, Ram!" Instantly he transferred to Sonia's quarters, unease and dread riding his back.

Anticipating rejection, he had not expected the third occupant. The second female with the 'Leader Pair' was of exceptional loveliness, apparently half-human, and at first Ram could not place her.

When she giggled self-consciously, he realized who it was. His eyes went wide in shocked recognition; his throat closed off, and he could not voice words.

"Ram," Sonia declared softly. "I give you your bride. You may touch her."

The room vanished from his mind; the world ceased to intrude. He saw only the ravishing beauty of the female he had desired. Their hands made contact; the room filled with a fragrance unfamiliar; and a multicoloured rainbow appeared above the two. Only distantly did Ram realize they had just enacted the pairing ceremony.

****

The buzz of vocal conversation filled the compound with excitement. Sonia had just allowed Ram to pair with Jamara, even though they were only fifteen and fourteen. The matriarch had decreed it was necessary for Ram's emotional balance, but Kara was aware it was also as beneficial for Jamara.

Kara felt both happy for them, and sad. To her way of thinking, she had just lost two of her best friends. It was easy to include Jamara as part of the 'Aopato' family, but though they were still like sisters, the relationship between them would be different. Jamara belong to the paired females; Nadia and Kara remained singles, and Kara now had no partner.

It was not that Kara still wanted Ram; he was a good male, but had been twice her age. When she had been younger, before the capture, she had been enamoured by him, but since her return, she had not considered him her possible pair partner...not since Ty. He was now good friend, nothing more.

Now he had Jamara. *Where does that leave me?*

I am alone, an undesirable 'Leader Female'. I have no possibility of ever pairing... unless Ty were suitable. Would Ty even have me? Would Great-gran even permit it?

Kara would have been happy if she had simply been allowed to see Ty alone.

Nadia appeared suddenly at her side. "Come cousin," she declared. "We need to go do something to take your mind off these distasteful musings. Would you like to go pick strawberries? I know you favour them."

Kara half-heartedly acknowledged the effort to cheer her, with a hesitant smile. Nadia was still trying to be her balance, yet they both knew, balance would always be allusive without Ty.

"Yes," she accepted unenthusiastically. "I suppose...I would like that."

CHAPTER 23

Lou couldn't wait for shift's end.

The day had been pointless from the very start. The lead had been a dead end, the case they were investigating going sour for lack of evidence. It wasn't that she didn't like her work; work was her life, but today she'd had more than enough of drug informants and shyster lawyers; lying spouses and devious cut throats. She needed a reprieve!

All this detective wanted was to leave the troubled at the station, go home, and soak in a tub of scalding water.

As they headed back to the city, Barney her partner drove. When they topped the rise, Lou had closed her weary eyes to rest them. Her head was splitting, and the setting sun was blinding.

"Looks like our day isn't over," Barney observed ominously.

Lou opened her eyes squinting, then winced at what she saw. "Aw, bummer! Well, it's not like I had plans for the night anyway. Pull over to the shoulder."

From the accident scene spread below, it appeared the semi had tried to stop, skidding sideways on the highway as it braked to avoid hitting the oncoming passenger car. On one side of the roadway, the six-wheeler was on its side in the ditch, the cab twisted upside down. No doubt, the driver was inside hanging by his seatbelt, unconscious, for as yet he hadn't gotten out.

"Must have just happened," Barney surmised, as he brought the cruiser along side the upended smaller vehicle in the ditch on this side.

It too was resting on its roof; had obviously rolled several times. From the looks of the front end it had hit something unexpected, but if it had been the semi, the car would have been a compacted cube. It wasn't; it was still somewhat intact. The windshield was shattered, a large portion to the right of the steering wheel missing.

These two vehicles didn't hit head on, Lou reasoned. *Did the car encounter something else first, then roll? And if so, what?*

There appeared to be no third vehicle.

"Better call it in," Lou ordered. As ranking officer, command fell to her. "I'll check out the car, see if we have survivors."

Lou never liked accidents. She was Investigation, not patrol, but from rookie days, the experience was there, and you couldn't just drive on by, a way out here.

A cursory observation, a quick assessment, and she moved back to the patrol car. Her partner was just getting out.

"They're on their way," Barney stated. "We're to sit the scene. Any survivors?"

Lou shook her head. "Two dead: the male behind the wheel; female went through the windshield. There is a car seat for a newborn in the back, gifts and baby articles, but no child."

"So, guess we'd better look for the infant."

"The mother might have been holding it, nursing. They never learn! If the woman didn't survive, doubt we'll find the baby living. Then again, maybe it wasn't with them..."

"We can only hope." It was plain Barney found the thought of finding a broken tiny body as abhorrent as she did.

"I don't think the semi hit the car," Lou added. "Damage would be more extensive. They hit something smaller; there is a deer crossing just below us, maybe a moose..."

"And what do you think caused the semi to jack-knife?"

Lou shrugged. "Maybe the driver can tell us?" she suggested. "Let's go see what we can find there? Maybe, at least, he's still alive. Then we can look for the infant."

The two officers made for the semi cab, but before they were half across the pavement, a gigantic man suddenly appeared out of nowhere directly in their path.

"Holy crap!" Barney exploded, and both officers went for their weapons.

****

Lance had been on outside sentry duty for the night, the most dangerous of all watches, but still he preferred it. It brought him outdoors, and with his history of confinement, the open air always felt good, even after so much time had past since his ten year incarceration in the human world.

The females had retired early. Sonia seemed unusually weary, perhaps because of the 'blood healing', and the excitement of the new pairing. He knew it always drained on his mother; healing was still the female bane that weakened them, most of all the 'Leader Female'.

Djura had been on sleep break during the day, and had yet a few hours of leisure still to go before relieving him.

Lance sensed the sudden drain on the species immediately. He would not normally leave his post, but he felt an urgency, as if the need was personal, someone close to him in trouble. This was similar to the effect on them, as when they first became aware of the loss of Kara and Ram.

Surely, the enemy has not taken another prisoner, Lance hoped. *It doesn't feel the same.*

The minds of the rest of the species were in deep sleep, and he would not seek the assistance of Djura until he was certain of what this was. The guardian followed his foreboding instinct to its source, coming out on a quiet hillside not many miles outside Sanctuary, materializing on the payment of a secondary highway.

This is an accident scene, he realized. *Why do I feel it concerns us?*

He had the nagging suspicion his mother was nearby. As he stood searching, reaching out for her essence, a police cruiser drove up. Lance went invisible.

He watched the female officer search the damaged smaller vehicle; listened while the pair debated, and as they headed his way, decided to interact with them.

To his mind there was no avoiding it. Sonia might be in jeopardy nearby, and these two could do more harm uninformed. It was crucial he disclose his presence.

Lance did not like police; he did not trust them!

He touched the band about his forehead, switching it on.

****

The large man turned to them before either Lou or Barney could clear their guns. His eyes narrowed in annoyance.

"I prefer you keep those where they are," he stated bluntly. "I will not harm you; I am not the enemy."

However Barney had ideas of his own. His revolver cleared the weapon cradle easily, and was trained on the intruder. "Identify yourself!"

"If you persist, I will be forced to render you powerless," the other man warned. "You may need your weapons later. A predator exists in the vicinity that could present a problem for you."

Something about this colossal male caused Lou to take him seriously. Not only was he much larger and obviously strong enough to subdue them, he had an air of authority about him she could not refute. It was also apparent this was not a normal human being. He wore a gold band about his forehead, was lightly dressed, as if the weather was no bother to him, and his eyes, though blue, had a dark vertical slit at the centre.

Lou motioned Barney to stand down; negotiation was always preferable to force in her book.

When they had relaxed the larger being addressed them. "I am Lance," he revealed curtly. "And as you surmise, I am not fully human."

Lou did not react to the fact he seemed aware of her thoughts; she came bluntly to the point. "Did you cause this?"

"No..." He answered slowly, as if he were preoccupied. "You have others coming... support?"

"Yes. Back-up is minutes away."

Lance sighed, then frowned. "Will you work with us?"

"Who is us?"

"My people... I think...one of us is injured up on the road."

****

Now that Lance had spoken it, he realized the worst had happened. He knew the others at Sanctuary were waking, the sudden awareness spreading across the species.

His brother Zane had awoken with a start, and even damaged Kara came up sobbing, had sense their world was teetering.

It had to do with Sonia!

****

Lou spun toward the darkening highway. In the dampness of the air and luminosity of a pale moon the roadway shimmered, but she saw no one. "Where?" she asked.

"We are not visible to you unless we use our headbands. Her's must be knocked off line, rendered inoperable. I do not know this for certain... I just got here."

"Then how do you know she is out there?"

"I can sense her... She is my mother."

Lou went cold with foreboding; an old lady, lying out there, invisible to others, in the middle of a busy highway.

"She's about ten feet forward. We'll need the area blocked off from traffic; reroute it."

Lou nodded. It was something that needed doing anyway, so officers could decide what had happened.

Another thought struck her. "If we can't see her, I'll need you to take me to her."

The alien male seemed reluctant.

"And," Lou added. "I'll be staying with you though all this, mister," she warned. "Just to make sure this isn't some sort of hoax."

Lance quirked an eyebrow. "Well then, don't be alarmed when others of our species arrive."

Lou took the comment in stride.

In the distance, a second patrol car squealed to a stop beside Lou's cruiser, parking sideways across the highway, its sirens winding down to a mournful moan, as if in grief for the dead nearby. The lights remained, slowly flashing.

Lou addressed her partner. "See to things out there," she ordered. "Tell the others as little as possible until we know more of this situation. Don't tell them what we think is up ahead. Have them concentrate on the semi driver, and look for the infant."

Barney acknowledged, and moved away.

"Okay, mister. Let's see if you are right. Was your mother what was hit by the car?'

Lance turned frowning, gazing up the roadway as if he could see his answer there. "She is unconscious…and the residual memory I pick up is fuzzy. The car hit a deer, flipped and rolled. I think human mother and daughter were thrown from the car…"

Are these people telepathic that they can see each other's memories? Lou wondered, then answered her own speculation. *Of course they are! Didn't he do just that with me before?*

The giant was still talking, seemed to be deliberating with himself.

"What I can't understand is why she was way out here. And where is Sky? If she was in deep sleep cycle…where is he?"

"Who's Sky?"

"Her pair…husband," he answered absently.

"Okay? Obviously, he wasn't with her, so it's up to us. Let's go find her."

And finally he admitted why he was hesitant to lead her forward. "Approach is too dangerous. When mom's down, she has this ugly reflex action…it would vaporize a human. That's why we need Sky…"

Lou tried to keep her face impassive. In her opinion, this was an evident attempt to keep her from the scene. "Well," she observed, with just a touch of sarcasm in her tone. "I can see why you'd want the highway curtained off."

As if he'd read her thought again, Lance scowled, but ignored the acidic comment.

****

He couldn't blame the human. Why should she believe what she couldn't see? Were he still human-like, he wouldn't have believed this either. It sounded too absurd.

Lance noted Zane's scent behind him. He knew he had just joined them, though his brother remained invisible.

"Show yourself, Zane."

Zane immediately knew to use his headband. His abrupt appearance caused the female cop to start violently.

"Man! You guy's could give a person a heart attack!" she exclaimed with annoyance. "Where'd you come from?"

But both the men had their minds elsewhere.

"Aw, mom," Zane moaned in sympathy, dropping unsteadily to one knee, and covering his face with his hands in his grief.

"Zane." Lance touched his troubled brother on the shoulder to comfort. "Keep it together. Help me... Do you sense her?"

Zane raised his head. Their eyes met, and he nodded. "I place her about ten feet to the left, forward." He pointed. "She's badly injured."

Zane got to his feet, a question on his lips. "Why would she come out at dusk like this? It exposes her. The darkness will reveal our presence soon as well. And where was Sky?"

Lance knew it best to not go there, the scolding tone Zane used bordered on anger.

"Zane we need to hide her, until we can safely deal with this. Any suggestions?"

His brother pondered the situation a moment. "We could use a guardian ring," he suggested. "They would appear as lights to a passer-by. We could leave Tech centre on 'Keeper' to blind the enemy until she is healed enough to move."

Lance agreed. "Where the devil is Sky?" he said in frustration. "He should have been the first to sense her danger."

Sudden realization hit both men cold in the gut. As one, they wheeled to the right. "Oh, man! No!" they cried in unison.

Panic paralysed Lance, as he grasped the implications to them all.

****

Lou was watching their every action. Both men seemed genuinely alarmed; they were not putting this on, or she was a very poor judge of character. If she had had any doubt this was genuine, it was fast dissipating.

She decided, something very serious was going down here.

"Well," she finally broke in. "If you guys really want our help you'd better explain to me what's going on. Unlike you, I don't read minds."

The look on their faces was one of sudden realization, as if they'd forgotten her presence. Lance looked at her for a second without comprehension. "Oh, sorry." He met the eyes of the other male. "She can hear us?"

Zane grimaced. "We forgot. We're using the bands."

"Oh, right."

It was Lou's turn to be perplexed. "And?"

"The bands not only keep us visible, they make us audible. We are telepaths, not speaking aloud."

Lou blinked. "Okay," she accepted. "So, what's got you boys all rattled?"

Lance pulled in a breath; Zane looked away and wouldn't meet her eyes.

"We still don't know how this happened," Lance finally admitted. "But both our 'Healer Ultimate' are down. And that means…we can not heal them."

"I gather her mate is out there as well?"

"Correct," Lance agreed, his tone preoccupied. "Zane…we need the guardian circle."

Zane nodded. "They can be here in seconds, but…it leaves the females unprotected."

"Leave Chad and Ram behind to guard them. The females are to stay away from here."

"That means only Eric, Djura and myself for the circle," Zane warned. "It is not enough; they'll be too far apart."

"Man!" Lance exclaimed in desperation. "This can't be happening. It can't end like this! She carries their first offspring!"

CHAPTER 24

This simply did not make sense to Lou. If the woman on the road was old enough to have two grown sons, this obviously was not her first child. Something didn't add up here.

And it seemed to her, at this stage of their mother's life, wouldn't she also be too old to have a healthy child? *Why risk it?*

Once again, doubts arose, at what she was hearing. To Lou's way of thinking, so far, there had really been no proof that anyone lay out on that road ahead.

Are these guys simply that good at the con game, or am I missing something?

It is time to put a stop to this immediately!

Her hand moved to her gun. But Zane was quicker. Lou felt his hand go to her shoulder, and she was suddenly frozen in motion, couldn't move a muscle even when she tried.

"Don't human!" he warned. "You do not have the whole picture. Hear us out...please. We are not deceiving you."

His brother tried to explain. "We...Zane and I are from another partnership, our father was human. And, in our species we age differently than human kind. When Sonia, our mother, took Sky in pair...the species had no children except from that human coupling. The child mother carries is special..." A tremble entered his voice, and he had to compose himself before going on. "Sonia is our oldest 'Pure' female, and uncle Joel is the only 'Pure' male…"

Lou did not know quite what to say at that disclosure. Evidently, the matter was extremely sensitive, the conditions taking place upsetting. She realized a lot was at stake here, and no doubt the woman would lose the precious child. She decided to cut them some slack. After all, even though she could not see the beings on the road, these men had the power to stop whatever she tried. It was best to go along with them.

As she relaxed, she felt Zane release her. Lou left the weapon in its holster.

"Bare with us," Lance pleaded. He shook his head as if to clear it. "We are having trouble…focusing…processing…reasoning this out." A second time, he shook his head, like a dog with water in its ear. "Our 'Ultimate Healers' are down," he repeated. "Sonia, our mother…is also our knowledge keeper…her being down befuddles us…confuses…"

Lou frowned. *What is he implying?*

"Are you saying, somehow this affects you; there's something wrong with you? Are you somehow connected to them?"

"Just give us time…please…to sort through this."

Lance dropped to one knee in apparent weakness. The younger one swayed dangerously, and wiped perspiration from his brow.

Lance looked up at his brother in fright. "Zane, I can't even think straight. Is mother really that low?"

"I can barely feel her now." Zane moaned, as if in pain. "I think we're in big trouble, bro. I can't feel any of the others either. Mom...always...knew what to do..."

Their actions were beginning to scare Lou. Both men were fazing in and out like a light bulb on its last legs.

"Don't you have another healer?" she challenged. "Or perhaps someone else able to tell you how to proceed?"

"Uncle Joel!" Lance burst out in sudden clarity. "But...I can't connect. He's on home planet. Only Sky or Djura can reach that far..."

"Why?" Lou asked to get him to think it out himself. She wasn't following his reasoning.

Lance sighed, seeming uncomfortable at having to admit weakness. "Because they are much older. "Zane and I are...too young."

"Too...young?"

Lance gave a shaky laugh. "Don't try so hard to understand, human. Just accept."

"It's not important," Zane cut in. "It would be too dangerous for uncle to come at this time. He'd be seen against the night sky..."

"So, what's so bad about that?" Lou wanted to know.

"Would draw...the enemy to us."

"What enemy? You're not talking about humans, are you?"

Lou felt cold dread crawl her spine when neither man answered.

****

Almost as if to speak of them had brought them into existence, the ebony sky around them lit with the glow of seven distinct luminescent giants standing in a circle, spaced fifteen feet between each, all around the section of road where the hidden victims were alleged to be.

Lou shivered. The spectacle gave evidence of impressive authority, strength and magnificence. *Is this their guardian circle? This is what real alien beings look like!*

Lance came shakily to his feet, and placed a hand on Lou's shoulder. "Let's just step inside the light circle, human. We will be much safer there."

Lou was curious, somehow not afraid, and went with out objection. As they walked about five feet forward to step within the ring, a third man appeared beside them.

This one was obviously older, but not nearly the elder Lou had expected. Compared to the two brothers, the new arrival was huge, standing only about half a foot taller, but with a girth twice that of his nephews, a body dense with muscle and evident strength. His eyes were unlike anything she had ever seen, the iris silver; the pupil a rust vertical slit.

Indeed a man to be reckoned with!

Lou slowed in misgiving, dropping back, but the three men stopped abruptly, circling her, as if it were their natural inclination to protect her. Yet they seemed more intent on each other, and their behaviour toward her simply conditioning.

"Joel, I am so sorry. We tried to keep her safe," Lance apologized in a voice of concern. "I'm not sure how this happened."

"Was your mother perhaps sleepwalking again?"

"Unsure. But it seems logical. We can see little from her memories. What made you aware we were in trouble?"

"Djura sent out the call for help as soon as he realized Sonia was down," Joel stated matter-of-fact. "When he could not raise Sky either, he realized this was a much more serious matter."

"Where is Djura?" Lance turned to gaze toward the guardian circle, and suddenly became aware of their number. "You brought guardians from home planet?" he exclaimed in surprise. "You only left two behind? Chi and Wade?"

"How else were we to do this?" Joel queried pointedly. "I've told Djura to remain at Sanctuary. If you boys are feeling confusion when in close proximity to her, how much more do you think this would affect him?"

Lou realized there was something these beings weren't telling her, but she was hesitant to interrupt. She stood between them listening, waiting.

She had a husky build of her own, but standing just over five foot three, she felt small and of little consequence among these giants who towered at least two feet over her. As an enforcement officer, the representation of law among her people, it could hardly be said she had matters under control, but there was little she could do about that.

"I will see what I can sense," Joel offered.

He dropped easily to one knee, closing his eyes to concentrate.

"Aw," he finally said. "I can see into Sky's memory."

Lou waited, as hopeful as the other two, for an explanation.

"She left the bed chamber..." He nodded knowingly. "And yes, she definitely was sleepwalking. Baby..."

"Was craving human companionship again!" Lance finished with a chuckle.

Lou frowned. *What are they saying? The baby has the power to make his mom sleepwalk?*

Zane was more serious. "Sky's been saying, that little guy will cause the death of us."

Joel seemed puzzled. "No," he disagreed. "Baby wasn't craving. He was sensing danger, and brought his mother here."

Brought her here! Lou thought in shock. *This baby can do that!*

"Why?" wondered both Lance and Zane in union. "Danger to what?"

"Whatever it was," Joel marvelled. "It lies protected beneath her."

Lou gasped. Suddenly she had the answer.

"The baby!" she yelled horrified.

All three looked at her in amazement.

"The baby!" Lou clarified. "The one from the over turned car."

"Ah…yes." Joel gave a soft sympathetic groan, and closed his eyes again. "It lay in the centre of the highway…the semi was baring down…she had only seconds to step between…"

Lou cringed. *She must have taken a direct hit from the semi. She should be dead! At the very least, she is very, very broken.*

"And what did Sky do?" asked Lance.

"He came upon them just as the truck cab was dragging Sonia forward. Sky ran along beside the cab, lifting it and turning the wheels away from his pair, but the back end of the semi jack-knifed catching him square on, sent him flying. Just before he lost consciousness, Sky threw the truck by kinetic as far as he could."

"He what?" squealed Lou. "He threw a semi that size!"

Joel opened his eyes, and grinned in amusement at her reaction. "If it had been my female," he said evenly, rising to his full height. "You'd never have seen the darn thing again."

Lou shuddered. "Did you ever think of the guy inside?"

"Well…" Joel conceded. "Sky has always been more generous that I."

What kind of creatures are these anyway?

"Djura?" Joel turn with a frown. "I thought I told you to remain…"

Lou was becoming conditioned to their sudden popping in, but she jumped back in dread at sight of the formidable new arrival. She had thought the first three large, but each new male seemed more enormous than the one before. This one appeared Arabian, was near eight feet tall at least, with the body of a weightlifter, and a scowl of threat on his countenance.

"She has need of me!" he objected with a hiss. "I will not refuse her."

Joel nodded, amazingly acquiescent.

Do they feel as threatened by this guy as I do? wondered Lou.

But the big warrior appeared suddenly submissive. His face went from menace to remorse. "Aw...female," moaned the powerful male. "What have these humans done to you?"

Lou frowned. *What does he think? That we did this!*

Then it dawned on her. *The driver is human!*

A shiver of apprehension ran through Lou. *What if these guys seek retribution?*

"Are you able to tell the extent of her injuries?" Joel asked.

Djura took a step beyond the group, and abruptly dropped with force to one knee, gasping.

"Be careful," Joel cautioned. "I would go no closer. We don't need you down as well."

"She drains only half...she's still able to control some functions."

"Is she okay?" Joel asked again.

"As okay as possible." Djura turned his head, looking to his right. "Sky is down too?" he noted.

"Yep." Lance agreed.

"And our healing powers are non-existent," Zane added.

"Sonia is in need of female balance," Djura declared firmly.

"We bring no females here!" Joel quickly disagreed. "It is dark! The site is too dangerous!"

Djura rose to full height, swaying weakly as he stepped back. "Joel...you need to rethink that," he warned. "She...needs Kara!"

Joel shook his head obstinately, refusing to even consider the thought. "She is our next in line, and she's already damaged!"

"Then Sonia must have another...one of equal stability."

"No females! Look what being near her does to you!"

"You wish then to just give up, warrior? You seek to end the species?" Djura met the eyes of the 'Pure' male without wavering, as if he were reminding of some past offence, and forewarning of a repeat. "Because we are indeed on such a brink...again."

Joel winced, and backed down. "There must be another way," he implored.

"We need at least one female," Djura persisted.

"The 'Opposites' will trace a female here; it will take seconds and they'd be on us... and we are basically defenceless!"

Djura grunted, and doubled over, as if in pain. When he again straightened, he declared, "I alone...am not enough."

Lou had no idea what they were talking about, was puzzled by the behaviour of this enormous new arrival. To her, he seemed to be ill, in a great deal of agony.

What is wrong with him? she wondered. *Sure hope this isn't contagious.*

As if he'd read her thought, the giant turned dark intense eyes toward her. "I am added strength support to the 'Leader Female'," he stated calmly, as if such a thing were most natural to him. "When she is too weak to support us she drains energy from me."

Lou ignored what she didn't understand of his revelation, and went right to what she thought was the most important issue. "Sonia is your 'Leader Female'?"

"Correct." Djura looked again to Joel. "It is unwise to wait, guardian. Without female support, we will all go down quickly."

"Can you at least isolate the guardian circle?"

"I have…but it does not mean they will not go down…in time."

"I'm not bringing a female here! Especially not Kara!" Joel decided firmly. "We just got her back, and we've fought too hard to get these females…"

"What about Amadeus?" Zane cut in. "Wasn't he a physician? Sky's been training him…"

The others all turned to look at him. Joel frowned. "What is your reasoning here?"

"Maybe he can do something we cannot? Sky is half human. If Amadeus could revive him…perhaps by conventional methods…he tended Kara for the past three years…"

"Then Sky could tell us how to better help his pair," Lance quickly agreed.

Joel pondered a second, finally nodded. "Go fetch him."

Zane vanished instantly.

One thing worried Lou beyond all else. *If this injured woman is their leader, and she dies…what will these powerful creatures do to humans in retaliation?*

What she least expected, was the answer relied upon the help of another human being.

CHAPTER 25

As they came visible Amadeus doubled with the sudden throbbing spreading through his every limb.

Joel spun upon them, scolding. "What is wrong with you, Zane? He's a human! You travelled too rapid!"

"Sorry. Sorry, Amadeus," Zane responded with contrite sympathy. "I didn't mean to hurt you, man. I figured the need was to hurry; didn't think of what it would do to you."

"It's okay. Guess I'll live." Amadeus straightened, as the hot pains subsided. "Now you get why I hate this teleporting."

Zane grinned widely.

Joel stepped forward. "I've heard much about you human," he said approvingly. "It's too bad we meet this first time under such circumstances."

Amadeus nodded in recognition, assuming this was Sonia's brother. "Zane filled me in, says you need my help. Don't know just what I can do."

Amadeus had noticed upon arrival the descending darkness, and the glowing rim of guardians. He knew that nighttime placed all present in extra jeopardy. The 'Aopato' stood out in stark silhouette against any ebony skyline making them easy prey for their enemies.

When they parted, he was surprised to see the human woman between the three guardians. He had not expected a police presence.

The stocky woman was Caucasian, shapely even in the bulky uniform. Because of the illumination of the males near her, Amadeus could make out her brown eyes and auburn hair. She appeared to be in her late forties.

Joel gestured out to the road, where lay two glowing mounds approximately ten feet apart and five feet forward. Amadeus could not make out the forms; only saw radiance over something more solid.

"Sky is the one on the right, Sonia on the left. We cannot approach closer."

"Their bands are knocked off line?" Amadeus quizzed. "All I see is a glow."

"Sonia is very low, unable to carry fully," Joel confided. "It is already affecting our cognitive abilities, among other things."

"What other things?" Amadeus probed with concern.

"I don't know how much longer we'll be able to teleport, we are weakened physically, and...our ability to resist and protect is near non-existent."

"You're stuck here...and defenceless?" he exclaimed with alarm.

"Whomever joins us from this point on will likely be unable to go back...until we remedy the situation."

"And that means?"

"Until Sonia has healed back."

My God, they are sitting ducks!

Amadeus went to silent communication, speaking only in thought. *I notice you have a police presence?*

That is taken care of, Joel reassured. *To limit such a thing is always our first priority.*

"Okay." Amadeus spoke aloud this time. "What do you expect of me?"

"I...we are hoping you can help us. Sonia places great trust in you..."

Amadeus looked out at the two injured beings on the pavement. "Well...as I understand it, if Sonia were too far down, none of you would still be visible. Am I right?"

Joel solemnly nodded. "Should we go down, it would be all together. In order to correct the downslide, we need Sky...so he can begin the healing process. As long as he remains unconscious, we remain in a holding pattern. Is there any way to at least revive his human side?"

"I suppose like always, he can't be touched?"

"That is correct."

"Well...without touching I can't determine the extent of his injuries, and if I don't know what I'm dealing with...one thing might work, another might kill him."

****

Lou was shocked when the man Zane brought proved to be a human. She was amazed as well, that he seemed so familiar with the creatures; was not in the least apprehensive of them or considered as less intelligent. It blew all world theories of alien abductions.

The man appeared to be on equal footing with his captors, unless…he wasn't a prisoner?

As Lou listened to the two men discuss the situation, a thought struck her.

"Aw…mind if I interrupt? I have a question."

The human man chose to address her first. "What would you like to know?"

"The big guy…Djura? Is that what you call him?" Joel took sudden interest as if realizing her disruption was not a mere ploy for attention. Encouraged, Lou went on. "If he supplies energy to this female, can the same be done for the injured male?"

"No," Joel declared bluntly, turning away again to the human man. "But, Amadeus, would energy be helpful?"

"Well…he's unconscious. In a full human, if his heart stopped, we could jump-start it to make it beat again. But, Sky's a hybrid…"

Joel's eyes narrowed in anger. "They tried that on Kara! That's what caused her disconnect from us; it's the reason she's damaged!"

Amadeus frowned in consternation. "Sorry. I wasn't responsible for that. I never realized our physicians had caused her condition. Is that why her energy was so low when I found her; they tried to jump-start her heart?"

Lou realized she had inadvertently caused this controversy. Obviously it was not Earth's first encounter with these beings.

How come we've never heard anything about this in the news? A warning premonition made Lou turn

269

to the darkness beyond. *Why haven't I heard anything from Barney? Why hasn't an officer at least crossed the barrier? What's going on out there?*

Her heart began to slam against her ribs in fear. *I'm in big trouble. I've been too trusting. Maybe it's already too late for me, but I won't go down without a fight!*

Yet her fright held her frozen; she could only stand and listen, unable or perhaps, due to curiosity…unwilling to take flight.

****

"Humans seldom realize our different physiology. Our energy differs from yours," Joel declared with frustration. He turned to study the mound to their left dejectedly. "If only Sonia would waken… Her mind contains the medical records; each blood group mixture is so different. We need to know Sky's proper balance."

Amadeus saw now this was going to be harder than he had thought. "You each need a different treatment?" he questioned in amazement.

"Indeed," Joel admitted. "It took us years to perfect the exact medical balance for each in the species. Even now, as we were thrown this curve with Kara, we still are experimental. Sonia is the only one who knows what's best, and once…Kara knew it also, but…"

"That's part of the lost records?" Amadeus asked, incredulous. "Why didn't you keep written records?"

"Normally, there is no need. It has no benefit. Sonia as holder keeps all stable, and Sky heals any injuries…"

Amadeus went back to the matter at hand. "Before, you mentioned you could not approach them. Why is that?"

"Sky and Sonia are connected even though unconscious. As she is at such a low intensity, and Sky is in junction, kept in existence by her, if we approach either one, step beyond our present position, she we simple drain our energy to maintain the balance. We won't die; our consciousness is simply held in storage, so to say, while she maintains living level for them both. As she is essential to our existence, this is the best method of our continuing."

"So complicate."

"Not really. To us, it is quite simple. Sonia gives us life; therefore she must always come first."

Amadeus pondered the situation a moment. "What if they became one physically, like they do when healing back?"

"That's what we need to bring about. The matter is how? We cannot help him to do that unless he is conscious."

"So…we need to bring him around somehow?"

"Why do you need the female?" Amadeus had forgotten the cop until she interrupted. "Before, the big guy wanted you to get a female."

Joel frowned, annoyed by the intrusion, but he explained none the less. "A female when so down becomes unstable emotionally. Another female

271

presents a guide to emotional equilibrium. Males have a different emotional nature..."

The cop quirked an eyebrow. "No kidding?" she stated sarcastically. "I never would have guessed."

Amadeus almost laughed outright, but Joel saw no humour in her comment. "What are you called, female? So I can address you properly."

"Lou."

"That is a male name! Your female moniker, please!"

Lou chuckled, amused by his reaction. "It's Louise. Why?"

Joel sighed, realizing instantly he was being irritable. "I would rather converse respectfully. May I address you by...Louise?"

She shrugged nonchalantly, as if it mattered little, but Amadeus suspected, for some reason, this mattered a lot to her.

"Females are considered very special to us," Joel explained. "We treasure them... because at one time we had so few."

"So, does that mean you prefer us bare foot and pregnant?" the woman challenged bluntly.

Amadeus chuckled. *This lady sure has a chip on her shoulder,* he thought, and Joel reading the thought followed his lead, the reaction of irritation swallowed by a half hidden smile.

"I doubt they would have a female leader if that were their attitude," Amadeus defended. "Believe me, these males protect their females staunchly."

"So what are you protecting them from?" Lou challenged again. "Us? Each other? What?"

It seemed she was intent on picking a fight, but this time she had hit below the belt.

"No!" Joel objected with vehemence. "We are unable to protect them out here."

"From what then?" Lou asked again.

"If we allow a female here, it will bring the 'Opposites' out. It's a wonder we haven't attracted them already."

"And just what is an 'Opposite'?" persisted Lou.

Amadeus too had always wanted that question answered, so he added his voice to the fray.

"I've seen what your enemy does to you. I wouldn't mind knowing what they look like myself."

"Big lizard-like creature, our opposite," Zane volunteered from the sidelines. "As deadly as we could be…"

"Without conscience or compassion," added Djura coldly, speaking for the first time since Amadeus had arrived. "And Joel, we still haven't solved that female problem."

Joel turned on him, ready to debate.

"You know, I've been thinking on that," Lance cut in, his words slow and thoughtful. "Maybe we can't protect, but…I know one who might be able to. I'm just uncertain he's ready for this."

"Ram?" Amadeus guessed quickly.

Lance shook his head. "No. Ty."

"He's a human!" Djura objected.

Lance met his eyes evenly. "Sonia has kept a secret from most of you…" he disclosed quietly.

Djura's eyes narrowed to mere slits. Amadeus knew immediately information was passing mind-to-mind, and he was not privy.

Djura exploded with fury. "An 'Opposite' has been among us all this time!"

Amadeus felt the cold dread travel his spine. *Ty is 'Opposite'?*

Now he thought of it that made perfect sense.

Djura had calmed a bit. "And I knew nothing of this. I hate it when she keeps things from me!"

"How come you alone know this, Lance?" demanded Joel.

"Sonia and I have been working together with Ram."

"And how does that concern Ty?"

"Ty and Ram were together at the prison base before Ty went dormant… There is another thing you should know, but it should not go farther than us."

"You have our silence," agreed the other men.

"Kara is 'pair connect'…"

"To him?" Joel thundered. "To an 'Opposite'!"

Lance soberly nodded.

"Aw…aw," moaned Joel beside himself. "This happened while they were with Amadeus?"

"Yes, that was why Sonia brought them all to Sanctuary."

"Just what do you mean by 'pair connected'?" asked Amadeus. "To my knowledge they've never been intimate. I would have picked up on that."

"We are not like you humans, Amadeus," Joel reproved. "You should realize that by now. Our first connection comes on an emotional level, when time is spent with a compatible individual. It can happen by a simple touch, without the awareness of those involved. Such a junction can not be broken once it develops..."

"To be separated too far from each other results in death," Lance added.

"Litterly?" Amadeus clarified disbelievingly. Joel nodded. "It can't be broken?"

"Only ends at death; both will die if one does," Joel admitted.

"You guys are really...unusual. The more I learn about you, the more it floors me. Puts a whole new meaning on life pairing."

Joel chuckled good-naturedly. "Someday, we will have to tell you the story of the guardian pairings."

"Which makes me wonder," Lance interrupted. "Where is your female, Joel? We could use her right now."

"She is 'Pure'! I left her at Sanctuary. I will not jeopardize her life by bringing her here!"

****

Lou was startled by the deep velvet tones spoken beside her. All had been so intent upon the conversation, none had seen the female materialize between them.

"And what if I should come on my own?"

Joel spun toward the sound, his face a mixture of consternation and threat.

"Ziva!" he growled. "I asked you to stay put!"

"Am I not a warrior female? Just as needed as any male when danger lurks?"

Her appearance was so stunning it even had Lou captivated.

The female stood as tall as her partner, dark and ravishingly beautiful, with long blue-black hair, smooth tanned complexion, eye lashes that swept over brown eyes with a silver slit, and lips that parted in a sensual pout, as she reached out to caress Joel's cheek.

"Do not be angry, lover," she cooed.

"Aw, female." He seemed to melt at her touch, stroking her hand lovingly. "I wanted you safe. And now in your impetuousness you will bring the 'Opposites' down upon us. Do you realize you cannot go back?"

As he lovingly caressed, he drew her to him, indulging in an embrace that caused visible static to pass between them. Just to watch them sent a shiver of longing through Lou's entire body.

Their love is almost tangible!

Ziva eyed her mate coyly. "It appears the 'Opposite' base had a sudden power outage," she declared with pretended innocence. "Funny how males don't think of the obvious solution."

Joel laughed delighted. "Oh, you have been a naughty girl. But...that will only delay them for a short time." He stepped back, leaving her standing, regal.

"I saw the need, and filled it." She shrugged. "What did you expect? When Zane took Amadeus, we all knew the situation was dire. Oh, and by the way, you won't keep Kara away for long either. She is right behind me."

"Oh wonderful!" Joel turned aside, and spoke as if to empty air. "Ram? Will you come? And bring Ty with you."

****

A young pre-adolescent girl became solid at the side of the alien woman. She appeared younger then ten, and was no more than four feet tall. Like day next to night, beside to the larger female, she was pale skinned with curly blond hair cut short, and eyes of the most unusual amethyst-purple Lou had ever seen.

This must be Kara, Lou surmised.

The lids over the black vertical slit were narrowed; the young female obviously livid with anger.

"I am not stupid you know!" she burst out hotly. "Just cause I can't remember doesn't mean I can't feel. I know great-gran needs me!"

Almost instantly at her words, as with Djura before her, the small doll-like features screwed up in an agony of torment. As the child sank to her knees doubling in pain, her eyes went to the injured beings on the road.

"Aw...great-gran," the girl murmured. "Ah, ah. She's hurt bad."

Joel stepped to her side, dropping to one knee beside her. "How serious, Kara? Are you able to see the injuries?"

"That beast contraption has broken her back!"

Joel winced. Those around sucked a sympathetic breath. Amadeus got right to the point of the matter.

"Does the baby live?"

"To which do you refer?" Kara straightened, as she adjusted to the new conditions. She remained on her knees, sitting back on her heels. "Both young ones are asleep. Unharmed."

"Both?" Amadeus frowned in puzzlement. "I thought she carries only one male."

"She refers to the human infant protected beneath her," Lou offered. "As I understand it, that's how she got in this predicament in the first place. She was trying to save the human baby from the semi."

His eyes met hers with a look of such astonishment she almost laughed. It was as if he had never imagined a baby lying in the middle of a roadway. "What on earth?"

"It was thrown free when her parents hit a deer; lying in the middle of the highway."

"My god." He let out a breath of sheer disbelief. "Well...that sounds just like Sonia."

It would have been interesting to get this man's perspective on the matters at hand, but as there was no time, they both turned once more to follow the course of the conversation between the aliens.

"Good," Joel accepted. "If the infants are both safe, we have one thing less to worry about."

And just at that moment two young teenage boys put in an appearance. One was an alien; the other seemed human. But if this was Ram and Ty, both humans knew other wise.

Is the human-like one the 'Opposite'? I thought they were lizard-like?

Lance stepped forward. "I'll handle this," he told Joel.

Joel nodded in agreement, and the two boys stepped away with Lance.

CHAPTER 26

Ty was trembling, his heart beating like a drum inside his chest. He had been told Sonia was down, and that he had some roll to protect her. But he had not expected she would be lying out here in the darkness exposed, with a guardian circle about her. It meant she could not be moved, and...she couldn't heal back.

It brought him near to tears, realizing she was like that, and though he knew he was not responsible, he somehow felt guilty, feeling he had contributed to the circumstances leading up to this.

And what really shook him was to find Kara here, as well. She did not look her happy self, her face lined with suffering, sitting on the bare pavement doubled over as if she had a stomach ache, and was suffering along with Sonia and Sky.

As a matter of fact, all those about her appeared to be in various degrees of empathy and mourning. He too felt for them; could feel the heaviness in the air; the pregnant waiting for something bad to happen.

What can I possibly do here? he wondered. *They are so much bigger, stronger, wiser. Why me?*

Lance dropped to one knee beside the human-like 'Opposite', and looked him in the eyes. "Ty...you once told my mother something..."

Lance waited, as if he expected Ty to read his mind. But the boy felt quite certain he could not do that without help.

He wants me to remember something I said. I said a lot of things to Sonia.

His eyes opened wide with horror as he realized what Lance referred to. His breathing grew instantly difficult, fear flooding over him; Ty began gasping for each angst-ridden breath.

Ram also quickly recalled the conversation in question.

"You know?" Ram rebuked defensively. "She promised not to tell."

"I know because I've been working with you too," Lance excused. "She did not betray you."

Ty dropped his eyes in shame. *They all know what I am.*

Ram was quick to encourage. "That's not bad, Ty. Only these few have been told, and they understand the situation better than you. They do not condemn. They know you saved Kara!"

****

Kara's head came up with a jerk as the words carried to her. Lance had failed to place a silencing shield about them as they talked.

"Ty!" she ordered curtly, with the authority of her station evident in every nuance. "Come to me, please!"

Ram and Ty fled to her, like obedient subjects, as if she had suddenly become their sovereign, which in fact was the case, as the 'Leader Pair' was incapacitated.

Out of the corner of her eye, Kara saw nearby Joel wink at Lance, but she would not be deterred.

"Look at me, Ty!"

The boy met her eyes, his filled with stark fear.

"Is this what everyone has kept from me?" Kara demanded. "It was you in the barn? It was you who rescued me?"

"I didn't remember; I tried to forget the evil of my past," Ty defended quietly. "I succeeded until Ram and I met at Sanctuary. Sonia helped us relive...my..." He faltered, and choked out the next words in a near whisper. "What...what I did...to him. She...she helped us both to heal...and forgive."

Tears sprang to Kara's eyes at the implication. "But, you rescued me! How was that bad?" She turned angry eyes to Joel. "Stop hiding his mind from me, Unca Joel! I want to know it all!"

"No, Kara! It's no longer relevant," Joel declared vehemently. "We have more pressing matters to attend to."

"Ty," she pleaded, turning beseeching eyes on her friend. "Will you ever tell me?"

Ty wouldn't look at her. Ram answered in his stead.

"He and I both suffered the consequences of that rescue. Let it go, Kara. It will only hurt him to tell you."

Kara felt a deep apprehension. *What has Ty done?*

"It no longer matters," Ram declared in answer to her thoughts. "I have forgiven him. Ty and I are brothers now."

Lance returned them all to reality. "This can all wait for another time. We are in eminent danger here."

He led the boys apart, to the side again.

Ty met the older guardian's gaze, fully expecting retribution for what he had done to Ram, but Lance was sympathetic, even gentle, though serious, as well.

"Ty, you are the only one of us with defence capabilities. Because Sonia is so low, the guardians have limited abilities. Are you loyal to the 'Leader Female'?"

It was the last thing Ty had expected him to ask. *They want me to protect her…and them?*

"You want me to defend the Lady?" he said aloud for clarification.

"Exactly," Lance confirmed. "Are you loyal to her or them?"

Ram didn't need to be told who them referred to.

"Just show me what to do!" He narrowed his eyes in deadly determination. "I will die for her, gladly do battle!"

Joel's thoughts came to them from afar. *It may well cost your life.*

"That's okay," Ty said aloud. "I have nothing, save what the Lady gives me."

****

Lou hadn't heard all they said, but she'd gotten the drift of the exchange. They expected the boy to fight a battle that most likely would cost his life.

Without thinking, she spoke aloud. "I thought you said…"

Joel spun on her furiously. "Sh! Be silent, female! They do not realize…"

And to her shock, the words continued in her head. *They are 'pair connected' but not aware of it. At this moment, it is best for them to remain oblivious.*

The telepathic encounter rattled her, but not enough to stop her next response. "Oh…oh, sorry." She dropped her eyes, knowing full well he was right to rebuke her for interfering in matters she knew little about.

****

Amadeus felt empathy for the woman. He realized the rebuke had gone to silent communication, and as it was her first experience of such non-verbal interaction, it must have shaken her foundations.

He too wondered what would happen if Ty were seriously injured or killed. Were the lives of the whole race teetering at balance here, depending on a mere teen, an 'Opposite' no less? Kara was meant to be their next "Leader Female' and damaged or not, they were risking her life not simply Ty's.

"I know," Kara stated quietly, apparently reading the unguarded thought of the human physician, something which she had always been most adept at doing. "Only he is unaware."

Lance came to attention, quirking an eyebrow questioningly.

"I am equally willing to take this risk," she went on defiantly. "Great-gran must be the focus for now."

Lance nodded acknowledgement.

"Eric!" he called. "Attend me!"

The stocky red-haired technician appeared at his side, and an empty space was visible in the guardian ring he vacated.

"Program Ty's belt to defend."

Eric dropped to his knees before the boy, touched the belt for a second, then stood up again. "Done."

As the guardian vanished once again, Lance gave further instructions.

"You will be fighting your own kind, Ty," he cautioned. "We would understand if you have misgivings."

"They were my kind," Ty declared staunchly. "I am no longer like them."

The guardian nodded in approval.

"We do not kill," Lance went on. "I am trusting you to use only enough force to stun, or…"

"I will send them back to their farm base. How does the device work?"

"It is powered by your will. Think of what you want done. Very simple."

"Kind of like the 'Opposite' glove weapon?"

"Exactly, except with more power behind it," warned Lance. "While you are at it, prevent their return…done by the same idea. Visualise and push the button at the same time."

Lance turned to Ram. "Guardian, you will be his support. Watch his back; he cannot sense them before they appear. Also, they will be after the humans for food. Protect them at all costs."

Ram nodded, then took Ty by the hand, and led him away. Together, they walked to the guardian ring edge, and stepped out into danger. Each dropped to one knee, back to back, one beside the other, and prepared to wait this out.

****

That dealt with, Joel turned to Kara. "Now mini-monarch." He used her nickname to ease her anxiety. "We need to know the exact extent of Sky's injuries. Can you feel him?"

Kara closed her eyes in concentration. She inhaled sharply as she connected.

"He's very low energy. I see only very bad bruising."

"That's good," Amadeus said relieved. "Any internal injuries? Is he haemorrhaging inside?"

"I don't think so…but, now I feel, his legs are both broken. Unca Joel?"

"Yes, dear?"

"I don't think I'm sensing well. I didn't notice everything at first…I'm unsure."

"Need a little boost?"

Kara opened her eyes, as the solid guardian went to one knee.

"Will you let me touch you?" Joel asked gently. "We will try this together. You are still relearning, gaining back full ability," he encouraged.

Kara frowned. "Why do you ask if you may touch me? Is there a reason you cannot, unless I allow you?"

Joel grinned. *This close to Sonia, her memory is affected,* he realized.

"You are a 'Leader Female'. Believe me when I say this. If your reflex is anything like my sister's, you will send me flying across this highway should I touch when you are not prepared."

"I don't want to harm you."

"Good. I may touch then?"

Kara nodded.

****

The minute she linked hands with her great uncle, Kara had vision as well as feel.

"Tell Amadeus what you see, Kara," coached Joel.

"Sky has a concussion, both arms are broken, as well as both legs. Right hip is dislocated. He is bleeding internally! In his belly."

"That truck must have been travelling pretty fast," Amadeus surmised. "Wonder what damage it did to Sonia?"

"Try your great-gran," Joel suggested.

Kara saw the female image in her mind; she felt numb and confusion, but she knew these were not her own feelings. "Her back is broken in two places, at the second and fifth vertebrae." Her own panic near overwhelmed her; she replaced it with anger. "It ran right over her!" she cried hotly. "Why was it going so fast?"

"Most likely the driver couldn't see her," Joel reasoned.

"Great-gran was visible; she had her band activated when he hit her!" Kara objected. "So did Sky!"

"It's pretty hard for a transport that big to power down quickly," Lou defended. "Shifting is manual, takes longer to stop then a car."

"He didn't even power down until after he hit her; he was half asleep! He shouldn't have been driving when he was drowsy!"

"Calm down, Kara," Joel soothed. "Forgive, little one. Concentrate. When you are emotional, the negative energy thwarts and blinds you."

Tears of frustration flooded her eyes; depression crushed in. "I am useless!" she moaned. "I've lost the records we need. I can't even control my own emotions. I can never be 'Leader Female'. I can't do this!"

"How old are you, mini-monarch?" Joel tried to comfort. "You are still only eight; you have much growing to do yet. This will right itself."

Ziva dropped down on her knees beside them. "She's going unbalanced, Joel," she cautioned quietly. "All the pain from Sonia and Sky is throwing her emotions off kilter. Let me give her balance."

Joel let go, and moved back. Suddenly Kara was not only blinded in second sight but in genuine vision, as well. Out of the blackness, Ziva's comforting hands found her own.

Kara was suddenly besieged by an unreasonable terror, not for herself, but for Ziva. *She is the only other 'Pure' female. If she isn't strong enough to be my balance, this will cost her life!*

"No! No!" Kara tried to rip her hands free. "I will hurt you!"

"Kara," Ziva said gently. "I am strongest female next to you and Sonia. Also I am older. Trust me. I can be your balance. Besides, you've remembered how to pull away in time. You won't do me harm intentionally. Let me do this!"

Kara went to weeping uncontrollably; then she felt the 'Warrior Female's' balance. The girl's tears stopped as abruptly as they had begun.

Kara sighed.

"Okay now, honey?"

Kara nodded.

****

" 'Opposites' are here!" Djura yelled, startling everyone. "On alert warriors! Those in outer rim, brighten image. Blind them! That will turn them toward you, Ram!"

"Inner defence ring, form," Joel ordered calmly. "Boys!"

Beside them, Zane and Lance joined Djura and Joel to circle the women and Amadeus, Ziva and Kara at dead centre.

Ziva quickly caught Kara's hands once again. "We are the only protection for the guardians, Kara," she insisted. "In order to keep the males balanced, we must cut our 'pair connection' to them. Do you understand what I'm saying?"

"No. Why? How?"

"I will give you added power…"

"But, I don't want to break from Ram," Kara protested.

"The males must be free! They need this to concentrate on the battle! Separate from Ty!" Ziva ordered urgently. "Kara! Disconnect from Ty! It is important to break away during battle for our own welfare, as well, or we will go unbalanced at the violence!"

"But...that seems so totally illogical," Kara objected.

"Battle is never logical! Just do it! Please. Our lives are at stake; your delay will cost us casualties."

At last Kara accepted, steeled herself, and obeyed. Even so, in a detached almost indifferent way, she was aware of every deadly beam that followed, those that Ty was sending out, and every blow that came his way.

CHAPTER 27

Ty heard Djura's warning, and it filled him with mind-numbing dread. Ram quickly touched his shoulder, and instantly the fear dissipated.

Redro suddenly appeared out of nowhere before him, and the monster immediately inflicted this world with an appalling odour, the lethal violence of his nature, and the resident evil that came with it. Ty trembled, near overcome by the stench, the fierce weaponry, and the memory of days alone with his nemesis, the unrelenting cruelty.

Recollections of past wrongs clouded Ty's judgement; fear of reprisal rendered him thoughtless. Ram pressed his shoulder to reassure him.

Ty compressed the button on the band at his waist. Nothing happened.

"I can't make it work," Ty cried out in panic.

Redro fired the weapon that hung by a strap across his chest; hot molten laser fire spit toward them in streams as lethal as any flame-thrower.

Ty became aware they were abruptly, unexpectedly in a bubble of protection. He realized only vaguely this was of female origin, but his attention was required elsewhere, and he had no time to contemplate the matter.

The dangerous missives bounced off the shimmering shield, away into the night beyond, sizzling out at a short distance, ineffectual.

Redro continued to fire in hopes the screen would eventually break down.

Ty began to fear that protection would fail, and memory overrode essential sensibility. As when in Redro's clutches, Ty used as his armour, the reflex cushion of accusation, hatred and vengeance.

He tried his belt again...to no avail.

Ram squeezed his shoulder a second time. "Calm," he suggested. "Think pleasant thoughts. Love, compassion...forgive him."

Ty turned to stare at him. *That's how they do it?*

"Like this," Ram suggested.

Ram's mind came into his consciousness; an overwhelming feeling of mercy emanated from the other teen. Ty knew he was expected to reciprocate in kind toward his tormentor, but he wasn't sure he had it in him.

"You can do it," Ram reassured.

Ty looked at Redro, livid now with anger, and about to charge. The male had recognized the boys.

And from somewhere deep inside Ty, came a mercy he hadn't known was in him. He realized Redro could not help what he was; he had never been taught differently. With that thought, forgiveness came easily, and after...even love.

As Redro leaped in fury toward the two boys, Ty envisioned him back in the barn held down by chains, asleep.

Ty depressed the small button at his waist; a dazzling beam of green light escaped his eyes...and his adversary was abruptly gone.

"Did I do it?" Ty asked in surprise.

Ram grinned. "Perfectly! You are 'Opposite' no longer!"

Ty laughed with delight.

"Here comes another one," warned Ram.

****

Lou shivered. She had seen the grotesque monster from a mere eight feet away. The reek of it was enough to gag her, its malevolence, tangible, as it towered over the two brave teens. She could not help but fear for their safety, and for her own life, as well. She had realized quickly, if she drew her gun and fired, the missive would not merely be ineffective, but would draw attention to her, and to the others hidden inside the circle of males.

How is it possible I can see out, but it cannot see through to those inside?

Her trembling began only slightly at first, a fright she couldn't push away, and as the battle raged outside, it spread through her body. Lou felt Amadeus slip a strong arm of comfort around her shoulders, and she didn't reject it. It felt too good. And she was long passed pretending to be the imperturbable cop.

****

"Scattered." Joel spoke softly, absently. "Detaching…"

Amadeus frowned. "What was that?"

Joel looked down at him confusion in his eyes.

With a sudden gasp, as if punched in the gut, Zane dropped jarringly to his knees, hitting the pavement with such violent force, he would have fallen forward on his face, had he not stopped the fall with outstretched hands.

"Oh, man! We're going down, Joel," the younger male cried out. "Do something!"

Amadeus' chest tightened in dread.

Joel pulled in a ragged breath; he shook his head as if to clear it. "Amadeus, has Sky taught you how Sonia's support works?"

"Yes. Is that what's happening here?"

"Sonia is too weak to support us…"

"But I thought Djura would be the first to go down?"

Zane fell forward, and vanished just before he struck the ground. Standing between Amadeus and the fallen guardian, Lou's face went pale with fright, but the physician had no time to reassure her.

"Normally, yes. But in such a case as this, it proceeds in reverse." Joel brushed a hand across his face, as if feeling faint. "I'm loosing my sense of knowing…the others. Do you follow?"

"Mind connection," Amadeus clarified.

"I need a type of conduit…need…you to be my…eyes. You must recount what is happening…think for us…while we are incapacitated."

"Okay. I'm willing. Could you explain that a little better? Just how will this go down?"

"Yes." His voice came slow, strained, a painful hiss, as Joel began to instruct. "Sonia's break of junction will begin with those junior and nearest of blood."

"Zane was her youngest child."

"Correct. Next will be Rhea...her family."

"Doesn't that put Kara next?"

"We must prevent Kara from going down..."

"Because, she is the next 'Leader Female'! How are you going to do that?"

Joel sighed in exhaustion. "I will go into a sleep mode..."

"How could that possibly help? Oh! I get it! Lowest energy."

"I will mind link to you...you will have my knowledge. Then some of us will deliberately...break our link to Sonia."

Amadeus was shocked. But when he looked to the sturdy guardian his eyes were already closed; it was obvious he was blind.

"How...what will happen when you do this?" Amadeus asked shakily.

"Three of the males from the guardian ring will go down leaving only four..."

"That leaves sections exposed. And won't that kill the men who attempt this?"

"Not...not if Sonia can come back on time. They will disappear Amadeus, but their bodies remain where they have fallen..."

Lou moved closer to Amadeus, as if she were afraid she'd step on the collapsed guardian. "Zane is still here?" she whispered, but the physician knew she did not expect an answer.

"I understand," Amadeus reassured. "I know what is at risk if we touch them."

"Good." Joel pulled in a laboured breath. "I do not have much time. Rhea's family will begin soon...starting with the new born...then Kara."

"Oh, my. Will you loose the new one?"

"Not...not if we can do this quickly enough. Because they are still at home planet there will be an extra delay...hopefully enough time...to act from here."

"Okay. Tell me what is expected of me?"

"Even when I seem incoherent, continue to tell me what is happening...and most important...Sky needs to be brought back to consciousness...so he can help revive his pair."

"How do I do that? When I can't even touch him! Joel? Joel!"

The big male seemed to sink to his knees in slow motion.

"Your human female needs to keep you...focused. Louise...don't let him panic."

Amadeus pulled in a sharp breath, and looked to Lou. Her eyes were round as saucers, and it was clear she was as fearful as he.

"We can do this!" he said, as much to brace himself as her. But he was at a loss how to proceed.

"It rests in your hands, human," Joel encouraged confidently. "We are counting on you. Our lives are now in your hands."

Somehow, that did not give him the courage he needed. Amadeus felt sheer panic.

"One...more...thing. The guardians who remain will be the last to go down...watch Ram...he will be first of the others to drop. Is he still standing?"

"Yes. He and Ty continue to defend; the battle rages at the top of the road."

"Ahhh...I must...leave you. Tell out loud...what happens. Talk...to...your human... female."

My female? Why does he keep calling her that? Amadeus almost laughed. *He sure is confused.*

Joel leaned forward easing his arms to his knees, going limp, as if his energy had simply depleted, and he had fallen asleep.

"Oh, man! Oh, man!" Amadeus cried out in panic, as the full implication of his situation hit him.

Lou touched his arm. "Calm down. Take a deep breath. Think!"

"Aw...yeah. That's easier said then done."

"You're supposed to keep telling him what's happening. Remember?"

Amadeus looked toward the outer perimeter. As if on signal, every second figure just simply blinked out.

"Half the guardian ring just went down."

Unexpectedly, Lance spoke from behind them. ""I too am going down voluntarily, Amadeus. Don't be alarmed. I am taking Rhea's place."

"But, aren't you Sonia's eldest," objected Amadeus.

"Exactly. It will break the chain reaction. Remember…Djura goes down last, should we fail. Of the guardians, Ram is the youngest."

Amadeus looked toward the enormous warrior he knew to be Sonia's last strength source. Djura had gone to one knee in a position of rest, his eyes closed.

"As long as Djura stands, you are all still safe?" he asked of Lance.

"Yes. And…whatever happens…don't allow Ty to touch Kara."

"Why?"

But Lance sank to his knees and folded like a rag doll. He went invisible without answering.

****

Kara began keening softly, trembling visibly. Amadeus realized immediately she was giving way to fear because of loss of male contact.

"Oh, honey. Don't panic," he pleaded. "Stay with me. We can't touch you."

"I am so afraid, Amadeus. I don't want to be this alone."

It was then Amadeus noticed Ziva also had gone sleeper-like. He had not expected it, though now he thought on it; her reaction was totally logical, as she was Joel's partner.

Kara's keening turned to gentle weeping.

"They won't be able to come back, Amadeus," Kara declared as her doubts again surfaced. "I can't take over for Great-gran. I can't support them! They'll all be lost!"

"No. No." he reassured. "This will work. Be calm, Kara. Keep calm. Control...you can do it!"

"It won't work..."

Amadeus drew a deep breath, trying to practice what he preached, racking his brain for what could be done.

"Ziva has broken away from me," Kara went on negatively. "I'm supposed to be this great "Leader Female', and all I can do is sit here waiting for the end."

"Stay balanced, Kara. Please," Amadeus begged.

Suddenly he knew the answer. "That is simply not true, Kara," he disagreed firmly. "You are not simply waiting for the end. I'm connected to you all now, through Joel, and I know this... Right now, you are actually carrying them all emotionally...they have given you that burden. They trust you can do it."

Kara blinked disbelievingly. "They do? I am?"

She pulled in a ragged breath, an obvious attempt to right herself.

"Stay balanced, Kara...for them...you can do it!"

But instead the young girl burst into tears again.

"They can't come back," she wailed. "Unless...unless, Sky can break free. Without energy, he can't wake up."

****

Lou could take it no longer.

"Oh, just let me give her a hug," she implored sympathetically. "That's what she needs. What can it hurt?"

"Don't you dare touch her!" Amadeus ordered curtly.

"Why not?" *I'm getting real tired of this no touching nonsense. Clearly, all the girl needs is some comfort.*

Amadeus hesitated only a second, then spilled reality all over Louise.

"Not only will it kill you if you touch her, but it will serve absolutely no helpful purpose, and…"

"And what?" she fired back hotly before he could finish, intensely perturbed by his imperfect reasoning.

"By touching one, you will kill the entire species!"

"Oh, bosh!"

"Want to test it?"

Lou went very quiet, realizing the power at her fingertips, if this were true.

"You're not joking, are you?" she asked quietly in a near whisper. "You're serious? We…we have the power to kill them all…right here and now?"

Amadeus frown, as if he thought for a moment, she might actually attempt it. Then soberly, he nodded. "We are more deadly to them at this moment, than the 'Opposite' enemy."

Lou felt shocked. "But, they are trusting you?"

Amadeus looked pointedly at her. "It has dawned on me, they are trusting you also, which I might add, is quite unusual for them."

"Are you sure these guys...are the good half of the species? Are they...worth saving?" she demanded, turning devil's advocate, just for a second, as if she were a judge with the power to shape the future.

"If you need to ask that, then they have misplaced their trust...and in my opinion, I'd say, it's the human race that's the one not worth saving."

Chagrined by his words, Lou dropped her eyes. "I'm sorry. Sometimes, I think I've lost my own humanity to this job. I can't even find compassion..."

"Remember," Amadeus pointed out. "You are first a woman. And, I've learned... females, of all kinds, are capable of great empathy. It was your sympathy that started this discussion. I apologise for being too blunt."

This gentleness brought the tears to her eyes.

****

What amazed Lou most, through their entire conversation, was the stalwart warrior Djura beside them. She was certain he had heard everything, yet he showed no reaction. At some point he had opened his eyes, but his face was passive, mirrored no judgement. Resting easily against one raised knee, he stared stoically out at the battling teens, Ty and his guardian Ram.

Is his attitude deliberate, or is he indeed powerless? Maybe it is both?

And the ultimate question was: *will he report to his leader what had been said and done; will the retaliation to humans come later, after these beings have recovered?*

Kara's quiet tears in the background also made Lou feel guilty. She turned to Amadeus in annoyance, returning to the subject that began their debate.

"If we can't touch her, then how do we help her?" she demanded.

Brought back to reality, Amadeus looked at the young girl.

"We control our emotions!"

That didn't make sense to Lou. "How can that help her?"

"I watched Sonia heal Ram…"

Before he could complete the sentence, Lou shook her head in rejection. She wasn't even going to ask how the young boy got hurt. With monsters like those battling the boys, and the weapons they were using, she didn't want to know. Obviously, these creatures weren't infallible; they didn't always win; they could be hurt, killed. Whatever Amadeus would disclose would be beyond imagining.

But the physician wasn't meaning to go there. "One thing they told me, while they were healing they sense the emotions of those around them, and it makes the healing more difficult if those emotions are negative. Kara is locked into our sensations as much as to theirs. We can help her by thinking pleasant thoughts, using self-control to even out our own feelings. That should help her stay balanced."

Lou frowned. *Why does he have to make such perfect sense?*

"Okay," Lou surrendered. "Kara…honey?"

The girl made an effort to concentrate on Lou. "Kara...think about something good that's happened. I'll go first. I remember when I was a little girl, I had this puppy..."

Suddenly, through her tears, Kara was laughing. "I see it in your mind. Such an ugly mongrel, but he was so loving."

Lou grinned at the memory.

"Do you know what Sonia did a short time ago?" Kara wanted to know. "She healed a puppy in her sleep...a little Shitsu."

Just about now, Lou would believe anything. She was just glad her attempt had been successful, and the happy light was back in the girl's eyes.

"It's true," Amadeus agreed, grinning. "The baby caused the whole thing..."

"That little tyke inside Sonia must be really something," Lou decided. "Anyway, Kara, did that help any?"

Kara nodded. "I know what to do to balance. I just forgot. You hit on the right method for balance. Thank you." She shuddered visibly. "I can do this!" she told herself. "They will not die because of my lack!"

"Good girl!" Amadeus praised.

"So now," Lou wondered. " What do we do from here? We need to find a way to revive Sky. So these guys can begin...what did you call it...healing back?"

Amadeus grinned at her change of heart.

CHAPTER 28

"What baffles me," Amadeus wondered aloud. "Why did they separate their emotional from the physical?"

Lou looked at him puzzled, not quite understanding what he was talking about. "They've done that?"

"Yes. Kara now holds them emotionally balanced. Djura is the substitute physical balance on the male side…it must be necessary, for them to do that."

"Why don't you ask the big guy?"

"Djura can't answer me. He hears but cannot converse with us. Takes too much effort for them to speak verbally, draws too much energy."

"So maybe it was done to supply extra strength. Like for in the battles," suggested Lou. "I heard the older female say they sever the emotional connection during battles."

"Okay." Amadeus thought on that for a while. "Well," he finally said. "If I've learned anything about these creatures, they never do anything without a reason, and most everything that takes place has a purpose and a counter balance, whether we as humans understand or not. In their world, they believe nothing happens by chance."

"Then, I guess all we can do is accept that they still know what they are doing, and get on with our part."

"Yes. And that's to revive Sky." In his mind, Amadeus went over scenarios, frantically searching for a solution. "If he were only conscious…I could give him something orally. I can't even give him a shot of something to bring him around. Besides, I have no idea what would be right for him."

"If he's part human," Lou reasoned. "What would you normally use on one of us?"

"I can't use what would work on us," Amadeus repeated. "They react. Sometimes in the opposite most violent way."

"No way to predict what would happen, eh?"

"Well, the only thing we can be sure of, what won't work for us would have the reverse effect on him."

"Okay. If he reacts negatively to a pick-me-up…"

"We need a downer!"

It was as if suddenly Joel was doing the thinking for him, sending signals and ideas to his mind.

"A downer to them would be an energy drink!"

"You're kidding," Lou laughed in disbelief.

Joel had said he could supply his own needs when away from the compound kitchen just by asking for it, and pressing a button on his belt. Amadeus depressed the knob in question.

"Energy drink…tasteless, high sugar."

The can of pop appeared on the ground near his hand.

"Wow!" Lou exclaimed.

"Now, just how do I get it into him?" Amadeus wondered.

Kara's voice came clear but strained. "I can transfer the liquid inside him."

"Be careful," he cautioned. "He may not be able to swallow."

"I will place it directly into the stomach."

"I just can't see how this will help?" Lou puzzled.

"Well, my reasoning is this: when we have an energy drink, it gives us a quick high…"

"So if he reacts opposite, won't he go deeper into coma?"

"At first. But after we have a boost from drinking such a drink, it wears off pretty quickly, and we feel very sluggish soon after."

"So you hope Sky will come up like a shot?"

"Precisely. Go ahead, Kara."

Slowly the can on the road began to deflate, folding in on itself, as if someone had stepped on it.

"It's done," Lou noted. "Now what?"

"We wait for the reaction."

Together they peered toward the luminous mound that was supposed to be the male 'Healer Ultimate'. Suddenly, Djura went rigid in shock.

"Does he feel what's happening?" Lou asked.

"Djura hissed venomously. "He is convulsing!"

"Oh, man!" Lou moaned sympathetically. "Maybe this wasn't such a good idea."

"Wait," Amadeus said confidently. "Just wait it out."

All at once Amadeus could see Sky in his mind. The sight was euphoric. "The seizures have stopped! He's awake!"

"How can you see that far?" Lou asked, amazed.

"I can feel him in my mind. But...he's very confused."

****

Joel raised his head, stretched and yawned, as if waking from a pleasant sleep. Lance and Zane were suddenly visible, coming to their feet as one. And when the humans looked toward the guardian ring, it was complete with all seven luminous beings.

There even seemed a lull in the 'Opposite' attack.

Ziva came awake.

"You did it, mini-monarch!" she praised, catching Kara by the hands. "We knew you could!"

Kara smiled shyly in reaction to the compliment.

Zane touched Amadeus on the shoulder. "Thanks, human!" he said with a grin of approval. "You've saved the day."

Amadeus felt warmth spread up his neck at such exuberant admiration. *All this from a mere can of energy drink!*

"We can take over now, Amadeus," Joel offered.

Amadeus chuckled. "I was kinda enjoying having such power over you guys for a change," he joked.

Joel raised an eyebrow. "Were you now? Perhaps, you'd like to continue? Complete this healing?"

Amadeus shook his head. He knew how grave the situation still was, and how ill equipped he was to treat the 'Aopato'. "I think you're better suited to the task."

Joel grinned; turned to Kara.

"Think you have enough power to turn on Sky's band from here?"

"Sure, great Unca." She closed those beautiful, enormous, amethyst eyes, tensed, and suddenly the glowing heap on the right became the broken figure of a man.

Lou gasped. "Man! He looks absolutely dreadful!"

Kara relaxed. Joel dropped to one knee again, closing his eyes.

"Sky," he said in non-verbal communiqué. The audio also came through his band, so all could hear the exchange. "Are you able to understand me?"

A weak voice came back, mostly mental, but audible again through the devices.

"Where...is...Sonia?"

It was Kara who answered him. "She's bad hurt, great-gramps. To your left."

"Give me a moment," Sky returned softly.

"More than a moment, Sky," Lance acknowledged. "Take all the time you need. You can't walk, anyway. You need to heal back."

The man on the road sighed. "What hit me, a truck?"

It brought quiet chuckles from all.

Amadeus felt the moment Sky's mind connected with reality.

"You've got to be kidding me," Sky declared disbelievingly. He went silent a few seconds as he caught up on events that had transpired. "Seems, I've missed a lot. Thanks, Amadeus."

****

Lou couldn't help but marvel. *They are communicating telepathically.*

It was evident that without verbal explanation, the man on the road now knew exactly what had transpired while he lay unconscious. He seemed much like the others, yet different somehow.

Is it possible he is part aboriginal?

"Yes, female," Sky answered her. "I am part native American; Navajo to be exact. Welcome to our menagerie."

Lou shivered. *He read my thoughts from over there.*

"Thought transference is a normal state for us. Distance is no problem; at least not for me."

Somehow she knew he wasn't meaning the statement in a boastful way.

For the first time, Sky seemed aware of the distant area beyond. "It's dark," he commented. "And...you have Ty defending? With Ram guarding him! What an ingenious idea..."

He lay for a moment quiet, resting. After a time he spoke again.

"Sonia needs female support...energy."

"We don't dare approach, Sky; she drains abruptly," Joel informed him. "We need to find a substitute."

Sky went silent, thinking. "Try chocolate," he suggested.

"I have a candy bar," Lou offered. "But there's a lot of sugar in it…and peanut butter." As an after thought, should they wondered why she carried it around, she added, "I keep one in my pocket for myself…just in case I don't get to eat."

"Sounds perfect," Sky declared. "Peanut butter is protein. The sugar is excellent."

"I thought sugar would be a downer for you?" Amadeus interrupted.

"Actually, our "Leader Females' need high energy. So do some of the stronger males. Such females, when in need, have used sugar as a quick fix for centuries. Even the support male, though half human, may safely use the method. And remember, Amadeus, Sonia has no human in her. The 'Pure' female make up, emotional energy, is in opposition to that of a male 'Pure'."

"That's why Kara so craved chocolate bars when I first found her," Amadeus realized. "It was the only thing she would eat at the beginning. So, how do we give the candy to Sonia?"

"Have Kara eat it."

"What?" Lou laughed, and shook her head.

"They are connected. 'Leader Females' have a special bond from birth."

"They never cease to amaze," Lou declared.

"Are you one of those high energy individuals, Sky?" asked Amadeus.

"You are most fortunate that I am," Sky revealed. "If I wasn't you would have killed me instead of your intercession being of help."

Even Lou understood the ramifications of that result.

"Remind me never to place myself in that position again," Amadeus declared with candour.

Sky chuckled good-naturedly. He was sounding much stronger.

"Watch Kara carefully. When you give her the chocolate she will immediately go high energy."

From her jacket pocket, Lou removed the candy bar, and handed it to the young girl. As Kara eat, Lou watched in fascination and expectation, wondering how a female might react at high energy.

Amazingly, Kara soon began to glow excessively bright, so luminous that Lou had to turn her head away or be blinded. As if at that moment, she had been directed to look elsewhere by another, Lou turned her attention once more to Sky.

His image shimmered, wink out, then back in again. He seemed to have moved closer, beside the second glowing mound.

"How did he move?" Lou whispered to Amadeus.

"Guess he's strong enough now to teleport short distances. Notice..." Amadeus pointed at Joel. "...How they've all become very still? They've each somehow become part of the working unit. The males are feeding him energy."

Lou looked at him, puzzled, yet amazed.

"Sonia's gotten stronger," he clarified.

311

"Is she awake? And how do you know this?"

"She's aware, but not awake. Still unconscious."

Lou frowned. "And you know this how?"

"My mind is still connected to them, from before when Joel used me. He is permitting me knowledge, keeping me in the loop, in case my help is need again. Do you have more of the bars should we require them?"

Lou grunted derisively. "You think I'm some candy factory, or something? If you need more, why don't you use that belt of yours? It seems to work just dandy."

"I'd rather not. It's powered by their energy, and right now to use it would be a drain on them."

"So, your saying, if they'd been down too low, the belt wouldn't have worked at all?"

Amadeus shrugged. "Never thought of it, at the time." He looked toward the boys defending the entrance. "Even worse would have been if Ty's belt hadn't worked."

Lou turned to study the two teens. The boys sat quiet, but still on alert. Apparently, the 'Opposites' had run out of attackers.

"Tell me," she asked turning back to Amadeus. "Why did they order the young fellows to protect us humans at all cost?"

Amadeus visibly shivered. "The 'Opposites' like to torture humans, play with their meat. I've seen what they do to the 'Aopato' when they are vulnerable…who knows what it would be like for a human with no defence against them."

Lou was inclined to agree. After see the formidable enemy, she'd rather not fall into their hands...or paws...whatever you called those things on the end of the creature's upper arms.

"Why haven't the people of Earth heard about either of these beings?"

"You know our governments. It's quite possible they know all about them, but they'd keep it from the general public."

Yes, Lou was familiar with the methods of those in power. She had never agreed with hiding true circumstance.

"Come. Let's sit," Amadeus suggested. "Most likely, there will be a long wait involved here."

When they found a spot on the still warm pavement, the two sat down cross-legged side-by side. Lou turned her eyes to the mound they said was Sonia.

Suddenly it shimmered, and a breathtaking beauty came visible. Lou was astounded, and somewhat startled, to see the female was so youthful.

Surely this ravishing woman is not a great-grandmother, an expectant mother-in-waiting?

It was hard to equate this slight, shapely creature with the power attributed to her. Nor could Lou see the helpless woman as having the ability to drain the energy of these powerful males without conscious effort, and for that matter, support their life force.

The woman on the road wore a nightdress, a grungy shapeless cotton shift. The wide tracks of the huge semi tires were starkly visible, imprinted on the thin material, where the truck had passed over her body. Sonia lay on her stomach, face turned toward them, eyes closed.

"Sky's turned on her band," Amadeus observed.

Presently, the female began to move, slowly at first, then more easily. Sonia rolled from her stomach to her side, then to her back. And clearly, she was in the final stages of her pregnancy.

"I thought you said she wasn't conscious? And I expected her to be paralysed."

"She didn't move by herself. Sky is doing that...with the help of the others. The couple is too weak to move under their own volition."

"You think?"

Amadeus grinned, amused by her sarcasm. "As a group, they have phenomenal kinetic ability. I still find it hard to believe Sky could throw that huge semi, and so far. He sure paid for it though."

"The beastie got him back," Lou observed, tongue-in-cheek.

He laughed.

Lou turned back to watch again. Now, she could see a small infant in a protective bubble between the two larger figures.

"Do you know anything about the condition of the human baby?" she asked, not taking her eyes from the scene.

"The child is sleeping, still unharmed. Sonia has kept it safe."

"How could she do that, when she's been unconscious this whole time?"

Amadeus shrugged. "I don't know anything about the techniques of their talents. I'm a mere human, like you. For instance, I can't even explain how it's possible to heal instantly the way they do. It blows my mind; same as you."

But Lou was still on the instantaneous healing. "They do? They can?"

The man nodded soberly. "I've seen them heal cuts so deep they were near to the bone. One minute it's there, the next, gone."

"How did you come to be with them?"

"It's a long story," he warned.

"Looks like we have time."

He sighed. "Well, it seems I'm this magnet for strays. First it was Jamara, then Kara, and last Ty..."

Lou listened with incredulity as the story unfolded, finding the tale fascinating, as Amadeus told of when he had met Sonia, how he eventually ended up in Sanctuary, and what had gone on from that point.

****

When Lou finally looked back at the victims on the road, the two figures had joined hands. It appeared the woman was either still unconscious or asleep.

"We wait now," Amadeus stated the obvious. "They will heal each other."

"What is meant by 'Healer Ultimate'?"

"As I understand it, that is the strongest healer in their species. To varying degrees, all of them can heal others, but when two 'Ultimates' combine they have unparalleled ability. They can support the entire group. If one goes down, the other is still capable of helping the injured one gain energy from the assembly at large in order to heal itself. However, what I was unaware of before this is that, when both go down the species completely looses it healing capability. It is no wonder they guard the 'Healer Pair' so zealously."

Lou looked to the couple on the road. It fascinated her how Sky was visibly healing Never had she seen anything like this. The broken limbs were slowly straightening; the cuts and bruises disappearing.

"They really heal instantly," Lou marvelled.

It suddenly dawn on her, she had been here for hours, but had had no interaction with the police presence up the road.

"I should check in," she decided. "They'll be wondering what's happening down here."

Amadeus chuckled. "Not really."

Lou knew by now, he would have information not relayed to her. She frowned in consternation. "Okay, spill it. Why not?"

"Out there, they are frozen in time. For those beyond Ram and Ty, only minutes have gone by; this is just a simple accident scene. They have freed the semi driver. He's unhurt, but they think he's on some drug, a bit over the edge because the story he tells is so unbelievable."

Lou couldn't keep back the laugh. *They should just be in here.*

"And…I'm afraid, you no longer exist to them."

"What!"

"Hope you didn't have someone waiting at home, because I think the 'Aopato' intend to keep you, take you back with us. It's either that, or…should you choose otherwise, they'll erase your memory of what happened here."

Lou blinked in shock. "They can do that?"

"Oh, yeah! Did you have living family?"

It suddenly didn't matter to Lou. "I've lived alone for years. Family? My husband? They're all dead. I haven't had anyone…for a long, long time."

"Aww…guess Joel picked up on that. Even I can see that loneliness…"

Lou dropped her eyes, uncomfortable with the scrutiny.

"See…Sonia's a bit like me. She picks up strays…and gives them a new life."

Tears welled in Lou's eyes. *Oh, how I wish…*

"I'm another stray?"

"Appears that way."

CHAPTER 29

The first streaks of dawn were brightening the horizon. Sky sat beside his female still holding her hand. The male side of the healing process was apparently completed, and successful.

An awareness of knowledge lost, the feeling of being separated; these were what registered first in the mind of the human man. "I think Sonia's awake, " Amadeus observed. "They've broken my connection to them."

From behind them, Zane spoke. "Amadeus? Sonia wants you. And Louise may as well come also." His next words were for the others. "Kara and Ziva remain at a distance, please. So also, Joel, Djura and Lance. She may still drain if you come too close. Sky says she's not fully cognisant yet."

Each alien gave acceptance by a nod.

Without considering the significance of the action, Amadeus reached to take Lou's hand, stood up, drawing her with him. He wasn't exactly certain if he needed the comfort of another human being, or he was offering her reassurance. He simply, automatically did it.

Lou gave no objection. She appeared to have thrown off any previous training, considering it irrelevant in these irrational happenings, as if it was no longer her function to represent law and order at this scene. She was going with the flow, although somewhat unsettled and off balance. Clearly, the woman was still a little stunned by her circumstances. Amadeus could not help feeling exceedingly sorry for her.

When they had walked forward a few feet, and were approaching the two casualties, Zane cautioned. "Not too close. Above all, don't touch. She has no control, and will shock you. Even though I am her son, I dare not make physical contact, just now."

Amadeus released Lou's hand; a foot away from Sonia, he dropped to one knee as the guardians always did.

"What now?" he asked.

And immediately, Sonia was in all their minds. Out of the corner of his eye, he saw Lou started and go rigid, shocked by her first experience of deep mind contact, felt her tension as she fought the intrusion, then giving way to acceptance, she relaxed. The humans had been included, incorporated into the group union.

The 'Leader Female's' voice came to them weak, with still a little confusion behind it.

"Sky?"

"Yes, love? I am here, right beside you," the Navajo whispered gently. He made an attempt at levity, pretending to scold. "You could have picked a safer place for your nightmare," he chided jokingly.

"Never pick them," she objected with a half moan. "You know who orders our ways."

Sky grinned. "Indeed. Always. The Almighty has the master plan." His eyes found Amadeus and

Zane. "She's good. Even balanced emotionally; just needs a little more time to heal back."

"Not yet," Sonia disagreed. "Baby first."

"As always, my love...others first."

"Amadeus..." Though she spoke his name in his mind, the voice was incredibly feeble, and he understood why she was using mind contact to enhance. The effort to go vocal was too much for her.

"Is she...conscious?" Amadeus wondered, looking to Sky. The man nodded. "How do I answer her back?"

"Just think."

As he continued the conversation in his mind, he was aware everyone else could follow what was said.

"What do you wish of me, my lady?"

A half smile fled across the pain filled features, at the use of his endearment of respect.

"When I release the infant..." Sonia sighed with the effort to stay focused. "...From the shield, examine...examine her quickly. I'll keep her warm, so she doesn't wake. She may feel the cool air...let Lou hold her while you do this."

"Only step closer to the baby. Avoid Sonia," Sky cautioned.

The transparent shield bubble around the child abruptly blinked away. Amadeus and Lou moved forward cautiously, stepping carefully between the 'Healer Pair'. Together, one on either side of the small newborn, they knelt beside it.

A blanket was suddenly in Lou's hands. She wrapped this around the infant as she lifted carefully, then cuddled the small one close for long moments. When Amadeus looked up into the woman's face, he saw tears were streaming down her cheeks.

And he wondered, frowning.

****

The memories rose to the surface with violent intrusion, like a beast from the bog: the brutal rape, the resulting difficult pregnancy, the botched abortion...and the irreversible result.

She had always suspected her father had ordered the sterilization; it had not been accidental, as they had said. No, she knew that had been deliberate, so his reputation would remain intact, so his spiritual leadership would not be questioned.

The trial had been the last brutal blow, the slash, the rip that had severed her from a relationship with those who should have loved her, supported her through it all, but had turned on her instead. It had seemed like she was the one being tried. Her father had painted her as the seducer, believed that a mere girl of twelve understood fully the lustful needs of a grown man, and so, she was considered guilty, rather than a victim.

She had lived with the judgement in her father's eyes, his rejection and control, until at the age of eighteen; she had found a boy to take her away from it all. But the hardest pill to swallow had come a year after the marriage.

When drinking together with her twenty-year-old spouse, her father had told him all about her alleged sordid past.

Then had come the ultimate betrayal. As her father before him, her lover judged her promiscuous, defiled, and incapable of trustable connection. From then on, their relationship had been in name only.

To her, each of her family had been dead long before the fact: the superficial partner taken at last in a biker accident; her father subjugated by his cancer sticks, wasting away in hacking misery at the end, and her mother…

At least her mother had apologized…before the second stroke ended her life.

But, the wounds never quite went away; all that had been stolen from her festered away deep beneath the tough cop exterior. Harm like that really didn't heal with time, at least not with her. It sat inside, buried, chaffed by circumstances and constant exposure to the ugly world of crime, until now, of all times, it thundered to the surface.

Offence, agonizing and crammed with longing, swamped her reality.

And Lou bawled like a battered youngster.

"Aw, dear. I know how this hurts," Sonia whispered softly to her mind. "Someday, you will have a child of your own."

"I cannot," Lou cried from the depth of her soul. "I cannot!" tore out from her in anguish. "Don't mock me," she pleaded desperately. "Please, don't mock…me."

****

He jaw hung open like a stunned fool; Amadeus was so shocked at the sudden turn of events, he couldn't remember what he had come to do.

As Lou sobbed and rocked, embracing the newborn as if holding a cherished memory, he realized once again, Sonia had found the hidden wounded.

"Amadeus," Sky broke in quietly. "We cannot touch her directly. Will you once more act as conduit? Take Lou by the hand."

With not the least protest, he did as he was told, all the while wondering what dreadful story lay hidden in this lovely woman. The agony in her eyes, as she looked up at him, cut to the very depth of his soul. He took her hand.

Who did this to you? Who would do this to such a brave, dedicated woman? Why...how?

He had no time to think the matter through, before Sonia gave him just one tiny clue.

"Lou, the damage done at the abortion has been reversed. You are no longer barren."

His jaw dropped in disbelief. *They have healed through me? And they've healed...in their condition?*

"And Amadeus..."

Still half preoccupied by his own churning thoughts, he answered with incomplete attention. "Yes?"

"Take care of her for us."

Do they mean the baby...or Lou?

"Yes."

She does mean Lou, he realized in astonishment. *Maybe, I misunderstood?*

He turned to look at the still form beside them; the eyes of the 'Leader Female' remained closed.

"And now…" Sonia came back to the matter that had brought them all together. "The baby…Amadeus."

He jerked to reality; released Lou's hand. When he looked up at her, he realized her eyes were no longer empty, the tears were dry, and she was smiling. She opened the blanket.

Somehow his hands found the infant; after that they made no further eye contact, as if both were but embarrassed teens.

His hands moved deftly over the baby girl, swiftly accessing, delicately prodding, careful not to wake the sleeping child.

"She appears unharmed, but I cannot attest to a lack of trauma from this experience."

"There will be none; she will have no memory of what transpired here. Zane?"

"Yes, mother?"

"I have sent Lance and Joel for the grandparents. They should arrive back momentarily. When they come…keep them at the outer edge, so they do not view the human casualties. You take the baby to them, then return the three to their home. Joel will see that they remember nothing; they will think the child was with them when the accident happened. That is the simplest and easiest way out of these circumstances."

When Zane stepped forward to take the baby from Lou, she was hesitant to relinquish the child.

"Must we erase your memory, as well, Lou?" Sky asked gently.

"No," she pleaded, shaking her head, tears in her eyes. "I want to remember this."

With one last long embrace, Lou gave the infant to Zane.

"Amadeus," Sonia requested. "Will you take Lou to Ziva and Kara? Let them give her comfort."

He did what he was told, as if in a dream. The words Sonia had spoken earlier still sat at the edge of his awareness, puzzling there. *What did she mean when she said to take care of Lou?*

Lou let him lead, tears falling silently again. It was as if the baby had been hers and she'd been forced to give her away. The woman had become like a lost child, no longer the shielded individual, the trained imposing officer. He wished he could simply put his arms around her, draw her close and do the comforting himself. But Sonia had said, it was best to do it this way.

****

They quietly waited, away from it all, Amadeus sitting like she did on his heels, continually searching her features to be certain she was all right. He still held her hand, as if he needed the contact, to express sympathy, but Lou didn't want to explain what had underscored the episode, the years of abuse, loneliness, exclusion. She only felt numb, calmness she couldn't explain.

It felt like she was home at last, loved, but unable to encompass it fully.

Somehow, whether done by Sonia, or Ziva and Kara, or all three, the deep agony and hurt that had tormented for so long, now seemed lessened, the memories softened, that desperate need for what she couldn't have, that had surfaced when she had touched the baby girl, in someway put on hold to possibly be fulfilled at a later date, if only she could wait.

Did the healer pair really take away my curse? she wondered. *Can I have children after all, after all this time?*

With the things she had witnessed here, anything was possible. And she would only know if it were true, if she were to conceive.

What possibility is there of that? I don't even have a boyfriend. Besides, seems like I am going with them. Actually, I'd rather be with them.

Twilight was descending again. Another whole day had passed.

Everyone must be very tired; they've been out here a day, and a half.

She looked toward Sonia. The female was sitting up now, supported in the arms of her loving mate.

Is she well now? How very pregnant she is. Why she must be only weeks from delivery.

"When is Sonia due?" Lou asked suddenly, turning to Amadeus.

"Sorry, I'm not privy to that information. I'd say from the looks of her, it'll be very soon…especially after what's happened."

From the area where the injured were recovering, Zane moved across the pavement to their side.

Dropping to one knee beside the humans, so as to be at their level, he addressed them.

"We need to move to Sanctuary before it gets dark again. The 'Opposites' will have freed themselves, and will be coming once night descends."

Amadeus rose, pulling her up with him. She was resigned to follow obediently. It no longer mattered that she wouldn't have that former life; she couldn't say she'd miss all that violence, death, depravity. She'd seen enough for more than one lifetime; was oh so ready for something different, better, she hoped.

Lou stood waiting for their next move.

When Zane stood up, she realized he had a belt in his hand, a duplicate of that worn by Amadeus.

"May I touch you, female?" She looked at him puzzled, wondering why the formality with her, a human.

But he waited, so she nodded. Zane fastened the broad band about her waist, then stepped back.

"Press the blue button when you wish to teleport." Then he turned to Amadeus. "Her belt is programmed to follow your trail. Take her hand. Do you think can come to Sanctuary on your own, or would you like guardian escort?"

"I think I'd rather jump on my own. Last time, coming here, was a bit rough."

Clearly remorseful, Zane grunted self-consciously. "Sorry, again, for that. The purely human make up is different. I'm not good at taking an unfamiliar on my own."

"You wish us to come back to Sanctuary right away? Both of us?"

"That is your choice, Amadeus. We've always said you were free to go whenever you wanted. But, might I warn you? If you go anywhere else, we cannot guarantee your protection."

Amadeus nodded. "Understood."

"As a group, we will be leaving directly. Do not stay behind in this vicinity too long. Wearing such belts, you are targets for 'Opposites'."

Amadeus nodded once more.

Abruptly, every last one of the bright beings vanished. The roadway before them was empty. Lou stood alone with Amadeus.

She turned. Above them in the distance, one lone police unit flashed its red and blue lights. An officer from it was beside the overturned car, as if he only just now was examining it. On the opposite shoulder, on the tailgate of a rescue vehicle, sat the driver of the semi; a paramedic ministered to him, and a second police officer was questioning. It was as if time had stood still out there, or simply rewound with different characters.

Now, Barney was walking toward the rescue unit to join those there. It was like he looked through them, though she and Amadeus were not more than ten feet from him.

"You could still go back. They've left you the option," Amadeus suggested. "I could take your belt and leave you here."

Lou shook her head. *Why go back to emptiness? Besides, I'd like to see this Sanctuary.* Aloud she stated another reason, a pull she hadn't realized until just now. "I'd like to come with you, if that's okay?"

He grinned enthusiastically. "You bet! You'll like it at Sanctuary."

Catching her hand, Amadeus reached to the button on his belt. "Press the blue one; on the count of three."

And Lou did just that, willingly leaving behind the cruel memories of her past, her old abrasive occupation, and the unfulfilled existence that had gone with it.

Sanctuary was just as Amadeus had depicted it, a safe haven for the wounded.

CHAPTER 30

Kara was determined, Ty would avoid her no longer. This was as good a time as any to confront him; Sonia was still incapacitated enough to be unable to prevent it.

She found Ty alone on the look out ledge, over looking the falls.

"Why don't you like me anymore?" she demanded, appearing abruptly beside the bench he sat on. "Why do you keep avoiding any contact…even now, after all that has happened?"

He didn't seem surprised to see her. "Don't be angry, Kara."

For a moment he was quiet, looking away out over the fields below, avoiding her gaze.

"You are a 'Leader Female'," he said at last. "And…I am not like your kind. We would not fit together… It's not like it was before, when we were with Amadeus and Jamara. A lot has changed…"

He is drawing away from me!

"Have I changed that much? Do you think it makes a difference to me what you are?" She shifted down to sit beside him. "You were always there for me, ever my protector. I never will ask any more of you," she pleaded. "And now I find that you, at risk to your own safety, set me free; you were ridiculed and forced to be what your nature abhorred. It tears inside me."

He winced, as if her forcing the memory to the forefront shamed him. "I couldn't let them hurt you, like they were doing with...Ram. I knew a female...would endure much worse... I couldn't watch them defile you... I loved you...even then."

"Then why hurt me now?"

He looked at her, tears brimming in the corners of his eyes.

"Sonia kept us distant at first...so I might become more the male I should have been, learn to protect as the guardians of your people do. I could not have learn what was needed, with you so near to distract me... Ram and Lance are excellent teachers."

"We were always okay before..." she disagreed.

"No! We weren't! I was stuck in the negative mindset, only had what Redro had taught me to fall back on. I had never experienced kindness...male gentleness, nor was I ever taught the value of a female...other than the obvious. The guardians have shown me a better way. How one can treasure the lovelier ones like you..."

Her hackles rose in defence of him.

"You have always been most respectful too me, never were abusive. You protected me! Fiercely!"

"And there is the problem. I needed to be gentled...they have accomplished that, smoothed out that aggression, so I...could be good for you."

"Then what is the problem?" she demanded, frustrated.

Ty quietly chuckled. "You are only eight, Kara. I am sixteen...human-like."

She fired back, indignant. "By our aging gage, we are the same age!"

"Aw, yes," he sighed. "But I am human-like, not like your side of the species. I come from the other side, the hell existence. It can never be, Kara. You need an equal!"

"I know, what you once were! I saw your life! And I don't care that you were 'Opposite'!"

"But, you are "Leader Female'," he argued. "Human-like I cannot give you the support, be all, you need…"

"Great-gran will find a solution!" Kara declared confidently. She was near desperate in her exasperation. "The Almighty Creator always helps her find a way. She'll be shown the answer! Don't reject me, Ty," she pleaded, tears forming, trickling unheeded down her cheeks. "I've 'Pair Connected' to you! Do you realize what that means? It is you I need; you I will always love!"

"We are too young!"

His desperation to find a way out, the excuses for what he thought a better way, irked her. She wanted not to listen, but he went on none-the-less.

"I do not refuse you, Kara. It would be my great honour, and proudest joy to pair with you, but…it's not in my hands!"

"Are you saying Great-gran is against us?" She had always had a hard time with submission, and her rebellious nature was rising to the surface once again. "What does she still hold against you? Just what was it you did to Ram?"

"No! No! You misunderstand," Ty cut in quickly. "It is my nature against us! I cannot change what I did. Though all is forgiven, I will always remain capable of doing the same." Frustrated by his inability to explain, he moaned audibly. "I cannot make me different; I want to be like the guardians around me. Then I will be whole! I cannot make that happen. Don't blame Sonia. She has been nothing but kind and loving...beyond what I deserve...she has done as much as she can..."

"Whatever are you talking about?" Kara puzzled. Her thoughts returned to what was hidden from her, and thinking there lay the answer, she pushed for revelation. "Great-gran still hides your memories from me. I can't see the why of this. Please? Please, tell me, what you've done? Explain...so I can understand."

"I cannot... Do not ask."

"Still, you keep it secret. Will this always be between us?"

"I fear so," he said dejectedly. "My guilt will always ride me. I will remember; it will haunt...unless, Sonia...can find another way."

Aware her tears were falling uncheck, Kara brushed at them angrily. "What is it you ask of her? To erase memory, to forgive, what? She has always come through, been most merciful to everyone of us..."

"I know she is that to all. But what I ask...I don't think she can fix my dilemma."

"What are you saying? You make no sense."

Steeling himself, it was clear he was resolute. "We can never be together...only as friends. I will always be an 'Opposite', no way out of it. I can not break from it on my own."

"Great-gran always finds an answer..."

His dejection was tangible. "Why should she even want to?" He sighed. "She should send me from this place…"

"But you just fought for us!" Kara tried to reason, growing worried about him now.

"Yes, and that fulfilled my purpose!" he retorted angrily. "Everyone here now knows what I am…it would be only right…she must cast me out of this place. She has no choice."

"Ty, she would never do that!" Her rebellion rose full force. "And if she does," she declared forcefully. "I will go with you!"

"You will not!" he shot back. "Your place is here! You are next 'Leader Female'!"

His reasoning brought her up short. It calmed her. "My Great-gran will find an answer," Kara whispered. "She always has before."

Ty shook his head, doubting still.

"I pray you are right, little treasure. I really do."

CHAPTER 31

Her recovery at last complete, Sonia sent her extra guardians back to home planet, all except for Joel, and Ziva, his pair. To be honest, her brother would not leave his sister's side, did not trust her care entirely to Sky alone, not this close to her due date.

Joel also insisted on the constant availability of the human physician Amadeus, almost as if her brother expected some unusual happening to rear an ugly head. Because of the 'Pure' warrior's foreboding, the doctor took his turn obediently; much as if he too were a guardian, his shifts and rest breaks, scheduled like any of theirs.

Because it was his time to attend her, Amadeus was present when Sonia finally summoned Ty. He knew he was a mere observer; it was not his place to object, comment, or interact in any way with those present. The matter was between the boy and his benefactors.

****

Arriving in the spacious library recreation room with the waterfall feature wall, Ty trembled visibly. To be called here was an honour, he knew, and at any other time, he would have been thrilled, but his dread spoiled the occasion; the tightness of his fear made his chest like stone, his breathing laboured.

He expected the worst.

Not surprised she was attended, he noted both Sky and Amadeus were present. Ty suspected others might be there about, as well, her hidden guards, invisibly waiting to deal with him should he prove a threat, now that he had the knowledge given him while defending.

He had never been so frightened as he was now, of what was about to transpire.

"Ty," Sonia rebuked. "Why are you so fearful? Am I more formidable then your brother 'Opposites'? I did not summon you here to reprimand, only to commend and reward you."

Not quite believing, Ty stood in uncertainty, waiting.

"Are other guardians present?" he finally dared to ask.

"No dear. They do not wait to pounce." Sonia chuckled. "Such fear in one so brave when it was necessary. You are a valiant warrior! Act like one." She patted the seat beside her. "Come sit with me."

Hesitantly, timidly, Ty inched to the two-seater where she sat. He looked up to Sky, standing behind, as if he needed permission from him. The Navajo simply grinned, and said nothing.

Almost afraid to turn his back on Sonia's pair, he turned sideways facing her, staying on the very edge of the seat, so as not to get too comfortable.

"I don't bite." Sonia smiled reassuringly. "What really troubles you, Ty?"

Ty took a deep gulp of air, and dared to ask. "Lady...do you want me to leave?"

"And, why would I wish that?"

"I am 'Opposite'," he whispered. "Everyone knows it now. I should be cast out for what I did to Ram."

"We are always most hard on ourselves. Since you've come, what have you done that is meant to harm us? Did your defence of us mean nothing, then?"

Ty had to think on that. *Didn't Kara say much the same thing?*

"I am 'Opposite'," he stated a second time, as if that were reason enough. He didn't dare remind her of the brutality of his past sins; if she had forgotten the memories, it seemed best not to revisit them.

"I was aware of your condition when I brought you to Sanctuary. And shouldn't it be, were 'Opposite'? You are no longer."

And then, because he felt surely indignant followers had approached her, he blurted out what he had hoped to avoid.

"But, don't the others want revenge; don't they want me to go? I tortured Ram."

Standing nearby, Amadeus registered shocked disbelief. Sonia frowned. It was then Ty realized the human physician had not known about his grievous deeds.

Sky, on the other hand, remained passive of face, yet his eyes held amusement.

"I thought we'd dealt with this," Sonia scolded reprovingly. "Such past crimes, done under duress, are irrelevant here, and are never to be brought up again. Unless, you wish me to tell Kara?"

His eyes widen in horror; he cringed at the very thought.

"Do you really want to leave us that bad, Ty?"

Ty shook his head, speechless, afraid if he voiced any other thought, it would jeopardize what little chance he had.

"Do you wish to remain?" Sonia prodded a second time.

In a small voice he dared an answer. "I would like to remain with you."

"Is that all you desire?"

"I would like it…if I could be near Kara."

"Why?"

She was forcing it out of him; making him speak it aloud, not just dwell on the daydream.

Ty considered his hands, moved them nervously, studying them as if he could find the answer in their restlessness.

"I think…I might…love her." He ventured a quick look at Sonia, to see if this made her angry, but the amethyst eyes held only sympathy, and they were dancing with amusement.

Surprised, he met her gaze more boldly.

Sonia chuckled. "So hard to ask for what you want," she said bluntly. "Oh, Ty…just ask."

"But…Lady. I am 'Opposite'! She is next 'Leader Female'! Look at me; I am human-like. How could I protect her now?"

It was all spilling out so up side down, he wished he'd kept silent. But then, she had initiated the conversation.

"Oh, Ty," she said in soft sympathy. "You never had to tell us. We've all seen your dilemma."

"What do I do, Lady? What should I do? Kara wants…and I would give, but…I can't be more than I am."

"There is an easy solution…if you are willing."

Hope expanded in his chest; his heart began to pound. Ty went very quiet. *Kara said Sonia would have the answer. Why did I doubt?*

"Only tell me, and I will do it."

"All you need is to be willing…"

"Whatever it takes."

Sonia looked up at Sky smiling. He winked.

"Is Joel ready?"

Sky nodded.

Suddenly his anxious worries resurfaced. If Joel was involved, maybe this was still a punishment? "What will you do?" he asked uncertainly.

Sonia shook her head at his doubts, chuckled. "Ty when will you stop being so timid? We'll have to work on that with you. Confidence, dear; all will work out."

But Ty couldn't throw fear away so easily. "Lady…what is Joel…going to do to me?"

"He will make you like one of us."

Ty gasped, amazed. "This can be done?"

Sonia nodded. "If you are ready?"

Ty's heart played leapfrog in his chest; he had not realized how badly he had wanted this.

"Yes! Yes! I would be a guardian! Will that please Kara? Do you think?"

Sonia laughed, her voice a jubilant bell in the room. "Ah, Ty. You do realize you will be only eight…a young boy, not yet an adult."

"Then I can…ah…" He dropped his eyes self-consciously, when he realized where his thoughts had gone.

Sky chuckled. "Be carefully what you wish for Ty. Courting a 'Leader Female' can prove dangerous."

Warmth spread up Ty's cheeks. "Lady…may I?"

"I think that will be up to Kara." Sonia closed her eyes to summon her brother. "Joel? Come."

****

Joel had been waiting anxiously to be called. It had been some time since he had broken a male from dormancy, and this young boy had been born total 'Opposite', never having the option of going this far into the good-light spectrum. It was unclear how this might actually turn out, and that made the guardian nervous.

In a way, the possibilities also excited Joel, but as he came visible, he decided to school his features as if the matter was not to his liking.

His resolve was quickly tested, when he realized Ty quivered on the verge of panic, because it was he who must deal with him. The boy was anxious to get the deed done, anticipating something painful, thrilled yet edgy.

It just wasn't the best working scenario. His emotions would impede, and block an easy progress.

How do I put him at ease?

Joel gave his sister honour by addressing her first. "My Lady."

"Ty would like to be guardian. Would you perform that function, brother?"

Formality then it would be.

"Indeed! It would be a pleasure."

Ty stood up, shaking so badly, Joel thought he would have to support him.

Oh, boy, I do not mean you harm, Joel projected, then realized in his fright the young male could not read. "Nothing to fear," he said aloud, and smiled.

When Ty relaxed slightly, Joel took his hands. At the touch, the light shield flashed between them, wavering through them. The 'Pure' warrior had the energy of the multiple guardians to give him power; Sonia was his balance. The process was instantaneous.

Joel stepped away, ginning at his success.

He turned to his sister, exclaimed in awe. "He is a 'Pure', Sonia! I did not expect that."

"The 'Opposite' side have never been able to interbreed with other species; thus it has remained an undiluted blood line."

"You, son," Joel exclaimed proudly to Ty. "Are Kara's equal. No wonder she connected."

Shyly, Ty looked up at the sturdy guardian. "Will that please Kara?"

Joel laughed. "Why don't we see?" He shut his eyes, found Kara among the females. "Come, Mini-monarch. Attend us."

****

Kara took but a moment to orient herself, to understand what had just taken place. Then she squealed with ear shattering, toe tingling, infinite pleasure.

"Ty! Ty! You are beautiful!"

Sonia chuckled. The stoic Navajo grinned widely. Joel pretended nonchalance; even Amadeus couldn't hide his smile of delight, but Kara's beam shone more brightly than all the others.

Ty stood, almost fading from their admiring attention, not an adult, a mere boy, yet definitely a guardian male. He stood up straight, strong, a stable alert mind that met her thoughts without confusion or trepidation. Proud. Regal. A prince!

He already towered near six feet, never yet full grown at eight. Ty was muscular, slight of build, but he would fill out, as he had done when first she had seen him that day in Amadeus' world. Dark brown hair, handsome face, silver slit in blue eyes.

Oh, she loved him!

He is 'Pure'!

****

Running to Ty, Kara opened her arms wide.

He smiled, still shy in this new formed body, self-conscious at the appreciation he saw in her mind. He felt a 'Pair connect' to her, as strong as her own now, and their thoughts opened to each other without effort, his full of adoration that placed a blush on her cheek.

It felt so good to touch her, his heightened perception causing the knowledge of her sensations to intensify his own. Ty hugged with an energy that near melded them, with all the affection he could muster, his mind shouting at him to tame his reaction, yet his body unable to obey.

Kara sighed, as if she had at last received her reward, like she'd been waiting all her life for him to awake.

Long moments, they held that embrace, then Joel cleared his throat. Ty knew, without being told, what was expected of him. He was guardian now, needed to be the manifestation of self-control. It took more will power than to avoid going 'Opposite'. He felt the other guardians as they supported him, eased his longing, his need to hold her close, supplying the self-possession he lacked.

Ty stepped away, went stoic, as if all his life he had been a guardian exemplary. He saw in her mind Kara's surprise, then approval.

She looked at him, puzzlement mirror in amethyst eyes. He still held her hand, as he turned to his monarch.

"My Lady? May I be Kara's new protector?"

Sonia smiled. "Are your intentions only to be her guardian?"

This time Ty did not hesitate; confidence had come with his junction to the other males.

"I am aware we have 'Pair connected', my Lady, but we are far too young…"

"We can wait Great-gran," Kara broke in breathless. "If Nadia and Chad can have self-control, we can do as good."

Ty kept his grin from peeking through…almost. His eyes would always betray his pleasure. "Besides," he said in all seriousness. "It is best to court a 'Leader Female' first."

Amadeus smiled, a twinkle in his eye. Joel and Sky exploded into laughter.

"Oh, I remember when I thought the same, Ty," Sky warned. "Be forewarned. A 'Leader Female' is always in control."

Kara faded; Sonia blushed a deep crimson. Ty could no longer keep his stoic stance.

Grinning ear to ear, Ty asked a second time. "May I be Kara's guardian, my Lady?"

Sonia nodded. "Go. Play like the children you are."

Kara let out a small cry of delight, her behaviour now tempered with the dignity required of her station. Before Sonia might change her mind, Ty jumped with his charge to the gardens in the valley outside.

****

Joel was still laughing. Sky gave him a reassuring clasp of the shoulder. "Well done, guardian."

Sky turned to his mate. "I'll take Amadeus with me, give you two some privacy." He grinned mischievously. "Don't fight now…like you used to."

Sonia wrinkled her nose at him. Joel pretended a frown, though he appreciated the humour intended. The look on Amadeus' face told him, the man knew he had missed something.

"I'll tell you the story over lunch, Amadeus," Sky suggested. "These two were not always so amenable with each other." He grinned and winked at Joel.

"Tale teller," Sonia shot back, but laughed in spite of herself. "Good thing guardians are incapable of lying. Enjoy the story of our pairing, Amadeus," she added, giving blessing to the telling.

Without another word, Sky vanished with the human physician.

****

Now alone with her brother, Sonia motioned to the seat across from her. As Joel took it, she observed, "You have something you want to tell me, brother?"

Joel nodded. "You should know, sis…when I changed Ty, I found an anomaly. I noted an unusual condition, a quality in him, one we have never encountered before."

Sonia lifted a brow questioningly.

"Ty is a male 'Record Keeper'."

It wasn't often Sonia was caught off guard; amazement showed on her face. "I thought that breed was all lost when they went 'Opposite'."

"Apparently the gene still passed down even though they went 'Opposite'."

"Do you realize what this will mean, Joel?" Sonia declared hopefully. "Why, such a mind is like that of a 'Leader Female'. It automatically records everything that happens, retains it, and transfers it down through the generations. The only difference from the female holder is we need a mature 'Leader Female' to transfer his records."

Joel nodded. "He is the perfect match for Kara; the last of his kind."

"Can you tell? Does he hold any data?"

"Either those from Kara were transferred to him when the prototype was turned on her, or he already was storing a duplicate of our recorded past. He has the statistics from both sides, theirs and ours. I can see it's there, but without yours or Kara's help, I cannot access them."

"However this happened, we have again at our disposal the records we miss, plus a recording of 'Opposite' histories, as well. It is best they should remain with Kara, but...at the moment, she cannot retain them."

"Will you watch them, and make them accessible to all?"

"Of course; as soon as it is possible. And if...when, Kara's abilities heal back, I will help her access and store a second set, just to be safe." Sonia shook her head, marvelling. "Joel, through the ages, our histories always were kept in duplication, so no one would ever forget; so we'd learn from our mistakes. What never ceases to amaze me, is how the Almighty Creator brings about our salvation, and just at the moment it is needed... always."

"I was astounded myself when Ty turned out 'Pure', and now this...the added bonus..." Joel went speechless in wonder.

"The Almighty Creator is always wisest," Sonia agreed. "And now Ty, a new treasure, is given us to guard."

"Yes," Joel acknowledged. "He, not only Kara, must be protected conscientiously. They are of equal value, to be cherished beyond measure."

Sonia smiled. "Now I'm most satisfied they are 'Pair Connected', though, we will need to shadow them... Ty could easily become distracted, as Ram did. Also, Ty is still so very young... The last thing we need is to lose them both..."

"Way too young to be paired yet." Joel shook his head, worried. "It will be so hard on them. We'll need to keep them occupied."

"Aw, yes. That should be a challenge. I hope the male guardians are up to this. Until now they've never encountered a provoked 'Leader Male'...except for you, of course."

Joel winced at the reminder, then rose to the test.

"You just keep Kara in line. We can handle Ty."

Sonia chuckled. "Ahhh...the next seven years should be so interesting."

Joel grinned as he watched the visions passing through her mind, waited while she looked at the future.

Finally, he broke into her musings. "Come, sister; you need to rest now. I'll escort you to your quarters. Soon you'll be much busy; a mother again," he teased.

Sonia wrinkled her nose at him.

CHAPTER 32

Morgan found her sitting by the pond beneath the waterfall.

"May I join you?"

Startled, Lou looked up in surprise. These creature were so stealthy, they made her jump every time they showed up.

"I thought this would be a safe place to escape to…outside, you know."

" 'Fraid not. This is actually a favourite spot for most of us. Lance and I first met here. Correction; that's not completely true, but here was our first alone meeting."

"Lance is your partner, right?"

Morgan nodded. "Husband. Partner. Pair is what we call it."

"This place is very beautiful. The whole valley feels so peaceful. It's like I've escaped earth's grasping clutches, gone to glorious heaven. Don't quite know what to do with the tranquility. I've always been so…in crisis all my life."

"I fully understand. When I first came, I detested where I'd come from."

"But…why would you? You are…"

"I was once a human…a cop, like you."

Lou's jaw dropped. "Really? I'd like to hear about that."

"It's a long story. Better I give you the short version."

"Why? We seem to have plenty of time; I'll gladly listen, unless...there is something wrong with the longer version?"

"The extended tale involves all the guardian pairings. What I'd really like to tell you is my personal story, and...maybe give you a bit of advice, if I may?"

"Okay. Have a seat then, if you don't mind hard rock, that is. I can't promise anything, but I will listen. I like to weigh things."

"That's fine, all I ask."

Morgan sighed, lowering herself to settle against the nearby boulder, as if she hadn't found the time for a private break in some time, and it felt exceedingly good. For long moments, she simply gazed about, taking in the lush vegetation, the flowering foliage about them.

"Been a while since I indulged myself," she finally said. "I'd forgotten how relaxing it is out here. Lance used to like to fish and just veg out by this pool.

"The day we met, he was on guardian watch, so intent on the distant border in his mind, he was unaware I was near. I snuck up on him, startling him. It was a good thing I wasn't 'Opposite', or he would have been dead before we could become unioned. He assumed it was safe inside the valley; felt too comfortable in going all mind. He was still in recovery then..."

Lou frowned in puzzlement, and Morgan must have realized she'd gone to ramble.

"Sorry. I promised…my story."

She waited a beat, as if it took effort, preparation, to go into this unpleasant task.

"My father, in a drunken rage, shot my mother, when I was a small girl of three. I witnessed the brutality, before and during."

Lou winced at her morbid, aloof recounting. It seemed the female was forcing her feelings to remain distant, keeping the remembered horrors at bay.

"It was traumatic for me…for a long time I blocked it away in denial. My dad was sent to prison…got life. And he died in there. I never saw him again, spent my younger years in foster care…"

"That surprises me," Lou said. "You would never guess it to look at you."

"Good. I am happy that is so. I have had the benefit of other's help and healing time."

"Time doesn't heal everything. Sometimes, it makes it worse…"

"Most times the individual hangs on to the hurt. It is the only way they know how to cope…"

Lou turned away, setting her jaw angrily.

"We know you hurt much," Morgan told her sympathetically. "We can help you with that…"

Lou said nothing, peering off at the distant waterfall.

Morgan went on anyway. "As with me, everyone here…each one of our kind, has a hidden past. And, every human, like wise."

Lou pretended she hadn't heard; yet she waited for the next words with a tenseness that made her shoulders ache.

"Each of us have our own personal story, had our own demons to relinquish...before we became what we are. What we hope you will understand is this...we may not be able to relate to your exact circumstances: the combination of rape, condemnation, parental abandonment, and rejection, but some of us have experienced in part sections of such torment...and we are angered by the treatment you received, empathize with your pain, and wish your hurt to recede."

"I doubt you could ever understand what I went through," hissed Lou, turning back to look the woman full in the face, her anger smouldering. "And, I don't want your sympathy!"

It seemed not to faze Morgan that she'd gotten such a negative response.

"Everyone thinks their own pain is worse, but each burden carried is equally devastating to that particular individual. Experiences cannot be compared. I only told you, because I think something I say may help."

"Never asked for your help," Lou said stubbornly, turning away again.

"True. You did not. But we feel you do need it. You think we cannot possibly understand, no one can...accept someone who has experienced exactly what you did. You are wrong. You say you do not want our sympathy, but you need it...crave it."

Lou pursed her lips, tears forming. She was too proud to cry again. The first time had been a definite misstep.

Morgan leaned close to her, lowered her voice.

"I am going to tell you something in confidence. I hope it will go no farther..."

What is this, a bloody soul-bearing pity-party?

"Some of us do know the rape feeling..."

Lou went tense.

"My Lance was...sodomized in prison. Karine was forced into prostitution...choked into submission...need I go on?"

The memories flooded in again, overwhelming, gut punching, and Lou was fighting a losing battle with tears.

"Don't say again, there's no way we can understand," Morgan hissed viciously. She leaned back against the rock again, going silent.

The sounds of nature took over: birds in the trees, frogs in the water, a bee buzzing, heard even over the muted waterfall.

At last the 'Aopato' spoke again. "As a species, our memories are combined; what one has experienced, all know and have felt. We soften the cankers, each other's grievous wounds...that is our function, why we are as we are..."

A meadowlark began to sing, as if it had not a care in the world.

"You will always remain human, never be like us," Morgan said softly. "Your healing must come through other means. We can help you, if you will allow us..."

Lou's shoulders sagged in defeat; tears slipped past her defences.

"You must let go of the past, let it conquer you no longer. Take another into your confidence; share your trial with a concerned companion. Learn to trust. As long as you keep it bottled up inside you, it will ride you, defeat you. Forgive! Then, let it go... forever."

Tears wandered down her cheeks like errant rain on window glass; Lou brushed at them, frustrated.

"Your need is for the human male...and Amadeus needs you...trust my word on that."

"What would a gentle, kind hearted man like that want with hard core me?"

Morgan laughed softly. "Aw, Lou. Don't be so hard on yourself."

As the female drew her into her arms, Lou began to shake with uncontrolled sobs. She buried her face against the bosom of the other like a small child who had just found her mother.

"Let it happen," Morgan soothed. "Amadeus is for you...you have the chance you never had. We see that in your future. Try..."

Lou cried brokenly for long moments, feeling like a small child at the knee of a caring parent. At last, she steeled herself, sat back, and brushed away the moisture on her cheeks.

"Are you willing to let go of the past?" Morgan probed. "Give the future a chance?"

Low nodded half-heartedly. "You...you really think he'll accept what I've been...what I did?"

Morgan chuckled. "You mean, the abortion? That was forced upon you. Let me tell you what I did. I helped do a murder. I was a jailor; let my prisoner have my gun. Sure her tormentor deserved it; that prison guard had his way with her, but to kill wasn't the answer...anyway, Lance accepted me. If we can find love with each other, why not you two?"

Lou smiled at that. "But it's different for you...you're not...human, anymore."

"No different. We started out human. Asked Amadeus someday to tell you about the guardian pairings. There are many examples there. Give your physician his chance. He needs it."

"I'll try..."

"Good. And now, I must leave you. I am expected inside. Sit here a while and think it through."

****

The night was already descending, the distant sky only partly dark, but here beneath the mountain peaks it was in deep shadow. Lou still sat alone beside the lake.

Her world had changed so abruptly, nothing was as it had been, and she had decided to take Morgan's advice. The problem was what to do from here on.

"Would you care for some company?" Amadeus' soft words, spoken from behind her, made her start. She hadn't heard his approach. "They've sent me to fetch you inside. The 'Aopato' have this inbuilt precaution about darkness; it's dangerous to them."

"I know," she agreed. "And after what I've seen, I don't blame them."

"We can stay out if you want…"

"No, that's okay. I've been out here long enough. Will you help me up?"

She reached out toward him, and he agreeably complied. "I think my legs have fallen asleep; I've been sitting on them too long."

"Well…why don't we take a walk in the gardens…until you get the feeling back."

"Sounds good to me…"

"You must be cold…"

He placed a light jacket about her shoulders, which she knew he'd come up with using the belt he wore. The device certainly came in handy when you knew how to operate one.

Passing through the flowering trees of the orchard, the black of night descended around them. Lou shivered, still a bit chilled, and Amadeus dared to put his arm around her to warm her. Weary from all her tears, Lou surrendered, laying her head against his firm, muscular chest. It felt so comforting.

They stopped for a moment, to gaze up at the stars.

Maybe Morgan has it right, Lou thought. *Amadeus might be good for me.*

CHAPTER 33

Sky gasped with the sudden force of the excruciating pain, as it quickly radiated from the small of his back to his shoulders. He dropped to one knee with violent force, and crunched over cradling his belly, as the agony spread across his abdomen. Being a physician, he knew to ease the sudden discomfort by panting short quick breaths. Still, the sensation continued a full minute.

When it ceased at last, he returned to a normal vigour, yet with a lingering feeling of tenderness just at the edge of his awareness.

He had originally come to the gardens alone to go walking, to ease a feeling of stiffness in his joints and muscles he could not account for. Now, he wondered if that had been a prelude, a forewarning of this episode.

He rose to his feet, continuing at a brisk walk for another ten minutes, to wear away the lingering ache. He was beginning to think the whole matter had just been a freak sensing of another's condition.

Perhaps, Sonia is in labour? Has her time arrived; and is this how she chooses to enlighten me?

He reached out for mind touch, but she seemed unaware of him, absorbed in her reading, unconcerned and unbothered by the pending birth.

If anyone should have a premonition, it would be my female.

Joel also sat across from her, intent on a novel of his own, oblivious as she. Being a 'Pure' male, he too should have sensed if something were amiss.

But both sat content in the waterfall common room, their favourite spot to indulge and rest.

Perhaps, it is nothing? Perhaps, I am the one coming down with something; like Sonia feeling the after effects of constant stress.

He preferred to keep such knowledge from his mate if he could, especially with her future holding the unpleasantness of childbirth.

Then, just when he thought the experience solo, a second, longer, all encompassing pressure spread across back and belly. He moaned at the agony, went to his knees, doubled over, panting rapidly. Again it finally subsided, and he went back to normal.

He rose, straightened; reaching in mind to his pair, knowing full well what this was now. She remained oblivious as before, appeared just fine.

What is this? Since when does the male feel labour first?

From the memories in the minds of the females of the species, Sky knew this was what childbirth felt like; in his earth practice, he had watch many a woman struggle in excruciating agony for days. He had expected Sonia to be plagued by what was to come, intended to ease and to share in the experience, but...not like this!

This was full blown labour, and the Navajo cringed in anticipation of the next contraction. Whether premonition or reality; imagined or otherwise, he neither wanted to share, nor have his

357

beloved Sonia go through this. He had never realized it hurt this bad.

For mere pleasure, I gave her this; he scolded his inner man. *Never again! Yet he knew his lover would disagree. I hope I can endure this.*

Sky knew it was time to go back inside, but how would he hide this? Nature had dealt this unimaginable blow; how, he could not fathom, but as long as he must suffer, Sonia need not know just yet. He had never expected to be the one to feel the other side of birthing.

But just as he prepared to teleport, a third contraction bent him forward, dropping him to a curled foetal position. He cried out with the force of it, screamed out in an anger he thought himself incapable of, and the wrathful response seemed to ease the agony. He wasn't mad at Sonia; he didn't blame the Almighty Creator for giving him this burden; it just felt good to express the frustration at the circumstance. Now he understood why women often yelled at their partners in venomous hate during such times.

****

Amadeus and Lou were sitting on a blanket on the sandy shore of the waterfall pool. It was a bright sunny afternoon, the air smelled of blossoming fruit trees and new spring flowers.

Lou had her head resting comfortably against his shoulder, relaxing. They had been in a healthy and heated discussion for hours, debating with teasing commentary the pros and cons of a subject they both felt adamant about. It mattered not who would lose or win; it was the pleasure of the controversy, their convictions that drove them. Their rivalry had cooled, and now they were simply enjoying the satisfaction of each other's company.

Comfortable that they minds were well matched, the exercise had been almost like an act of love between them, though they had not yet reached such a level of intimacy, nor did they seem to require to go deeper. As yet they were simply friends.

Amadeus loved the feel of her soft hair against his shoulder. Lou sighed with a form of ecstasy that pleasured him.

From across in the orchard, a scream tore at the air, tensing them both with dread. Amadeus quickly pushed her forward, and they both sat listening intently. In Sanctuary a scream was never harmless.

The sound came again, fraught with agony, desperation, like a tortured animal in a trap. Except in Sanctuary, they never were so cruel as to snare the animals. It sent shivers through the two humans, and brought back visions of the night of Sonia and Sky's deadly encounter with the semi.

Amadeus pushed to his feet. "Stay here, while I go see what's happening."

But Lou disagreed. "I think not! I'm coming with you."

"Then hurry," Amadeus ordered. "This might be an 'Opposite' attack. They might have gotten into the valley somehow."

"And you would handle them on your own?" Lou demanded. "With what? You don't even have a weapon."

Amadeus had learned this much since coming to know Lou. Her personality was such, that when determined to do something, it was pointless to argue, or for that matter to remind her, she also had no gun.

"Whatever. Let's see what's wrong first. Then we can work from there."

He took her by the hand, and headed at a fast walk, out across the field to a nearby garden path.

"It sounded like a man's voice," he reasoned. "I can't believe I'm saying this, but I'm almost certain that was Sky. And he's not one to cry out unnecessarily. Never in all the healings I've witnessed him do, has he ever vocalized his pain. It must be really excruciating for him to cry out like that."

"Could the enemy's laser weapon cause pain like that?"

"It didn't sound like a weapon was involved. And none of the 'Aopato' cry out when it slices; something in their make up keeps them mulishly silent. And if Sky has been hurt in that or any other manner, I worry what it will do to Sonia so close to her time. They keep her pretty excluded from unsettling circumstances now, but that empathetic female's first reaction upon sensing this will be to try to heal him immediately. Could be he's hiding his pain from her by remaining out here."

By now Lou knew him well enough to realize he was deliberating out loud to ease his worry, and as they made for the orchard, she said nothing, simply let him talk. Amadeus knew he and this woman made a good fit, anticipated each other well, and he appreciated that.

As the two broke through into the trees, they found Sky just rising to his feet. He appeared haggard and gaunt, unsettled and confused, but seemed unhurt.

"What's wrong?" Amadeus demanded without preamble. "Are you hurt?"

"If I could figure that out, I'd not be standing here!" the Navajo returned testily.

Now, that was decidedly unlike Sky!

"Do the 'Opposites' have some sort of weapon trained on you?

"No... You will find this difficult to believe..." The male hesitated; as if he not only found what he had to share embarrassing, but incredible himself. He looked about him at the bushes, then off toward the waterfall from which they had just come, as if he might find his answer there, or he was waiting for something else to strike him again. "So far to walk," he said with confusion in his tone. "Don't think I can make it...if this keeps up..."

"Why can't you teleport?" asked Amadeus.

Sky only shook his head, disconcerted.

This must be really bad if he can't do that.

"What wouldn't I believe, Sky? Explain it," Amadeus prompted.

"I never thought I'd have to say something like this...I am...experiencing child birth."

Amadeus laughed out right; it sounded so ludicrous.

"Very funny, Sky," he shot back without thinking. "And I'm not a human after all."

And as if to prove his point, Sky doubled over with what appeared to be just that, a labour contraction. He went rigid and stark white, dropped to his knees cradling his belly like a pregnant woman, panting short quick breaths, as tears formed at the corner of pinched closed lids.

He had never known Sky to exaggerate; it was said 'Aopato' were incapable of lying. *Surely this isn't for real?*

Amadeus and Lou stood there disbelieving, there mouths open in shock.

He had attended many a woman in the birthing process; he'd watched them all in the throws of eminent delivery, and Sky had the actions down to exact. Amadeus was appalled, as he waited for the cramping to pass. He was aware if he touched the man he might kill him, even should he attempt to stroke his back to comfort him.

"How is this possible? Are 'Aopato' that different?" As Sky stood to his feet when the spasm had passed, Amadeus wanted to know, "Do your males always endure the labour with their spouse? I take it Sonia is delivering?"

"No, males do not usually feel it this strong. And I am unsure if this is birth itself; Sonia feels nothing…totally oblivious. It's like I am separated from the others, isolated."

"So, whatever these are; how far apart are these pains?"

"That was my fourth in less than an hour…unbearably strong."

Sky never complained. The very fact that he was doing so now worried Amadeus."

"Well, we need to get you inside before the next on comes. Where is Sonia?"

"In the common room…as usual. But I don't have the energy to jump there."

"Can we safely touch you? What if we used our belts; can they support more than one?"

Sky looked from Amadeus to Lou, debating.

"I think it's safe to touch me. If I was between the two of you…perhaps we could jump it together. Hurry, another is beginning."

Sky began to pant, doubled forward.

"Lou take his other side; press the button on the count of three."

CHAPTER 34

Joel started to his feet as the two humans, with Sky between them, materialized in the library common room. Then an involuntary yell escaped the 'Pure' male, as his empathy caught him up on what was happening, the excruciating pain spreading up back, down and across the belly, the agony that was in Sky, the incredible pain he was enduring. And Joel also bent double, joining the Navajo in his misery.

"Oh, man!" Amadeus cried, stepping away from both males, pulling Lou with him.

With great effort Joel pulled back from the immediate area around Sky, to ease the intensity of what in his empathy he shared. At last, distance enough brought relief, at least for him. Sky was still doubled over with this strange phenomenon.

Upon the appearance of her pair, Sonia looked up in incredulity; her jaw dropped as she noted his weird behaviour, the book in her hand sliding to the floor unnoticed. Yet still, she showed no symptoms pertaining to delivery herself.

"Whatever is happening?" she asked in bewilderment. "Why are you in such agony? Did something happen? I cannot see in your mind. Why do you hide this?"

Sky still on the backside of the contraction, took a moment to answer. "I believe," he gasped. "You are in labour, my Love."

"Oh, don't be silly," Sonia disproved. "I feel nothing."

"I know. Isn't it most peculiar?"

As Sky stood to full height again, moving back to a corner away from all others in the room, Joel asked the question uppermost in their minds.

"How long since this began?"

"Approximately an hour. The pains are closer together now then at first...about ten minutes between the last two."

Not doubting the fact, or the evidence in the least, Joel assumed Sky was right.

"Any idea why you feel the labour and Sonia does not?"

Sky shook his head.

"Oh, this is foolishness, Sky," Sonia reproved. "Somehow, your will has produced this unusual experience. Subconsciously, you wish to spare me such discomfort, and have overridden my ability to prevent you doing so." Sonia rose from her seat approaching her partner. "Now stop it this instant; there is no need for you to bear the entire burden alone."

"I know that!" Sky retorted testily. "Believe me, I would not willingly take this on. What man in his right mind would? Were your other births this painful?"

Sonia grinned, and giggled, which only served to infuriate Sky further, resulting in his withdrawing mentally, as well as physically from her. He backed deeper into the corner to avoid her.

"Sky, give me your hand," Sonia ordered. "Enough of this!"

Before they could effect the touch, a visible static energy spat between them, arching around the two with colourful blue and white lightning-like bolts.

Amadeus and Lou scampered to the opposite corner away from this action.

"Ouch!" complained Sky. "How does it help me for you to sting me?"

Shocked, Sonia defended determinedly. "I am not doing that!"

"Yes, you are! That's your reflex!"

"No, it isn't! I wouldn't do that to you under these circumstances."

As if feeling a sudden weakness herself, Sonia back away. The energy output stopped immediately, so she went and sat down again. Joel moved to the third corner, realizing more was amiss here than first thought.

Sky moved to a chair, as if anticipating another eminent contraction.

"I can't touch you?" Sonia frown perplexed. "Even your mind is hidden from me. That means I can't put a stop to this…I can't even help you. Whatever is going on here?"

"What a wonderful predicament," Joel declared with candour. "Two 'Healer Ultimate' and both seemingly incapacitated by the birthing of their son…and as that also renders the healing powers for the rest of us useless, we are all in quite a quandary."

"I think…" Sky broke in tentatively. "This might well have something to do with our unborn son. That little culprit is a 'Double Healer', able to override his mother, and do what he wishes with me..."

"You think?" Joel stated sarcastically. "A union between two 'Ultimate Healers' will always create a 'Double Healer'! I can't believe you didn't foresee this. Did you not plan ahead?"

"How could we plan for this, Joel?" Sky retorted angrily. "We weren't even certain he was 'Double Healer' until recently. There is no precedent to go by; we fly blind in this matter. All we know is a 'Double Healer' is strongest just before birth. It was impossible to predict how he might act when the birthing pains began. It is my assumption, he is aware his mother will have discomfort; he considers me responsible, and so he's transferred to me what he feels I deserve. He is doing this!"

"Are you saying the child is stronger than his mother at this point?"

"Not merely stronger than Sonia," Sky reiterated. "More powerful than both of us together! And...he is operating without knowledge, by sheer emotion...unreasoning instinct."

"Is there no way to thwart the infant?"

"No," Sky admitted. "He has this mixed up..." Tears formed in the Navajo's eyes as the cramping began for another round. "To his credit...he can't stand to see his mother suffer, and...I am secondary."

As Sky doubled in agony, a sheen of perspiration standing out on his brow from the effort to endure without voicing his fury, it was Sonia who cried out in frustrated sympathy at watching her mate's torture.

"Oh, Kyle, stop this! Please son. Daddy can't bring you outside to us. Mommy needs to do it. She needs to help him." Sonia burst into tears. "Please, Kyle, please," she pleaded of her unborn child. "I don't want to see your daddy hurting. That hurts me!"

But it seemed the rascal was ignoring her.

****

Amadeus chuckled; their predicament was so absurd. "The little fellow has actually overruled his parents? Is there anything we could do to help?"

Sonia sighed, as if it were an effort to form a reasoning thought.

Is this affecting her more than it outwardly appears? Is she unable to find the solution?

"Yes, Amadeus," Sonia answered softly. "This influences my reasoning faculties. I may not appear in physical labour, but my thought processes are becoming confused, disjointed. As far as I can see, there seems no way in this unusual state of affairs that I can actually give birth. I need to think the matter through..."

"Sky needs physical support, sis," Joel interjected. "Can we bring another in for balance? Obviously, the imp will not let his uncle near Sky."

Sky relaxed as the current contraction ended, while Sonia struggled with an effort to speak. "No one else can come near, if you can't...the result would be the same. He doesn't want Sky to be helped."

"Then is it possible to help you?" Joel asked seriously. "This cannot go on like this. It is impossible for Sky to give birth."

"We have to trick the child…so he allows nature to take its course."

"We could knock Sky out," Amadeus said, tongue in cheek. "He is half human."

Sonia chuckled despite herself. "Perhaps…let me think. There just might be a way to do something like that."

****

Sky was just coming down from another contraction, when Sonia finally spoke again.

"Joel," she declared with gravity. "We have only one choice here. We again must rely on human hands."

Her brother winced visibly. "Why? How did you come to that conclusion? This matter is most delicate."

"Always, in the visions I have seen, Amadeus saves us."

"Hasn't he already fulfilled that function?"

"There is no time to argue, brother," Sonia warned him. "We are in a holding pattern at the moment, but Sky will exhaust beyond recovery soon. The space between contractions has shortened."

Joel looked to Sky. He now sat on the floor beside the chair, having remained there after the last episode, too weary to rise. He leaned back against the seat, resting, but extremely pallid, his hands lowered, limp at his sides.

Joel curtly nodded. "Very well. I'll back whatever you decided. What do you plan on doing? How do we proceed with this?"

Rather than hash over the details, Sonia turned her attention to Amadeus.

"Human, are you willing to again put your life on the line?"

Amadeus hesitated. A short time ago, he would have answered yes quickly, but Lou had now entered the picture, and he knew their relationship was progressing. To risk his life now not only involved him but also her. He had to seriously consider what his death might do to her psyche.

Sonia reading his dilemma easily wisely nodded. "I fully understand." Her gaze turned to Lou. "You, human female, have a choice to make for us…"

Lou, who had been watching Sky, turned her head in surprised shock. "Me? What do I have to do with this?"

"Amadeus loves you," Sonia declared bluntly. "And…I believe you have feelings for him…"

Lou's cheeks burned crimson at the realization, she was being asked to verify this.

"Oh, geesh! Is anything private with you guys?"

A silence heavy with expectation filled the room.

Tears filled the human woman's eyes. "Yes, I am growing fond of him, and I wouldn't want to lose him, but…this decision is for Amadeus to make. I…I have no hold over his life."

"But his death would hurt you?" Sonia clarified.

A tear wandered down the cheek of the former stalwart law enforcement officer. She was more fragile female at this moment than at any time in her life. "I doubt I would ever be able...to fill the hole he would leave in my life."

"Will you...are you able to trust us enough...to save his life, should it come to that?"

"After what happened on the highway, I know miracles can happen." A second tear followed the first. "If you think this plan can work, and Amadeus is willing to do this...I can't, won't ask him to hold back because of me. If it were my choice, I'd say this baby is more important than a couple of humans."

"Ah..." Sonia sighed, pleased. "And Amadeus, what of you?"

Amadeus steeled himself. "Put like that, I can't help but agree. Baby comes first. I'm willing. What do I do?"

"Much the same as with Joel on the highway, I ask you to be my intermediary host."

"Aw! No, sis!" Joel objected vehemently. "Not that! The birthing has confused you."

"Joel," Sonia pleaded softly. "This is the only answer. As you've noted, I cannot think clearly enough. I have lost most of my mental junction to others of the species, and as you've said before...Sky cannot deliver this child!"

"Aw, sis!" Joel moaned. "Not this! Not only are you going female to male, but..."

"It is the only way..."

Joel stood tensed, the struggle to submit obvious; equally apparent was his surrender when it came.

He nodded. "I obey," he agreed quietly. "What do you wish of me?"

Sonia gave him a sobering look, then she delivered the gut punch. "You…must go back to home planet."

"Aw, no," he pleaded. "Don't send us away."

"I need you there…to support. You are second coffer."

Tears filled the 'Pure' male's eyes as he nodded acceptance. "This maybe goodbye…"

"Never, brother! We will always be together."

"Your orders then as 'Leader Female'?"

Joel appeared calm now, stoic, as if this duty asked of him was merely to fetch a companion for his monarch. Had the others not witnessed the moisture previously in his eyes, they would have thought his sorrow imagined.

"When all go down," Sonia counselled. "You must be linked to our second infant. She is our weakest link, and must heal back first."

"She'll be squalling like the dickens until an adult awakens."

Sonia chuckled softly, picturing it in her mind.

"Go, brother. I love you."

"And I you…" With that Joel vanished.

Sonia turned to the business at hand.

"Joel will need at least an hour to arrive and prepare. Until then, we wait. When that time is up, remind me."

As Amadeus agreed, Sky bent forward cradling his belly, in agony once again

CHAPTER 35

Amadeus checked his watch for the umpteenth time. Sonia had said to remind her when the hour was up. It was time!

Sky was visibly trembling, a sheen of sweat standing out on his arms, neck and forehead. He had just come out of a very long contraction, and Amadeus was timing them. They were now three minutes apart, obviously nearing the point of delivery.

He and Lou were alone with the pair, and it was most unpleasant to watch them suffering while unable to help. Though Amadeus had cautioned Lou that their personal emotions affected the birthing couple, Lou found it impossible to keep from crying softly in sympathy.

Sonia appeared totally out of it, neither aware of the two humans or Sky. Incapable of helping her mate, it appeared she had retreated deep inside her mind, escaping where the harshness and intolerable pain of her partner could not reach her.

Amadeus feared for her. The pair was so intertwined, depended so completely upon each other, it was beyond a human's understanding. He remembered Sky sharing in confidence, that without that intimate connection Sonia would be driven to insanity. He hoped she could stay stable long enough to do what she had planned.

"Sonia…" He tried to get her attention. "Sonia!"

After numerous loud shouting of her name, she finally stirred. He did not dare touch her.

"Sonia!" She looked up at him, confusion evident in her eyes.

"It's been an hour…"

She frowned, puzzled.

"I'm to be your intermediary host, remember?" He had no idea what that entitled; only that Joel had feared it enough to give Amadeus personal qualms.

Recollection brightened the amethyst eyes. "Ah, yes." Sonia sighed with the effort to bring her thoughts into focus, then explained the working of what would take place. "I will separate my thought processing…put it inside your mind…"

He shivered in spite of himself.

"You will have my knowledge, think like me, but not have the powers. My physical body left behind will operate on instinct; you will have to guide it. I will be much like a robot with you in command…and I will be obedient to your will."

Terrified by such a prospect, Amadeus almost withdrew his agreement, then remembered it was already too late.

Sonia articulated the words from his thoughts.

"We place our lives in your hands once again, human. Please…" she pleaded. "Do not take advantage. Do not fail us."

Before the physician could comment, or even prepare, the world as he knew it became suddenly much more expansive. He was aware of a second presence with him, saw a vast expansive universe; incredible knowledge at his disposal; his to command, his to control. The blatant manipulation available to him humbled and made him tremble.

Questions were now irrelevant. He knew all the answers he might seek.

She had prepared to implement his direct instructions; even her powers were available to him simply by commanding her. He could tell her, 'Destroy the universe', and she would do so without questioning.

Does she realize there is this flaw in her plan?

If he'd harboured animosity toward them, been of a vicious sadistic nature toward his own world, he could right all the wrongs he supposedly saw there. He could start over... be King of creation...

And for a brief second, he toyed with the idea; saw the dilemma and the temptation Sonia struggled with daily, near gave in to it, then his good nature, that which was in the best of mankind, took over and...conquered.

Amadeus made his choice, decided irrevocably; it would not benefit him, nor any other, universe or private humble human world, if he should surrender to evil intent.

"Sonia? Can you hear me?"

"Yes."

"Release the rest of your people; carry their consciousness, obtain their energy. Take Sky last of all."

Amadeus watched as it was done, heard Sky moan at the loss of connection with his kind, felt the unbearable aloneness in the male, and regretted having ordered it.

"Now, make it complete. Liberate Sky," Amadeus prompted.

With a sign of pure ecstasy, at the release from constant agony, the Navajo folded gently like a rag doll to the floor.

Immediately, Sonia gasped with the shock of the first real feeling of her own labour. She let out a scream, then pulled in a gulp of air, as if about to push, but Amadeus quickly intervened. "Not yet! Not yet. Quick, short breaths."

Lou swiped at the tears on her cheeks, coming to attention. "What are you doing, Amadeus?" she asked, as if for some reason she didn't trust him with this sudden manipulation of others. "Was it necessary to put Sky all the way out? He'll miss the big event."

"His body needs the rest. Don't question me," he ordered curtly. "Sonia gave me her reasoning abilities. I know what's best right now. Sonia could not feel as long as Sky was in the picture."

"Is he…dead?"

"By all intents and purposes, yes! But Sonia will restore him when this is over."

"If she can," Lou reminded.

"Don't, Lou! I don't have time to argue. Time is vital here."

With that, Amadeus turned his attention to the 'Leader Female'.

"You need a birthing chair, dear Lady.

Abruptly, Sonia was seated in a wooden chair, the stool of which was but a gaping hole much like that on a commode. Beneath the female's feet, on the marble floor, appeared a soft white blanket.

"Now, I need you to neutralize your reflex. Don't fight me on that, Sonia," he warned. "I know it is not natural to do that and it makes you vulnerable, but it is necessary. We need to be able to touch you."

"Only…if the female is the only one to touch me," Sonia objected.

Well! Her will is still intact, observed Amadeus. *A safe guard, after all. Good!*

"I agree," he decided. "Lou will do it."

Sonia, though at the moment in the heavy end of a long contraction, was muting her reaction to the pain.

Man! This lady is a trouper.

"Lou, come forward. Try to touch her."

Lou, shivering visibly with fear, moved to Sonia's side obediently. When touch was instigated, and nothing happened, the human sighed relieved.

"Okay, next step." Amadeus relaxed, and moved away. "Stay there."

At least now we are able to help her.

"Sonia. Do you think you can neutralize the baby's powers now?"

"Yes. With no one else to be responsible for, I can concentrate on him, and override."

"Then, do so."

Tears slipped from beneath Sonia's closed eyelids, and a mournfully sigh escaped her. "We are separate." She swallowed the groan of loss; an agony of withdrawal, nearly crying, as if her baby was dead.

"He's still there, still alive," he reassured. He felt for her. It was not normal for them to be apart.

"I would suggest you go naked at this point. If you maintain a shield around you and Lou, I won't be able to see."

A curtain of light came between the women and Amadeus.

"Lou, I'll need you to tell me what's happening. Can you see how close the head is?"

"Crown is visible," came from behind the shield.

"Good. I guess the rest is up to you, and nature. You ever delivered a baby before?"

"Once, in the back seat of a cruiser. I know what to do."

"Let me know if you need my help. And just tell Sonia to sever the cord when you get to that part."

Then Amadeus sat down in a chair to wait out the next stage.

CHAPTER 36

It seemed far too quiet behind the light curtain. It worried Amadeus. By now, they should have been hearing the lusty cry of a newborn.

Did Sonia mute sound, to give her more privacy? Why is it taking so long? She was in the delivery stage an hour ago.

It was so hard for him to wait this out, unable to take part, feeling useless, and ineffectual out here. It appeared as if the women had excluded him since they had taken over.

Is my part really over that easily?

****

A small 'Keeper' floated into the room, hovering just above eyelevel, like a pesty fly he wanted to swat.

"Master?" it queried.

Why is this thing bothering me now? Everyone is unconscious except for Sonia.

Amadeus chose to ignore the machine.

Once again it repeated the enquiry.

He was curt when he answered, worried at the silence behind the curtain.

"What is it? Can't you see we are busy? Surely this can wait?"

"This is most important."

"Then spill it! Get on with it, whatever! Just tell me what you want!"

"The compound has been breached. As you are the only conscious being, and have the matriarch's reasoning knowledge I have been programmed to come to you for instruction."

Only conscious being, obviously this thing is faulty or something.

Amadeus frowned as the words finally sunk in. "Are you telling me Sanctuary is under attack? The 'Opposites' picked now to launch an offensive?"

"Correct, master."

"You're certain? Any chance your equipment is malfunctioning?"

"Our units are self-repairing. It is not possible for us to be in error. Only our destruction will cause us to cease function."

Okay? reasoned Amadeus. *And this thing expects me to command it. Perfect timing!*

Uneasy at the idleness of waiting, Amadeus was actually glad to be so distracted. He willingly turned his mind to this new problem.

"Are you capable of defending?"

"Most certainly; we are programmed to protect, and are doing so as we speak."

"Then what do you need from me?"

"It is required to seek clarification, master?"

"Okay. Then continue on. Protect! Do whatever it takes! Your masters are helpless here, and Lou and I are needed by Sonia. We have our hands full."

"And what level of defence should be implemented?"

"Protect with everything you've got!"

"Clarify, please?"

What is the matter with this thing?

Becoming exceedingly annoyed, Amadeus tried not to let his temper get the better of him. "Destroy the bastards once and for all! So they can never hurt these beings again!"

"To kill is not in the programming; this compound is under peaceable governance."

That brought Amadeus up short, caused him to remember the 'Aopato's' merciful nature. It shamed him to realize he'd just about ordered the annihilation of a species that had fathered Ty. He took a deep breath to calm himself.

"Okay. Just what are you programmed to do?"

"Deactivate enemy weaponry. At death of our mistress' race, extreme measures are to be implemented: we are to send enemy from this planet, isolate each, then explode enemy outpost."

"Then do that for gosh sake! What are you waiting for? Destroy everything that is evil!" Amadeus ordered tersely. "Be done with all this torment!"

"Mistress still lives," it objected. "And please, define evil?"

Exasperation got the better of the man. Inside his mind he felt more than frustrated. The wishes of Sonia were warring with his own, two minds together in there, his own on the verge of loosing control, at odds with the gentler, more compassionate nature of Sonia. She wanted leniency; he was angry at the injustices he saw.

"Anything," he declared hotly, "that means harm or poses a threat to your masters."

"Does that include humans?"

"What?" Amadeus had been caught off guard. It hadn't dawned on him, the human race matched the criteria.

Who was it had said the 'Aopato' considered his genus as predatory to them as the 'Opposites'?

"Said species is also opposed to and adversary to my makers," clarified the 'Keeper'.

Amadeus stared at the machine in utter shock. To hear it speak what he already had realized did more to fuel his temper then the obvious label.

"What are you?" he exploded in fury. "A machine that takes orders, or...or a thinking being that acts of its on volition?"

"I am both a device equal in knowledge, and a being of reasoning capabilities."

"Well...well," sputtered the man. "Humans are not 'Opposites'! Why would you lump us together with these nasty lizards?"

"You are both aggressive to my masters."

"But, man has good in him as well as evil?"

And the machine answered him as the programmed teacher, much as a professor enlightening a contesting student.

"Indeed, sir, as it is with all creatures. That is why our mistress has cautioned for non-violence. Without life, the balance of good and evil cannot be brought to maturity."

"Oh, for crying out loud!"

He couldn't believe he was arguing a morality issue with a machine, at a time like this.

"You are implying that evil is needed?"

"You understand me correctly. Controversy is required. Struggles are necessary to gain the proper perfection. This is the basis of my programming."

Amadeus digested this information with the realization he could never bend what was designated before hand. Besides, the "Keeper' had a point.

"So…what does your encoding suggest for this situation?" he asked, admitting at last to inadequacy in his makeup.

"To keep at bay that which means harm, and allow good to predominate."

Quietly serious now, Amadeus surrendered. "Then do that."

"It remains still to clarify the method."

Back to square one, Amadeus mused.

Aloud, he sighed. "Okay. What would you suggest for the ultimate solution?"

"Stop the attacking 'Opposites'. Destroy their weaponry. Then remove from Sanctuary and the nearby site all elder 'Opposite' who display apparent aggressive tendencies toward my masters. Put these in their ships, in a cryo-suspension state, at the edge of the universe, until such knowledge be gained as to turn them back to productive good behaviour; free beings capable of interacting once again with the 'Aopato' species. The young left here should be given a choice to find this best path willingly."

"Wow, you've got it all worked out, haven't you."

"This will be Sonia's plan."

To the human ear, such a future scenario sounded quite impossible, idealistic to say the least. This machine had no idea what it would take to carry it out, nor did it consider failure.

Amadeus contained Sonia's reasoning mind, and at this point a thought from her seemed to surface.

Is something else controlling this device?

"And just how did you come by this scenario?"

The answer that came back was the one least expected.

"The Almighty Creator has orchestrated this from the beginning."

Amadeus went cold.

That machine really didn't say what it did?

"Are you saying…this is God talking through this machine to me?"

"The Almighty Creator is also called God, but I am not that being. Yes, It will talk to you, but I simply obey Its directives."

Amadeus let out a stuttering breath, shivered.

Is it really possible this Maker can reach down and intervene in our lives at this moment? To guide me through this machine, just when I was about to change the balance of power?

After quiet deliberation, he made up his mind.

"Proceed as you suggested," the human ordered. "And just to clarify, you did say you were leaving the youngest 'Opposites' here?"

"That is correct. Those below the age of five will be left at the farm base. These young ones have not yet been schooled in warfare; their aggression is latent. Left to itself, that generation may possibly choose the better path. They will simply need the proper guidance."

"And this was all in your programming?" Amadeus marvelled astonished.

"I, as well as you, am linked to the reasoning thought processes of the 'Leader Female'."

"Should Sonia die during this delivery, what will happen?"

"All mechanisms will cease to exist, but...the Almighty Creator will always be with you."

Silence held the room, as Amadeus waited, thinking.

"Your order still stands, master?"

"Yes."

"And is the human species included in this command?"

"Are you programmed to include the human race as an adversary?"

"Only upon the order of the 'Leader Female'."

"Then there you have your answer."

For a beat there was silence, as if the machine were searching its records.

"She has not commanded the inclusion of humankind."

"Then quickly deal with the 'Opposites' before they succeed in causing her demise."

"Yes, master."

The small orb vanished, leaving Amadeus with his previous task. And as life and death hung in balance in this room, he could hear the battle raging outside.

****

Another half hour passed before Lou's uncertain voice came to the waiting physician.

"Amadeus? I think this baby is caught up on something. It has stopped coming. What should I do?"

"Sonia?" Amadeus probed. "Can you give me a vision of the baby inside you?"

He abruptly had a visual: an obviously male infant swimming in the embryonic fluid. He had never thought he'd have such a close experience; it was as if he was there inside the woman.

"The cord is tangled around the child's leg," he noted. "Sonia? Turn the baby clockwise until the cord slips off."

Amadeus watched as the infant was slowly rotated; he even felt the liquid slosh around the unborn child.

"Now, make him bend his knee."

The fleshly rope slipped away, and the boy was free.

"Good. Now move him back to his original position."

For an instant, Amadeus felt the beginnings of a contraction, then Sonia shut him out. The abrupt loss of visual, as well as feeling, had Amadeus nearly falling from his seat, but at least he had no further need for alarm. With the baby positioned correctly, the birth should proceed quickly…unless something else went wrong.

"The baby is coming!" squealed Lou exuberantly.

The next sound was a strident cry of indignation, just as with any human born for eons past, and it brought tears of joy to the listening man.

Finally, this is over! Amadeus thought, and sighed in relief.

****

"There's my 'Double Healer'," Sonia cooed softly. "My Kyle."

And suddenly, the proud mother appeared, fully clothed and holding her small infant swaddled in a warm blue blanket; Lou stood beside her. The light curtain had dropped.

Amadeus had expected to see blood everywhere, and at least a half naked Sonia, but true to her own modesty, all mess was erased; no birthing chair, only a soft cushioned rocker that glided silently in answer to the 'Leader Female's' gentle guidance.

"He is so beautiful, Amadeus," Lou exclaimed in wonder. "Oh, I can hardly wait to have one of my own!"

Amadeus felt the room suddenly go unusually warm, and knew it had nothing to do with Sonia or her baby. The expectation of future performance had him rattled.

Can I even be a father still?

"Amadeus.' Sonia broke into his reverie. "We must part company now. I gratefully thank you both."

It wasn't until she said that, that he realized she was of sound mind, and his own lacked the former clarity.

Abruptly, both he and Lou found themselves beneath the waterfall, on the shore of the small pond. The fields around them were silent now, the raging battle of the past hours seemingly over.

Sonia's voice came with one last command, heard in both their minds. "Do not enter the caves for at least two days, please. We need the time to heal back. We will summon you when it is safe."

He felt both elation and extreme loss. His mind seemed utterly inferior now, empty, inefficient, and...primitive, compared to what he had experienced with Sonia.

But...they had birth a special baby together...and he would never forget that.

CHAPTER 37

Kara awoke as if from slumber, yet that had not been natural sleep. The experience of being lost in emptiness, drifting in a deep, cold abyss…a space confined, yet seemingly not present. It was disconcerting.

Is that what it feels like to die, to be non-existent, the absence of other minds…of being nothing…a nobody?

Kara shivered. They were back unified. It felt good! But she realized they were all teetering on the edge of weakness.

She was meant to hold the others…the way her great-gran did.

But the memory of how it was done, escaped her. Gone. Lost.

Kara burst into tears, softly crying at first, then gulping in uncontrollable grief, terrified and trembling.

I want to remember so badly…to be what I should be. Why can't I do it? Great-gran needs my help.

She still lay on her back on the couch where she had placed herself in preparation, but though she wanted to rise, the agony of inadequacy that filled her now, paralysed and prevented it.

Suddenly Nadia was at her side, comforting, embracing, holding tight while Kara sobbed her heart out.

"I just want so badly to be whole again," she mourned. "I don't ever want to be separate from the others. I desperately need to be…right in my head again!"

"I know, Mini-monarch," Nadia whispered softly, stroking the girl's back. "You will be…soon, now that you want it so very much."

"Believe me, I'm not keeping it from happening. Really, I'm not!"

"We know. There's something blocking it."

Sonia's voice came in mind command to them. "Kara." The words were whispered, soft and soothing. "Come here to me. Come alone."

Kara sighed in resignation. Nadia stepped aside, and Kara sat up.

"Okay, great-gran. I'm coming."

****

Kara had taken the time to collect herself, by walking the corridor to the library common room, instead of making a jump. Sonia was cuddling a small bundle wrapped snugly in a blanket, when the young girl entered the room that held the waterfall feature wall. Sky stood behind his mate, his features alight with a proud grin.

Kara's heart gave a great stuttering leap in her breast.

Her great-gran had hidden what was happening, and Kara had not realized this was why they had all gone down. She had simply been obedient, trusting the matriarch knew best, a step of confidence that was important in itself.

The baby is here!

"Come," Sonia whispered softly. "He sleeps. Now is a safe time for you to hold him."

Kara stepped to them carefully, holding her breath less she awaken the slumbering infant. She felt the fatigue that emanated from the elder 'Leader Female'; her great-gran was barely holding it together. Even Sky was exceedingly weary. Both 'Healer Ultimate' desperately needed more healing back time, or the species would go down again.

"You need to go to your chambers, great-gran…to rest," Kara encouraged, as she eased to her knees before mother and child.

"Oh, dear…not there," Sonia objected. "Come sit beside me."

Kara obediently switched positions to the seat of the couch, beside her great-gran. Suddenly, she felt so old, like a century had passed while they had been in mental limbo, and she had aged way past her meagre eight years in the 'Aopato' reckoning. The process of suspension always had that effect; it matured, especially those who should have been children.

Without my support, our species is so unstable again, Kara realized. *If only I was able to heal my own mind.*

"Here Kara. Why don't you take him," Sonia requested. "Easy now. Try not to wake him."

They made a cautious, slow and gently transfer. Kara went all soft inside, at the silken touch of newborn skin and hair. His healing essence was powerful; she felt it flood through her: peace, love, joy…a helpless baby reliance. She sensed his need to feed…and to pass his water; he let it go, and the diaper around his bottom soaked.

Laughing, Kara dropped her cheek to the smooth downy mane, eased her face caressingly over the silken cheek. He smelled of fragrant powder, a new baby aroma.

Oh, such a treasure. An infant held is beyond pleasure.

As she lifted her head again, Kara realized he was awake. He was staring wide-eyed, with a searching gaze so penetrating; she knew he was probing in her mind. His eyes were deep turquoise, like those of Sky Hawk, with the vertical slit in Amethyst, the mirrors of a 'Double Healer'.

Kyle was only one hour into their reality, living, breathing, whole…but incredibly powerful.

"Well," Sonia beamed in pleasure. "Kara, meet baby Kyle. The youngest, yet first born of a new generation."

"But…" Kara objected. "Didn't my baby sister come first?"

"Yes. But he is the first 'Healer Ultimate'. Through him passes not only the healing gene, but also the seed of ruling."

"He carries the 'Leader Female' genome?"

"Indeed."

Kara marvelled. *There is much hope placed in you,* she thought, studying the infant.

"He is aware of me, great-gran." Kara pointed out the obvious.

Sonia chuckled. "Isn't it amazing? This little boy is your uncle."

It sounded so ludicrous it made Kara laugh too.

Her eyes met those of the infant. He made no sound; only his slit widened, and then he was inside her mind probing, crawling over every inch as if searching for an errant, defective area. Like fingers, he manoeuvred through her memories, felt the painful regrets, knew her hidden desires. She could hide nothing from him.

So very innocent, yet already caring too much.

Kara felt the sudden sadness in him, as he found what he sought. Then his scent came, overpowering, the bouquet of healing.

Sandalwood, Kara thought vaguely. *So masculine!*

It made her body tingle, tremble, as if with sensual desire.

Kara closed her mind against him, came once more to reality. "The ladies will adore this little male when he is of age." She smiled softly at Kyle.

A sudden hot heat flooded over her, and Kara gasped at the intimate feeling. *Surely, a child this young...is not healing?*

Sonia laughed delighted. "Oh, I suspected he might try to do that if he could!"

"Great-gran!" Kara squealed breathlessly. "He's trying to heal my mind. He will hurt himself!"

"Let him try, dear," Sonia encouraged. "He must learn his limitations soon enough. At this point in time, his power is the most potent. It will even out from now on, as he grows older. If he cannot correct your imbalance now…you will be left as you are."

Kaleidoscopic images flashed through Kara's reawaken mind: scenes of past battles, medical procedures, instructions long buried.

It was as if a door had slid away.

"I remember!" she cried out jubilantly. "I see my records! They were not lost! Only hidden."

Unbidden tears crawled her cheeks seeking a dropping place from her chin. "I see how to heal, to balance, how to hold the others. I can help you now, great-gran. I can hold, as you do. Let me; give me the younger ones…so you can heal back properly."

"Just for a little while, dear," Sonia agreed. "You are not old enough, strong enough yet, to hold for long periods."

"Just let me do it long enough so you can repair yourself. And at other times too…so you can separate to just be mother."

Tears of gratitude filled the matriarch's eyes. "Okay, dear one. Give the little one to Sky."

Sky dropped to one knee before them. As they gently shifted Kyle to his father, Kara realized the baby had gone quiet in slumber, weary now, healing back from the difficult procedure he had manipulated.

Kara felt distressed that he would never again have at his disposal the force he'd used on her. He would still be the most powerful healer in the universe, but it would always take its toll from him.

After Sky had jumped to their sleep chamber with baby Kyle, Sonia turned to her great-granddaughter.

At the touch of their hands, the transfer of power was instantaneous. It was not near as heavy as Kara had expected; it seemed easy, natural…a labour of love. But she also realized Sonia was right; she could not maintain for long.

Sonia vanished, to join in rest with Sky. Kara was left sitting quietly in the enormous cathedral-like room, listening to the muted waterfall cascade down the far wall.

Her great-gran needed these few hours of down time; Kara felt pleased at the purpose she fulfilled.

Kara knew it was best to remain stationary, not to try to do much else this first time. She was not surprised when Ty materialized at her side. He stood a slight distance away; knowing instinctively it was unsafe to touch her. Taking a stance of fierce defence, he stood guarding her against the chance touch of any other. From now on, it would always be so.

Ty was her soul mate…always and ever. It had been ordained by the Almighty Creator, and no being 'Opposite' or human could prevent that from happening.

Kara was 'Leader Female' as much as Sonia, and Ty, though born 'Opposite' was meant to be her partner.

CHAPTER 38

Amadeus and Lou had just been summoned to the common room, the one with the beautiful feature wall made of an indoor waterfall.

They came together, walking hand in hand. The days together outside, the shared experience of troubles and triumphs, had blossomed their relationship beyond mere friendship.

It was in this room, baby Kyle had taken his first breath of Earth's atmosphere. To the human couple, the memory of that birth still seemed like an impossible dream.

Sonia looked up with a smile, as they entered the huge library. Relaxed, she held in her arms baby Kyle, cuddled close, as any human mother would treasure her young.

Sky stood, ever guardian, beside mother and son, protective, filled with obvious pride, a fierce tenderness fighting for dominance with stoic aloofness over the features of his face. It was evident the Navajo would give his life to keep his family from harm.

The humans realized also, this room, a favourite even before, had become the comfort place of this core 'Aopato' family.

"Ah, Amadeus, Lou. Come in," Sonia bubbled enthusiastically. "Come see the baby, Louise! I think in the last week he has grown half again."

Lou giggled thrilled. Sonia was such a delight, acting like a child with a new toy. If she had not known better, she would have assumed this female new to motherhood, and all that it entailed. It was equally amazing to believe, here was the ruler of the species.

Lou scampered across the marble floor, dropped to a crouch before Sonia and her infant. Amadeus followed more slowly.

"Oh. Yes. He is so very beautiful," Lou cooed softly. "I do think you're right. He's filled out a lot."

"Want to hold him?" Sonia offered.

"Is it safe?" Lou whispered. "I'd love to."

Sonia chuckled. "Oh, yes. He's just like any other infant now."

"Pretty powerful little creature though," Amadeus observed. "Got to watch out for this little guy."

"You know, there is very little human in him, Amadeus," Sonia declared proudly. "He's almost completely 'Pure'."

"That's good, right?"

"Makes his mental power stronger," Sky added from behind them.

"Yeah," Amadeus agreed. "We've experienced that."

"Come, Louise," Sonia prompted. "Sit down, and I'll hand him to you."

Lou moved to a second soft plush rocker across from Sonia, and the baby was handed carefully across.

"Don't you sting her now, little one," Sonia scolded softly. "She may be human, but she helped birth you. All the while you were forming inside me, you craved human presence …so no need to fear this one." She looked up at Lou. "Don't tense like that, dear. If he senses you are not relaxed with him, he will try to heal you. Also," she added. "He does have this wicked little reflex…"

"Just like his mother," Sky declared proudly. "When he wants to feed, he'll shock me pretty good, till I give him back to his mother."

Lou grinned. "You think he could heal, already? He's not much more than a week old."

"Age makes little difference," Sky revealed. "His healing abilities are very evident, and though he's yet to be trained, he sure knows how to use them. If we were not stronger than he is now, so we can stop him, he would be giving up his life before he was three."

"And because of that, we must take him back home quickly," Sonia stated. "We need to keep him from human contact…until he learns to control and balance."

"Humans have many defects," Sky added. "He'll want to heal whomever he meets."

"Besides, even though only the young 'Opposites' remain, they may try to kill Kyle. It is imbedded in their nature. My baby is safest at home."

It suddenly registered what these two were saying. "You are leaving?" Lou said with disappointment. "When? And what will become of Sanctuary while you're gone?"

"Now, there is the reason we have asked you in." Sonia looked to her pair. "Why don't you tell them Sky?"

"We have decided, when we leave, Sanctuary should be put to some use," Sky revealed. "It is wasted and foolish, sitting here all idle, only maintained by 'Keeper'." He looked back to his mate, and winked. "How would you two like to be its caretakers?"

"There is only one condition," Sonia broke in. "We would like to be able to visit once in a while."

Flabbergasted, the humans were having a hard time taking it in. "But, this is your place!" Lou objected. "What are you meaning here?"

"We are giving Sanctuary to you," Sonia declared. "If you will take on that responsibility."

"The whole valley?" Amadeus exclaimed in astonishment. "Whatever will we do with it?"

Sonia chuckled. "Let's see. How about: feed the hungry; mend the injured; comfort the battered; house the homeless? Isn't that your specialty, Amadeus? Here you have the means to do all that."

"Oh, man!" the human man said softly, the prospects clearly travelling through his mind.

"We will still help you," Sky declared. "We will set all up, and maintain the 'Keepers' for you, the barriers, etc. And if you have a problem..."

"Just call out with your mind. I will always hear you," Sonia finished.

Amadeus went quiet; Lou rocked the baby silently.

"Will you bring baby Kyle back to visit with our children?" Lou asked, timidly.

Sky grinned, not in the least surprised by the plans implied. "When he is old enough to use self-control; it will be a pleasure."

"Well, I'm certainly game," Lou agreed. "It's up to you, Amadeus…"

The man looked up with longing in his eyes, as if all his dreams were coming true at once. Lou knew there was more in his mind than just excitement at the project.

"There's no negative from this end," he agreed with a grin.

"Good. That's settled then," Sonia decided. "You will have to work in secret, as we always have. The 'Opposite' base is still close by, and could be problematic in the future, but…maybe you will be an influence for good there…even, some 'Opposites' may turn back as Ty did," she added hopefully.

"We'll call out for guardian help, should we need it," Amadeus agreed.

Sky grinned. "We will always keep in touch."

Lou sobered. "Just when are you leaving?"

"Tonight," came from the Navajo.

"So soon," Lou bemoaned with regret.

****

The night sky was clear and cool, the stars above bright and twinkling back toward Earth. Lou and Amadeus sat alone on the lookout ledge watching the darkness of space, while the streaks of light sped away, and eventually faded out.

It had seemed one stream was missing, but that had only been because the light of his mother hid baby Kyle.

****

Two lonely figures studied the valley, like Adam and Eve alone in the Eden garden; the vastness of their new empire spread before them, impacting the enormity of what they had agreed to do, near overwhelming them.

They had pledged their love for each other, before the 'Aopato' in that valley garden, just before the take off. In the not to distant future, he and Lou would get to know each other more intimately, they would work together as man and wife, their family would grow. They might even adopt needy others.

One day at a time, Amadeus reasoned. *With the Almighty Creator to guide us, who knows what can come of this?*

EPILOGUE

Nothing was visible in the ebony room save the ghostly glowing figure seated on a chair at centre stage. When the lights came up, those at the front found the visual of the raised platform, the high ceiling above, and the storyteller.

She was of taupe complexion, with jet-black hair and small delicate features; though seemingly from the humanoid planet of Earth, a region called India, her eyes said otherwise. It was known she was from the 'invisible ones', 'Aopato' they were called.

She was soft spoken, yet clearly understood by all, as she completed the weaving of her tale.

"And that, dear ones, is the story of how baby Kyle was birthed to the hands of a human. I state this account as factual, by the inability of my people to lie. I was there as it happened, a witness from afar. I am Jamara."

She paused, holding her listeners spellbound.

"And as we return to the present, many will ask, what has become of those in this tale?"

Again the mixed adults held their breath, captivated by the bright being.

"On this very ship, our resident physician serves. He sits in the audience as escort to a human woman. These two have met just recently, seemingly quite by accident. But as proclaimed in my story, the Almighty Creator guides unbeknownst to us. Wonder you; who is this physician? He is the baby Kyle, grown to manhood, while the female human is the second infant from the highway, protected by

Sonia from harm. Perhaps from their chance meeting another future account will come to pleasure my fond listeners. And with that, I bid you pleasant dreams."

Oh, thanks, female, for blowing my cover, Kyle mind projected. *I owe you one for that.*

The Light female chuckled softly, just as she vanished from the stage.

Standing, Kyle offered his arm to his companion. "Shall we go then?"

As they moved into the crowd, the woman at his side turned to him. "Was that all true, or did she just use the two of us to give it a personal touch?"

"Light beings are incapable of lying. If this was from our memory records, it was factual. My mother has kept very silent about the time of my birth. Until now she has kept this memory hidden from me...and I do not remember it. After all, it took place before I was born."

"How old is your mother now?"

"Sonia? In human? I guess she'd be coming up on one hundred thirty-six years."

"And that makes you how old in human?"

"Perhaps, it is not wise to ask age?"

Yet, she persisted. "Will you not tell me, anyway? Just so, I might at least judge if there is some truth to the story weaving?"

He chuckled. "In human...I am over fifty."

Intrigued, the woman probed again.

"And...in your years?"

"I am twenty-eight."

"And…why have you never married?"

"Paired, is what we call it. And…perhaps…I was indeed waiting for you…"

###

About the Author:

Margaret Afseth, a Canadian novelist, lives in Saskatoon, Saskatchewan. She is a widow with four grown children, and five grandchildren.

An avid reader and clandestine writer since her late teens, she only recently stepped to the publishing stage. Though she has training in both art and as a freelance writer, she is self-taught, her expertise gained mostly from observation and life experience.

From an error in judgement early on, she learned a hard lesson. A narrow-minded counsellor burned the only copy of her first novel. Perhaps this man did Margaret a service, as when one of the manuscripts destroyed was later rewritten, a single novel became the trilogy she now offers for your enjoyment.

Discover other titles by Margaret Afseth at
Amazon.com
Aopato
Remedy
If you enjoyed this book and have not read the first in the series, here is a sample.
Aopato
By Margaret Afseth

Prologue:
1902 Northern Canada

The settlement consisted of the lumber office, a trading post and the row of connecting log houses everyone called the motel. It was in the cabin, third from the left, that the man and the boy had spent the night.

Inside, the room smelled of alcohol, stale cigarette smoke, dirty socks and urine, which emanated from the chamber pot in the far west corner. Littering a small table, three feet from the dingy bed, were two dirty aluminium plates, two tin cups, one still half full, and pages of newsprint scattered across the top.

It was dim, the window shades drawn.

Sprawled upon the tousled cot was a tall, extremely thin man; his salt and pepper hair matted, his unwashed red chequered shirt ragged, and the coveralls worn. He was shoe less.

In his right hand he held a half empty bottle of cheap whiskey. Near his left hip, a small loaded pistol waited for his courage to be fortified enough that its owner might actually carry out the purpose for which the weapon had been purchased.

The man wondered *how did I come to this place?*

He lifted the bottle to his lips drawing deeply. The amber liquid burned as it travelled down his throat.

First he had killed his favourite son while working in the bush, the tree falling with such finality, ending the child's life before it began. He had felt that last breath leave his slight frame, and as he grieved his loss beside the mounded earth they had come.

The man had seemed just like any other, but it was hard to make out features for the light that shown behind him. In his arms he carried a sleeping boy near the age of Jake's lost son. He offered to give the child to Jake…said that one could take the place of his treasure.

Would Jake take the small one, raise him as his own; keep him safe from something that hunted the child?

Jake had agreed, too numb from his sorrow to think ahead to the consequences such an action would bring.

A night bird called from outside the window. Darkness was closing in.

That child would never replaced his own, though he had so resembled his son in face and features. The new one acted strange, different some how, peculiar.

Jake had given the new boy his son's name. Avery.

The outside door rattled in the wind.

Is it here? Has it found us at last?

But though he listened hard, only distant sounds of revelry came from outside in the night.

They had travelled together, he and the child, moving from place to place, the man always feeling hunted, though by what he could not tell. They had just kept running.

The bottle found his lips once again, but it did not drown his fear.

I am tired of running; I can do this no longer; I will flee no more. This is over. Finished. Let someone else protect the boy...

He had sent Avery to the store.

"We need supplies," Jake told Avery, handing him money. "Go to the post. Pick up some grub... spend time looking around."

Jake raised the bottle, draining its contents.

The smell of the room was becoming overpowering; added to the usual stench was now the odour of sulphur, rotting flesh; the metallic taste of blood.

The air filled with overwhelming anger, rage; utter viciousness.

It is here! I can feel it!

He could not see anything; never could, only felt the presence of something so evil his heart threatened to stop with the fear.

I will face it this time.

A hollow voice, as though someone breathed through a tube, sounded about him.

Too loud! It was more inside his mind than around him.

"What have you done with him?"

"He's gone," the man answered. "Go find him yourself."

A hard derisive snort, and Jake began to tremble.

"I will kill you first, so you can no longer hide him."

Jake did not care anymore.

Let the creature have its way. I am tired of running; I am ready to die.

Trying to wear him down, drawing out the minutes, the being meant to torture him.

Silence dragged in the room.

Suddenly, without Jake's will or control, his hand released the bottle, and picked up the gun. He raised it to his head, pointed to his temple, pulled back the trigger…and fired.

Simultaneous with the loud report, a blinding flash occurred, flooding the cabin in light. On either side of the room, two small bright star-like orbs appeared in mid air.

Beside the bed, a huge grotesque shape shimmered to visibility, a reptilian creature, reeking of hatred and revenge.

"You will not stop me!" it thundered.

A beam of red light zapped from the reptilian to the star shape on the right, while at the same moment another of blue went from the star at the left to the monster.

The first star object exploded with such force the room went almost dim.

Beside the bed, the ugly being began to melt slowly, as a hot candle melts in extreme heat, turning to dark vapour, then at last fading from sight.

As the outside door began to open, the second star vanished. All went still…and dark.

A slight boy of seven entered, a bag of groceries in his arm.

Avery pondered the darkened room; set his burden in the chair by the door. He made his way to the bedside; fumbled to light the lamp. His hands came away sticky, and wondering why; he turned up the wick.

The scene accosting his senses stunned him. The man upon the bed had only half a face; the pillow beneath him was covered with chunks of brain matter; the faded blue blanket was spattered with bright red blood, as was the yellowing walls. The lamp dripped with dead tissue and gore.

At first he did not comprehend. He raised his hands and pondered them. He looked up, gazing about the room.

It sure stinks in here, he observed.

He looked again at the man he knew, sprawled upon the bed. Realization finally hit him; what had just happened in this room; why he had been sent away.

The young boy screamed.

From then on, he entered a world of numbness from which he would never quite recover. As from a distance, his screams continued...on...and on...and on.

Outside alarmed voices called to one another. The door was rammed in hard; it banged against the wall.

Finally, someone was leading him away.

Outside. Fresh air. Someone folded him in comforting arms...

But forever, that memory would visit him in dreams.